CHILDREN *of the* DAY

by the same author

THE RUSSLÄNDER

NIGHT TRAVELLERS

LADIES OF THE HOUSE

THE MISSING CHILD

THE CHROME SUITE

THE TWO-HEADED CALF

(for children)

THE TOWN THAT FLOATED AWAY

Children

OF THE

Day

A NOVEL BY

Sandra Birdsell

RANDOM HOUSE CANADA

 Published in 2005 by Random House Canada, a division of Random House of Canada Limited. Distributed in Canada by Random House of Canada Limited.

Random House Canada and colophon are trademarks.

www.randomhouse.ca

LIBRARY AND ARCHIVES CANADA CATALOGUING IN PUBLICATION

Birdsell, Sandra 1942–
Children of the day / Sandra Birdsell

ISBN 0-679-31369-9

I. Title.

PS8553.I76C44 2005 C813'.54 C2005-902312-0

Text and jacket design: CS Richardson

Printed and bound in the United States of America

2 4 6 8 10 9 7 5 3 1

This book is dedicated to my brothers and sisters,
Marie, Robert, Norman, Lenore, Joan,
John, Peter and Betty

And to the memory of my sisters, Annette and Judy

—

Time used to live here.
It likes to find places like this
and then leave so quietly
that nothing wakes up.

William Stafford, "From the Wild People"

ONE

The Vandals

IN THE MORNING, sunlight stretched like cellophane across the doorway of Sara and Oliver Vandal's bedroom. The ticking of a clock beneath a heap of clothes on the bureau became louder as Oliver gathered them up and quickly dressed, his back turned to Sara in the bed. Throughout the night the clock's muffled *click, click* had underscored the fist of worry in his ribs, and he had told himself, don't jump to conclusions. But his worry hadn't diminished or vanished, as it sometimes did when he awakened to the sight of the turquoise walls awash with daylight, the sound of his children's voices in the kitchen below telling him that they were up and breakfast was on the go.

Sara moaned and turned her face to the wall, the memory of their quarrel a sickness pressing against one side of her ribs. The baby sleeping in the crib stirred, then poked her almost bald head up from a blanket to regard her mother hunkered in bed, her father across the room, his dark head crooked as though he was listening to himself slide the knot of his tie up under his shirt collar. She flopped back down, sensing that it was futile to try to gain their attention. The baby was Patsy Anne Vandal, the day June 14, 1953, in Union Plains, Manitoba.

Halfway across the room, Oliver was stopped by the

sight of the shopping bag lying on the floor, shoes spilling from it, maroon calf-leather flats, navy slingback pumps, a pearlized bone-white sandal holding the imprint of a woman's toes. The shoes conjured the image of Alice emerging through the darkness of her yard last night, bringing him the shopping bag, and Oliver relived the surprise of her breasts, as small and unyielding against his chest as they had been when they were kids. Her kiss, however, with its urgent appeal, was unlike any of her kisses that he'd chosen to remember.

In comparison to the tiny shoes, his feet were ungainly and used up. He regarded them. Spidery threads mottled the skin around his ankles, the pads of several corns were swollen and sore—they were the feet of a man much older than his forty-five years. It occurred to him that his father had been his age when the lung disease had overcome him.

Men and women can't be just friends, Sara said, her tongue thick and coated and tasting like a peach seed. She took up where she had left off during the night, when Oliver had begun to snore, stranding her with her mind boiling for hours.

You don't say. Well, in my opinion they can be. Oliver stepped round the shoes. He knew that eventually the footwear would wind up at the bottom of the closet, along with all the other shoes Alice had sent home with him over the years, shoes she dropped off at the hotel—a friendly call at his place of business, he'd told Sara, a white lie, knowing that she was apt to turn molehills into mountains.

Why shouldn't I pay a friend a visit? he'd said last night, when there was no way around it other than to admit that he hadn't stayed for the entire public meeting at the school, but had fled. Couldn't sit there listening to all the down-in-the-mouth talk; and the next moment he found himself on the ferry and crossing the river. He hadn't planned on going to see Alice, that was just the way it had turned out.

Dragging the girls along, Sara muttered into the wall.

I didn't drag anyone. Oliver sighed heavily. I had me a walk, and they tagged along.

A walk to see that woman.

I don't have time for talking in circles, Oliver replied, and stepped towards the door.

You can make your own breakfast, Sara said, her voice sounding as though it came from the bottom of a barrel.

Will do.

Sara's presence in the kitchen wasn't as crucial as she seemed to think it was, given her usual early-morning hustle to get downstairs first thing, hair rolled up in the style of Wallis Simpson, a freshly ironed housedress cinched at her still-narrow waist. She was charged and determined to conduct the business of her household, emanating a purposeful energy. An energy that sometimes had the effect of throwing a monkey wrench into a smooth and well-running machine. Her arrival in the kitchen had the power to induce quarrelling and tears.

This morning, however, she was worn out by her night-long fuming.

Some of us have to get to work, Oliver said, reminding her, as he often did, that his time was not his own. He couldn't dally in the morning over a second cup of coffee, or the list she'd made of what needed fixing, or the remnants of a quarrel. This morning the word *work* was a raft being swept away on a fast current. His occupation; vocation, several long-time customers said, given that Oliver was a natural, the kind of man at ease with princes and paupers alike and therefore well suited to the hotel business.

Suddenly Sara was up, swinging her legs over the side of the bed, her eyes burning with rage. All these years, she said. Going to see that woman while I waited half the night. Going to see a woman who thinks she's better than I am. Showing her off to the girls. She hissed the words, her fists raised and shaking. Then she gasped and clutched her ribs.

She'd been watching for him at the kitchen window last night when he returned home with the girls, staring into the darkness of the yard, her lit face betraying a raw fear. But once he entered the house, quick as a snake she lashed out, one hand on her hip, the other stirring the air to send the girls on upstairs to bed so she could have her say.

You went to see that woman.

Yes, I did.

The startling admission had left them both speechless for moments.

Sara broke the silence to accuse him once again. You went to see that woman, and took Ida and Emilie with you.

I already said so, he snapped. And I didn't take the girls, they tagged along. But why not, eh? Why shouldn't they meet my old school friend? Heat rose in his neck as he remembered Alice's kiss, the searching flick of her tongue. The girls had stayed out on the veranda the whole time, he was certain they hadn't seen.

Sara balled her nightgown in a fist beneath her ribs, her slate-grey eyes growing wide and watery, like blobs of melting glass. The sight made Oliver turn away. There's no need to cry, he muttered, although in the almost twenty years he'd known Sara, he'd never seen her cry.

I'm sick, she said, piqued, gone huffy that he would think she was about to bring on the tears. She hadn't cried during the births of their ten children, each baby weighing over nine pounds, their oldest son, Sonny Boy, coming out into Oliver's hands at eleven and two ounces. She hadn't wept when Oliver hoisted a duffel bag onto his shoulder and boarded a train for Halifax, where he was stationed to barber in the army during the Second World War, leaving her to cope with four small children.

Throughout Sara's young childhood in a country that had become Soviet Russia, she hadn't cried once during what had proved to be an entire season of weeping. She hadn't cried when she'd boarded the train along with seven hundred other Mennonites who, like her, were fleeing their homeland. They'd cried for wanting to leave the country and then cried when they left it. They wept when their ship entered the Gulf of St. Lawrence.

In Sara's opinion, crying was a waste of tears, and she wasn't about to start wasting them now. Over Alice Bouchard? That whore? Huh! I guess not. A pain shot round from the back of one side of her ribs to the front, and she gasped.

The colour drained from her face and her skin took on a pasty sheen. Beads of perspiration began popping out across her forehead. Holy Mother of Christ, the morning sickness, Oliver thought, and looked about the room. He saw the metal wastebasket on the treadle of the sewing machine, took it up quickly and put it on the floor between the crib and the bed, and got out of there.

Downstairs in the kitchen, Alvina, the oldest of the Vandal children, was at the Rangette, stirring the oatmeal to prevent it from sticking, her auburn hair still wound up in large rollers. Ida and Ruby, two equally capable girls, scraped soot from bread slices they'd left too long under the broiler. Four big-eyed Vandal boys, Simon, Manny and their older brothers, Sonny Boy and The Other One, were energetically engaged in the task of waiting for their breakfast to appear.

Because the Vandal boys were boys, they'd been the first to use the wash basin and fresh towels. Consequently, as they sat at the table their faces radiated cleanliness, good health and what they were too young to recognize as contentment. Their scrubbed necks sprang up from their starched shirt collars as though to give them a loftier view of the world than their sisters could lay claim to.

Simon had clipped a bow tie onto his collar in anticipation of receiving a perfect mark on a test, this one being in arithmetic. His milk-chocolate hair was arranged low across his forehead in the same way Sonny Boy combed his. Everything the two younger brothers had learned in their short lives, they had gained from watching Sonny Boy and The Other One, who were in their early and mid-teens. And so, although their mother was nowhere in sight, because they were boys they had good reason to be confident that food comes to those who sit and wait.

Their duty of waiting for breakfast this morning included the extra chore of directing Emilie, their anemic-looking sister, through the precariousness of cooking basted eggs. Sonny Boy preferred the yolks to be slightly congealed at the edges, while Simon and Manny wanted to be able to bounce them on the floor. The Other One was easily satisfied, and would eat eggs prepared any which way, providing they were not raw. His real name was George, as in King George, and he was a silent, ruddy-complexioned boy possessing a strong and square jaw.

Add more water, Simon advised Emilie, mimicking Sonny Boy, who'd earlier made the same suggestion. The suggestion had been ignored then, as it was now, Emilie's attention absorbed by the voice droning from the radio. Although nearly two weeks had passed since the coronation, the news broadcasts still replayed portions of the service in Westminster Abbey. *Bless we beseech thee this crown and so sanctify thy servant Elizabeth.* Moments later the ensuing cries of God Save the Queen! buzzed in the radio speaker, and then came the booming sound of guns that Emilie felt in her spine.

The thundering cannons and a choir's carolling hymn faded, and the announcer's voice cut in with the news of the day, releasing Emilie's attention. Her pale eyes searched beyond the kitchen window for sight of Charlie, her new friend, the Arizona boy who had come to Union Plains to visit his grandmother. She anticipated being given a ride to school on his bicycle, clasping her hands over his midriff and speaking into the cusp of his ear. She would show him the coronation coin whose presence in the pocket of her pedal-pushers had warmed a spot against her thigh. Where he came from, they didn't have a queen.

Move, dipstick, you're blocking the light, Sonny Boy called out to Emilie. On sunny mornings—and the sun was strong that day—light came blasting through the window and turned the Arborite counter and tabletop, along with Sonny Boy's eyes, the colour of abalone. Emilie moved away from the window, and her brother's eyes lit and his hair shone yellow, like corn syrup.

Open the steam vent, Simon directed Emilie, adding, dipstick. Which brought the anticipated snickers from the two oldest brothers.

Yeah, and close your mouth or you'll lose all your air. Manny laughed at his own joke, the sound like a stick playing against a chain-link fence. Fifteen months separated the younger brothers, and while Simon was usually earnest and enterprising, this one, seven-year-old Manny, had an out-of-the-ordinary sense of humour. His private and sardonic fits of chuckling were somewhat beyond his years, and unsettling to those who thought they might be the cause of it.

Nine of the ten Vandal children were in the kitchen that morning, the baby, Patsy Anne, being upstairs in the crib. A toddler named Sharon sat at a play table beside the mammoth Servelle refrigerator that Oliver had ordered from a company in Grand Forks, North Dakota. The appliance had proved to be a brand not serviced in Canada, and ever since its door handle broke off, the handle had been a pair of vise grips.

The Vandal children breathed one another's air, shared the same parents and a kitchen whose lime-green floor tiles shone like a freshly flooded skating rink. The wallpaper was dotted with cherries, and busy with the plaques Alvina had guided her sisters through making—plaster pears, peaches, clusters of grapes and strawberries, green apples, tomatoes—and hung diagonally across the wall. The radio on the counter was not yet a year old, but its maroon plastic case was cracked and its knobs were missing and replaced by clumps of adhesive tape. The newscast ended. The radio vibrated with a song about Dutch Cleanser. *Wash those germs right down the drain, Dutch Cleanser, Dutch Cleanssserr,* the choristers sang with an unnatural cheerfulness, their voices trailing off in a hollow echo.

Turn that off, Alvina called to Emilie. It makes me want to scream.

So scream and get it over with, Sonny Boy said, his sneer being appropriate for his age of sixteen.

Emilie silenced the radio. Two or three eggs for Dad? she asked. Oliver's preference was dipping eggs, yolks the consistency of clear honey that he mopped from his plate with toast. Alvina spooned steaming porridge into bowls that were arranged on a metal space-saver beside the Rangette, and was too preoccupied to answer.

The ceiling shuddered now as feet pounded across the floor in their parents' bedroom, but Alvina seemed to be the only one to notice her mother's flat-footed and resentful gait. A little gut began chasing a big gut in her abdomen as she anticipated Sara's arrival, the push of questions and directions. Did you—? Yes, I did. Don't forget to— I won't forget. Make sure you— I will.

There was a moment of quiet above, then the bedsprings reacted suddenly and violently as Sara threw herself onto the mattress. What sounded like crying beat through the ceiling, but it couldn't be crying, oh no, because Sara did not cry. There hadn't been anything worth shedding tears over in the early years of her life, she said, and later she didn't bother, because when had bawling ever changed a thing? Go ahead, cry. See where it gets you.

The sound coming from the upstairs bedroom was harsh, a bark followed by a cough. Moments later it gave way to what, unmistakably, was throw-up.

Turn the radio back on, Alvina called to Emilie. Turn it up loud. There was no sense in spoiling everyone's appetite, she reasoned silently, as the retching rose in volume and ended in a crack of air exploding in the back of Sara's throat. Clear and sunny for the remainder of the day, the radio announcer predicted.

A growing wariness tightened Alvina's scalp, and her metal hair rollers became a transmitter of anxiety. Throwing up in the morning meant, in her experience, one inevitable and irreversible fact. It meant another diaper pail of rank water, bleach stinging her nostrils and burning her fingers raw. It meant more presents for her to unwrap, the flannel bundles rolled in newspapers, and layers and clumps of baby mustard, a brown stew of undigested peas and carrots for her to scrape free with a putty knife.

Holy Toledo, Alvina muttered, as she muttered during the warm months of the year when she brought the diaper pail up from the cellar and took it outside to the cistern. At such times, she hoped for a breeze to chase away the odour as she sat on an overturned log and scraped and kept an eye out for any objects the current baby might have ingested, a penny, a length of narrow bonnet ribbon, a button. Once upon a time, she'd found three cat's-eye marbles pressed into the muck, and not encased, and so she deduced that the baby hadn't swallowed them, but rather hidden the agates in its diaper nest. Holy shitty Toledo. *Shitty* being a word Alvina, understandably, had acquired at an early age. This shitty job, my shitty life, she thought. Hallelujah, Mother's woofing up her insides again.

She ran water into the porridge pot to soak it and, remembering that the water man was due to come and fill the cistern, took the key for the cistern padlock down from a top cupboard shelf and sent Ida to hook it on its nail beside the back porch door. Then she began yanking the rollers from her hair, poking them into a cloth bag whose ties she'd strung through the belt of her skirt. She toted her personals around in the drawstring bag to prevent the children and her mother from snooping; she shared a room with four sisters, and for the sake of privacy dressed and undressed in a closet.

Sonny Boy swore in disgust, as Emilie dished eggs from the fry pan onto her brothers' plates. Rubbery-looking eggs, curled and crispy brown around the edges, obviously not what he had ordered. Manny echoed his older brother's disgust, although the eggs on his plate were exactly as he liked them.

Their attention was drawn then to the sound of Oliver's heavy tread on the stairs, and for a brief moment they were still, Alvina staring at the wall as though she was counting the number of steps, her brothers' and sisters' bodies rigid with awareness. Oliver's arrival in the kitchen this morning was unlike any other morning. Simon muttered, Dad ruined my boat. Nine pairs of eyes swerved towards the kitchen door and its smashed sill, a long and deep gash that looked like an open wound. Simon's wooden tugboat lay to one side of the door, shattered and unrecognizable.

That'll teach you to leave it lying around, Sonny Boy said.

Don't say anything, Alvina cautioned them. She raked her fingers through long heavy ringlets that she hoped she'd have time to coax into an Ava Gardner style. Oliver's footsteps grew louder, and then stopped. Alvina turned to the counter, busy wiping smears of butter and toast scrapings from the breadboard.

Oliver paused at the bottom of the stairs in the front hall to gaze out the screen door at the town, the several narrow, tree-lined streets turned into tunnels moving with light and shadows cast by the new greenery. A shaggy-looking mongrel emerged from a yard, ambling aimlessly along. The stray had wandered into town and stayed, either because there was a bitch in heat or because someone, who should've known better, had fed it. The dog was marking, stopping here and there to lift its leg against a fence post, a bush fronting a yard.

He thought about coming home at suppertime last night, wanting to take Sara to the bedroom and sit her down on the hassock. Tell her, See here, I don't mean to cause worry, but this afternoon a man and a woman came round. From what they said, I suspect that Henri Villebrun has sold the contents of the hotel out from under me.

During supper the kids had been jabbering all at once, it was like being in the middle of a three-ring circus, and he couldn't get a word in edgewise. Sara adding to the racket, going on a mile a minute about the meeting, telling him that he must speak strongly against the proposed closing of the school. Emilie and Ida whined to go with him and Sara agreed. At least there'd be two kids out from under her feet, she said, but he knew it as a ploy to ensure that he would come straight home.

He'd made a spectacle of himself. Gone off half-cocked and fired his rifle into the doorsill. Scared the wits out of the kids and Sara. He wasn't proud of that.

The ditch beside the gravelled street was still marshy from a week of rain that had caused everything to grow in a hurry. The RCMP officer emerged from a side door of a two-storey house, wearing his scarlet jacket, which usually meant he had official business in either Winnipeg or Alexander Morris, the nearest large town, minutes away on Stage Coach Road. Constable Krooke was new in the municipality, a rookie who went by the book, and another ball of wax entirely.

Oliver passed through the living and dining rooms, where the blinds were still drawn and the light was as serious as a Mennonite funeral. The usual clutter of crochet, dark varnished furniture seemed to be purposefully unwelcoming. As he entered the kitchen he noticed some of his kids staring at him, and others trying not to. He thought, the girls, they were out on the veranda, on the swing, and the swing was off to one side of the window—they couldn't have seen me and Alice.

Howdy-do, he said, not making eye contact with any of them. He went over to the washstand, in a corner of the room near to the back door, which opened up to the porch.

He glanced at his image in the splattered mirror and saw the bachelor he'd once been, a man women had made excuses to seek out. In his mind, he wasn't who his children took him to be—middle-aged, slightly rotund—and there were women still attracted by their father's generous dark hair. In the eyes of his children, the way he combed it straight back from his brow, and the baggy, off-white trousers he preferred to wear, made him aged and pathetically out of fashion.

Oliver picked up the wash basin, whose soap-curdled water had cooled, and went out through the porch. Water splashed against the earth, and he returned, stumbling on the gash in the doorsill. He felt his children's eyes turn to him, waiting to see what he would do.

It's not my fault, Emilie thought, being accustomed to having fingers pointed in her direction. She hadn't ruined the doorsill. That pale Vandal slip was Emilie, and not Emily, as teachers preferred to spell her name. Sara had once worked for a woman named Emily Ashburn. She had borrowed a blue silk scarf from the woman and failed to return it, and entered her name in a diary along with all the other names she collected for the time when she'd have children. Emilie and not Emily, as Oliver had insisted. If you're going to saddle the girl with an old woman's name, then at least give it some class. Which pleased Sara, as she was determined that her children's names would be not at all like the names she'd grown up with in Russia. I named you after Emily Ashburn, a rich woman who was good to me, Sara said. But she neglected to say anything about stealing the woman's scarf.

Was it my fault? Emilie now wondered, beginning to question her innocence, as scapegoats are known to do. She knew she was responsible for wanting the Arizona boy,

Charlie, to be outside his grandmother's house waiting to give her a ride to school. She was responsible for having spied on her father last night, leaning forward on the veranda swing and swivelling her head to look into Alice Bouchard's living-room window.

Emilie's lips tingled, and the more she struggled against it, the more a guilty smirk pulled her mouth sideways. It was understandable that she was the first to be suspected of having committed various transgressions, and that she eventually found herself owning up to them. A dot in the fry pan's handle glowed red as she plugged it back in and began furiously scraping at congealed bits of egg. If Oliver ran off to live with his school friend, she'd go with him.

Oliver looked into the oval frames that captured his children's features. Strong and dainty noses, dark- and light-coloured eyes, white and coppery-tinged complexions. They seemed gratified by his embarrassment, and he understood that kids might relish catching their parents doing something wrong. Perhaps they hoped for a show of remorse, hoped he would go for his change purse in his back pocket. A dime for each of them, two-bits for Simon, whose boat he'd ruined.

At the squeaking sound of bedsprings, Oliver glanced at the ceiling and made the sign of the cross, muttering a promise to fix the ruined doorsill. Then he handed the emptied wash basin to Ida, a frizzy-haired and high-complexioned girl a year into her teens who'd inherited Oliver's love of skating. She was pleased to now own a flesh-coloured latex girdle, and prayed that she'd soon grow into it. She poured water from a kettle simmering on the Rangette and returned the basin to Oliver, her green eyes swerving with a mixture of pride and shyness to have been the one to do so. Evidently she hadn't witnessed Alice's kiss, Oliver decided, with considerable relief.

Crack two eggs into the pan for Dad, Alvina instructed Emilie. Once Oliver was done at the washstand, it was her turn.

No, no. Toast. Toast is all, Oliver objected, his face rising from the basin. Water dripped onto his white shirt as he groped for a towel that should have been hanging on a hook alongside the washstand mirror. You girls don't need to bother none with eggs for me. Sugar toast will do, he said, as Ida set a towel into his hands.

Alvina saw the troubled thoughts roaming beneath the surface of Oliver's smooth face, his dark eyes darting about the room, looking for someplace safe to rest. Last night she had tried, unsuccessfully, to shut out her parents' quarrel with a pillow. Burning with indignation all the while, and wanting to shout, I have exams tomorrow!

In despair she'd crept from the house, climbed onto the shed roof and hugged her knees, imagined that the sky was made lighter by the lights of Winnipeg, that the air hummed a beckoning refrain. A refrain Alvina was ready to take up. She would disappear into a junior secretary position, if only she could pass her typing and shorthand exam. She felt the seductive draw of stillness in the grounds of the Trappist monastery west of town. A silence that sometimes drew her to a grotto there, near a creek, to plead for a means of escape. Please, please, please.

She'd returned to bed and managed to fall asleep through the give-and-take of her parents' quarrel, the long silences in between. As usual, halfway through the night Sara's call prodded her awake, Alvinnnaa? Her siblings enjoyed the peace of oblivion while Alvina stumbled down the stairs to check if the locked doors were locked, as they always were, although no one else in Union Plains bothered.

Alvina had seen the muscles in her father's jaw and neck working when he came home for supper last night, while her mother, preoccupied with complaining about the ladybugs, missed the signs of his inner turmoil. She went on and on, clueless, griping about the ladybugs streaming into the house all day. She'd given up on having the kids tromp on the insects, and had dusted the sill with poison. But still they kept coming, found a way into the house by going under the sill to avoid the dust.

Sara had prepared a light meal, as she didn't want Oliver to be in his usual after-supper stupor. Sit near the front, she said, so you can be seen and heard. How can closing a school be called progress? I don't want our kids riding a school bus three hours a day. During the winter they'll be leaving and coming home in the dark. When will they do their homework? They'll be up half the night and tired the next day. I won't be able to get them to bed, or out of bed. And before you go, you've got to do something about the bugs. I found one climbing up the flour barrel in the dining-room closet.

His chair crashed to the floor as he leapt up from the table and went down into the cellar. The clink of cutlery and chattering of voices gave way to silence. Sara swivelled in her chair, her ear cocked towards the open cellar door. Moments later Oliver stormed up the stairs with his rifle, which he aimed and fired at the doorsill, Simon's tugboat catching the brunt of the impact.

Alvina didn't know what had been worse, the deafening blast of the gun, or the animal sounds Sara made when she scrambled up onto her chair, covered her ears and screamed.

My boat, Simon had protested in a quavering voice.

I'll get you another boat, Oliver said, and the floor shook beneath the force of his feet on the stairs as he descended into the cellar. He returned long moments later without the gun, his hands trembling and chest heaving as though he'd just run a mile.

That should fix the frigging bugs, he said, and left the house, Emilie and Ida hurrying after him.

This loony bin of a house, Alvina thought now, and dipped her hands into the water Oliver had just used. She splashed sleep from her eyes. With any luck, she'd be out of this shitty family by the end of summer.

TWO

Oliver going around with a shadow

OLIVER WAITED IN THE STREET in front of the house for his children to join him. I'll walk you kids to school, he'd said, feeling that he owed them an explanation for having fired his rifle in the house.

Boston ferns pressed against the front windows in the living room as Alvina drew the blinds. She peered out at Oliver for a moment, her hand coming up as though she might rap on the glass, and then her moon-shaped face turned away. He had to work hard these days to get that girl to smile. She'd been named after his grandmother, and had inherited her bushy dark hair. A good woman. Unfortunately, Sara and his kids hadn't been privileged to know her.

The house looked awkward and top-heavy. The two windows in the girls' bedroom were like baleful eyes this morning, with the blinds half drawn. Hang on to your hat, he'd say when the wind got up and the house shook, fearing that the top floor might one day be wrenched loose. Near to twenty years ago, when he'd chosen this house, it hadn't had a top floor. He'd been drawn to it for what it was, an unpainted two-room dwelling of split-log construction, sturdy and substantial.

Its front door looked out across Union Plains and the back door opened onto the prairie. The dwelling seemed to have one foot in the wilderness and the other in society. Like

Oliver, a French Cree Metis—mixed blood or half-breed, as he was sometimes called—the house appeared to be welcoming the possibilities of both worlds. Given that not a single nail had gone into its construction, he imagined that the history of the people who'd lived in it long ago was like his, one of make-do and invention.

When for the first time he went through its two rooms and felt its tongue-and-groove floor give beneath his weight, he fancied that the dwelling had been waiting to be inhabited by the likes of him, an elastic-natured and loose-jointed man, weathered to a dusty brown. Its location so near to a string of early settlements along the Red River suggested it might have been a wintering place for *hivernants* who had once followed the herds.

That possibility suited Oliver, as he'd been a cold-weather person from the start. As a boy, at first snowfall he'd run out into it immediately, and felt his blood quicken in the brittle air, anticipated the inevitable hot gush of snot cresting on his lip, its familiar taste satisfying. At the first hard frost, the bachelor Oliver had cleared a path on the river, and anyone looking towards it after sundown might have seen what appeared to be a shooting star streaking round a curve of frozen water—Oliver Vandal, his skate blades strapped onto his boots, the light of a headlamp bearing down on that black corridor of winter.

The house had always been there, long before his time. But he hadn't given it more than an occasional curious appraisal when passing by, until it appeared he might be faced with the possibility of raising a family in a moribund hotel. Come and see this house I found, Oliver said to Sara, and she was as eager to view it as he was to show it to her.

The five short streets of Union Plains were laid down north to south. The abandoned house was on the edge of town, facing a rutted road that went east and west; the southerly ends of the town's five streets butted up against it. There was one other house near it, belonging to Florence Dressler, a widow, who would become their closest neighbour. The Dressler house was a neatly kept yellow cottage, its back turned to the rough-hewn dwelling as though wanting to ignore it.

As they neared the house, Oliver sensed Sara's growing disquiet. What do you think? he dared to ask. They stood before it, Sara cupping her hands and blowing to warm them, the biting November wind sweeping grainy snow across the road in front of the house and down into the overgrown yard. Licks of snow climbed up the weathered wood; in the dead of winter they would grow to three- and four-foot drifts. Sara shrugged and made for the door. Oliver followed.

She stood in the main and largest room, struck silent as she stared at drawings on a wall that would eventually become a wall in her kitchen.

Pictures, Oliver explained, unnecessarily. He'd asked round and learned that, years ago, a family of Assiniboine had squatted for a short time before being encouraged to move on. Likely the pictures were their doing. The drawings were red, and looked as though they'd been made by very young and artistically inept children. Stick men mounted on horses shot arrows into a herd of buffalo. In another, men killed each other with lances and arrows.

An Indian war party, Oliver said, when Sara wrapped her arms about herself and shivered.

A killing, she said.

We'll throw on some whitewash. Is all she needs. For sure, I know there's mouse dirt and the rabbits have got in, he continued, when she didn't seem convinced. The house, she has somewheres to go, he allowed.

From what little he knew of Sara, Oliver sensed that potential inspired hope. That was why, like most immigrants, she'd come to this country in the first place. For a new life. For the reason of hope.

We'll get a Quebec heater for the small room, a cookstove in here, he said, and you'll see, we'll be snugger than a bug in a rug.

He began pacing, his hands slicing the air as he spoke too quickly for her to fully comprehend; nor had she understood the concept of snugness in a rug. The two rooms would be filled with fiddle music, he said, and sit-down dancers, when his St. Boniface relations came visiting in winter. He vowed that he and Sara would cross the Red River to the French side to attend the winter carnivals, the snowshoe, horse and dog races a new priest in the parish of Ste. Agathe had taken to organizing. Go from house to house on New Year's Eve, and celebrate the French way, as he used to do, firing his rifle into the wind, begging the favour of a drink and a kiss. I have relations coming out of my ears up and down the river, he told her. As far south as St. Joe and Pembina. The Carons, Berthelets, Branconniers, Dubois, St. Germains, Delormes. He recited the names, the syllables like a church bell tolling across the snowbound land.

No guns. There won't be any guns here, Sara interrupted, as though laying down a condition to her agreeing to make the house their home.

She had promised her older sister, Katy, there would be no guns. No crosses either, she now added, meaning crucifixes on the walls. No strong drink. No dancing, she said, reminding him of who she was, a Mennonite, one of a people who throughout the centuries had fled various countries for the freedom to practise their religious beliefs. Russia having been the latest country. Thousands of German-speaking Mennonites like Sara had called Russia home for over a hundred years, and then had been forced to flee, following the revolution.

You don't say, Oliver said, after a moment of silence.

But Katy didn't say we shouldn't do That, Sara said. Her smile was a suggestive one as she spoke, her grey eyes a radiant hardness beneath the brim of her hat. You and I know the things we've done, her eyes told him. Her felt hat was the colour of pigeons, its band of feathers iridescent shades of blue. It was too large and the rim rode low on her forehead, making her eyes look perpetually watchful.

Her hips shifted beneath her dark wool coat as she went to the open door, the pear shape of her bottom emerging when she stooped to pick up a wooden crate. She set it down in the centre of the room, stepped onto it so that she might look Oliver eye to eye. Then she raised her arm and proclaimed in German, There will be no drinking! You must not have any fun!

Although Oliver knew she was mocking, he heard her sister Katy's admonitions echo in the frost-tinged walls. It wasn't necessary for him to understand German to know that Sara's people considered him to be rough around the edges. She stood with her hands at her hips, looking down at him for a moment, before stepping off the crate. Her round young cheeks were rosy from the crisp air, her small pink mouth turned up with the beginning of a self-conscious smile. He remembered the incredible softness of her skin next to his, her heat; the blue crepe dress she wore beneath the coat—a new dress, he'd noticed before they'd set out—its tiny pearl buttons marching up between the mounds of her breasts, which were surprisingly full and heavy for such a small woman.

He wanted to make her sweat and moan on his narrow bed in his hotel room under the stairs, stealth, the necessity for quiet, driving his blood hot, her teeth grazing and nipping at his palm. But the hotel was at the other end of town, and they were here, and he was ready.

He caught Sara by the window, was driven by her protests to chase her across the room. Not here, not now. It's too cold. Someone will come. The floor's dirty, she said. She tried to twist out of his arms, reached to steady herself, and her hand came upon a leather thong looped onto a nail beside the window frame.

Was ist das? she asked. For moments their hard breathing was the only sound as she held the pouch up between them, its leather stained and smelling of strong tea.

You got me buffaloed, Oliver joked, knowing that the beaded orange-and-white pouch was a strike-a-light and held the means to spark a fire. Sara burst into laughter. You understood me, she said. You can understand German if you want to. Then she turned and threw the pouch out the broken window into the yard, where the bleached grasses of summer lay flattened under a hard covering of snow.

Liebst du mich? Sara asked, and then once again, in English—Do you really love me? When he nodded she removed her hat and hooked it onto the nail beside the window frame. Her light brown hair was a cap of soft waves tucked and pinned under at the back of her head, revealing the shape of her small skull. Then she untied the belt of her wraparound coat and let it slide from her shoulders onto the floor.

Oliver clasped Sara to his chest and thought, with a pang of worry, she wasn't much taller than the day he'd first seen her on the ferry. Eight years later, that girl had become this woman he held in his arms, though she didn't look grown enough to bear children. Beyond the window the strike-a-light pouch lay on the snow, its *babiche* thongs crumpled beside it. He said, My own little pig, my dear, of course I love you. Sara, satisfied for the moment, stepped out of his embrace and began unfastening the buttons of her dress, lest he try to do it for her and half of them wind up scattered across the floor.

A little while later Oliver Vandal, Sara Vogt's gypsy-looking man, her thin-as-a-rail man with wild dark eyes, lay on the floor beside her, spent, drifting towards a gentle snore, dreaming of his house, its open doors and windows welcoming a bit of rain; the scuttle of autumn leaves, a fox crossing its doorsill. He dreamt that he would take Sara roaming in the country. Take her out amid the booming and echoing dance of the prairie hens, among the red dogwood. He'd show her its bark, pulverize it, put it in a pipe, and they would smoke what his grandmother had called *kinnikinnick*. He was about to become a *chef de famille*, and would see to it that the children they brought into this world, the baby already sparked to life inside her, grew up to be children of experience, and were not, by God, taken over by civilization.

Whose house is this? Sara asked, her eyes growing heavy. Despite the chill of the room, she wanted to sleep.

Her hairpins had worked loose and strands as fine as cobwebs tickled his neck as she breathed. Your guess is as good as mine, he said. What does it matter? It's empty, it should be put to good use.

Water under the bridge, Oliver thought, as Sonny Boy and George matched him step for step. The two youngest hung on to his thumbs and hippety-hopped, mullets tugging on the end of his line. When they'd left the yard, Ida had hurried on ahead, eager to join her friends gathering on the school steps, while Emilie headed off in the opposite direction. I'm going to see a man about a dog, Emilie said, when Ida inquired.

He stopped for a moment and ruffled Simon's hair and straightened his bow tie. The way the kid looked at him made Oliver want to turn away.

For the most part, his children encountered in him what the patrons of the Union Plains Hotel encountered—a generous and amiable broad-faced man who, despite the stories he liked to tell of a wild and desperate childhood, seemed to be a cautious person. He dispensed warnings of rabies and distemper whenever a stray dog ventured into town. He warned swimmers to beware of the river's unpredictable currents, hikers of inclement weather he didn't need a barometer to predict.

Although he didn't own an automobile, for a time in his youth he'd driven taxi in Winnipeg, a city he swore he knew like the back of his hand. He did not have a bank account, but he did have a cash register at the hotel, with compartments that kept his money accounted for and secure. He didn't join his children and Sara on Sundays, when her brother-in-law took them across the river and inland into Mennonite territory in order to attend church. He seemed more charitable and forgiving than the people his children encountered in church, and so they accepted him for who he was—different, diffident and sometimes gregarious. But most of all, in their experience, he was absent.

See here, Oliver said, and cleared his throat before continuing. I knew what I was doing when I shot at the doorsill. I was testing the rifle. Turns out she's shooting low, that's how come I got the boat. A gun needs to be fired now and again. But it's not something I want you boys fooling around with, you hear?

We won't, Simon said, speaking for Manny too, who was at the age of being interested in fire and quietly eager to start one. Manny had borrowed his father's eyepiece, a loupe Manny now carried in his pocket. Oliver kept it in a buffet drawer and used it to better see the splinters he plucked from their skin and the specks of debris he dabbed from their eyes. Sonny Boy and George remained silent, anticipating the arrival of a black Chevrolet in front of the school, the Bogg brothers coming to pick them up and take them down the highway to attend the Alexander Morris Composite High.

Along the way, children straggled from yards, their voices like the twittering of anxious sparrows as they headed towards the two-storey red-brick schoolhouse that in years past had been near to bursting with students. Half of its eight classrooms were empty, and the building was feared to be a hazard as it sagged at one side under its own considerable weight.

Once I shot at a mouse in my mother's pantry with a twenty-two, Oliver said now, hoping to capture his older son's attention, I put a hole clear through a crock of corned beef. That was before mousetraps were invented. He was rewarded with a snort of what might have been withheld sarcasm from Sonny Boy, while George seemed lost in his thoughts, clutching his binder and books against his chest. Even to himself Oliver's laughter sounded tight, a smoker's wheeze, and he wondered if his sons detected the lack of mirth in it.

Sonny Boy was wearing his knife, the belt of his blue jeans threaded through its leather sheath. He was good with that knife, he had a sharp eye and steady arm, but there was nothing around about that required sticking, Oliver thought. Sonny Boy wanted danger. He wanted to rescue people, to save himself, to test his courage. It went against some people's natures to sit for hours in a classroom. Sonny needed to know the bellyache of hunger and to have no one but himself to rely on. He wasn't learning any of that at the high school.

The two younger boys entered the schoolyard without a backward glance, dashing off to join the games already in progress. Having the time of their lives, Oliver thought. Which amounted to such a short time.

A horn tooted as the Bogg brothers' car came to a stop in front of the school. Several small kids ran over to it, likely thinking to write *wash this car* in the dust on the door, and were scared off by the loud warning—Touch this car and we'll break your arm—from the two burly sons of a local farmer.

Don't you forget, you boys come round to the hotel for chores after school, Oliver reminded Sonny Boy and George. They would sweep up, wash the tumblers and ashtrays, dust the mirror and the buffalo. Wipe tobacco smoke from the picture glass of a photograph hanging above the bar, a portrait of Fine Day, a Cree war chief. A picture that might one day soon wind up in a second-hand shop, or in a museum.

I'm setting pins after school, Sonny Boy said, and Oliver remembered he was now employed part-time at the bowling alley in Alexander Morris. He would be late coming home and would hook a ride on the highway.

Sonny sprinted off to climb into the car, as though he'd escaped a confinement. He and the Bogg boys called for George to get the lead out, but he seemed reluctant to leave his father.

They aim for Sonny Boy, George said, in a monosyllabic mutter. Sonny's bruises? he added, referring to the angry-looking yellowish-and-blue marks on Sonny's arms and shins. When he sets pins, the Alexander kids try and get him with the ball, George explained, when Oliver appeared not to understand. They think we're hicks. The French kids are frogs. Anyone with a Low German accent is a square-head. The Chartrand kids get called chiefs, he added, the Chartrand family being the only Metis family living in the predominantly Anglo-Saxon town.

The school of hard knocks takes some getting used to, Oliver said carefully. It'll put hair on your chest, he thought. He watched George shuffle off to the waiting car. He had yet to prove what he might be good at, except at being quiet, his cheeks burning brick-red at the threat of being noticed.

You're not a hick, Oliver thought to call after him. The Bogg brothers, they were hicks, farm boys who could be counted on to hit a home run nearly every time they came up to bat.

Oliver waved as the car sped off, thinking he should have told his boys that he'd once shot at a privy knowing his mother was inside. Knowing she would come out fighting mad with her underclothes down around her ankles. Shooting at the privy had been the quickest way to get her attention before the truancy man hauled him and his brother, Romeo, away. He also hadn't told his sons about once being at Romeo's house in St. Boniface and taking a shot at a church steeple to see if he could make its bell ring. Like most children these days, he supposed, they were not interested in their parents' stories, or his grandmother's remembrances, either, which he sometimes took out and read, although he knew them by heart.

As he walked towards the hotel, her warm voice ran through his head. *Me and my man loaded two carts. The children rode in one, while we took what we could with us from Red River. We was leaving Red River and St. Jean where I was raised, for Batoche, as my man's health was not good, and I had a sister there. Monsignor Tache and our Father of St. Norbert called a meeting of all Catholics. I remember that the Priest told us that our country was sold to the Orangemen. These Orangemen was going to harness the*

Black Dresses and Black Robes and make them plough the land. It was decided to send for Louis Riel. Those who wished to defend their country and religion went to Fort Garry to protect it from the Orangemen. Mr. MacDougal was coming. So my man went with fifteen or twenty others on horseback to meet him at La Salle. MacDougal was scared and went back to Pembina. There he told them that there was around a thousand men holding him up at St. Norbert and he couldn't possibly get through. Of course, it was a miracle that he should turn when there were so few men to stop him, and so my man and others erected a cross at that point. After the trouble at Red River was all over, we loaded the two carts and my husband and myself and four children went to join my sister at Fish Creek, near to Batoche. By this time, my man's chest was bad and he was pretty well useless.

Sara and the children were indifferent to the history of Union Plains, and of the French towns dotting the *plateau de coteau* of the Red River, which had been predominantly Metis settlements, and among the first towns and villages of the North-West Territory. Aubigny, where Oliver had spent his youth, St. Adolphe, Ste. Agathe, St. Jean Baptiste—the birthplace of his grandmother, and where she had ended her days.

The French towns across the river from Union Plains possessed similar churches to each other whose spires were visible from Stage Coach Road. The histories of these settlements harked back to the fur trade, to the Metis freighters who stopped to trade on their journeys to and from St. Paul, going east and west, their oxen-drawn Red River carts a shriek of sound announcing their arrival and departure.

Their histories, and those of the Oblate fathers and Trappist monks, the Red River rebellion led by Riel, the histories of the Cree women peddling their hand-crafted wares in the towns along the river, most people, including his own family, didn't care to know.

History, for his children, was recalling the concession booth beside the highway where they'd been able to purchase ice cream, and which had been swept away by high spring water. The Second World War had ended. King George VI had died and they must now sing God Save the Queen. Long ago, a train had jumped the track at the train station and caused the death of two men. A man had become lost in a snowstorm while delivering a load of ice, and perished. More recently, a booth Florence Dressler operated during the summer months as a nip-and-chip takeout stand had been shut down by health regulators for its lack of running water. That was history to them.

When Oliver entered the hotel, he was struck by the heaviness of the air, the odour of must retreating to the corners of the room as he drew the blinds on the poolroom windows. He heard footsteps in the hall above, and knew the old gentlemen were up and would soon want to wet their whistles. What would become of them, if the hotel shut down? They wouldn't find accommodations for what he charged them. What would become of Union Plains? A ghost town, likely, the hotel a falling-down relic of the past, a shell people would poke about in while out on a Sunday drive into the country.

He'd come home for supper last night thinking to tell Sara about the man and woman who'd stopped by the hotel to see him, the woman catching him by surprise in his broom-closet office under the stairs late in the day, when he'd already turned the lights off over the pool tables and in the parlour, as he usually did over the supper hour.

The woman said she would appreciate it if Oliver would sell her a bottle, as her old codger got mean when he was dry. He was waiting for her in the car, she said, and nodded at the shelves in his closet, indicating the poolroom beyond that wall, its large windows and the street where, Oliver feared, the man waited in plain view.

She'd come to purchase bootleg liquor on the say-so of a barber in Alexander Morris, she told Oliver. A town they'd stopped in as they returned from a trip south of the border. The barber, Delorme, had said just to mention his name. My hubby is one thirsty bugger, she said, as though this might help to sway Oliver, as though thirst was his next of kin.

Usually these transactions went on after work and from the back door, but there was something doelike about her that tempted him to take a chance. She was good-looking, with soft dark eyes, dark hair, her stomach rounding out the front of a green tailored suit. A drinker's belly. He noted that her handbag was large enough to hold a bottle, or two. The odours of fried bacon and tomato soup wafted down from the second floor as the old gents began preparing their evening meal; the lights had been turned off, anyone going by would think he'd left for supper. Oliver reasoned that it should be safe to sell her a bottle.

He wanted to pull the light chain in his under-the-stairs office, lock its door, make the woman wait among the pool tables in the semidarkness while he went into the cellar. He didn't want her in his room, whose shelves were stacked with the towels and sheets Sara laundered for the gentlemen boarders. His shaving basin rested on a middle shelf with its ring of soap, the mug and brush beside it. A buffalo robe hung from two hooks beside the door, a robe that had once covered a cot where he'd slept as a boy and then as a young man, in what had now become this broom-closet office under the stairs.

You sell me a bottle, I'll tell you your fortune. One good turn deserves another, the woman said.

She took his hand, turned it over and cupped it, her fingers clammy against his hot skin. A sour odour wafted from her nostrils and pores, and he stepped back. Likely she needed a drink more than the man. She peered into his palm, her lashes thick with mascara, some of which had come off on the skin beneath her brows and looked like the tracks of insects. From the lobby came the sound of the door opening and closing.

Oh gosh, I shouldn't have started this, she said, and dropped Oliver's hand.

The footsteps faded. Whoever had come in had gone into the parlour. Connie, where in hell are you? a man called.

Oliver followed the woman and the odour of cigar smoke through the lobby, and as they entered the parlour a shaky smile covered half the woman's face, revealing lipstick-stained teeth. He could smell her fear.

I was in China, where did you think I'd be? she said.

The man standing in the centre of the room wore a fedora crooked to one side of his head and shadowing his face, but as he came over to the bar, the light through the curtains revealed his bulbous features. A bulldog. Once he clamped onto something, this man would shake the life out of it. Oliver noted the off-white suit, soiled at the cuffs and in need of pressing, a Masonic ring on one hand, two gold rings on the other. Likely he was a gambler. He recognized the type from his taxi-driving days.

So, you're Vandal, then? the man said, sizing Oliver up, and when Oliver nodded the man turned away as though to dismiss him. Where's the bottle? What's the holdup? he asked the woman, and Oliver thought for a moment that his deep voice sounded familiar.

The air in the parlour was oppressive with the acrid odours of lives being sloughed off for near to a century. The velour curtains held the smell of weather, excitement and desolation. Oliver indicated where the couple should sit; he wanted them to stay put while he went into the cellar room behind the furnace.

But the man strolled the length of the parlour and back again, jingling coins and keys in his trouser pockets, the hint of a smile playing on his blunt features as he surveyed the room, its arrangement of square oak tables and hoop-backed chairs, the gilt-framed mirrors, the shaggy buffalo head mounted on a wall. He tipped his fedora to the back of his head and whistled. My God, it's just as Villebrun said. Nothing's changed.

The age lines in the man's grey face softened and Oliver finally realized, with a start, that he had seen him before, years ago, when he was just a boy. There was always a single voice pushing through all the others, laughing more uproariously, while he tried to fall asleep in his room under the stairs. This man's hoarse and gravelly voice.

This isn't your place now, is it? I take it you're just running it? He turned to Oliver as though wanting to clarify this point.

Oliver was about to say that it was his place. To tell the man its history. The hotel had begun as an inn where

Minnesota stagecoaches, traversing the land between St. Paul and Winnipeg, stopped for a change of horses. The coaches carried mail and money, settlers, politicians, speculators, surveyors, who dined on boiled potatoes and warmed their insides with bitter tea. Paddlewheel steamboats brought latecomers up the river from Illinois, from as far away as New Hampshire. Mennonites stopped to water their horses at the stables before going on into Winnipeg with their wagonloads of produce and grain. The town's name, Union Plains, testified to the expectation that it would always be a hub, a centre through which mail was routed, goods passed, people arrived and departed.

Oliver replied after a long pause that Henri Villebrun was the owner, not him.

He said he was, noted the man, nodding. But you never know what Villebrun might try and pull. I'd heard he retired to Florida, but you could have knocked me over when I came across him on the golf course in Palm Springs. Small world, the man said, and his jaw began to work as though his thoughts were ball bearings he shunted from one side of his mouth to the other.

How much for a bottle of whisky? He reached for an inside pocket of his jacket, his apparent interest in the hotel giving way to a twitchy impatience.

Oliver remembered this man more clearly now, a heavyset man whose sprawling legs had threatened to trip him up as he moved among the tables. What're you doing here, kid? he always demanded. What's your name? Speak up, kid, speak English. Get wise. You're in an English-speaking country.

That'll cost you fifty, Oliver said. It was more than twice what he normally charged—Delorme had no business telling these two to look him up, and he wanted the man to know it.

The man blinked in surprise, and then dug into his wallet and fanned several bills across the bar. I suppose you've got to make hay while the sun's still shining. Just go and get the damned bottle.

Oliver went over to the bar and gathered the bills, folded them and stuck them into his back pocket. You betcha, I'll be right with you, he heard himself say, and thought that he sounded like a scared twelve-year-old kid.

Look at all this stuff, will you? the man said to the woman. And to think I got it from Villebrun for a song.

Oliver went down into the cellar, his stomach churning. Got what for a song? When he returned with the bottle, the man was gone. The woman tucked the whisky into her handbag and patted it. Don't mind him, he can be such an arse, she said.

Then she turned her attention to the photograph of Fine Day hanging above the bar, indecision shifting in her dark eyes. I agree with that, she said finally. She nodded at the picture. There's no reason for a person to be shy of where they come from. But I suppose you have to be choosy about who you let know.

Oliver saw the reflection of Fine Day in the mirror, saw his own white shoulders, the almost square shape of his dark head. The photograph was a relic he'd rescued years ago from a heap of garbage in the cellar. Villebrun had told him to get rid of it. The chief was from a band called Strike-Him-on-the-Back, according to an inscription on the back of the picture. Oliver had been taken by the name, the man's distinct and intelligent-looking features, the way he crouched, a rifle held across his chest, one foot in front of the other as though at any moment he might stalk away.

That's not my history, Oliver replied. It's something that came with the place. I fancied it, is all.

Well, she said, and hesitated. In any case, if you want to keep it, if I were you, I'd stash that away.

You saw Henri Villebrun? Oliver asked.

The mean codger saw him. I only heard about it. About nothing else, since. Listen, you should know. My old man's going to come and take an inventory of what's here. Real soon. He might not notice if a few things went missing. She winked, and the door closed behind her.

Oliver stood listening for a moment as the car's engine started up. When he went into the vestibule he felt a weakness in his legs. He opened the door a crack to watch their car, a white Cadillac, lumber down the street and turn at a corner. Heading for the access road and the highway, he knew.

This morning it was as though he were seeing the vestibule for the first time, the scarred mahogany panelling and the battered chairs lining the panelled walls. The leather that wasn't cracked and peeling had split open revealing horsehair padding. The parquet was scored with a criss-cross pattern of slashes made by the town kids' skates when they came in to warm up while skating on a vacant lot across the street. They begged for their blades to be sharpened, and Oliver obliged. He'd bought an electric motor and mounted his father's stone on it to give them the pleasure of watching the sparks fly.

He took down from the vestibule wall the notice of the meeting to be held at the school that evening, and an out-of-date announcement of an auction. There was a scuff of slippered feet on the stairs, the sound of Cecil's phlegm-filled cough preceding him, and Oliver realized that he hadn't entered into the books the four hours Cecil had spent tending the parlour last night. At the end of the month he'd deduct the sum from what Cecil owed for his room.

Jesus, God, he thought. At the rate things were going, he'd wind up owing Cecil. He felt turned upside down, suspended above the ground in a rocket tumbler, the ride the kids pestered him to take them on during fair days at Alexander Morris. He went with them for the pleasure of having his pockets emptied of change, and their stomachs turned inside out. He felt that the ground lay far below him and he was about to come crashing down into it.

Minutes later, he found himself going along the path beside the access road that would take him to the highway. Prickly spikelets of wild oats snagged his trousers and let go, creating a wake, a silvery current of movement behind him, as though a small animal scurried through the weeds trying to keep up. He needed to feel the ground moving under his feet, to fix his sights on a point and just keep going. In this way, he supposed, he was like his uncle, Ulysse, needing to move, freed from any backward or forward pull.

He reached Stage Coach Road, which seemed a funnel for the quiet coming off the land. He crossed the highway and was well onto the river path before the silence was broken by the dull hum of an approaching vehicle. It grew as loud as the roar of the creek swollen in spring and rushing to the river.

The car passed and again quiet descended. The nearby cawing of a crow seemed to be a calculated attempt to disturb it.

Years had gone by, maybe five, six, since he'd fired a gun while hunting. There was no sense in hunting any more, no one wanted the meat, he couldn't give it away, couldn't get Sara to cook it. The kids screwed up their faces. He didn't know why he had gone for the gun last night, except that the man in the cream-coloured suit had made him want to smash something. To put his fist through a wall, sweep the dishes from the supper table.

The RCMP cruiser drifted by on the highway and the young constable, Krooke, seeing Oliver, tooted the horn lightly. Although Oliver waved in return, he knew that the shave-and-a-haircut greeting wasn't meant to be friendly. The constable might have seen the white Cadillac either arriving or leaving Union Plains, and suspected that he'd bootlegged another bottle. Free traded, was all. He didn't sell hooch, because he didn't want blindness on his conscience. His brother, Romeo, and a couple of Romeo's friends in St. Boniface kept Oliver supplied with the real stuff, which he resold for a tidy profit on holidays and weekends, when the government stores were closed.

A roll of fat chafed against his belt and his buttock muscles cramped as the path began angling downhill. What he had a mind to do was to haul his kids off. With or without Sara. He should take them up north to the bushland, where they might become people of experience. For sure, Sonny Boy would benefit.

What do you mean, experience? Sara had wanted to know when he'd once made the suggestion, speaking his daydream aloud. He admitted that he'd never lived in the bush. That digging for seneca, berry-picking, cutting wood for fire and fence would likely not see them through. Nor would trapping, of which, except for rabbits and raccoons, he also lacked experience.

But he still had the traps; his grandmother had kept her entire family going for a year with those traps. When once he'd caught Sonny Boy and George using the trap chains to hook their bike onto the wagon, he'd shown them how the traps worked. You see this? He demonstrated with a piece of firewood how the jaws of a trap were sprung, its teeth almost severing the wood. This isn't something I want you boys fooling around with. He'd known men to lose a limb. He knew of instances where men caught by a winter storm were found frozen inside a carcass of an elk, a horse. Men in the bush had gone half-crazy from loneliness and blackflies, from the pain of an abscessed tooth.

Even so. His instincts told him that his children would be better off living in the country. He'd take them up to the North Saskatchewan River, maybe. Near Batoche, Fish Creek, where his grandma had once lived. There were still some Vandals up there last he heard. Take his kids away from people who would want to dirty them with their hands, steal the clearness from their eyes. Sara demanded that they be given an education, which she'd been denied. Especially the boys. But it wouldn't matter none what they took up, they'd just wind up being joe-boys to some rich man.

And what would he put his hand to at this late date, if the hotel was shut down? Sara was suspicious of the French, and the priests, and she wouldn't hear of living in a French town. And it wasn't likely that he, a hotel-keeper and bootlegger, would be at home among her people, either.

He smiled despite his worry, recalling a Sunday afternoon when he'd sat down to dinner at his sister-in-law's table and taken an onion-and-sardine sandwich from his pocket. He unwrapped it before Katy's and Kornelius's astonished eyes and set it on his plate, fooled them into believing that he preferred the pungent-smelling sandwich to their farm fare. This was what people of his kind preferred to eat, he said, this, and fish eyes fried to a crisp. Fish eggs, wild mushrooms and CNR strawberries, he added. They might want to go along the track looking to pick the berries sometime, he said. When they failed to laugh, he realized that they didn't know that was what the locals called the turds flushed onto the tracks by rail passengers.

He was surprised, now, to find that the memory made his eyes wet. His kind of people. Those people of his. Dose people. When you're with dose people of yours, your English, she falls apart, eh? Sara liked to tease.

Yes. And sometimes he heard his kind of English coming from the mouth of one of his daughters. Emilie. Ida, too. His people were all gone now. His mother only a scant few years after his father. Romeo was sucked into the bottle and the drinking crowd at the Belgium Club in St. Boniface, the drudgery of a meat-packing house. His sister gone into marriage to a Ukrainian, and he hadn't seen her in over twenty years, although only a hundred miles lay between them. She'd married a bohunk, for God's sake. A confused fella who, on a trip to Winnipeg during the curling season, had seen so many people carrying brooms on a city bus, he'd gone out and bought a barrel of them, thinking there was going to be a shortage.

Oliver strained against the recurring prod of guilt. He should return to town, drop by the house and see if Sara was up and about, check on Ruby and the little ones. Perhaps he'd stop at the municipal yard on the chance that Stevenson was there. Find out if, in spite of being owed for the last filling of the cistern, the man would come to do it again today. The fifty dollars Oliver had received from the souse and her man was a reassuring thickness in his back pocket, and it came to him that perhaps he should use some of the money to pay for the water.

Then he thought that it might be better to put a bit of cash down on the grocery bill; if the grocer was going to be persuaded to stay open, he had to be paid. The Good Maker knows I've done my part to supply the school with students, Oliver had said at the meeting last night, attempting to lighten the atmosphere. To lighten his own atmosphere, his stomach feeling as though it were filled with lead sinkers. Maybe he'd square up for a load of coal from last winter, see what was left over for the water man. Grease the squeaky wheel, Stevenson being less squeaky than most, a good-hearted Anglican. He wouldn't let Sara and the kids go without water.

And then Oliver's thoughts were disturbed by a faraway call. The silence among the willow clumps and stunted oaks on either side of the path was a shifting pool of deadness and he had to concentrate in order to listen through it. Once again, someone or something called. The sound was sharp, like the point of a pencil piercing a sheet of paper. A bird, perhaps, warning others of a predator.

He saw in his mind the quick flutter of a sparrow coming to rest on a snowy windowsill. The memory of the bird, a candle flickering in the early morning room, filled his head. The prayers of the priest mingled with his mother's weeping, with the sound of his father struggling to breathe. Oliver, come away from the window, come and say farewell. Your father is passing.

Yes, and the bird knew it too.

He recalled that winter of his ninth birthday, crossing the river in the late afternoon darkness, his white breath pulled sideways by the wind. The lit-up windows in Aubigny receded as the river curled, its ice cracking in the extreme cold and echoing along the tree-lined shore. The jars of pickled eggs he was meant to deliver to Henri Villebrun's hotel in Union Plains clinked together in the sled box, and the sled's runners rasped against the ice road, whose ruts were polished as smooth as marble by the passage of dray horses and wagons going to and from the ice harvest.

His courage was such that he didn't fear this lonely trek across the frozen channel in the fading light; rather, he drank in the look of the sky banded faintly with shades of violet and pink, the tree branches along the riverbank a filigree of silver. From Winnipeg to the border in the south, winter roads crossed the breadth and length of the river, gleaming white scars. Snowdrifts banked the shorelines, and cast down royal blue shadows in the disguise of slumbering animals.

His mitts smelled of the brine seeping through the cheesecloth his mother had wrapped around the chunks of corned beef she'd placed in the sled, along with the jars of eggs. He paused to taste his leather mitt, and then threw himself backwards onto the snow-packed ice and looked at the sky, at the toenail sliver of a moon. He thought of his father laid out in a cold shed on a block of ice, his white and still face, his work-worn fingers blackened at the knuckles. Oliver wanted to speak. His body swelled with a desire for someone to feel what he was feeling. And all he could say was, Oh God, his voice a puny whisper.

He scooped up snow and pressed it against his mouth, the stinging cold bringing him to his senses and to his feet. He took up the sled's rope and continued on, facing his apprehension of arriving at the hotel, of seeing a lantern lit and hanging from a post beside Stage Coach Road, which meant that the establishment was open for business. Without understanding what the temperance movement was about, or the word *prohibition*, Oliver sensed restriction and danger, the unseemliness of the aspersions cast upon Villebrun's establishment, the kinds of things that were likely to go on behind its velour curtains and in the rooms upstairs.

He shivered in the darkness cast by the shadow of the livery stable while he waited for Villebrun to answer his knock. The back door swung open to a long, narrow room, revealing a pale orange light, releasing a pent-up and mouth-watering odour of venison stew bubbling in tubs on a stove in the kitchen. Oliver wanted to draw away from Villebrun's proprietary clasp of his shoulder, refuse to respond to his pleasantries while he unloaded corned beef and pickled eggs from the sled.

When he climbed the stairs to the second floor, the voices of the patrons in the room below echoed, and a sudden burst of laughter seemed to confirm the presence of the sinister. The corridor at the top of the stairs was lit by wall lamps, circles of flickering light that made the pattern on the carpet swim as he went towards the suite of rooms where Madame Villebrun spent her evenings playing solitaire and sipping at dandelion wine his mother had made, the air in the kitchen tainted all summer with its perfumed must. He knew, as he waited for Madame Villebrun to open the door, that she would be wearing a green kimono.

She greeted him with a smile and a run-on cooing of sentences meant to disarm a shy child, which only intensified that shyness. His face burned in the heat of the room and a spicy scent made his nostrils sting. The windows were hung with what looked to be tasselled shawls, opaque material the colour of skin. Ecru crocheted cushions were scattered across a copper-coloured velvet settee, and on every table was a collection of gewgaws—tiny glass clocks, their inner works spinning, music boxes, porcelain dancing ladies and dandy men, coy and majestic animals.

She went into the adjoining room, where she kept the strongbox, and when she returned, she bent towards him and he looked away, knowing that the kimono would gape open and reveal the pendulous sway of her breasts. He didn't understand why she always wanted to touch him, to stir his hair with her fingers, to pat him on the back. He had put the money she'd given him into his mitt, was turning and had almost made it out the room, when her fingers brushed against his cheek. You're a good boy, she said.

You're a good man, Henri Villebrun said years later, when he came looking for Oliver at the taxi garage in Winnipeg, as though he was underlining the reason behind his generosity in offering Oliver the opportunity to manage the hotel in his absence. Oliver didn't know that Villebrun had tried and failed to interest buyers in the flagging business, and that Oliver was his last hope to supplement his and Madame Villebrun's retirement income in Florida.

Except for the three old gentlemen bachelors, the guest rooms were vacant, and many years had passed since anyone had turned off from the highway in search of accommodations. The rooms had become home to mice who were nibbling away at the wallpaper, while outside, rabbits burrowed in the holes they'd dug all along the foundation of the building. Years had also passed since Oliver had been able to honour his agreement with Henri Villebrun to send him a biyearly accounting of the hotel's intake and output, and deposit fifty percent of what was left in an account at a caisse populaire.

He stood on the path leading down to the river, listening again for the call. He held his breath, and when the call didn't come again he carried on, feeling that the air about him had become charged, and that static drew on the hair on his arms.

THREE

—

Emilie the opaque

EMILIE WATCHED as Manny and Simon latched on to Oliver's hands, her older brothers slouching along on either side of him. Ida clomped on ahead of everyone in a pair of Sara's shoes, the blue wedgies she'd dug out from a corner of the porch because her sandal strap had broken. The wedgies were Sara's garden shoes, and although Ida had wiped them with a wet cloth before leaving the house, the shoes looked used up. Likely they pinched Ida's toes, but the heels made her taller and so she felt older, or so Emilie judged from her sister's self-important walk. When Ida thought no one was looking, she tilted her face to peer down the neck of her blouse, admiring her new freckled breasts. Barf city, disgusting, Emilie thought.

Her family turned at the corner, their murmuring voices fading, while Emilie went towards the oldest residential street in Union Plains. Its grown-up trees formed a canopy of greenery that shaded the boy from Arizona as he straddled his bike in front of his grandmother's prim-looking house. Emilie hurried towards him, the day expanding like a book opening flat against a table.

He waved and dismounted, the tree branches reflecting in his eyeglasses; the wedge of sand-coloured hair lay against his forehead like a hand. A robin called out, its cheery sound suiting the June sky. The coronation coin was a spot of heat moving against her thigh, and she thought to tell him that the Queen of England had sent it to her in the mail, but she knew he wasn't just any kid she could tease.

Charlie was wearing a white T-shirt and jeans that looked to be new, and an expansion bracelet engraved with his initials. Something I wouldn't be caught dead wearing, Sonny Boy had scoffed, when Emilie described it. The veranda curtains were drawn, as they always were, inviting the suspicion that Charlie's grandmother spent most of her day spying on people. She turned the lights off on Halloween, too, as though the town kids didn't already know to avoid her house. The clipped look of the yard and the lack of flower beds suggested stinginess. Sonny Boy said the woman was so tight, her ass squeaked when she walked.

Look, the Queen of England sent this in the mail, Emilie said, despite herself. The coin was light in her palm, unlike a silver dollar.

The Queen of England must have sent one to everyone then, because I've seen other kids with the same thing, Charlie said.

The veranda door of the grandmother's house opened, and Charlie's older brother came down the stairs, a tall, ginger-haired young man who walked like a cat, and whom Emilie had seen only fleetingly, when he drove past her house in the car.

So, where do you guys think you're going? he called.

What's it to you? Charlie replied, and Emilie was surprised at the unpleasant tone of his voice.

The brother wore grey-blue trousers flamboyantly wide at the knees, and a silver belt that looked like crinkled metal. He circled Emilie and Charlie as they stood on the street, the bicycle between them. Emilie felt shabby, her red checkered pedal-pushers worn at the knees; the tails of The Other One's cast-off shirt were so long she'd knotted them to hang like moth-eaten rabbit ears from her waist.

The brother said to Charlie, So, how old is your girlfriend, anyway?

None of your business, Ross, Charlie answered.

Ross glanced back at the veranda before speaking. I was just wondering, see. Dad's going to let me have the car for the day. We could drive to Winnipeg. Maybe Emilie here would like to show us around?

Emilie felt Ross's eyes pass across her body, glance away and then back again, and resisted the urge to cross her arms in front of her chest. She didn't want to admit that she didn't know Winnipeg, except for the several blocks on Portage Avenue between Eaton's and Hudson Bay department stores. She might also be able to find her way to the zoo, but that was it. I'll have to go to the hotel and ask my dad, she told Ross, confident that permission would not be granted.

Ross can go sightseeing on his own, Charlie objected, and Emilie said, It's okay. There's nothing but art and phys ed at school today, anyway.

Charlie gave Emilie a ride downtown, his shoulder blades see-sawing with effort beneath his white T-shirt. Who are you? he'd wanted to know days earlier, when he appeared out of nowhere, coming up behind her on his bicycle. He hadn't asked, Which one are you? Or stated matter-of-factly, You're one of the Vandals, as though there were nothing more to be said or learned. She was Emilie, she told him. He introduced himself as Charlie, from Arizona. He'd driven up with his parents and brother to help their grandmother pack up her house and move to an apartment in Winnipeg.

He dismounted from his bicycle to walk beside her that first day, and when she spoke, he crooked his head to look into her face. His arms were downy with sun-bleached hair and his skin deeply tanned for early spring. No, she hadn't heard of Arizona, she replied to his next question, although of course she had. She was rewarded by a flare of pleasure in his face as he went on to recite the various statistics about Arizona, ending by saying that when he returned to Phoenix, he'd send her a horned toad in the mail to prove they existed.

Charlie had since talked about guided intercontinental ballistic missiles whose trajectories would one day carry them beyond the atmosphere and back to earth, where they'd obliterate an entire city in Soviet Russia. Push of a button, he said. Emilie didn't mention that Russia was the country of her mother's birth. Aunt Katy received letters from relatives and friends still living there, and brought them with her when she came on a visit. Letters crying out with requests for prayer, for clothing, for rescue. Katy replied to those letters, although she said she had nightmares of being kidnapped and spirited out of Canada. Of being sent into forced labour in a Siberian gulag.

That's what happens to people over there who believe in God, Aunt Katy declared. Which Emilie thought was stupid—they should just say they didn't believe, and everything would be copacetic. That doesn't mean God stops believing in them, she said, voicing her opinion in Sara's presence and being reminded swiftly to watch her mouth, as there was such a thing as an unpardonable sin. The entreaties Aunt Katy translated from the soft grey paper hung around like weary ghosts, and often sent Emilie to a field beside the schoolyard, a large open space where she could practise running. She wondered what could be more unpardonable than a cleverly concealed gopher hole, the possibility of breaking an ankle.

What she appreciated the most about Charlie was that he ignored the fact that the back of her hand was never without a bandage of some sort, and she didn't need to explain that there was a colony of warts underneath it. He didn't seem to notice that she was female, either, and that left her free to take him in. To grow to love the flashes of pleasure in his caramel eyes, the wetness of his small mouth, the light beaming in his face when she told him something he didn't already know.

They rode past two girls who were going to school, one of them being June, Emilie's best friend. See you later, Emilie called, and was rewarded by June's eyes going large. Since Charlie had come to town, Emilie hadn't gone to June's house after school to hang out in the lean-to they'd built by nailing boards to a fence.

The sign on the hotel vestibule door was turned to OPEN, and the poolroom blinds were drawn wide to let in the morning sun. Emilie went up the steps, imagining herself returning to Charlie moments later with an appropriate hangdog expression and saying, My dad said I can't miss school. She went into the poolroom calling for Oliver, and heard the sound of coughing coming from the parlour.

She entered the dingy, ill-lit room and found Cecil, the youngest of the three elderly boarders, the decrepits, Emilie called them, seated at a table. Cecil had the gout, Oliver said, which meant that his bunions were painful and he swore a lot. His red hair was going grey, and pouches of pebbly skin hung under his eyes. He hacked phlegm into an already stiff handkerchief, his rheumy eyes peering at her.

Where's that Christly daddy of yours? Cecil asked. I thought I heard him putting on the coffee, but when I came down, damned if he wasn't here. My pump needs priming.

Sometimes, when Emilie came looking for Oliver, Cecil or one of the other decrepits would tell her that Oliver had gone to see a man about a dog. He's gone to see ABC the Goldfish, they sometimes said, a joke they had between them, which she took to mean that Oliver had stepped out on business. Or he was on the toilet reading the newspaper. But now, of course, she knew what it really meant. She knew ABC the Goldfish stood for the French lady in Aubigny, Alice Bouchard.

Emilie wasn't aware that sometimes, if her father saw her coming, he'd step into the broom-closet office and hold his breath while she rapped on its door. Or that he stood listening at the back door as the old gentlemen put Emilie off the track.

Oliver stayed out of sight because Emilie always wanted something, and Oliver found it hard to say no to her. She wanted money for Band-Aids to plaster over her warts, or she'd been sent on someone else's behalf. Alvina needed a box of cornflakes, which was how Alvina instructed Emilie to ask for money to buy the monthly box of Kotex. Now Ida needed a monthly box of cornflakes too. Emilie's sisters sent her to ask for money to purchase socks, school supplies, a mother-of-pearl compact Ida had seen in the grocery store window. The boys sent Emilie to beg for advances on their allowance. Sara sent Emilie when her grocery money ran out and there was no meat in the refrigerator for their supper meal. She sent Emilie with the kids' shoes when they wore through at the soles, and Oliver would be required to walk to the highway and flag down a southbound bus and have the driver drop the shoes at the depot in Alexander Morris, where Otto, the shoemaker, would retrieve them.

Or perhaps the sharp-boned and see-through Emilie came to lodge a complaint, rattling and loose like a half-full sack of marbles, her eyes glittering and casting about for something in the room to fix her attention on while she delivered it. The buffalo staring into the past, its beard hoary with dust and worn from being tugged and patted. Yes, that. The multiple reflections of Oliver in the gilded mirrors on opposite walls, head and shoulders turning towards her and at the same time turning away.

She might be coming to complain that Sara had smacked her across the face, pinched her arms, switched her legs with a belt. Sara had been known to turn on her suddenly, her arms swinging about Emilie's head. The thing is, Dad, Emilie said, winding up her complaints with a question that the constriction in her throat made difficult to pose. The thing is, the thing is, Dad, why doesn't Mom like me? Of course your mother likes you, Oliver would tell her, knowing that the words were as satisfying as a warm beer on a hot Saturday afternoon. Most of the time it was better to hide when he saw

Emilie coming, as there was nothing in his experience that he could draw on to ease her hurt. Sara could not abide this girl, and for the life of him, Oliver didn't understand why.

Emilie and Charlie left the hotel and went rattling through the streets of town in search of Oliver. Now, as they rode down the access road towards the highway, she saw him. She watched her father glide effortlessly along the river path, as though drawn by a magnet. His shoulders were equal to the height of the treetops, a fringe of greening bur oak, poplar and the Manitoba maples that marked the river's presence below the path.

There's my dad, Emilie shouted into Charlie's neck, not understanding her reluctance to call out to Oliver while he was still within earshot. Charlie swerved to avoid a pothole and they stopped, but she kept her arms about his ribs. He smelled like a dog, the odour a pleasant twist in her nostrils that made her want to sneeze.

I've seen that guy before. That's your dad? Charlie asked, in an incredulous tone of voice.

What was he implying? Did he think Oliver should be taller or shorter? Was that admiration she detected in Charlie's voice? She decided that he was amazed they were so dissimilar in appearance, not knowing that Charlie's grandmother had pointed Oliver out to him one day. You see that man? He's a half-breed, she'd said, the word dripping with the implication that Oliver was a mongrel.

If Emilie had called out to Oliver then, he might have put his hands at his hips and watched for approaching vehicles while she and Charlie crossed over the highway. He would have been peeved that she'd tracked him down, but only mildly. He would have sent Charlie packing and marched Emilie back to school, and himself to the hotel. In doing so, Oliver might have stopped the onward flow of that bright onward-flowing day, which wound up with Emilie finally learning what people were saying about them.

Oliver was nearing the place where the path forked, one narrow trail leading through the trees while the other continued on south along Stage Coach Road, as far as a person was inclined to walk. To Alexander Morris, to St. Jean Baptiste and Pembina, as far as Kansas City and the Gulf of Mexico. Moments later Oliver turned towards the trees and the river, his back to them now, only his shoulders visible as the trail descended. And then he was out of sight.

Emilie said to Charlie, My mother's sick and so I can't ask her, either. His heart beat against her palm; she imagined that she felt him fizzing, that he was effervescent with the ideas and information he'd gained from reading, and from the discussions he carried on with his scientist father. Emilie hadn't met anyone like Charlie, someone so intensely pleased just to be breathing, so pleased with himself.

Should I take you to school? Charlie asked. He jabbed the bridge of his brown-rimmed glasses with a finger, the movement releasing another wave of wet-dog odour.

The school bell began to ring, a brittle clang that echoed.

I'll walk to school, Emilie said, and watched as Charlie rode away. He stood on the pedals and leaned over the handlebars, raising a smoke of dust that lingered along the road. And that was the last she ever saw of Charlie, that smoke, a silence settling between them.

—

Florence Dressler had once remarked to Sara that Emilie reminded her of a flower that had been pressed between the pages of a book. The girl's washed-out blue eyes and pale skin, hair so blonde that it was near to being silver, were like the flower's petals when they became opaque enough to read through.

There was no reason to suspect that Emilie's extreme thinness was caused by anything more than a cranked-up metabolism. The flick of a finger against an arm was enough to raise a bruise. Emilie read the story of the princess and the pea, and thought she might be a descendant of royalty, Russian perhaps. Then a teacher drew her attention to the tale of the ugly duckling and Emilie perceived that, if the teacher thought she was in need of encouragement, there must be something wrong with her. And indeed, not long afterwards, the first wart appeared on her hand.

It's like she's Swedish, her uncle Romeo said, when his wife, Claudette, suggested Emilie's paleness might be caused by anemia. They'd come for a weekend visit without their five children, their oldest being twin sons older than Alvina who were employed at the meat-packing house and able to hold down the fort. Throughout their weekend visit Romeo referred to Emilie as Sonja, but the nickname refused to stick.

That Emilie, she's too slapdash. She's mouthy, too careless, Sara complained in Romeo's presence. It's no wonder people don't like the girl, Sara said, as though this were a proven fact, as though people had drawn up a list of Emilie's deficiencies and presented the results to her mother.

I like that girl fine, Romeo said. When Sara left the room, he winked and gave Emilie two bits. Then he raised a mug of beer in a mock salute and drained it.

Romeo was responsible for Sonny Boy being called Sonny Boy and not Norbert, Oliver's father's name, which Sara had bestowed on her first-born son out of a sense of obligation. Beer talk, Sara said, when Romeo became expansive and gregarious, caught the children on the run and swung them to his shoulders. Yes, yes. He's a barrel of fun, Sara said. It's the drink. It's the beer talking. But she was secretly pleased and beholden to Romeo for the name Sonny Boy. He had been the most beautiful of all her babies. His presence in her sphere was perpetual sunshine. That Romeo recognized this tempered Sara's judgment of him, and she quietly endured his and Claudette's periodic weekend visits.

Romeo was also responsible for George being known as The Other One. It was simply a forgetfulness on his part but the name had taken. As a small boy, George had crawled into a culvert to avoid speaking to an adult approaching in the street. He hated having to answer lame questions, he said. By calling George The Other One, his uncle had afforded him a degree of anonymity, and if he ever objected he never made it known.

On another visit, Romeo called Emilie Angelique, but that name didn't stick either. The wan and see-through Emilie was as near to being angelic and ethereal as a wood tick. She vibrated with an energy that threatened to mow people down. But as she watched Charlie going away down the road, a lethargy set in that made her limbs feel stretched and useless.

A stillness hovered above the town and she knew that its streets were empty. She was already late for school, and would find herself on the periphery of activity and instruction for the remainder of the day. Even her best friend, June of the perfume breath, would ignore her for a time.

She told herself there was no point in hurrying. She could have taken the fire escape and entered the school from the emptied second floor, and claimed that she'd been present all along but hadn't heard the bell. But to do that she'd have to get past Alvina, parked in a classroom, seated at the typewriter, the words-per-minute speed pins she'd already earned lined up across her cardigan breast.

Emilie didn't understand how Alvina did it. Where had she found the gumption to study by correspondence, and the brains to teach herself how to type? Alvina had fashioned a paper keyboard, which she placed on her stomach at night. While she lay in the top bunk, her fingers tapped against the keyboard in the dark as she whispered the alphabet; whispered, Now is the time, now is the time, now is the time.

As she had been doing last night when Emilie and Ida undressed in the dark, Ida crawling into the bottom bunk and instantly falling asleep. Emilie joined Ruby and Sharon on the mattress on the floor, and listened to Alvina practise typing. The street light beyond the window illuminated the row of pictures hung on the wall where it met the sloped ceiling. Waves washed along a shoreline, poplar trees bent over lake water, a sailboat skimmed across a water horizon.

Now is the time for all good people, Alvina whispered, and Emilie longed to interrupt. She wanted to tell Alvina about Oliver leaving the meeting at the school and taking them to Aubigny. From the angry sound of Sara's voice in the kitchen, likely by the end of the night Alvina would know. But she wouldn't know that their father and ABC the Goldfish had kissed.

Instead of going home they had crossed the highway and gone down to the ferry landing. Oliver, Emilie, Ida, their lips sewn shut. Silent as fieldstones as they waited for Oliver's uncle Ulysse to bring the ferry across.

Ida took Emilie by the hand even before they were underway, as though it were Emilie she feared might spill into the water, and not herself. The engine and its spinning propeller vibrated in the planks, and Emilie knew they were moving by the reflection of the stars on the water advancing and retreating beneath them. Water lapped against wood, Ulysse's pipestem clicked between his teeth as he sucked on it, the *putt-putt* of the engine filled the silence.

Oliver hawked and spat into the river, and Emilie was astounded that he would do so, given that he called spitting a filthy habit. But there were no terms of reference for what was happening. Oliver leaping to his feet during the meeting and leaving. Now this journey across the river to Aubigny, the town of Oliver's youth. Ulysse sat on a chair that had been screwed into the wall of one of the ferry's two motor sheds, his legs crossed.

Emilie watched as the blackness of one shore retreated and the other advanced. Ulysse had recovered from his surprise at finding them waiting on the ferry landing, and he spoke to Oliver now, in French, but she discerned the question—Where was the Deetch? Deetch meaning Sara. His tone of voice implied that he was wondering whether something untoward had happened.

Oliver's reply was curt.

Emilie and Ida stood between the two men, Ulysse seated on the chair, Oliver leaning on the other motor shed. They had nothing to hang on to except each other. Emilie felt a tremor in her sister's hand, and saw that her eyes were cast down to avoid looking at the water, or so Emilie thought. But then Ida blurted what was on her mind. Aren't we good enough? Aren't we good enough to have our own school? she asked Oliver.

By cracky, Oliver said. Only fools believe everything they hear. And I didn't leave the goddamned meeting just to be hauled back to the subject. So keep your trap shut.

The ensuing silence vibrated, Ida shrinking into herself over Oliver's uncommon harshness. She let go of Emilie's hand and lurched over to the guard chain, stumbling on the broken sandal strap. She leaned into the chain and covered her face with her hands. Emilie went over to her, hooked a finger into the waist of her sister's skirt to encourage her to come away from the edge. She thought, the trouble with Ida is that she isn't used to being in trouble.

During the remainder of the river crossing they didn't speak. At the sound of water rushing against the landing, Oliver pushed himself upright. Emilie and Ida followed him up the incline of the ferry road, the ditches on either side of it an eruption of sound. Frogs burped and cleared their throats, falling silent when they passed by, and erupting again behind them. But as they reached the town the cacophony ended abruptly. Street lights burned holes in the darkness, the main street of Aubigny opening up before them.

The sidewalk undulated beneath Emilie's feet, a wavy tarred walk that was pitted with stones, and not a wooden sidewalk as she was accustomed to. Wooden sidewalks revealed the state of a pedestrian's mind, Emilie had discovered from listening as she lay on the made-up bed on the girls' bedroom floor. Revealed Sara's impatience, Oliver's reluctance to return home, Alvina's worried hurrying, the heels of Sonny Boy and The Other One coming down hard in a quarrel.

Here in Aubigny, she was in danger of putting a foot down and finding air, of being pitched onto her face. The bow of her dress had come undone and the ties trailed against her legs, but she didn't want to risk disturbing the unravelling of this unusual night to stop and fasten them. She didn't want to risk falling behind Oliver's determined steps as they passed a church, its steeple casting a narrow shadow across the street, and a machine shop whose dusty windows were dimly lit. When a window suddenly brightened with a cascade of white sparks, Oliver stopped to take it in.

The place where my father worked, he said. Dead, long time ago. Tuberculosis, he added, telling the girls what they already knew. The pauses between his sentences were filled with other sentences, entire scenes, the scent of his mother's hair falling across his face as she bent over him in bed, listening as he recited the rosary. No use looking for the house, she's long gone, he said, although Emilie and Ida already knew this too.

They approached a cinder-block building, the caisse populaire, and Oliver's forward march began to waver. His muscles unclenched and his shoulders dropped, as though he was fatigued. The impulse that had propelled him to his feet and out of the meeting seemed to be wearing thin.

Our house was there, he said, where the credit union now stood, which Emilie also knew but wouldn't say, because she understood that he was talking to himself. They continued, passing through rectangles of light from the windows of houses along the street. They didn't come upon anyone out walking or in any of the yards, although the night was warm enough. Just as they were approaching a large and square two-storey house, its front door opened. A woman crossed a wraparound veranda and came down the stairs. She went over to the gate and leaned across it, her head a flash of maroon and the brass buttons on her burnt-orange shoulders glinting in the light of a street lamp.

At the sight of her, Oliver turned round quickly and headed back where they had come from, Emilie and Ida needing to hop-skip in order to catch up. He stopped and looked down at them as though emerging from a daze, as though he'd just realized they were present. Damn foolish nonsense, he muttered, and Emilie thought he was harking back to what Ida had said on the ferry. It did not occur to her that he realized he was about to visit an old flame with two of his daughters in tow.

Alice called out to them. She called Oliver's name as a question, and then again, as an exclamation. Oliver turned towards her as she came through the gate and stood still for a moment, looking at him. She called again, and this time his name was an expression of pleasure.

Alice, Oliver said, as though he too were surprised and pleased.

She hurried to meet them, speaking in French, and Emilie thought the sound of it was as lively and lilting as her step, the gentle sway of her body. She'd almost reached them when she became aware of Emilie and Ida, and hesitated.

This is very nice, Alice said moments later, in English, as she closed the gap between them. She hooked an arm through Oliver's. You've come calling on your old school friend and brought along two charming visitors. As they went towards the house, the street light illuminated her vivacious features, accentuated by her short curly hair in a poodle cut. The tight curls framed her heart-shaped face; the mandarin collar of her orange dress and the shoulder epaulets gave her a squared look.

Alice went into the house to call her parents, and Oliver repeated the description—we're old school friends, he said, as though wanting this to be clear. And then his features lit up with pleasure at the sight of Alice's mother, a diminutive white-haired woman coming to meet him with a string of run-on sentences, her voice lively and young. They embraced, Oliver bestowing a kiss on both her cheeks, while a bald and grossly overweight man in a dark suit presided over the scene from the top veranda step, his eyes briefly passing over Emilie and Ida, before he turned away and sat down in a wicker chair.

For near to an hour they sat in the quiet of the veranda, illuminated by a light shining through sheer curtains on a large window. Emilie and Ida rocked on the porch swing, Emilie nearest the lit window, and when she turned her head she could see through the sheer curtains into the room; a lamp highlighted pages of music spread across a piano, there was a glass tank glowing with the greenery of water plants. Stained-glass flowers unfurled across the top of the window and seemed to change colour with the motion of the swing.

The light from the window illuminated Alice's hair, the deep colour of her lipstick. She seemed carefully drawn, a mole on a cheek an exact circle, her eyebrows matching thin arches that rose and fell as she listened to her mother talk non-stop. Sometimes her mother leaned towards Oliver, closing the space between them to tap him on a knee. That familiarity startled Emilie, the right this woman seemed to think she had because she'd known him in another life.

The toboggan of run-on sentences swooped up and down, sometimes ending in a spill of laughter or a click of her tongue, while Alice looked on, turning a charm bracelet on her wrist, fingering each piece, her impatience obvious. Her father didn't ever speak, except when he greeted Oliver with a kind of grunt and a curt nod, taking his watch from a vest pocket and glancing at it pointedly.

As the hour passed, his breathing grew laboured and his walrus moustache began to droop towards his chest. Then his head dipped and the wheezing gave way to snores. Alice spoke sharply to her mother, who appeared not to hear what she'd said.

At last her mother's talk subsided, and Alice broke the silence, speaking to Oliver in English. When I was in Winnipeg a couple of days ago, someone cut the tires on my car. In broad daylight, can you imagine? Two tires cut to ribbons, she said, her voice plaintive and her tiny hands coming towards him, their palms turned up as though she held the tires up for him to see. Two brand new tires, ruined, she said.

Her mother sucked air between her teeth and nodded. It's true, she said. My God, what's it coming to, eh? Can you tell me?

Punks, Oliver pronounced. He'd read in the newspaper that there were gangs of kids hanging out in downtown Winnipeg. They've got nothing better to do than— He was stopped mid-sentence by a trickling sound.

A puddle grew under the old man's chair. Alice became stiff with anger, while her mother leapt to her feet and said, Hey! Hey! Hey! She went over to her husband and jostled him awake.

The two women then helped him up from the chair, and with much manoeuvring and effort they assisted him into the house, while Oliver looked on, shaking his head. Remembering how this man had intimidated him throughout his young life, how the creak of his heavy steps in the house had been enough to make Oliver stumble through a song he played for Alice and her sisters, his fingers gone cold on the piano.

He lit a cigarette and drew on it, the spark of light accentuating the hook of his strong nose. He exhaled a stream of smoke, as though releasing pent-up pressure. All the king's horses, he muttered. And then he said, Well girls, your mother's going to be in a snit. Better hit the road.

Emilie was about to get up from the porch swing, when Alice returned. She stood in the doorway for a moment, and then stretched out a hand to Oliver. With painstaking care he ground out his cigarette with the heel of his boot and flicked the butt over the veranda railing, into the yard. He followed Alice into the house, Emilie and Ida remaining on the swing, intuition saying that the invitation didn't include them.

Emilie saw Alice enter the living room and go over to sit at the piano, her body swaying in time to the music she played, which was charged with melancholy.

Oh great, Ida complained. Although she too was a piano player, she was impatient for the visit to end. She couldn't see into the room and, unlike Emilie, she had no sights to entertain her except for the dark shrubs crowding the fence beyond the yard. Emilie watched Oliver roam about, stop to look at pictures hanging on the walls, to peer into the fish tank. He moved out of sight, and reappeared a moment later behind Alice, watching as she played, and then he reached across her shoulder and flipped the music book shut.

You! Alice exclaimed, and in mock exasperation she got up from the bench and swatted at Oliver's hands, advancing as he retreated, his arms coming up in surrender.

He turned towards the door as though he might leave, his smile fading, while Alice remained in the centre of the room, her hands pressed against her stomach. She spoke, but Emilie did not hear her say, Why would someone cut the tires on my car? It makes me feel so old, so small.

Emilie saw Alice's features crinkle, and realized she was about to cry. Alice stepped up behind Oliver and slipped her arms around his waist and they stood like that, Alice's rouged cheek set between Oliver's shoulder blades, he with his arms at his sides. She released him and went round him and turned her face up to his. They looked into one another's eyes, and then their bodies came together.

Emilie went through the gate behind Oliver and Ida, and into the street, her heart a hamster running in a wheel. The night air was a press of wet tissue against her legs that made her shiver, the darkness beyond the sphere of the street light seemed a deep well she might fall into. Their mouths had touched. Hurry up, she urged Ida, and grabbed at her arm. Alice called out to them and they all turned to see her coming across the yard and over to the fence, carrying a shopping bag.

I've been holding on to these, hoping I might see you, she said. The bag bulged with several pairs of shoes. Shoes that Alice had grown tired of, that were out of fashion or no longer suited her wardrobe. Shoes that she had purchased in Paris and Florida the years when she accompanied her parents on their vacations. Shoes that she had purchased on a whim, because she was bored, whose soles were sometimes barely scuffed from wear.

Shoes that Alvina, Ida, Emilie and Ruby in turn would wear. They'd gone slapping about Sara's bedroom in a pair of velvet mules, teetering on spikes that gouged crescent imprints on the soft linoleum floor. When they weren't fighting over the shoes, they made off with them. Took them to a friend's house as a kind of bring-and-brag, as the shoes were unlike any to be found in Otto's shop in Alexander Morris, or in any of the department stores in Winnipeg. To them the shoes were art, objects to be admired, puzzled over and then abandoned. Eventually they lost a shoe here, a shoe there, and Sara would get dressed for church, for a day of shopping in Winnipeg, with a particular shoe in mind, only to discover that its mate was gone.

—

The dust the boy from Arizona raised when he rode off on his bicycle settled, the school bell stopped ringing. A car swept by on Stage Coach Road and Emilie watched it pass, the sound becoming a thin line that snapped, and once again the dense silence descended. Oliver has gone to see a man about a dog. He's gone to see ABC the Goldfish. AB being Alice Bouchard. The goldfish the fish in her aquarium, of course. The decrepits had been talking in code. And that was where Oliver was headed now, she was certain. He'd taken the path leading down to the ferry and the river. He was going off to see ABC the Goldfish. The need for Oliver to return home became a burning coal in Emilie's brain.

Dad! Dad! she shouted, and began to run, her flimsy canvas shoes sliding on the loose gravel. Wait up, wait for me. What would she do without him?

She called again. A vehicle was coming along the access road behind her. She pounded at her thighs in frustration, knowing that Oliver had likely reached the ferry and was out of earshot. Tires crunched through gravel and she felt the heat of the car's engine as it approached and came alongside. Even before its passenger door swung open, she sensed that the person behind the wheel was Charlie's brother, Ross.

FOUR

Ruby the tightrope walker

RUBY CLIMBED THE STAIRS, leaving behind the familiar and comforting odour of winter still clinging to the parkas and coats hanging from hooks on all the walls of the downstairs hall. She counted the steps silently as she ascended into the dimness, her heart beginning to thud. The music playing from the radio was a river of muffled sound, and the quieter it became, the more she was aware of being alone, of the kind of feeling she had when she played blind man's bluff, stumbling and groping the air, desperate to touch someone and know that she hadn't disappeared along with the world when the blindfold came down over her eyes.

She slid her palm against the wall, anticipating the bend in the stairs where that wall ended and another began, and then six more steps to the landing of the upper hall. There were thirteen steps in all, eleven, twelve, thirteen, Ruby counted, and at last she was home free.

The dove-grey walls of the landing were illuminated by the pale northern morning light coming from the girls' bedroom doorway. Alvina had made the bunk bed, rolled up the bedding on the floor and set it on a trunk. *We're all in our places, with bright shining faces, oh this is the way to start a new day. But you'd better not go alone, for every bear that ever there was—* the songs came to Ruby unbidden, their words returning now that she was home free. Their presence was as natural as the sound of her own breath.

She went along the hall, passing by the door of the boys' bedroom, where Alvina's hand was also evident in the smoothed and tucked-in blankets of the army cots, pajamas folded and set at the foot of each one. A bed should be made up so tightly you can bounce a coin on it, Oliver had once said, in jest, citing his army days, and Sonny Boy kept putting Alvina to the test. The girls can do it, Sara said, when Oliver suggested that the boys might learn to make their own beds. Sara's job, according to Sara, was to teach the girls how to care for the boys, and for the house, while she reigned over the kitchen. She taught them that a boy's appetite was a raging furnace that required to be stoked with the largest of the pork chops, mounds of mashed *patates,* pudding desserts she arranged on the space-saver according to size, the boys' being the largest and having an extra dollop of jam. More for the boys! More for the boys than for the girls! As it should be, as God intended.

Ruby thought of the rope that was strung between two trees at the side of the yard, and she said, I'm a type-rope walker, and she teetered along the hall one foot in front of the other, aiming for the sunlight shining in the doorway of her parents' bedroom. She expected that at any moment she would lose her balance, that at the end of the hall she would come face to face with an argument: Alvina said I should come and get the baby. When it's time to get the baby, I'll be the one to tell you, and not Alvina.

Her heart thumped faster than the clock ticking on the bureau in the room beyond. Like the other children, she never entered her parents' room without hesitating, and she was propelled now only by the affection she had for Patsy Anne and the anticipation of her sister's hot hands against her neck, the clutching and hanging on, as though Ruby's freeing her from the crib meant she had saved her life.

Ruby pushed through the doorway, her inner music stopped as her eyes adjusted to the outpouring of sunlight. She squinted against it and noted a shopping bag lying on the floor, shoes tumbling from it. New second-hand shoes to be added to the jumble of footwear at the bottom of Sara's closet. The shoes were expensive and frivolous, and almost small enough to fit Ruby's foot.

An overstuffed maroon chair in a corner, a matching hassock and the floor lamp on one side of the chair were for the convenience of Oliver, who endured long hours when he couldn't sleep by reading *Field & Stream, Reader's Digest.* The hassock was where Oliver sat when he shaved Sara's armpits. She claimed not to be able to do it, and so, monthly, Oliver obliged. She carried a basin of water up to their bedroom and he joined her while she stripped to her petticoat and perched on the arm of the chair. Oliver sat before her on the hassock, drew her pebbly underarm skin taut and said, Kootchy, kootchy, coo, as he brushed up a lather of suds. He scraped away the hair and said it was getting curlier. Lately he'd been telling her that it was not as thick as it used to be.

When he finished shaving Sara's armpits, he said, So what's next, eh? I'm just getting warmed up. He threatened to have a go at her pubic hair, should she so choose, her laughter girlish as he chased her around the chair brandishing the razor, knowing that Ruby and several other Vandals crouched outside the door, listening. Their curiosity overcame their apprehension of intruding, the closed door being an invitation to come sniffing about, just as a locked diary was an outright invitation to invade privacy.

An ancient sewing machine beneath the window provided an hour or so of quiet for Sara, whose children knew she was out of bounds when she mended, unapproachable while she bent over the machine, sometimes singing a song in German.

There were the familiar heaps of clothing on chairs and draped over the open closet doors, and Ruby was engulfed by all the various adult odours emanating from the closet. Perspiration, tobacco, a musty smell of dried roses—roses that, according to Alvina, Oliver had sent to Sara when he was away barbering during the war. The bouquets were delivered from Winnipeg on a mid-afternoon Greyhound bus, and dropped off beside Stage Coach Road, along with various other packages and the usual bundle of daily newspapers.

In the closet on a shelf was a chocolate box holding pots of rouge gone chalky and rancid-smelling, hair combs and velvet bows. The box held the blue silk scarf Sara had borrowed from Emily Ashburn, and several bottles of nail varnish Oliver had purchased when Sara fretted about the look of her hands, which had never been opened.

Unlike her older sisters, Ruby hadn't reached the age when her inquisitiveness would not be denied. She had yet to come upon the box containing packets of letters that smelled of her parents' fingers. *My dearest Sara, my beloved pigeon, how I wish I could stroke your breasts, and that you were here to warm my lonely cot. Dear Oliver, don't forget that you promised the boys, on your next leave you said you would see to it that they got a wagon. Sonny's too small to be carrying the newspaper bag all over town.*

Ruby didn't know that the closet held the entire history of her parents' lives. A hand mirror tucked beneath a stack of bed linen on a shelf on Sara's side of the closet was the sole keepsake of her dead mother; a homemade fiddle whose strings were missing had once belonged to Oliver's grandfather. In a jacket pocket of Oliver's army uniform there was a wad of papers folded down into a square, official documents he had come upon in a tobacco tin in his mother's house after her death. The documents had been issued by the Government of Canada some seventy years ago, when Manitoba became a province.

With these documents the government had hoped to settle the land question of what to do about the Metis nation that had come into being along the Red and Assiniboine Rivers. The bearer was entitled to either land or money, but few claimed either right, mistrusting the intent, or they were hornswoggled by land speculators, or they went to claim the land and found others, usually English-speaking settlers, already farming it. *I am a half-breed head of a family resident in the Parish of Ste Agathe, in the said Province, on the 15th day of July, AD 1876, and consisting of myself and wife and children and I claim to be entitled as such head of family to receive a grant of one hundred and sixty acres of land or to receive Scrip for one hundred and sixty dollars pursuant to the Statute in that behalf.*

There she was, Ruby thought. There was Patsy Anne, the diddle, diddle dumpling, sitting in the crib that was jammed into a far corner of the bedroom. Patsy Anne, in person.

When she reached the age of two, or if in the meantime another baby came along, she would be ousted from the crib to join Ruby, Emilie and Sharon on the made-up bed on the floor. On the outside edge of it, so there wasn't the danger of someone rolling onto her. Until Patsy learned to stay put, as Ruby had done, she would crawl off across the room during the night, to be found in the morning, a chilled damp heap in a corner of the room, or tucked away under the bunk bed, her diaper lumpy with the night deposit.

What little hair Patsy had was pasted against one side of her head and stuck out the other. She peered through the rungs at Sara, her baby face a study of glumness at the sight of her mother leaning over the space between the bed and the crib. Sara's hand grasped the rungs, and the other clutched her forehead as she dry-heaved into the wastebasket.

At the sight of Ruby, Patsy Anne squealed with relief and scrambled to her feet. Sara reared up, sweeping hair from her eyes in order to see who had come into the room. Her complexion had a yellowish tinge and gleamed with sweat. She belched loudly and long, and then lunged for the side of the bed and began retching anew.

Ruby asked, Should I get some water?, which was the prescribed treatment for stomach upset, fever and colds. For growing pains, toothaches and whooping cough. Depending on the degree of illness, the water was sometimes topped up with grape juice.

Either Sara hadn't heard, or she was too busy to reply. *Roll, roll, roll your boat, gently down the stream.* Beyond the window the sky was the same blue as the ocean pictures Emilie made, sunsets on water, clouds, boats. She taped the drawings on their bedroom walls. Ida complained, as she had been born with a fear of water. Alvina wanted one wall for the photographs she cut from movie magazines. Bickering, always bickering, Sara said. The boys didn't bicker when Sonny Boy plastered their walls with Joe Palooka comic strips.

Alvina said I should— Ruby thought, not finishing that thought, as Sara came up for air. She gathered a corner of the sheet and pressed it against her face, as though wanting to shut out the room. The muffled sounds coming from the bed sounded like crying, and the idea tore a hole in Ruby's desire to speak.

Patsy Anne's mouth begin to quiver. Yah, yah, Ruby's coming, Ruby assured her sister silently, and anticipated the warm stickiness of her chubby body, her bum shining with wetness when Ruby peeled the sodden diaper away, Patsy Anne eagerly lifting her bottom so Ruby could slide a fresh diaper under her.

There was movement beyond the bedroom window, which proved to be Florence Dressler coming out from her house carrying a basket of wash, which she began hanging on the line. *They all ran after the farmer's wife, and she cut off their tails with the carving knife. Did you ever see such a fright in your life?*

Sara slid down in bed and lay on her side, the sheet bunched beneath her chin, her hands curled there in gentle fists, in the same way she had slept since being a child the age of Ruby, as though she was protecting her throat. There was nothing left in her stomach to bring up except for bile, which was harsh-tasting and green.

That whore, Sara thought. The woman had used the shoes as a way to keep her hooks into Oliver. She pictured

Alice Bouchard as she'd seen her only days ago, when happening upon her in the city—her carefully painted kewpie-doll features, the flare of recognition in her face, small brilliant eyes flickering across Sara's stomach before she turned away. No, I'm not pregnant, Sara had wanted to shout. As she sometimes wanted to shout while pushing a carriage along the street in Union Plains, her children hanging on to it on all sides. She felt eyes turning in her direction. There goes the baby manufacturing plant. Why don't you try crossing your legs?

We're just friends, Oliver had said last night, admitting that he'd gone to see Alice. All these years, while I waited up half the night, you went to see that woman, Sara said, and at the same time she had wished, hoped, willed that Oliver would say that wasn't so. But he hadn't. With his silence he'd as much as admitted that he'd been to see the Bouchard woman all those nights when she had hoped that he truly was out stretching his legs, had stayed past closing to have a game of cards with the old fellas. Is all, is all, he said. Had me a walk, is all.

With his silence, Oliver had stolen her refuge of uncertainty. Knowing left her shaking and confused about what to do next, except to stay where she was, in bed, struck down by what might be a gallbladder attack, but more than likely it was jealousy.

Mom, Ruby called, and watched a ladybug crawl across the oiled veneer of the sewing machine under the window. Alvina said I should bring the baby downstairs, Ruby dared to continue, and held her breath, expecting to be buffeted by objections.

Well take her! Take her, for Pete's sake, just take the baby downstairs! Sara cried out, her voice sounding as though she had the croup.

All right, Ruby would take Patsy Anne downstairs. But how could she? She couldn't get at her. There wasn't enough room to squeeze into the narrow space next to the crib to let its side down, without coming too near to Sara.

As if realizing Ruby's dilemma, Patsy Anne pulled herself over to the end of the crib and held up her arms and wrinkled her nose to make herself more appealing. Sara lay curled in bed recalling Alice's mincing step, her hips shifting beneath her narrow skirt as she lifted the lid of the trunk of her car and set the packages down inside. Sara cringed, seeing herself as she'd seen her reflection in the shop window that day, her suit crumpled from the bus trip, the hat she'd put on before the bureau mirror that morning, which had made her feel stylish and sophisticated, so obviously a cheap imitation of the real thing. Sara groaned now, experiencing the desire she'd had to kick her shoes off in the street, unable to pretend any longer that they'd come from a woman whom time had rendered a faceless stranger.

Okay, okay, Patsy. Ruby's going to take you downstairs, yah, yah, Ruby said. She needed a chair. That was about the only way she'd be able to lift Patsy Anne over the end of the crib.

I'm strong, Ruby reminded herself as she swept clothes from a chair and carried it across the room. There wasn't enough space between the sewing machine and the crib to set the chair down, so she set the chair off to the side and climbed up.

The yard beyond the window seemed farther away as she stood on the chair, like a picnic set down on a blanket. Toys and roller skates littered the huge pancake circle of the water cistern. She might clear off the cistern later, put on skates and practise on the cement surface, although it was only large enough for two short glides before she stumbled off the edge into stringy weeds that got stuck in the wheels. One day soon, Oliver had said, I'll take you kids to Alexander Morris and you can skate on the car dealership lot. This time we'll ride the goddamned bus, he'd said. And not in the back of the water man's truck, as they had done the last time.

Ruby riding with two others in the cab, struck silent to see her father shifting gears, the engine revving and blowing blue smoke, the differential squealing as the truck jounced along the highway. *We'll be coming around the mountain when we come, yahoo! We'll be coming around the mountain when we come.* Only they weren't riding six white horses but the water man's rusty truck, and maybe the television in the garage window would be turned on. They were almost there, almost at the sign that said, *Welcome to Alexander Morris, population 1,350 and growing! Drive carefully.*

Then, poop, along came the constable, his police siren screaming, sticking his sweaty face in the truck window. Don't you know, mister? Didn't anyone ever tell you that when the light's turned on you're supposed to pull over? If you care about your kids, then don't take them riding on the highway in the back of a truck. Don't take them riding six white horses. I don't want to see this happening again. You betcha. The next time they'd go on the bus.

Patsy Anne snuffled and yanked impatiently on the crib railing.

I'm strong, Ruby reminded herself, her attention once again fixed on the task of freeing her baby sister from the crib. If she grit her teeth she could lift a mountain, and mountains were made of rocks, as most people knew. She believed she could do anything she wanted to, except tell time. Her sisters had tried to teach her, but she couldn't understand how to count by fives, although she should have been able to, they told her, given that she was five years old. They had said, Now Ruby, you don't want to be a dunce when you start school, do you?

Just as Alvina had taught her young sisters, they in turn were bound to teach Ruby to read. They'd cut letters from a magazine and taped them to the refrigerator door, formed words such as *CAT, DOG, ICECREAM, RUBY, POOP.* Which was in keeping with what the Vandals were known to do. They could read and spell and tell time, run the fastest and jump the highest when they entered the first grade. Their artwork dominated the wall above the blackboards, their singing voices were true of pitch and sweet of sound. They set track-and-field records, following in Sonny Boy's footsteps. At five Ruby could read the newspaper, and she was strong. But she couldn't tell time.

She pulled at Patsy's arms and felt her rise from the crib. The baby's expectant grin became a surprised O as her belly slid across the cold metal railing, and she wound her arms about Ruby's neck. One more little tug, one more tug, and just as Ruby thought, the baby swung down and thudded into her chest. A firecracker of triumph exploded in Ruby's ribs, and then she felt the chair tip backwards.

Sara called out from the bed, a screeching *eeeek!*, but was unable to move. Frozen, as she usually was in an emergency, although, as a child the same age as Ruby, she'd been quick to act. In a slashing white moment of terror, she'd known what to do, while her sister, Katy, had not. Now, as a grown woman, she froze and made this childish, cartoon-character-like sound, and relied on others to come to the rescue.

When Ruby realized they were falling, she tightened her hold on the baby, resisting the reflex to flail to try to break their landing. They were going to hit the floor hard, Patsy Anne's weight might knock the wind from her lungs, but she knew what that felt like. She'd once fallen off the shed roof and lain on the ground gasping. She knew from experience that the sudden inability to breathe was frightening, but eventually her lungs would open and fill.

The air parted as they went down, the room dropped away, a Palm Sunday leaf on the wall above the bed vanished. Ruby felt a smack of pain as her head struck the iron wheel of the sewing machine, felt it, solid, a ringing sting behind her ear.

She opened her eyes and found Patsy Anne lying on her chest, her brown eyes startled, apparently unharmed. It's okay, Patsy's okay, we're okay, Ruby said loudly, to cover the threat of tears in her voice. She struggled to her feet, grunting extravagantly with the effort to lift her sister and hoist her onto a hip.

See? No one got hurt, Ruby claimed, although the side of her head had begun to throb. *Beautiful, beautiful brown eyes.* Oliver sang the song to tease those of his kids who didn't have brown eyes, which was almost all of them, except for Patsy Anne, Ruby, Manny and The Other One. *Oh, beautiful,*

beautiful brown eyes, I'll never love blue eyes again, Oliver sang, which made Ida hide in the closet and weep. What a baby. What a, what a baby.

I'm sick. Tell Alvina I'm not coming down, Sara said, while Ruby puffed and grunted to make herself strong enough to haul Patsy Anne across the room to the closet and a shelf of folded diapers. *For every bear that ever there was.* Ow, ow, ow, ow, Ruby thought, in order to keep from crying, because she knew that Sara hated tears.

FIVE

Sara now and then

THE SUN ROSE, its rays slanting through the window of Sara and Oliver Vandal's bedroom, turning a picture of a windmill hanging beside the doorway shades of grey. Earlier in the morning there had been the suggestion of a clay-coloured sun pressing through storm clouds, but in the diffused light, it was no longer visible. Sara lay across the bed and massaged her ribs, studying the foreboding and gloomy print and puzzling as to why she had ever found it appealing. She was thankful that her stomach had settled, but disquieted by the unusual stillness in the house; through it she could hear her ears ringing. A dismal sound that aroused loneliness. The sound of sickness. Gallbladder, likely, Florence Dressler had suggested days ago. Fair, fat and near to being forty, she said, Sara, that's two out of three.

Near to being forty. The words were jolting—not that she wasn't well aware of her age, but that someone else had noticed. Throughout the years her neighbour, Florence, had correctly guessed the sicknesses that befell Sara's children—chicken pox, red and German measles, scarlet fever. Pinworms. Florence didn't have children, but Sara had to admit she was good with them. Just as Katy was good with her own children, and tried to train Sara to be good with hers. Speak softly and they'll need to be quiet to listen. Yell and you'll only need to yell louder and louder. Spare the rod, you'll spoil the child. But Sara's children were unlike other people's children. This was plain as day, starting with Alvina, whose crying as an infant went on for as long as four hours at a time, and she cried so loudly Florence could hear her bawling clear across the yard, and came to investigate.

She came calling in mid-afternoon and caught Sara by surprise, the unexpected sound of her knock raising Sara's heartbeat and riveting her to the floor. Who? Who is it? She and Oliver had been living in the house for six months, and this was the first knock. A flood of relief sent her bounding to the door as Florence announced herself. Sara pulled out the breadknife she'd wedged behind the door's frame, unmindful of her frowziness until Florence stepped into the room.

Throughout the winter Sara had watched Florence plodding back and forth between her woodpile and the back door, going off on errands downtown or returning. A widow. A woman only ten years older than she was, who'd lost her husband in a train accident. The plain-faced Florence was strongly built but moved slowly, resolutely, her perpetually sloped shoulders looking as though her sorrow were water she carried in two brimming pails—a stoicism Sara was firmly acquainted with, having seen it in the bodies and faces of the women she'd known in Russia.

When Florence stepped into the house, it became a home. Sara's home, her first visitor. A guest. The woman's cheerful greeting trailed off as she saw the knife in Sara's hand.

Oliver's going to get a lock, Sara said, knowing that anticipating a lock for the door sounded strange and perhaps unfriendly. She knew the custom of not locking doors in Union Plains. Her parents and grandparents hadn't locked their doors in Russia, either, not until the troubles started. And then what use was a lock? It was easily broken. But not before a warning, the shoving and pounding that would alert a person to escape through the back door, or a window.

I've brought coffee, Florence said, indicating the bundle she carried, her eyes taking in the bathrobe Sara was wearing in mid-afternoon, the fact that her hair hadn't been combed. Then Florence looked about for someplace to set the pot, the table in the centre of the room being taken up by a large basin of water, a stack of folded diapers and a quilted pad.

I would have come sooner, Florence said, but I noticed that you've had people coming and going. I'm dying to see the wee girl. Her eyes came to rest on the piano, with a look of surprise.

My sisters were here, Sara explained. But there's colds at home now, and so they won't come back until that's over. Her voice was barely a whisper, as she hadn't used it much since Katy and Annie had left. Except to sing when Alvina wouldn't stop crying. She'd tried swaddling Alvina the way Katy had done, binding her in a blanket with her arms tight to her sides, and then walking the length of the room and back, rocking, jiggling, singing. As Katy had shown her, but without receiving the same results. Alvina had cried herself hoarse, and stopped only to drink greedily from a bottle of warm water for a moment, and then spat out the nipple and resumed howling. Hour upon hour.

Florence unwrapped the coffee pot and set it on the water boiler of the cookstove, then folded the blanket and presented it to Sara. For the baby, she said. And noticed the basket on the floor beside the stove, Alvina tucked down into it, asleep. May I have a peek at her? she asked.

She's sleeping, Sara said, and thought, please don't wake her up. She received the blanket and felt the usual flush of shyness. Although she tried not to appear shy, it was always so near to the surface. She unfolded the blanket knowing that she was meant to admire it, but couldn't think what to say, and so she draped it over the basket, then realized that it looked as though she wanted to deny Florence even a glimpse of Alvina.

She stood for a moment gazing down at the covered basket. The baby doesn't like me, she heard herself say, speaking what had just occurred to her. Alvina obstinately refused to be comforted. I can't make her stop crying, she said to Florence. I don't have a hand with children, she thought, with a flutter of panic.

It sounds as though your baby could have colic, Florence said. I gathered as much from the way she cries. I can hear her clear across the yard. I could set my clock by that girl.

Katy had said gas. Alvina's stomach became a hard small melon and she drew her legs up against it. Katy had taken a tiny sliver of candle wax and slid it in and out of Alvina's rectum to make her expel the gas, but that hadn't worked.

I'm sure she has colic, Florence said, with more conviction. She came from a large family and knew about babies and what could ail them. Union Plains' only store sold gripe water, she said, a teaspoon of that sometimes helped. She won't always cry. They usually grow out of it when they reach three months.

Colic, Sara repeated, wanting to remember the word for the next time Katy came over.

I'm sure the coffee's still hot, Florence said, her attention drawn across the room to wall shelves holding battered tin pots and various crockery, a row of cups and bowls Oliver had brought home from the hotel.

I have not cupboards, Sara said apologetically, following Florence's gaze. She tucked her hair behind her ears and smoothed the front of Oliver's plaid bathrobe, knowing that she had just brought attention to her frowzy appearance, and not improved it.

Rome wasn't built in a day, Florence said, leaving Sara confused as to what she meant.

Sara looked around the room wanting to see it through Florence's eyes. The bleached cotton window curtains she'd spent hours embroidering looked absurdly earnest. But she was satisfied with the red braided oval mat at the centre of the room, its colour vibrating against the green floor—which she should not have painted, Oliver said, given that she was expecting. He'd heard someone once say that women expecting should not paint. And so she'd painted with the windows and doors open, snow blowing into the room. What was worse, paint fumes or the cold? But sometimes she wondered, with a stab of guilt, was that why Alvina cried so much? Because she had painted?

I'll come back another time, Florence said. You may keep the coffee pot. It's a wedding gift, she explained. I'm a member of the Women's Workers Club, we do the same for all newlyweds.

Yes, Sara had heard that from Oliver. And she'd also heard that, for a first baby, the women threw a shower in the Anglican church basement. While she didn't want one, she'd come to expect it would happen, and had thought and thought about what she might wear and what she would say. Thinking that she would ask Annie, her young sister, to make another smock. She suspected now that once the women found out how pregnant she was, they'd decided against it.

Please stay—I want to wash my hair, Sara blurted, surprising herself and Florence with the request. Would you? Please? she added, almost apologetically. She'd been trying to wash her hair when the knock came at the door, had shoved the knife in the frame to give her courage.

Of course, of course, Florence said, barely concealing her curiosity.

Danke, Sara said, the word uttered in relief. She rushed over to the shelves to cover her embarrassment at having spoken German, and took down a cup. Then she pulled a chair out from the table, indicating that Florence should sit down. Moments later she returned from the stove, the cup brimming with steaming coffee she'd poured from the shiny new pot.

Do you have other family? Florence asked, as Sara rubbed a bar of soap through her wet hair. Other than the two women Florence had seen coming and going.

They're in the old country, Sara said, groping blindly for the dipper beside the basin and then rinsing the soap from her hair. Doing it quickly, imagining someone entering the room, a knife plunging into her back. An arm around her neck, and being thrown onto the floor. A man wanting more than a taste of the soup on the stove.

My hair is so— Sara stumbled for words, snatched up a diaper from the pile and dabbed at her eyes to clear them. My hair is so heavy, she said, turning to Florence, meaning that her hair was oily. Usually I wash it when Oliver's here, but today I couldn't wait.

Your house is looking very nice, Florence said, and then a whimper rose from the basket beside the stove. Within moments Alvina was howling, and Florence pushed Sara aside to rescue her, picked her up and put her across her shoulder. Florence rocked, jiggled, sang, just as Sara tried to do, and miraculously, Alvina grew silent.

All these years! Sara called out to the ceiling now, her jaw so tight she could barely form the words. Sometimes she felt as though she'd only just had Alvina, and yet all these years had flown by in a blur of nine more children and keeping this old house going. She'd rescued a house that truly was abandoned, she discovered from the courthouse records in Alexander Morris. When Alvina was just four months, she'd bundled her up, walked to the highway, hitched a ride on the bus, somehow managed to make herself understood to the clerk. I'm not dumb! she wanted to shout as loudly as he shouted at her. Her planned triumph was diluted when her brother-in-law insisted on seeing the records for himself before he would plunk down the money for the amount of taxes owing. Then, every step of the way, she'd had to argue and reason and persuade Oliver that the changes to the house were necessary, take it upon herself to arrange for a carpenter to build a room onto the front of the house, a porch onto the kitchen. A place where, in summer, she could fill a washtub with water to bathe the children, wheel out the wringer washer and do the laundry. When the piano's wavering and uncertain tune made it unwelcome in the living room, there was space for it in the porch, along with the mound of footwear, broken toys, sleds, scooters and other paraphernalia of all their varied lives.

While Oliver escaped to the army in the war, she skimped and hoarded the pay the army sent to her. A cellar was dug out beneath the house and a coal-burning furnace installed, a potato bin, shelves built for the hundreds of jars of preserves she canned each year. She raised the roof to accommodate a second floor, and by the time the fifth child arrived, the rough split-log exterior was covered with cedar siding and whitewashed, the window frames trimmed with red. The abandoned house had become a reasonable facsimile of the other houses in Union Plains.

And what was all that for?

And what was the purpose of giving birth to ten selfish and obstinate children who sometimes made fun of the way she talked, scoffed at any advice she tried to give them? They pilfered her chocolate bars, the treats Oliver sometimes brought home because he knew she craved dark chocolate. It was an insult that she had to hide them or else she wouldn't get a taste, not even a measly crumb would be left in the wrapper. As if her sweet tooth didn't count. I'm a person too, she sometimes told her kids, the notion as startling to her as it was to them; her need for dark chocolate pronounced because it was something about herself she knew for certain—I like dark chocolate. All these years her body had betrayed her again and again, no matter what jellies or appliances she used. What great lesson was she meant to learn from that?

Yes, yes, I know. I'm supposed to try and become a mountain flower, she muttered. Trials and troubles are sent to shape a person, yes, yes, yes, according to the gospel of her acquaintance Coral.

She laughed wryly, a rat-a-tat-tat sound. As if I haven't learned enough by now. I'd rather be a common weed, a dandelion, she'd once said to Coral, and she thought now, yes! Why not? Why *not* be satisfied to be a dandelion like everyone else, rather than try to become a rare and exquisite blossom that only God and the mountain goats would ever see? A velvety and brightly spotted lady's slipper, which every year, near to Easter, she could count on appearing in the window of a Winnipeg flower shop. The blossoms resembled a purse more than a slipper, and they were susceptible to sucking insects, the store clerk said.

She raised an arm now, opened her palm to shield her eyes against the brightness in the room, and was caught for a moment by her freckled firmness. It was a lithe, narrow arm that seemed to belong to someone else, a girl's arm, it didn't match her face. What a shock to glimpse her face in the store window before she'd had a chance to arrange it! That washed-out person is not me, but yes, it *was*. And then there was Alice Bouchard's kewpie-doll face looking out the window through her reflection.

Again the image of Alice emerging from the store gripped her. Alice's self-containment as she set her parcels into the trunk of the car. The lid coming down in a solid muffled *thud!* spoke of more money than you could shake a stick at.

Okay, okay, she whispered to the ceiling, wanting to steady her breathing. Okay. Her chest rose in a shudder, and she wiped her nose on the back of her arm, frowning as she noticed the collection of dried insects in the light fixture, the grey footprints on the ceiling's fresh white paint, going from one end of it to the other. The kids couldn't or wouldn't say how the footprints had got there. She thought she heard someone coming along the hall, raised her head and saw Alice Bouchard's latest endowment of second-hand shoes on the floor, and once again she was struck through with a bolt of pain that left her gasping.

If what she was experiencing was gallbladder, as Florence Dressler suggested, then it had started acting up days ago, during the bus ride home from Winnipeg. The dull pain set in as the bus left the city limits, the neon lights of the motels and hamburger joints giving way to houses whose lit windows sometimes afforded her a glimpse into rooms. The two nuns who'd been on the bus when she boarded it that morning sat in front of her, their heads almost touching as they talked in French. Unlike most of the passengers around her, the nuns seldom returned from Winnipeg carrying bags or packages, which raised the question, where had they been all day? Underneath a priest, likely, Oliver said, when she'd once posed the question, and he was serious, not teasing. Of course, they're no better than I am, Sara thought, but the idea did not give her any satisfaction.

Anger is a sin, Coral had said, and Sara wondered if the nuns would agree. Wasn't there ever a time when anger was righteous? She thought of Alice Bouchard—that bitch—her hips swivelling in her pencil-narrow skirt as she went off down the street, and realized that the lingering ache was the residue of anger brought on by Alice ignoring her. Anger's a sin, Coral had said when Sara once admitted to being short-tempered. Read the scriptures and search your heart.

And she'd been doing just that for almost a year now; every day she read the Bible in an attempt to make herself feel bad. She'd discovered that she regretted giving herself to Oliver before they were married, regretted chasing after him, her craving for the sight of him like a toothache, a pulsating need that had her begging to accompany Katy when she delivered eggs and cream to Union Plains. To put her face up to the hotel window, hoping for a glimpse of his slim silhouette moving among the pool tables. Once she'd heard someone call to him—Oliver, it looks as though that German DP girl has an eye for you. Now, there's an itch begging to be scratched. I made such a fool of myself, she'd confessed to Coral, her voice echoing in the grey washroom cubicle at the bus depot, its walls and doors scratched with graffiti. The air freshener on the wall above the toilet tank oozed a medicinal odour that made her throat scratchy, and she'd staved off coughing in fear that Coral would think it was a cover for crying.

One way or another, a person reaped the results of anger, and Sara supposed this shifting dull pain that began as the bus left the parking lot and went lumbering through the city streets was her reward. Black puddles in the ditch beside the highway flashed by, the ditches being full from a recent downpour of rain. She belched into her fist and recalled the bag of Planters Peanuts she'd consumed while shopping. *Do unto others as you would have them do unto you. Love one another as you would love yourself.* Huh! Easier said than done. She would never wear another pair of Alice Bouchard's shoes, even though that would mean shopping in the kids' department in order to find ones that would fit.

All right, so she had committed sins that couldn't be undone. But there were others that she *could* make right, according to the gospel of Coral, the bus depot's cleaning lady, big in the derrière, a woman from Trinidad. Sara could return the scarf to Emily Ashburn, that was a start. She had been on her way to do just that when she took the bus to Winnipeg that morning.

The scarf and a shopping list were tucked inside her handbag as she got on the bus early in the morning, the land still shining wet with dew. Half an hour later, she disembarked at the oil-stained bus depot parking lot in Winnipeg and hurried through a blue cloud of diesel exhaust into the waiting room, feeling smart and purposeful. She knew where to go in the city without needing to think about it, and felt a mixture of pity and benevolence for the country people who wandered about the depot looking lost and afraid to venture out the doors onto Graham Street.

She anticipated the sound of Coral's singing, the sight of the large woman pushing a broom and a pile of Dust Bane between the rows of benches, but saw instead the thin, nervous-looking cleaning woman who went about with a cigarette in her mouth as she worked. Sara figured that Coral was on the second shift and she would come upon her in the coffee shop at the end of the day.

By one-thirty she sat on a bench beside a trolley stop, looking down at two bulging shopping bags at her feet and thinking, that's thirty dollars' worth. Not quite believing that she was near the end of Oliver's money and hadn't got to the end of her list. She'd decided against purchasing a new brassiere for Ida, although she was growing so quickly she'd soon be larger-breasted than Alvina. She'd promised Ruby a harmonica, but not if it left her short of money to buy running shoes for the boys.

Her handbag lay open on her lap as she sat on a bench, and inside it was the nest of blue silk. There was more than enough time for her to catch the trolley and ride as far as the park gates and return downtown. Enough time to ring the doorbell, to deliver the scarf and an explanation. Enough time for a cup of tea, in the unlikely event that Emily Ashburn requested that she stay for one. Time enough, but the determination to humiliate herself was beginning to wane.

Across the street a Union Jack fluttered from a standard in front of the Winnipeg Auditorium, and Sara's attention was drawn to it, and to a woman about to enter the building. As she reached for the door handle, sheets of paper came flying out from under her arm and went skittering end over end along the sidewalk. The woman dashed about collecting them and was soon joined by other people, the men among them stiff-legged and awkward as they ran in fits and starts. Their laughter at being caught like children at play rose above the sounds of vehicles passing in the street. Sara was left feeling hollow after her own laughter subsided, knowing that, given a similar circumstance, she would let the papers blow away rather than risk looking foolish.

The trolley slowed to a stop in the street, but she resisted the impulse to gather up her shopping bags and push through to the front of the crowd. While the passengers began filing from the trolley she remained perched on the edge of the bench so that her feet would touch the ground. Her plastic overshoes were mud-splattered and so were her legs. I didn't go because my stockings were dirty, she imagined explaining to Coral when she got back to the bus depot, and she cringed inwardly, anticipating Coral's reply, Honey, that's flimsy talk.

Sara always dressed carefully for a shopping trip to Winnipeg, but this morning she'd been more particular than usual: a navy shantung suit, its jacket open at the neck to reveal the ruffled collar of her blouse. The short jacket and long narrow skirt made her look and feel taller. Thanks to the sewing talents of her younger sister, Annie, the suit was stylish and expensive-looking. She knew Emily Ashburn would appreciate her appearance, the wrist-length gloves, the pink scalloped-brimmed hat with its half-veil.

However. While eating lunch at a coffee bar, she had managed to get a spot of mayonnaise on her skirt. That and the mud-speckled stockings made her less than what she had hoped to present to her former employer. She decided now that she would board the trolley car on the condition that she wasn't required to stand. If all the seats were taken, she'd do the rest of her shopping and return to the bus depot early. She'd feed her curiosity on the sights there, the different types of people coming and going, the regulars, the low-downs shuffling in the front door and out the departure gates, returning again and again. Sometimes Sara recognized a woman from another town waiting for a bus, or from Union Plains, or one of the nuns who travelled frequently between Winnipeg and Ste. Agathe. She would ponder what they wore under their habits, whether or not they were having their period, if they were bald, and what they had to talk about so animatedly.

The first shall be last, and the last first, Sara recalled a line of scripture as she waited for the people ahead of her to board the trolley. She wouldn't fool herself into thinking that she wanted to board the trolley out of a desire to be last; rather she hoped that all the seats would be taken. This was not the case, she realized, as she stepped up into the coach and saw an empty seat beside a window. She sat down thinking that there couldn't be a clearer sign; her fate was sealed.

The trolley lurched and glided through stop after stop, until the buildings and pedestrians were fewer and far between. Moments later the trolley entered Crescent Road, an archway of greenery. The man beside her opened the window, and she recalled that the silk scarf felt like a moist breeze against her skin. I've been meaning to return it for ages. How it wound up among my things, I don't know. A mistake. She would offer Emily Ashburn an explanation, not a confession. What sin had she committed in failing to return the scarf? Wanting what didn't belong to her, coveting?

But there had been more to it than that.

Male voices drifted up the stairwell from the sunroom and Sara stood listening, her hands trembling. Beyond the dressing-room window she saw Emily Ashburn crossing the lawn, at her side the man who'd come to tend the garden. She turned to the dressing table, startled by the reflection; the seventeen-year-old round-faced girl looking back at her; the muslin band flattening her hair against her forehead, the band's centre rising in a scalloped crown; the uniform, a crisp white apron over a black dress. Sara had cream-fed cheeks, Emily Ashburn teased, country girl cheeks, and a high complexion, unlike the pasty-faced city girls.

Emily Ashburn's crystal box wasn't in its usual place in the top side drawer of the dressing table, but had been left out. The casual-looking clutter of pins and earrings, the absence of its lid, suggested a carelessness that invited Sara to pick through the jewellery. To choose a pretty pin and hold it against the bib of her apron for a moment, before putting it back. The whole dressing table was in disarray and had the look of impatience and hurry. Sara arranged an ivory vanity set in its usual order, and lined up the jars of creams and cosmetics, a decanter of toilet water, against the table's mirror.

A clock chimed from the room down the hall, the bedroom of the Ashburns' only son, a young man who had failed to return from the war. Beside the mantel clock in that room was a photograph of him in uniform, and a brass vase of silk flowers. The mellifluous chiming of the clock never failed to catch her unawares, and left her chest aching for air. She deliberately avoided winding that clock, but apparently someone always noticed, Mrs. Ashburn, likely, although the woman never mentioned it. During the night Sara could hear the chimes from her room on the third floor. That far-off counting of the hour would awake her, pitch her down a well of despondency and leave her flailing to right herself by the morning.

The clock and the dressing table in Emily Ashburn's lilac-print room seemed familiar to her—perhaps her family had owned similar items in the old country. But when she'd told

Katy she remembered sitting at such a table, remembered someone unravelling her braids and pulling a brush through her hair, her sister became terse with anger. They'd never owned anything like that. Sara shouldn't confuse what she might have seen elsewhere with anything that had belonged to them. We were workers. Only workers. Our father didn't even own land, she insisted, as though she were on stage and speaking to someone in the wings—a Soviet spy, perhaps, standing in the shadows, writing her name down in a book.

There was something new lying on top of the jumble of jewellery in the crystal box, Sara noticed, a pair of pearl cluster earrings. She reached for them, her fingers suddenly chilled. *Brazen, shameless, vain, shallow,* the words leapt to mind. Women who resorted to using cosmetics and jewellery attracted the wrong kind of attention. A more fitting adornment for someone like her was beautiful hair, a clear complexion and a clean heart and mind.

She held the forbidden jewellery to her ears, her heart racing, as the voices in the sunroom suddenly grew louder. Mr. Ashburn and a visiting nephew, she realized. She expected to see Katy in the mirror, arms crossed against her breasts. *Ja, ja,* so this is what you do when there's no one watching. You forget that the Heavenly Father never sleeps. The sheen of pearls made Sara's grey eyes appear larger, and her face brightened with a vivaciousness that the maid's uniform thwarted. She set the earrings in her palm, enjoying their heaviness for a moment before putting them back into the box.

She'd investigated the velvet-lined and lidded compartment where the whatnot box was kept, but had never gone beyond that drawer. Today she dared to pull open a second drawer, releasing a scent of citrus and cloves and revealing a wild toss of undergarments, among them a flag of blue.

It was a scarf frayed at one corner, the colour blue of the Russian sky that had been in her eyes ever since she could remember. It felt like cool water in her fingers, but when she wound the silk about her neck, her skin instantly warmed. She crossed the room to the window in time to see Emily Ashburn and the man who came to tend the flower gardens going round the corner of the house. A blond spaniel followed at their heels, its presence an abrasion. Sara had been taught that animals belonged outside, but Mrs. Ashburn wiped its paws and runny eyes on towels that were meant for kitchen use, and the dog left hair on the bedspread in the son's room.

Sara returned to the dressing table and picked up the earrings and, this time, managed to screw them into place. She savoured the bite of metal against her earlobes, the strangeness of the weight drawing them down. Impulsively, she unscrewed a lid from a pot of rouge and dipped her fingers into the russet powder and rubbed her cheeks. Her fine light brown hair, cut short since she had come to work in the city, had a natural curl, and she fluffed it. She stepped back from the mirror, heat rising in her neck. She saw that she was lovely.

She went down the hall, the dog barking now as Mrs. Ashburn entered the foyer, the blue scarf a soft thickness in her uniform pocket. She hurried up to her room on the third floor and stuffed it into the toe of a shoe before returning to her chores.

Throughout the day she was aware of her body, her buttocks shifting beneath the confining and heavy fabric of her uniform. She was certain she had grown up in a similar house. Somehow she'd become susceptible to beauty, had learned to appreciate the sensation of fine material against her skin. Surely she'd once been indulged, waited on by others. As she passed by doorways opening up to pastel-coloured rooms, light shone through the curtained windows. There was order and peace. She believed she was at home.

Sara had come to work for the Ashburns in Winnipeg during the first month of the winter of 1928, a winter that proved to be severe. Near to Christmas there was a cold snap, but the roads stayed open and Sara was still able to travel to the farm on weekends. When the cold days broke in mid-January, the change in weather brought intense blizzards that left the city streets impassable for days.

During one of those storms, the snow drifted halfway up the windows and doors of the Ashburn Edwardian house, imprisoning everyone until late afternoon, when at last they were freed by a party of young men going house to house, rescuing snowbound residents. The unpredictable weather prevented Kornelius from travelling to the city to fetch Sara, and for the first time in her memory she found herself passing time alone.

She spent her off-hours in her third-floor room, the day broken by the meals she took in the kitchen. While Irene, the cook, went about her chores, she sat at a huge table eating without tasting the food while a radio played somewhere in the house. The male announcer's voice seemed buffeted by high wind and waves, as though it were crossing an ocean. She thought that the speech of the people around her sometimes sounded the same, a billow of distortion out of which a sentence would emerge, complete and clear in its meaning.

During the time of the blizzards she was often joined at meals by Penny, the downstairs maid, and Irene, both of whom hadn't been able to reach their homes in the north end of the city. Those meals were more leisurely, not the usual hurried gulping of food, Irene leaping up to tend something on the stove. The constant battering of the wind against the house, the hurl of snow against the windows, made Sara grateful for the warmth of the room and their company.

Penny and Irene chatted about people they had known, events that had happened in the household before Sara's time. When they included her, their talk became abrupt, simplified for her benefit. So then, what was life like in Russia? Irene asked one day, in a manner that suggested the question could no longer be avoided. The cook was large and florid, her eyes always reddened as though perpetually stung by onions.

Most of the people in Sara's world did not ask such questions. Occasionally they offered their own remembrances—only fond ones—of life in the old country. They repeated stories of the idiosyncratic antics of a person they had all known, without mentioning that the man had met a brutal end. They reminisced about a journey made to the Crimea; a grove of oak trees halfway up a hill above the town of Rosenthal where they had gone on May Day picnics.

Ja! Ja! Hans and Frank, Sara's grandmother once chimed in, interrupting a story to speak the names of young martyrs who had chosen to jump from a bridge into the Dnieper River rather than deny their faith. She was near to the end of her life then, her jaw swollen and bruised from a recent fall. Over three thousand of their people had lost their lives during the season of weeping, including seven that the grandmother called her own. But it was the young men's names she brought forward to the new country, wanting to say them before she could no longer speak. Her visitors grew silent, as they did whenever anyone ventured too close to the edge.

You wouldn't want to live there, Sara told the cook. Why not? Irene wanted to know. You just wouldn't, Sara said, emphatically. A see-saw of ambivalence tied her tongue. The women's averting of eyes told her that she'd sounded mysterious. Fine. It was better to sound enigmatic than risk sounding deficient.

Had her father fought in the war? Penny finally asked, speaking loudly, of course, as though this were necessary to make herself understood. Immediately Sara thought of the photograph in the vacant upstairs room. Had the Ashburns' son been in the same war as her father? Had men from Canada gone across the ocean to attend the same war? She recalled her father's departure to Moscow for training as though it were yesterday.

My father was in the war, but he didn't fight, she told the women. We don't believe in fighting. He was a nurse. She gathered from their raised eyebrows that either they didn't approve of what she'd said or they questioned her truthfulness.

We don't believe in fighting, she'd said, and for an instant she'd felt taller, made of finer stuff than they were. Then she felt deflated—she couldn't say if that was her own belief or not. She sat at the cook's table, near the wood stove in the wide kitchen, its radiant heat pressing against one side of her body, leaving the other chilled. Outside, the snow slanted across all the windows, casting the pale white light of midwinter over the room.

He who lives by the sword dies by the sword. Sara had almost spoken the maxim she'd heard so often while living in Russia. Memory of the tragedies that made the creed of pacifism a topic for daily consideration back home had been buried beneath the Canadian soil. The line of scripture suggested judgment, punishment; she was silenced by the photograph of the Ashburns' son in the upstairs bedroom as much as by the knowledge that many people who'd never lifted a sword had wound up dying by it.

When the weather cleared, Sara sometimes caught sight of a skater gliding along a path of ice on the river. From her third-floor window she watched hikers thrashing through the drifts on snowshoes. In the early evening, the sound of sleigh bells drew her to the window. Lanterns illuminated a swirl of light snowfall as a team of horses drew a wagon of tallyho riders. The horses, the light moving through the darkness, made Sara's throat constrict in a memory of home that was quickly receding into the twilight of a winter spent in a strange city. Distance transformed the skaters beyond the window into geese flying low across the ice, the hikers into black bears. The suggestion of a city was only that, a shapeless possibility, a smog of chimney smoke, an idea.

During the ensuing months of a sudden wet and rushing spring, the river turned yellow and viscous with silt. It swelled and overflowed its banks, its current becoming a torrent that heaved sheets of ice into the underbrush, shearing off many small trees and carrying them away. Sara struggled to read the books she borrowed from a bookcase in a hall outside her room, books Mrs. Ashburn had placed there for that purpose. There were books her daughters had once read as children, and several that had been left behind by the maids who'd preceded Sara. Their presence was made known in the dog-eared pages of the books, in rust-coloured stains on the mattress and in the messages they'd left behind, which Sara came upon by chance when she retrieved a pencil that had fallen behind the bed and found several scraps of paper wedged between the baseboard and the wall.

Good riddance to bad rubbish.

In this room, Hannah Johnson spent an entire year, an entire lifetime.

Ruth the good-hearted, soon to be departed.

My heart belongs to Robert, the final message declared, in handwriting that was such a flourish of curlicues it was difficult to read.

As the weather warmed, Mrs. Ashburn began sending Sara downtown on errands, writing precise instructions regarding what she should say to the trolley operator under every circumstance, and her address and telephone number should she become lost. She wrote down where Sara would find a card of shirt buttons and a packet of bias tape in the Hudson Bay store. When such missions proved successful she began to send Sara farther afield, to the Eaton's store, whose goods were less costly than the Bay's. The distance between the two stores was only several blocks, but seemed to be greater as, for the first time in her life, Sara walked among a throng of people on a busy street, her heart quickening with the sight and energy of the motor traffic. For whole moments she forgot who she was, and where she had come from.

One day she returned, to the surprise of Mrs. Ashburn, with a poem she'd painstakingly copied from a café window near Eaton's: *I'd rather be the gayest mortal, that ever walked the street, if I could be the lucky dog that makes your pulses beat.* Emily Ashburn read the poem aloud several times, as though she found it puzzling.

Why does he want to be a lucky dog? Sara asked.

He's wanting to be her beau, I suppose, Emily Ashburn explained, a smile tugging at her rose-coloured mouth. Her thin russet hair was arranged in a swirl at the back of her head that reminded Sara of a bird's nest.

Her intended, her husband, Emily Ashburn explained further, when it was clear Sara didn't understand.

Sara had been caught by the poem's illustration as she went by the café window, that of a woman stretched out on a lounge, a book opened on her lap, and a man sitting beside her on a chair, holding her hand. Curious and then mesmerized, while at the same time taken aback. She'd attended the weddings of couples who hadn't sat near to one another in church, not even after their announced engagement. Once they were married, they might as well have not sat together, for the space between them.

And why would he rather be the gayest mortal, if at the same time he wanted to be a lucky dog? The poem didn't make any sense. Or else it was the language and its double meanings that eluded her.

I *would* be the gayest mortal, Mrs. Ashburn corrected gently, suggesting that Sara had made an error when she'd copied down the poem.

Sara suspected the errands were a test of whether or not she would prove to be both intrepid and prudent, whether or not she would return with the correct amount of change. Kornelius says to tell you that the lady of the house is finding out if you can go fetch, Katy had written in a letter.

Katy had also written that Kornelius would come at Easter to take her to the farm. The news of his pending arrival made Sara feel as though she'd been bedridden for months and now her illness was over. She was hungry to talk her way out of her loneliness, to stand beside him and know who she was. But the idea of Kornelius was unlike the real man who appeared in the foyer to wait for her, the hem of his dark coat streaked with mud. He hadn't removed his overshoes, and the carpet around him was smeared with clay footprints. Kornelius had been known in the old country as The Wild One, for daring to go against the grain of common Mennonite practices and beliefs. Canada had turned him shrewd, and less willing to tip the boat of convention.

He nodded a curt greeting, as if preoccupied. He seemed as oblivious as always to the size and opulence of the Ashburn house, and once again had used the front entrance despite Mrs. Ashburn having suggested that in the future he might want to come round the back. He jammed his hat on his head, impatient to leave, and was already turning to the door when Mrs. Ashburn came into the foyer.

She said, Now you take good care of our Sara. And bring her back, you hear? Her voice trailed off as she noticed the mud on the carpet. She gave Kornelius an envelope containing Sara's wages, minus the small weekly allowance she paid Sara directly, which was the agreement. As he took the envelope, Sara thought he was rougher-hewn than she remembered, his wrists chapped and his knuckles reddened and enlarged.

She went to the back door, where she'd put her satchel, and met up with Kornelius around the front, going on ahead of him over the crusted and frozen slush, the satchel cumbersome with the gifts she'd purchased for Katy's children. Although Kornelius was swift to assist Katy with a heavy burden, he didn't offer to carry Sara's bag and she didn't expect him to. Tree branches along the crescent were glazed in ice, and clacked in the wind as she looked up and down the street for Kornelius's car, a dark blue Plymouth, and saw instead a new Packard, its chrome fenders and sides splattered with the mud of country roads. Kornelius came up beside her and clapped her on the shoulder. Well, what do you think? he said. I thought a visit to Buckingham Palace deserved only the best. His grin was sarcastic.

On the way to the farm, several times they nearly slid into a water-filled ditch, Kornelius becoming the old-country Kornelius, whooping loudly and relishing the danger. Man oh man, he exclaimed with pleasure, while Sara feared they would never reach the farm. Not so fast, not so fast, she pleaded, but no, he told her, speed was necessary. It was the only way to drive when the roads were soft. He'd no sooner spoken when the car fishtailed out of the deep ruts and they found themselves stuck up to the fenders in Red River gumbo.

She watched him plod down a lane towards a barn in search of someone to come to their assistance. Her heart raced and she clenched her fists as she prayed to be spared.

Spared from what? She didn't know. She was old enough to realize that it was unlikely that she would spend Easter in the car, mired in the mud. But her bowels churned as she waited to be rescued, and when at last Kornelius returned with two men, the sudden release of tension made her want to sleep.

They soon pushed the car out of the muck and back into the deep ruts, which eventually led them to the farm and to Katy, who came running to meet them, a kerchief tied over her head and the muddy lane sucking at her rubber boots. To meet Kornelius, Sara assumed, and was surprised when it was her door Katy wrenched open, and herself Katy engulfed in a fierce embrace.

You're home at last, Katy said. And for a brief moment, Sara was home. She leaned into her sister's body, inhaled the odour of nutmeg in the skin of her neck and remembered that, for a time, home had been Katy's body, the curve of her back, their spooning together wherever they slept. Then Katy held her at arm's length to take all of her in, joy streaming in tears down her face. Kornelius called from the car, Say, you two, there's enough water around here without you adding to it. Sara stiffened and clarified, It's not me, I'm not crying.

Moments later she wandered through the rooms of the farmhouse, looking for changes and finding none. Her feeling that she was home vanished. What little furniture Katy possessed, arranged around the walls of the rooms, made the house feel grudging and cold, the only adornments being the cuckoo clock that had once hung on a wall in Kornelius's house in Russia, and a hand-painted porcelain pitcher belonging to her dead grandmother, its pale roses gleaming in the dimness of a corner shelf.

Later in the day, Sara went walking on the land with Annie, and Susan and Jake, a niece and nephew who ran on ahead towards a dilapidated log cabin that Kornelius had inherited when he had purchased the land, and for a time had used as a pigpen. Its stone hearth had been smashed apart by the previous owners, the stones piled in a heap that Katy's children raced to meet, the first to climb to the top becoming the King of the Castle. The log cabin was built to last, Kornelius had said, in admiration. The previous owners had likely tried to bring it down and failed. It brought to Sara's mind the houses they'd left behind in the old country. She sometimes wondered who might now be living in her grandparents' large and solidly built house.

Finally, during the Easter church service, Sara felt surrounded and comforted again, the familiar people around her being like a feather tick she wanted to sink into, as soft and giving as her grandmother's feather bedding, which was now packed in a trunk in the farmhouse attic. When her grandfather had died, Katy had sent Sara to sleep with her grandmother to ease her loss. Sara had forgotten that she'd once feared the feather tick—feared that her grandmother's movement during the night might cause her to sink too deeply into it and suffocate.

Later that evening, Annie gathered Katy's children to be bathed and put to bed. During their four months of separation,

Annie had grown suddenly from a shy twelve-year-old girl to a thirteen-year-old woman quietly pleased about her achievements at school. Katy was her usual bustling self. Although she was prematurely grey-haired, she hadn't turned sour, unlike many of the women they knew who had come from the same town as they had, who had passed through similar circumstances and fled Russia in the same manner. Rather, Katy remained young-looking, much more so than Kornelius.

Come, let's you and I have a good visit at last, Katy said, leading the way into the dining room.

Sara joined her at the table. A bowl of rye wheat, grown tall, was placed at its centre, next to a paska bread on a plate with coloured eggs arranged around its base—Easter traditions Katy adhered to. What was life like in Russia? The cook's question was on Sara's lips and she remembered her own unsatisfying reply.

She remembered their last Easter in the old country, when, for the last time, they visited what was known as the Taras Bulbas cave, after the famous story by Gogol. Sara, Katy and Annie, Kornelius, her spent and broken-hearted grandparents; a red-haired aunt, an uncle and their three children, whom Sara would never again see in this world; they were like a string of obsidian beads being drawn across a trestle bridge. The sky was a grey-blue, and as distant as the Dnieper River appeared to be, one hundred and fifty feet below them. Her grandmother stopped on the bridge to peer down at the undulating currents and whispered, This is where those two poor young men were made to jump. She hadn't known the young martyrs, but their names were silver spoons she constantly polished.

When they had crossed the river and climbed an outcrop of rock to the cave, they crawled inside it and arranged themselves in a circle. *Faith is the victory,* they sang, their voices as patched, threadbare and mismatched as their clothing. Their hymn resounded within the confines of the ochre-coloured cave, their teetering song growing harmonious and strong with conviction, while Sara covered her ears and shut her eyes against the sight of tears coursing down her elders' faces.

She clearly remembered that last Easter in the old country, and she was beginning to recall their life on the estate.

Your letters haven't told me much about what it's like working for the Ashburns, Katy said.

Katy's question immediately brought to Sara's mind the dressing table; the memory she had of being a child and sitting at a similar table; the chiming of the mantel clock in the Ashburn house, similar to her family's clock striking the hour while moonlight fell across floorboards the colour of butter.

It's like being in our house. The Ashburn house is like our old house. The one we lived in when we lived on the Sudermann estate, Sara said, the words coming out in such a gush that she realized how much she'd been wanting to say them.

Phfft! Katy said, after a moment of startled silence, as though she needed to clear the air of what Sara had said. You were five years old when we left the estate. Obviously you don't remember much, or you'd know that our father was a poor man. He was a worker for the Sudermanns. He didn't have even an acre of land to call his own. The house we lived in wasn't as good as this one.

Katy got up and went over to a window that looked across the yard to the barn. Kornelius walked towards the barn, a lantern swinging at his side. Sara Vogt, get your nose out of the air for once, Katy said to the window.

Yes, accuse me, Sara thought, her sister's unfairness making her throat tighten. Make me feel in the wrong for wanting to know.

There was a sound, and both Sara and Katy turned to see Annie in the doorway looking at them, her cheeks flushed with anxiety. She gestured to Sara to come with her. You never said what you thought of our room, she said. Meaning the bowl of crocuses she'd set on the apple box beside their bed, the new cover she'd made for their quilt during Sara's absence.

Our room, Sara thought, as she got up from the table, hooked her arm through Annie's and went upstairs to at last dig out the gifts she had brought, having waited until the end of Easter Sunday, as Katy wished, so as not to distract the children from the reason why they celebrated Easter. Our room. Our room in Kornelius's house. As much as the barn and outbuildings belonged to Kornelius, so did the house. She'd come upon the envelope containing her wages tucked alongside a stack of plates in the cupboard when cleaning up, her contribution to Kornelius for what he'd provided.

The following morning, when Sara was to return to Winnipeg, Katy surprised Kornelius and her sister by insisting on accompanying them. It was a two-hour trip back along the same deeply rutted road, and then a gravel road that followed the course of the Red River. Kornelius stopped after a time, the car's engine idling as he looked out across the land.

You see that? He indicated a path cut through a stand of trees. That land belongs to me now, he said. He had recently purchased a strip farm from a Frenchy, a father of six girls and no sons. The man had been crippled by a falling tree, and was no longer able to farm. Someday I'll build you a castle there, eh, Mother? he said to Katy. Kornelius would harvest those trees and build Katy the kind of house he had once owned in Russia, a large A-frame that looked out for miles across the prairie in all directions.

Sara watched them from the back seat, thinking that Katy was broad-shouldered to the point of looking clumsy unless she held one of her children in her arms or on her lap. Then she softened, her eyes rising to meet Sara's, saying, See this? This is what tenderness looks like from the outside. The outdated dark hat she wore aged her. How like Kornelius, Katy had become much like Kornelius, calculating, choosing her words carefully for fear that she might reveal something her husband had cautioned her not to speak about. Plans for their future, a new purchase that might incite envy in fellow Mennonites, or raise questions as to how he could afford to buy more land, a new car, when the same rain and hail fell on his crops as on the others', the same pestilence of grasshoppers.

When the broad city streets began opening up before them, Sara recognized several buildings along the route to Crescent Road. But although much of what she saw had become familiar, she didn't feel as though she was being taken home. Neither here nor there, Sara thought, a favourite saying of Irene's. Not here, not there, but somewhere in between. Somewhere in between the city of

Winnipeg and Kornelius's farm was a place that Sara might someday begin to call home.

Katy grew increasingly silent as they drove along the wide crescent, passing by horse-drawn delivery wagons, her eyes taking in the houses and drawing private conclusions. Well, yes, she said, as though the spectacle confirmed a long-held suspicion. Later, her disapproving eyes swept around Sara's small room on the third floor, noting the clutter of clothing her sister had failed to put away, several books lying face down on her bed, the wardrobe door open, revealing clothes hanging askew.

I didn't teach you this. You know better, Katy scolded, as she began picking up the clothing, folding it, putting it into drawers, while Sara sat on the bed watching, amazed as always at how swiftly her sister could make order out of disorder.

How do you spend your free days? Katy asked, opening and closing doors with more energy than necessary, hangers clacking in the wardrobe as she rearranged garments. Then she sat down beside Sara on the bed, opened her purse and took out a slip of paper with a woman's name, address and telephone number.

Sara recognized the name. It was the person who had recommended the job and been present during the interview with Emily Ashburn. Frieda Wiens, a middle-aged childless woman who, along with her husband, had started a mission in a boarding house on William Avenue, the Home Away from Home Club, a meeting place for Mennonite girls who'd come in from the country to work for the wealthy. She'd invited Sara to attend the weekly meetings, and when Sara made the excuse that she didn't know her way around the city, had offered to send someone to fetch her. Not yet, Sara had said. Not now. She hadn't persuaded Katy that she was ready to take up working in the city in order to be put back where she had come from.

You need the company of other Christian girls, Katy said now. When it appeared Sara would object, she insisted. Either you go, Sara, or we'll have no choice but to bring you home.

Which meant that Sara would be sent down the road to work on the neighbouring farm. She'd been allowed two years in the one-room schoolhouse and then, at twelve years old, had been sent to work for Low-German-speaking Mennonites, *Canadieres,* as they referred to themselves, who had immigrated near the turn of the century and were stubbornly entrenched in their backward ways. Katy had understood that Sara would be employed as kitchen help, or caring for children, not hoeing sugar beets or stooking hay in the fields during harvest. The sight of Sara's blistered hands had struck Katy with remorse, which she stifled as she smeared them with Vaseline, bound them and sent her back to the fields wearing a pair of Kornelius's work gloves.

All of the following summer, Sara reluctantly attended the weekly meeting of the Home Away from Home Club, slipping away as soon as possible without risking offending the host or raising questions among the twenty or so young women. She preferred the solitude of her cozy third-floor room, where she watched the constant flotilla of boats and canoes going up and down the Assiniboine River, the women wearing broad-brimmed hats and muted Sunday finery while the men worked the oars. The river, in late afternoon, looked like milky amber.

She lay awake in the sweltering third-floor room, wondering about the writers of the notes that were wedged between the wall and the baseboard. What drove the girls to leave the messages, what did they hope to gain? She knew that Katy had written down her thoughts in a notebook—*Kornelius is going to ask me to marry him, I'm certain. My dear Kornelius*—she'd written, and later she had spoken those words aloud in her and Kornelius's curtained-off room. Sara had tried to shut out her whispering, their muffled laughter, the sound of movement in bed.

My heart belongs to Robert. Had the writer brought Robert up the back stairs to this room? Had they lain together perhaps, he on top of the girl, just as Kornelius had been lying on Katy when Sara had entered their room and demanded to know, What are you doing? What was Kornelius doing to Katy that made her cry out?

Sara wondered the same now, as she touched herself, felt her slipperiness and heat. She wanted to experience, for once, what she sometimes experienced in dreams, an agony of pleasure that roused her from sleep. She put a finger into herself, felt her own pebbly insides, which was what Kornelius must feel when he put his sex into Katy. Her fingers smelled yeasty and the scent was comforting, and she fell asleep with them curled beneath her nose.

She awoke hours later to the heat of the room, the dim light of early morning beginning to creep along the river. She swept her nightgown over her head and lay in the sudden coolness, her skin prickling with the sensation of air. She let her knees fall outwards, felt the air cool against her wetness and wanted something to be there, to touch her. Kornelius, she said, her fingers pressing and working, the other hand muffling the sound of an ensuing moan.

On Saturday afternoons she was free to go walking along the crescent as far as the gates to City Park, where she stood for moments, looking at the people strolling along the pathways, at the picnics taking place beneath a canopy of canvas, before returning to her room. Then she began to venture through the gates, to walk among the trees, each time going farther, drawn by the sunlight moving on the surface of the river, but always heeding Mrs. Ashburn's advice not to stray from the paths.

On one of these walks, she got to the point where the path opened to a clearing and to a large building with flags fluttering from posts. The pavilion, Mrs. Ashburn explained later. On the second floor there was a dining room where Sara might purchase ice cream, or a sandwich, Mrs. Ashburn said, forgetting that the small weekly allowance she doled out would hardly allow for such an expense.

The next time she went to the park, Sara brought a book and a sweater, which she spread across the grass in the field facing the pavilion. She was surprised at how chilled the air had grown—already it held the distinct odour of a pending frost. Several branches of trees had turned chokecherry-red and bright gold. She opened the book, intending to read, but her attention was drawn to a man running through the field towards her pulling a kite.

The yellow kite kicked along the grass and then lifted. It soared straight up, its tail snapping as the man reeled out more line and young boys around him shouted encouragement. The kite began to dip and climb across the sky, while the children gazed heavenward. Gerhard, Johann, Daniel and

Peter. Sara's brothers, wearing middies and knee-high socks, just as these children were wearing. A photograph in Katy's trunk showed her brothers dressed that way too, laid out in their narrow caskets, throats and heads bound, hands folded and still against their chests.

Sara snatched up her sweater and looked about, her breath rising. The book lay open on the grass, its dense paragraphs of print, walls erected to shut her out, each word a stone that needed to be pried loose and examined before she could go on to the next one. Devil! she shouted, and heaved the book, watched it arc and thud to the ground, its pages fluttering. Quickly, she left the park.

SIX

By chance

THE TWENTY OR SO GIRLS who attended the Home Away from Home Club had become upstairs and downstairs maids, chore girls, assistant cooks and nannies, in order to repay the Canadian Pacific Railway company for their passage. Like Sara, they were required by their families to do so, leaving their brothers free to go to school or to work on the farm. Sara had to repay her passage fee and to help with those of her sister Annie, and her grandparents, who'd barely survived the trip. The Mennonite girls' reputation for honesty, intelligence and meticulous cleanliness made them suitable to become servants to coal barons, land speculators, grain dealers and proprietors of large commercial enterprises.

The girls had once benefited from the cheap labour of Russian servants in their own homes, and now they were servants. The Home Away from Home Club provided a place for them to air their concerns, any instances of mistreatment or misunderstandings, or unusual or embarrassing requests made by their employers.

Concerns and needs and embarrassments of which I have none, Sara wrote to Katy. I have nothing I want to air. Least of all her underwear, she did not add, which in her opinion was what the young women were doing.

She was especially unwilling to take part when the hostess, Frieda Wiens, encouraged them to talk about what had happened to them and their families in Russia. The other young women did so eagerly, hushed and forlorn, seated in a circle in the small room, several on the floor with their legs curled beneath them. They all assumed that because Sara was forced to listen to their stories, she was obliged to tell them her own. Most of them knew what had happened to her family, but hoped for some new detail, something they hadn't already heard, which they could take back home and spread through their towns and villages. Their body heat warmed the room, which became overpowering with the mingling odours of talcum, crepe and wool, the sweetish thick smell of menstrual blood. Their swollen features and tears made Sara want to slam doors.

She began leaving the room during these moments of sharing, climbing the stairs to the second floor to use the bathroom and then daring to venture down the hall, sometimes hearing a cough, a shuffle of sound behind closed doors.

Once she was startled to come upon an open door and a man seated at a table with his back to it, his sand-coloured and bristly hair accentuating his decidedly square-shaped head. The floorboard creaked under her foot, and he turned to look at her. A square jaw, too, rough with whiskers. He moved his chair away from the table to face her, a friendly curiosity lighting his features, his arms coming up to cradle the back of his head.

Well, what brings you here? Are you lost? he asked, speaking in Low German, a language she returned to whenever she went home to the farm. His grin revealed large even teeth and an apparent good nature.

The young women's voices rose up the stairwell, dominated by that of the hostess.

Nein, not lost, Sara told him. I'm just tired of sitting.

What's your name? he asked, as she turned to leave.

She knew the girls would be glancing towards the staircase, sending silent messages between them, as they did whenever anyone was absent from the room for an undue length of time. Every time she returned to her place, someone would touch her lightly on the knee as she passed or pluck at her sleeve. It was meant to signal their concern—concern being a wedge they used to lever their way inside another person for the sake of being able to say they had done so.

Their concern was a way of keeping Sara safe inside the Mennonite family, the chorus of rosy-cheeked females whose beauty relied entirely upon the whim of nature and their crocheted and lace collars. The girls' descriptions of a sunset, a favourite Christmas, could be counted on to be similar, right down to the choice of words. They sang the same songs, and married their own kind, or remained single if necessary. They hoped to perpetuate in Canada a way of living and believing that had begun centuries ago, during the Reformation.

The square-headed man's features softened as she told him her name. You're from the Vogt family, *yes?* From the Abram Sudermann estate. It wasn't a question but a knowing, and Sara thought that likely he'd been told. Yes, from the estate, she thought. A place she barely remembered. A collection of buildings, a big house, her father singing as he went across a barnyard, *Praise God from whom all blessings flow.*

When she nodded, he said, I knew your sister. Margareta. My name is Peter Goosen. Margareta and I were baptized in the same church and on the same day. You resemble her very strongly.

Yes, I know. There was a box of photographs in Katy's trunk at the farm, though her sister seldom took it out; she hoarded the images as though the family had belonged only to her.

Did you know my father? Sara thought to ask. She became aware of the rumple of blankets on his bed and his shoes tipped on their sides in front of the bureau. She took in the length of his body, the soft-looking mound at his groin, and she imagined putting her hand against it. She had to leave before her eyes gave away what she was thinking.

Sara, you'll come and talk to me again, won't you? Peter Goosen asked.

From then on she anticipated the weekly meetings of the Home Away from Home Club, feeling the time passing too slowly between them. Each week she watched her reflection in the trolley-car window, her hands cold as she screwed the pearl earrings into place and then slid the blue scarf under the collar of her dress and knotted it. She was aware of the new luminosity of her eyes, the enigmatic pout of her mouth, and the presence of a man sitting across from her, attentive with admiration. I'm pretty, she thought, the realization always new. Her act of daring, however, was always eroded by apprehension, and whenever she neared the boarding house she took off the earrings and scarf.

Peter Goosen. She repeated his name while looking out at the display windows of the stores on Portage Avenue, the people strolling along the sidewalks, just as she and Peter Goosen would do. During the weeks she occasionally stopped whatever chore she was doing to say, Peter Goosen. He knew Kornelius too, and remembered her grandparents. But I don't remember you, he'd said, in a teasing voice, when next she had come upon him in the upstairs hall. You must have been just a *schnigjelfrits*, he said, meaning a cute little person.

She replaced Kornelius's face with Peter's while she indulged in her nocturnal manipulations. She winced with the agony of intense pleasure, the release of it, then rubbed her stomach and breasts to feel her hands against her skin. She took in the sounds of life going on beyond the house while she, Sara Vogt, lived in this tiny room of her body and longed to enter the huge beating heart of the city.

Peter and Sara Goosen, she said to herself. Where would they live? She realized that she didn't know what he did. All she knew was that he was often reading, and there always was a pile of books on the floor beside his bureau. He wasn't a farmer, and that, for now, was enough to know.

On this warm autumn day, the trolley rounded the corner and entered Main Street, where crowds of people milled about. She was taken by the air of festivity, the cars nosed into the curbs, many festooned with banners and ribbons. Men stood leaning against the cars, their shirt sleeves rolled to their elbows.

It's the Labour Day celebrations, the man sitting across from Sara said, his admiration making him bold as he leaned towards her, his features narrow and slick with humidity. He'd read her mind, guessed that she didn't know, surmised that she wasn't from here.

The trolley came to a stop and as several people got on, before she had time to argue with herself, she rose from her seat and stepped into the street. Into a cacophony of people jabbering, calling to one another overtop the sound of music, a brassy jolting tune coming from a gramophone on a table beside a shop door. She swerved to avoid a black dog threading its way among the legs. The day was the colour of a ripe apricot, the light diffused, softened by moisture-filled air that smelled of overripe fruit. There was a resulting mellowness in the faces of the men, women and children collecting in groups beside the bedecked cars.

Usually she got off the trolley at William Avenue, having watched for a large red-and-gold sign on a saddlery store that had a relief of a full-size white horse. She began to walk, confident that she'd soon come upon the sign and know where to turn. But as time passed, the scenery she had viewed from a streetcar window became unfamiliar in its details. She hadn't noticed this wrought-iron gate across the entrance to a bank, or the lamppost at its door. Or the impish-looking faces peering down at her from the cornices of a building, or the particulars of the wares displayed in its windows.

She crossed through several intersections, walked for what seemed longer than necessary. The heel of her foot burned where the skin had become abraded as it rubbed against her shoe. Now she was nearing a large building with an ornate façade, which she should have remembered seeing from the trolley. Its white brick trim reminded her suddenly of another building, of going walking with her father in Russia along a tree-lined street. I've gone too far, she told herself, and felt her heartbeat rise.

She retraced her steps, thinking that she'd somehow missed the saddlery sign and the horse; the stores she'd just passed by moments before remained unfamiliar. Her own stricken features reflected in a window, with the pearl globes at the ears and eyes wide with fear, seemed to belong to someone else. In the street behind her, balloons bobbed, and when she turned she saw that they were tied to a vendor's cart. Standing beside the cart was a man wearing a top hat and a black-and-white striped jacket.

Why hadn't she noticed the vendor the first time? The ornate building, the garish-looking vendor, seemed as unreal as apparitions from a faraway land, a dream. There were ice-cream vendors in St. Petersburg, and in Alexandrovsk. In Montreal, where they'd stayed for a little while before boarding a train, an unrelenting stream of vehicles had passed by in the streets and they'd been afraid to cross. Here, there was a similar noise of engines, of car horns honking.

This was not the Winnipeg she'd come to recognize. Nothing here was familiar, not a word on a sign, not the colours of a storefront. Where was the green awning that should have identified the hotel entrance; the barber pole in front of a shop? A man and woman came towards her, holding hands. They separated to go around Sara, and she felt their heat as they went by, heard their laughter. So this wasn't a dream—she could walk out of this strangeness if she kept her wits. What she needed to do was return to the stop where she'd got off the streetcar.

At last she recognized Portage Avenue, which meant that she had gone past that stop. Again she retraced her steps, her heel now blistered. The vendor's multicoloured balloons bobbed in the distance, and she became aware of several people sitting on the sidewalk near the vendor, where, only moments ago, there hadn't been any people.

The men sat cross-legged, their long hair matted and heavy-looking, their coppery features unreadable as they squinted against the sun and seemingly ignored the crowd of people beginning to gather on one side of them. There was a burst of laughter, and several among the crowd called out to the men, who didn't reply. As Sara grew nearer, she realized that the men sitting on the sidewalk were Indians.

She'd seen Indians before. Occasionally there'd been a straggle of stoop-shouldered people going past the farm, the dog raising a hullabaloo. Sometimes the women among them ventured down the lane in the hope that Kornelius's cattle dog was out working, or asleep. The women begged for food, for water; took notice of what was in the yard and in the house that might be worth stealing, according to Kornelius. If Katy saw them coming, she headed them off, made them wait at the top of the lane while she went back to the house and returned with a loaf of bread.

A red-haired man in a gold houndstooth jacket stepped out from the crowd. He strutted rather than walked over to the Indians, and looked down on them. He turned and spoke to someone among the crowd, and then he set his foot against an Indian man's shoulder, and pushed. The Indian toppled over, as though made of wood. The ensuing laughter was cruel. Sara had heard similar laughter, seen similar acts. People wearing rags, their faces gone stark bony from hunger, the unseeing eyes of men who were drunk.

She turned from the scene and ran out into the street, into the path of an oncoming car. From a corner of her eye she saw it, and she threw her arms up in the air. She felt the engine's heat, the car's fender passing through the inches of air between them. She stood frozen, on her tiptoes, arms raised as the car came to a stop. Something was falling through the air towards her, something grey and transparent, a turmoil of motion, a sphere of bladelike wings that wheeled both counter- and clockwise. She felt the air moving as it descended, and then suddenly it stopped, backpedalled and disappeared.

The driver came round the front of the car, his voice raised in a question and sounding as though it came from a distance. Her eyes remained fixed on the air above her head as she relived the swirling movement she'd just witnessed, the transparent sphere of grey wedges tumbling towards her. Whatever had come falling from the sky had a mind that realized at the last moment that it had made a mistake. During that instant of hesitation, Sara had felt its surprise, before it gathered itself up and away.

That could have been a guardian angel, Katy would one day tell Sara when, in a moment of weakness, Sara described what she'd seen. Sara had just given birth, and Katy had come to Union Plains to assist, bringing with her a Mennonite midwife. Oliver had delivered Alvina by accident, but when he'd delivered Sonny Boy by design, Katy had said it wasn't fitting. Oliver had graciously acquiesced, and awaited news of the next birth at the hotel. The birth of son George, which proved to be more difficult than usual. Forty hours of labour, the last ten hard.

Afterwards, Sara wondered if her life was going to ebb away, slow and hot, into the bedsheets. Was this the time it would happen? Now? She gazed into the rafters of the unfinished room, remembering the swirling sphere of wings. Would the ball of wings descend today, as it had on the day when Oliver almost ran her down in the street? Katy entered the room, bringing the swaddled baby, Sara's second son, and set him into her arms.

Why not name this one Johann? she suggested gently, her eyes brimming.

Because I wish a better end for him, Sara replied, the words coming out like wooden blocks. Likely there had been many swirling balls of knives descending from the sky on that November day in the old country. She didn't need a constant reminder of it. Of her brothers and sisters standing out in the open, unprotected, while she and Katy cowered in a hole in the ground.

Oliver leapt from the taxi and hurried round the front of it, and when he saw the shaken Sara, pale, her arms outstretched as though to embrace the sun, he swore a string of French in sheer relief. Collecting himself, he removed his cap and nodded, his thick dark hair falling across his forehead.

What's happening? Sara said in German. She had meant to ask where she was, who she was. Oliver came towards her, a hand extended, as though offering her an explanation, comfort, begging to be pardoned.

And then she was in the back seat of his taxi, and they were going along the street. She hugged herself, still in shock, more from what she had seen falling from the sky than from the near accident. Gradually she began to notice Oliver, a blue birthmark on the back of his neck in the shape of an acorn. He would take her wherever she needed to go, he said. She objected but he wouldn't be denied. Mademoiselle, it's the least I can do.

As they drove along the street, the buildings became familiar to Sara again; the green awning over the entrance of the hotel appeared, then the barber shop. As they went past, a man leaning against the barber pole waved, and Oliver tooted the car horn in reply. He pushed his cap to the back of his head and began to whistle a tune softly, through his teeth.

Everyone's going to the train station, he said moments later, likely heading up to Victoria Beach for the last weekend of the season. I'd give my eye teeth—whitefish the size of washtubs, he said, as though Sara understood what he meant. Where was she from? he asked. Before she could reply, he added, Everyone in this city comes from somewheres else. The Jews, Ukrainians, Icelanders, Poles, Hungarians, the English, he recited, his hand rising from the wheel to indicate both sides of Main Street. This hadn't been the case when his people came, he said. The French had settled early, near a town called Aubigny. His family was the first of three families that settled there. I'm a Vandal. A fifth-generation Canadian, he told Sara, as though trying to convince her of something.

The name *Aubigny* had jumped out at her. She took hold of what was familiar, leaned forward in the seat to interrupt him. To tell Oliver that she knew of Aubigny. Her brother-in-law's farm wasn't far from there, and a sister sold eggs and cream in that town, and in Union Plains, too. Had he heard of Union Plains?

For sure, yes, he was acquainted with the place. A nice little town. It appeared as though he might say more, but decided against it.

There's going to be a cheese factory built at Union Plains, Sara told him, eager to push their conversation forward. To show him that she'd recovered, convey that the near accident hadn't been as serious as all that.

You don't say, Oliver replied, as though she'd said something important and interesting.

He sounded different from most Canadians she'd met, his voice husky and full of air. He grasped the wheel lightly, with hands that were almost dainty, and so unlike the broad and scarred hands of a farmer.

What brought you to Winnipeg? he asked.

I came to work, she told him. Like everyone else, she thought. The clerks she sometimes dealt with in the stores. Like them, she rinsed her stockings at night and hung them to dry, but unlike them, she did not have to choose what she would wear, could not anticipate any lively chatter in the lunchroom, or in the restrooms where they tidied their hair and freshened their faces and talked about—what? Where they would go after work? Who they might see? She really didn't know.

Nevertheless, she was riding in a taxi and having a conversation with a man. A person who didn't ask her to repeat herself. Who hadn't started in surprise when she spoke and then become wary and distant, or treated her like a child, raising his voice and choosing his words carefully. The street unfolded in its familiarity, and beyond she saw the shining white rump of the horse on the saddlery store sign.

You don't say, Oliver said once again. And where do you work?

I work at the Hudson Bay store, she heard herself tell him, and for the moment it took to speak it seemed true. He sat up straighter and she saw his dark eyes looking at her in the rear-view mirror, appraising, approving.

As they drew up in front of the boarding house, Oliver turned to her, indecision working in his face. Say, I wonder. Do you like picture shows?

I don't know, she said, answering without thinking and revealing that she'd never been to one.

There was a flutter of movement in the curtain on a window at the boarding house. Oliver got out of the car and she resisted the impulse to open the door, waiting for him to do so. She had thought Oliver was tall, but now, as she stepped from the taxi, she realized he was medium height. Her mouth quivered as she said, My name is Sara Vogt. His teeth were the colour of old ivory, and wet, and when he smiled at her they shone.

The door opened quickly to Sara's ring, and she attributed the startled expression of the hostess of the Home Away from Home Club to the fact that she was so late. Then she realized that the woman was staring at her ears. Without thinking, Sara brought her hands up and touched her lobes, which were numbed by the clamp of metal. From the curb came the sound of the car's horn tooting, and she turned to see Oliver wave as he drove off. The woman's shock gave way to disapproval as she took note of him.

Well, yes. You're here at last. We wondered and wondered what could have happened. What's keeping our Sara? The woman's veneer of concern did little to conceal the chilliness of her tone.

Sara entered to the buzz of conversation and laughter coming from the living room. For an instant she thought, Take off the earrings, the scarf. She would enter their presence as plain and as unadorned as they were. The odour of coffee brewing seeped out from the kitchen at the end of the hall. She was in time for the customary mid-afternoon lunch of cheese and buns, for more depressing stories.

Our Sara has arrived, the hostess announced at the living-room doorway, loudly, as though giving the women a warning.

When Sara told Oliver about what she had seen falling from the sky on the day he had almost mowed her down with the taxi, he suggested that it had been a bat. Her description included pantomime when her English failed, her hands moving in counter-circles in the air. You can't predict the movement of a bat, and they're quick as a wink, he said. More than likely, that's what you saw.

Cigarette smoke streamed from his nostrils as he exhaled; then he crushed the cigarette out in an ashtray resting on the arm of the sofa where they sat, in his brother Romeo's tiny living room somewhere in St. Boniface, on a short street of rundown houses. A street that ended near a large stone cathedral, and the muddy banks of the Red River.

I've seen bats, Sara said. In that other place, while she was being carried on her father's shoulders across a compound towards a lit-up house, the hair on the top of her head had lifted, and a bat had dipped down on the path in front of them and disappeared into the twilight. Bats were suddenly present, and suddenly gone. She'd seen bats when she brought Kornelius's cows to water at the dugout pond, and their flight was an erratic swerving and darting, not at all like what she'd seen falling towards her from the sky. But she didn't tell him that. She did not say to Oliver, Don't tell me what I saw, as she would do after they were married. Don't tell me what I meant to say.

Well then, maybe a pigeon, Oliver responded.

No, no, no, Sara said, shaking her head. The wings were larger, and transparent. She struggled to say more, while seated beside him on the sagging couch in Romeo's rundown house, rain pinging against the tin roof, twin boys romping in a crib in the bedroom beyond, causing the crib to bang against the wall. She wanted to tell Oliver that she'd come close to dying once before. But she was quieted as his hand came near her face, his fingers combing through his hair and releasing a scent that reminded her of the smell in the air when the train taking her to their ship neared the ocean.

She was wearing the silk stockings of a dead sister on that train trip, the flesh-coloured hosiery folded down and drawn tight around her scrawny girl thighs with large wool stitches. The pucker of material, the grasp of garters, was noticeable through her skirt. Throughout the long journey the stockings kept twisting, and they rumpled like a second skin at her knees. Sara had left that sister, her four brothers and her parents behind in their graves. The train crept through the Russian border and into Lithuania, a drawn-out moment that went on longer than Sara was able to hold her breath, while all around her people broke into song and weeping.

She breathed Oliver in, aware of the crepe of her dress shifting as she moved closer to him, its weight like water sliding across her stomach and thighs. My brother's having a small get-together, Oliver had said to her earlier in the evening, when he met up with her at the Bay store entrance. She had expected that they were going to go to a movie, as he'd suggested, as an apology of sorts for having come near to running her down. She'd told Mrs. Ashburn that was where she'd be, and with a friend, neglecting to say that the friend was male.

Romeo studied them from across the room as he leaned forward on a kitchen chair, a burning cigarette in the fingers of one long hand. Oliver's usual easygoing self had been trimmed and spiffed. He looked uncomfortable in a new shirt and tie, his boots shined to the limit and planted on the floor as though he needed to feel it beneath him.

Sara was small, and she was pretty, as Oliver had said. Her face was unblemished, and even without the benefit of makeup her skin glowed, as did her eyes as she took in the room. Her quickness brought to mind the fluttery movements of a finch, but there was nothing flashy about her that would have caught Romeo's eye if he had passed her on the street. Her jitteriness, the heavy material of her dress, its tailored and carefully pressed appearance, made her look like a convent-school girl about to give a piano recital, and having a case of the butterflies.

Sara thought Romeo seemed to have a fire going inside him, the way his features flared one moment and darkened the next. He went from silent laughter, as he listened to her and Oliver talk, to guarded puzzlement. He didn't seem to understand much of what she said, and when the brothers spoke French she tried to guess from their expressions, the movements of their bodies, what they were saying.

Dishes clattered in the kitchen, where Romeo's wife, Claudette, prepared food for the guests they were expecting. Likely there's going to be music, Claudette had said, and chuckled at the thought. Her nostrils were slits, not holes, and her voice was squeezed thin. She'd worked for a longer time at Canada Packers than Romeo, filling boxes on the conveyors. It was a coveted job, and therefore there were more English girls than French ones working with her. As a result, Claudette's English was better than her husband's.

After the guests arrived, Oliver and Romeo spoke French for the remainder of the evening. The small house quickly filled, became jammed with bodies, and the air blue with smoke so thick Sara could barely breathe. Cheers went up when a small wiry man with a thin black moustache arrived carrying a violin case, soon followed by another fiddler. Within moments, out came a lively jig that stopped all conversation.

People's smiles grew wide, were almost conspiratorial, as though they'd agreed beforehand to become devil-may-care and comfortably soused. Sara was a dull spot sitting on the couch, not knowing where to look, wearing a dress gussied up with a limp-looking scarf knotted at her breasts.

These men and women from St. Boniface were meat-plant workers, Canada Packers being a major employer for people lacking in education. But they'd educated themselves in a more necessary way than what might be found in books.

They knew how to be flamboyant, to spend the money they worked so hard to earn. They played the horses until their pockets were empty. Went dancing at the Belgium Club and flirted with each other's spouses, attended mass at the cathedral the following day, bleary-eyed, contrite, a handshake forgiving a bruised chin, a woman blushing to recall the illicit caresses of the man now standing in line in front of her, waiting to receive the body and blood of Christ.

Alice Bouchard arrived near the end of the evening. The music stopped and the room grew still as the door closed behind her. Alice swept a green cape from her shoulders and gave it to Claudette, as though this were the reason why she had rushed to the door. Alice was petite and small-boned, and more polished-looking than the other women present. Her eyes found Oliver and Sara seated on the couch, and her smile seemed forced as she came to greet them. A cloud of sweet-smelling scent wafted from her as Oliver rose to meet her, and to receive her kisses, first one cheek and then the other.

How do you do, Alice said, greeting Sara in English, in a tone that sounded as though she was withholding laughter. Her olive eyes grazed Sara's face and her body once, and then she ignored her for the remainder of the evening.

Who is she? Sara asked Oliver, as Alice went away from them.

She's an old friend from my school days, from Aubigny, Oliver replied.

Sara grew quietly agitated as the hours passed by. Close to midnight she said to Oliver a second time, I have to go, and got to her feet, thinking that she felt the others sigh in relief as she did so.

Oliver walked her to a taxi stand and insisted on paying the driver to take her home. And so she had her second and last ride ever in a taxi, speeding through the streets, the houses all along the crescent like dark sentinels, until the taxi drew near to the Ashburn residence, whose front entrance was lit.

This just won't do, Sara Vogt, Emily Ashburn called to her as she went up the stairs at the back of the house. Proper girls don't come home at such an hour.

Not long afterwards, Katy and Kornelius arrived at the Ashburn house to fetch Sara, Katy's face grey with disappointment. She didn't speak the entire drive to the farm. They entered the house and the children scattered like chickens in a barnyard, Annie's eyes filling as she came from the kitchen to greet Sara and was stopped short by a pointed look from Kornelius. Immediately Kornelius made Sara sit down on a chair, as though he meant to interrogate her, the cuckoo bird in the wall clock shooting out from its door to count the hour.

For a moment Sara thought Kornelius would strike her, and steeled herself against it. Go ahead, do it, she thought. Let me feel the sting of your hand against my face, something more than disappointment, the feeling she had of falling backwards.

Take the silver spoon out of your mouth, Kornelius said. It doesn't belong there. He would finish paying off the passage fees, he said, and in return she would help Katy raise the children, and take on more of the farm chores, now that Annie would be attending high school in the nearby town of Steinbach.

High school? she did not ask. Why had she been given only two years and Annie got to go to high school? Katy had retreated to the kitchen and began to sing now, her voice filled with vibrato; Kornelius left the house, slamming the door behind him. She would run away, put on her coat, boots, and go running for the road. And go where? Into the kitchen to help prepare the meal. She felt numbed, her feet heavy. But she entered the kitchen singing, *When the moon shines over the mountain. Katy, beautiful Katy, I'll be waiting at the kitchen door.* She sang merrily a song she'd often heard playing from the Ashburns' radio, and drowned out her sister's hymn.

She became a prisoner of winter then, the long cold months that stretched endlessly into a white horizon without the relief of a city unfolding beyond the front door. She remembered hearing Katy once say that their grandparents had died of heartsickness, disappointment coupled with a loneliness that had no foreseeable end. In the old country her grandparents had lived in a town while farming the lands beyond. In Canada there was nothing to see for miles around and nowhere to walk, no neighbours they could visit at the end of the day, they complained, albeit apologetically, not wanting to risk sounding ungrateful. Sara understood their loneliness now. It was like a voice echoing from a deep stone well.

Winter isn't any colder this year, Katy said, as she and Sara hung laundry on lines strung through the attic of the farmhouse. Meaning it was no colder than the previous four winters Sara had already experienced in Canada. Sara's knuckles were bleeding, chapped as rough as a rasp, and paining with the cold. Four winters of hanging clothes out to dry in the bitter cold had permanently curled two of Katy's fingers, but still she only resorted to using the inside lines when the temperatures dipped below minus twenty. On a recent frigid day, Sara's niece, Susan, had drawn her outside to watch as she threw a cup of hot water into the air, delighting in the spectacle of water instantly turning to snow.

Winter makes me lonely, Sara said, speaking round a lump in her throat as she pinned a bedsheet to a line in the attic. When the clothing dried, she would need to bundle up once again, come up here to the wind-racked top floor, whose boards were thick with frost, and put the bedding, towels, tablecloths through the mangle.

Lonely for what? Katy asked, worrying that city life had got into Sara's blood. The rafters shuddered as the wind pelted snow against the house.

I met a man in Winnipeg, his name is Oliver, Sara blurted, wanting to make him real by speaking his name. She sometimes thought she'd imagined him and the failed party at Romeo's house. She'd returned the earrings to Emily Ashburn's dressing-table drawer, but kept the scarf, a reminder of the events when she had worn it, the freedom she had had to go about the city as if she was a normal everyday person.

And? Katy asked.

Sara sensed her immediate and careful attention.

I think he was fond of me, Sara said recklessly. Would Oliver have taken her to meet his brother if that weren't so? And I'm fond of him too, she said, thinking of the poem she'd copied from a shop window. Oliver, for a short time, had been her beau, her intended, my financier, she thought, meaning fiancé.

So that's it, Katy thought, relieved once again to have brought Sara home.

Spring finally dawned, bringing sleet pellets that stung Sara's face as she dashed between the car and the church; then a week of freezing rain glazed the remaining shreds of snow and made the roads treacherous. Soon after, pools of water collected on the fields, and Sara looked out the window one morning and saw a pair of mallard ducks flying above the dugout pond.

Katy attributed Sara's restlessness to having lived in Winnipeg; she'd been spoiled by its commotion and noise. She'd become a person who needed to be entertained, who liked to see herself in a mirror and hear herself talking. It would be good for Sara to be married, and soon, she concluded, failing to realize that Sara sought confirmation that she was alive. She had no sooner experienced joy at being among the living than that joy had been thwarted.

Her conclusion that Sara should marry was confirmed the following summer, during a get-together of several women from church. Come and visit us for a change, Katy had framed her invitation. It will do us all good. They would have a songfest in the way they used to amid the walnut grove in the old country.

The women arrived all together, six of them, spinsters and widows nearing middle age, driven to the farm by one of the women's nephews, Henry Friesen, a young man who was the son of a watch repairer from the large Mennonite town of

Steinbach. While the women went off for their songfest, he stayed to visit with Kornelius under the open veranda he'd built onto the back of the house so that Katy might watch twilight descend, the children playing while she shelled peas, the cows coming to the dugout to drink. The fair young man was pleasantly stout and boyishly handsome, and Sara didn't fail to notice him.

The women went through the field of blooming wild mustard, whose garishly bright flowers would have hurt their eyes had it not been for myriads of white butterflies, a confetti of flitting wings rising in a billow as the women made their way to the elm tree and the blankets Katy had spread down in its shade.

Sara recalled being with several of these women in Russia. Their dresses had been softer in colour and material then, and had revealed the shapes of their bodies as they ascended a hill single file to a grove of walnut trees at the end of a day. In Russia these women had dressed in the latest of European fashions, copied from magazines that the well travelled and wealthy among them brought back from their journeys to Germany, Italy and France. They copied fashions they'd seen women wearing while they strolled in the parks of St. Petersburg and on the boardwalks of Odessa.

As they went through the field of wild mustard, these same women seemed awkward and unlovely, swishing away the butterflies with their songbooks. Their dresses were jersey and cotton-print homemade shirtwaist styles, or a kind of A-shaped tunic worn with a white blouse. All of them wore white sandals and socks rolled down at their ankles, copying what their own people wore here so as not to offend their fellow

Mennonites who'd come to Canada sooner than they had. The Canadian Mennonites were known as Little Church, Mennonite Brethren, General Conference, while Sara, Katy and the women were First Mennonites, high brow and worldly.

These once-proud and educated women did not have to speak to be apologizing. They apologized with their demeanour. Apologized because some among them had buried young husbands or their betrotheds in Russia during the revolution. Several among the six women who came to sing that Sunday afternoon had been raped. They accepted the blame that they might have lost so much because of their desire to be fashionable, to dance, to play cards, to look in the mirror, as suggested by their more conservative cousins. Likely these women would never marry. They certainly would never speak English well enough to find employment as other than what they had become: servants, cooks, farmhands. Housekeepers and nannies for their younger sisters, who were obliged to make them part of their households.

They arranged themselves on the blankets under the tree, glancing up at its branches, which were spitting droplets of moisture, choosing to pretend that this was not the case. Sara leaned against the trunk, a songbook opened on her lap, as Katy led the singing. The other women joined in, their voices quickly blending. Their voices were both sweet and sad, and filled with a resignation that Sara found irritating. She'd begun to suspect that, while the beliefs of her people had been necessary to sustain them during their time of danger, in this country those beliefs had become heavy old coats, bulky and too hot.

The women harmonized as they sang the final amen. Katy then recited the Lord's Prayer. Sara half closed her eyes, her attention drawn to one woman who continued to work on a piece of crocheting while saying the prayer. Her fingers deftly looped and twisted the yarn while her eyes remained shut, her lips moving in silent recitation. *Give us this day our daily bread.* Her bosom heaved, and a sigh escaped.

Sara knew that like Katy, like herself, the women around her struggled to keep their memories at bay. They assuaged their night terrors with weak tea and honey. Forgiving those who had trespassed against them meant not remembering what had been done to them. These women had experienced desperate things that she'd escaped, and she suspected they might resent her for that. *For thine is the Kingdom,* they prayed, while Sara concentrated on the way her ankle looked; she wished it were more slender. These women had forgotten how to dream. She knew that if she was ever going to be able to dream, treason might be necessary.

They returned to the house and gathered in the parlour, Sara leaving them to go to the kitchen and help Annie prepare the lunch. It's time that girl was married, one of the women said, confirming what Katy had already concluded.

But to whom? Sara hadn't shown an interest in any of the young farmers attending church, those scrubbed and slicked men, sunburned and hardened by physical labour. They cast sideways glances in her direction, engaged in horseplay when she could see them, but failed to earn her attention.

Sara is too fussy, one of the woman said. Another recalled Sara as a child living in the town of Rosenthal, Russia, where her family had stayed for a time at the grandparents' house. Remember how active she was as a little girl? When she played with other children she sometimes stamped her foot to get her way, she said. Another woman remembered that Sara would enter their house and open drawers without asking permission, just as the dirty and sick little Russian children had done during the time of thievery. Sara had refused to sing for her unless she was given a cookie. Katy's eyes filled with regret as she listened. For a time following the deaths in her family she'd been away in her mind, and perhaps during that time Sara had been alone too much.

Sara once kissed me, a woman broke in to say. This was Nela, who had been a neighbour to Sara's grandparents in Russia. I didn't ask for a kiss. I was sitting on a bench outside thinking of my father. His pear tree had been chopped down for burning, and I thought how this would have hurt him so. I felt these little arms go around my neck. Sara kissed me. Sara said, I love you, Nela. It was as though she knew what I was thinking. She knew what I needed.

In the silence that followed, Sara's and Annie's voices rose up from the kitchen, over the murmur of Kornelius and Henry Friesen as they visited on the veranda.

When Henry Friesen came to visit again he did not come with his aunt, but on the invitation of Kornelius. Sara watched from the window as he walked down the lane to the house, his jacket slung over his shoulder, and she decided that she liked that. He's older than Sara, of that I'm sure, Sara had overheard Kornelius saying to Katy. But he seems younger. She'll eat him for breakfast.

And although Henry was expected, just before he arrived Kornelius took the little children for a ride about the country to look at the crops, while Katy sent Annie to the garden with two chairs, which she was to set down near a tangle of wild rose bushes.

Henry told Sara immediately, I work for my father, as though, if he didn't, he would not be able to speak, his blue eyes blinking rapidly behind his wire-frame glasses. His shyness made Sara bold. Made her want to touch him and say, Don't worry, I won't bite you. She liked the way his face had lit up with pleasure when they were first introduced. As they sat in the garden and talked, she appreciated that his ears turned red when she laughed.

There wasn't enough business in clock and watch repair to keep him and three brothers going in their father's shop, he explained, and so his brothers were going to Normal School to become teachers. He didn't have the patience for teaching, he knew. He wanted to build onto his father's store and sell furniture and household items. It was as though he'd rehearsed what he would say, beginning immediately as they sat down side by side on their chairs, Sara needing to turn slightly in order to look at him, to see his shirt moving with his heartbeat. Rose petals were strewn about the ground beneath the bushes, and she watched for a moment as several red ants began carrying one away.

I so terribly much want to buy a car, Henry blurted, the first thing that did not sound as though it was an item on his list. The day was hot and perspiration beaded his upper lip and forehead. The scent of wild roses mingled with the rich smell of decaying vegetation from a nearby compost heap.

His shirt strained at the buttons across his stomach, revealing a slash of skin and a feathering of gold hair. Sara thought about sliding a finger between the buttons and tickling him. A pink ribbon gathering the neck of her blouse had come undone and she played with it, rolled it up like a frog's tongue and let it fall loose. She knew not to look directly at him, but to be occupied with the ribbon, which left him free to look at her. She felt his myopic gaze, his yearning. It seemed to her that her hands were delicate, and that when she rolled up the ribbon again, they spoke to him.

If I had a car, would you go riding with me? Henry asked, which was tantamount to a proposal of marriage.

Sara knew this and yet she could not consider the proposition seriously. She grinned and said in a teasing way, You want to take me for a spin? She laughed. The English word, *spin,* stepped out from among the German. Once, when Emily Ashburn had sent her to order coal, there had been two men leaning against a car near the coal shed, their caps pushed to the backs of their heads. They'd called out, Hello there honey, would you like to come with us for a spin?

Annie came through the garden carrying a tea tray, choosing her way carefully among the rows of vegetation, the dog following at her heels. Sara felt the space between their chairs widen as she thought of Katy sitting in the shade of the veranda, watching; hovering over all the details of her and Annie's lives, the unspoken history of the violent end of their family.

Annie stood in front of Henry, colouring as she offered him a glass of tea, and it occurred to Sara that Annie had grown taller. Then she realized that it wasn't that Annie had grown, but rather that Henry had become shorter. During the night there had been rain, and the earth in the garden was soft. While they'd been talking, the legs of his chair had started to sink. He sipped cautiously at the tea, worrying, she could tell, that his nervousness might cause him to spill it. The legs of his chair were sinking minute by minute deeper into the earth, and he pretended not to notice, although he crossed and uncrossed his legs, trying to get comfortable.

He lived at the back of his father's watch-repair shop, as a window had been broken and his presence discouraged that from happening again, he told her. He planned to enlarge the living quarters back there, once he had added onto the business. This was where they would live, Sara knew. As he talked she willed him to get up from the chair. To pull its legs free and make a joke out of it. But he simply gave up trying to cross his legs, and now his knees jutted up level with his chest.

She noticed that his fingers were pudgy, and likely too blunt for the minute workings of a clock. A muscle jerked in his face as he talked, his stomach was fat, there were bracelets of fat around his wrists. Fatty, fatty, two by four, Sara thought; she had heard young children chanting the verse at school.

What's so funny? Henry asked, and Sara realized that she had laughed.

You, Sara told him, wanting suddenly for this to end. *Fatty, fatty, two by four, can't get through the kitchen door,* Sara said, as she went away from him through the garden.

Returning to the farm meant becoming the egg girl once again, going to the town of Aubigny with Katy. Waiting on the doormat while women went rushing about looking for the correct change, and then counted it out into her hand as though she couldn't make change. She welcomed the chance to peer into rooms, sometimes startled by the dirt and clutter, and sometimes admiring an arrangement of pictures on a wall, a vase on a table. Children peered at her as though she came from the moon. What's your name? she once dared to ask, and the children ran screaming to find their mother.

She watched for Alice Bouchard when they delivered eggs and cream, but apparently the Bouchard house wasn't one they called on. She crossed the river on the ferry with Katy, went trudging up the access road to Union Plains to sell their produce, not knowing that, shortly after her failed date with Oliver, he'd left the city too, and returned to run the hotel. On one of those Saturdays, Sara was shocked to come upon him leaning against the door frame, chewing on a piece of straw. Both of them were riveted in the moment, uncertain if they should acknowledge one another's presence. Oliver was the first to do so, with a slight smile and a nod before going inside.

After that she was feverish for Saturdays to come, for the sight of Oliver. Her eyes were drawn to any man she happened upon with dark hair, her body instantly coming alive. When she stood beside Oliver, she could barely keep from touching him, and went away hot, an ache between her legs that she pressed against when she had a moment alone, in order to feel normal again.

On their third encounter, Oliver invited Sara to attend a dance in Aubigny. I can't dance, she said, shifting from foot to foot, swinging the egg basket to cover her fear of Katy coming upon them talking in the street. She only meant to warn him that she didn't know how; that wouldn't stop her from going.

There's nothing wrong with letting your hair down, Oliver replied. He knew now that she was Deetch, and how peculiar they were. Straitlaced and pious, to the point of being offensive. Alice would be at that dance, he was certain, and there was nothing wrong with keeping her on her toes.

Sara agreed to meet him at the ferry, thinking that she would wear the blue dress Annie had made as a welcome-home gift to soften the disgrace of her return.

Throughout the week she performed all her tasks without complaining. With an eagerness to do them well, as though she somehow knew she'd soon be freed of them. Not knowing that, upon agreeing to meet Oliver to go dancing, she had agreed to become the mother of his children.

Her hand shook as she dabbed lipstick on her mouth and cheeks. The dress was flattering, its shoulders softly shirred and padded, accenting the curve of her breasts and her flat stomach. Children's voices rose up from the yard at the back of the house; Annie was with them, Sara knew. Kornelius was busy in the machine shed and Katy in the kitchen, and so she was able to climb down the ladder she'd placed against the house earlier in the day, unseen. And run through the garden towards a windbreak that would screen her from view.

She half ran the distance to the ferry road, and down the road where it dipped into a wet gully and then rose to a crest. When she reached the crest she saw the river below, and the ferry on the opposite shore reflected in its surface. As her breathing stilled, she became aware of a rustling sound behind her and turned towards it, expecting that Oliver had already crossed over and waited now among the trees. But what she heard was the sound of a tree shrugging off summer, its foliage churning outwards in a sudden gold rain, the swishing sound of it like running water. Several moments later, the ground was carpeted with leaves and its branches were almost bare. It was unsettling to witness such a thing, a tree's season ending so quickly. In this country there was sweltering heat and overnight, a hard frost, and the desolation of winter descended.

Someone called, and she turned to see Oliver and the ferry operator emerge from a path among the trees and into a clearing on the other side of the river. Oliver's voice echoed, cupped by the embrace of trees whose foliage was brazen yellow, cranberry and brown leather. The ferry's engine spurted to life and the operator ducked out of the engine shed, a small hunched man missing half an arm. Oliver leaned against the other motor shed, wearing a short maroon tie knotted beneath the collar of a white shirt and a brown suit jacket.

Small waves lapped at a sheath of rubber tires nailed to the front of the ferry as it reached the shore, the rippling water staining the planks of the landing a dark grey. Oliver stepped off and came towards her, and she waited for him to speak. She expected to be greeted in his usual teasing manner. My God, lookee here. Look who you see when you don't have a gun. In this joking manner, he always veered away from any attempt she made at conversation when she happened upon him in Union Plains, leaving the hotel, or at the nip-and-chip stand, ordering a hamburger and chips to go, and stopping for a smoke and a visit with the woman who ran the booth.

At last, she thought. Throughout the week she'd feared something would prevent her from meeting him. A fall, a twisted ankle, a raging flu.

By God, he said softly, after a long moment of silence.

She saw admiration shining from his eyes and didn't know where to look.

She thought they would return the way she had come. Go on back up the road and enter the town of Aubigny and walk to the end of it, to the dance hall, a lumbering, square building set in a field of grass. But instead Oliver glanced back at the ferry and called to the man in French. What he said caused the operator to start with surprise, and with a shrug he returned to the engine shed. A moment later the engine started up.

Oliver didn't ask whether she was coming or not. But Sara knew that he was inviting her to cross over to Union Plains. Yes, she thought. Go with him. She was a child daring to leap from the top step for the sake of experiencing the moment of flying, for the uncertainty of the landing. He didn't offer his hand to help her board, and kept his back turned as they rode in silence. She leaned against the guard chain, watching the shore retreat as she had watched the coastline of another world grow distant and dissolve into the horizon. Halfway across the channel, they entered a stream of moist warm air that was replaced by a stillness as they came near the other shore.

She followed Oliver as he took the path through the trees, both of them silent, unmindful of the deadfalls, the rich stink of decay amid the underbrush. Oliver crossed Stage Coach Road and Sara crossed too, following him into town and down a street, passing several children along the way, children who called to one another when they parted and went into their houses. She followed him into the hotel, and he took her by the hand and led her to his room under the stairs.

She could not have imagined the ferocity of his desire, his hunger, how he would consume her in a moment, or the tearing, the sudden raw pain; his panting and calling out, the gush of hot wetness, both hers and his. She was stunned by the largeness of his desire, then equally stunned by his tenderness. His tears as he nuzzled her neck, hands sweeping down and up the length of her body.

She could not have imagined how the distance, the strangeness between them, would dissolve instantly. She felt that she knew his body, its odour, its smooth skin and deep colour, as though it were her own. She came to learn that a touch, a certain expression, a glimpse of her nakedness was enough to make Oliver desire her, to lose himself for a moment and then return to her, soft with love.

A mist was rising on the land when Oliver walked her home, a dog barked, and then Katy came running down the lane towards the road. She grabbed Sara's hands and took in her dishevelled appearance. Fix yourself, Oliver had said, and given her his comb to pull through her hair. But there was nothing she could do about her dress being torn, its buttons missing. There was a rawness between her legs; a stickiness of blood, his fluid gluing her pubic hair to her undergarments so that it prickled and pulled when she walked. She had set her shoulders as Katy ran towards her, knowing that her sister had been waiting up all night.

Where were you? Katy asked, seeing Oliver retreating, walking smartly despite the mud and ruts.

That's the man I told you about, Sara said. The man who'd nearly run her down. The man she was fond of.

He loves me, she said. Katy's face twisted in anguish. She pressed her hands to her rib cage and said, For shame, Sara. Our dear father!

SEVEN

Ruby and the water man

IT LOOKS LIKE Mom's going to be late coming down this morning, Alvina said, and took Patsy Anne from Ruby's arms and plunked her into the highchair. Then she cajoled the baby to quickly spoon her porridge down. Moments later Alvina lingered in the doorway, tugging at her bottom lip as she glanced at the kitchen ceiling. I just can't miss school, she said.

Mom's sick, Ruby said, remembering to deliver Sara's message.

I know, but she won't be sick for long. She'll be down soon, and if she isn't, you go and poke her. With that, Alvina headed off for school and her typing exam.

In a way, Sara's absence seemed a less tumultuous event than her presence would have been. The Vandals' flat line of give-and-take became a pyramid when Sara joined them in the kitchen. A person singled out by their mother for praise or recrimination, or favourable or unfavourable comparison, threatened to knock over a glass of milk, threatened to send a dish crashing to the floor. Their pyramid toppled and they went off, all in their own direction, wary, too anxious to please and full of contradiction.

Ruby struggled to drag the playpen through the back porch and outdoors. The sun's heat released the scent of herbs hanging in bunches from the rafters, and a broth of chemical fumes emanating from tins of shoe polish and pesticides lining the windowsill. *Roll, roll, roll your boat, gently down the stream, merrily, merrily, merrily, merrily, life is but a scream.* She mistakenly sang Manny's made-up words, as she was preoccupied with the momentous task of moving the cumbersome playpen, pulling it while Sharon, the toddler, pushed. She was consumed by her monumental responsibility, and relief that the bump on the side of her head had stopped throbbing.

Music played from the radio in the kitchen, while Patsy Anne struck the tin tray of the highchair with a spoon. The porch windows vibrated as a heavy vehicle approached in the street, and Ruby felt the buzz in the lump behind her ear. She was too late, the water man had come before she'd had a chance to prepare. Before she was able to assemble the pen and put Patsy Anne inside it, leaving her with no one to watch but Sharon, who might wander too near the cistern's open lid. The vehicle went past the house and beyond it. It wasn't the water truck, Ruby realized with relief.

The water man doesn't have eyes in the back of his head, Ruby said to herself, aloud. She, Sharon and Patsy Anne had to steer clear of the cistern until it was shut and locked. Kids could drown in three inches of water. In a rain barrel. Once upon a time, water went down the wrong hole when a man drank from a dipper and he died of pneumonia, which was the same thing as drowning.

Ruby resumed the task of easing the playpen through the clutter of winter and spring footwear in the centre of the porch. She paused to catch her breath, and pointed to a grass-cutting whip that someone had left lying to one side of the heap. She warned Sharon, Don't, don't. That blade is sharp, stay away. That's something you never want to fool with, she said, repeating what had become a common household phrase.

The wooden playpen was as wide as it was tall, and as tall as Ruby, but she managed to pull it past the piano parked beneath the porch windows, veneer cracked and flaking from the elements of summer and winter. Whoever had last played it had failed to push the bench back into place, and it was piled with jackets and sweaters, which slid to the floor when Ruby squeezed by.

Oof, she grunted, to gain strength, kicking aside the clothing, and then, in one swift movement, she pulled the playpen over to the door and outside, leaving Sharon empty-handed and stumbling across the sill. The door snapped shut behind them, the key to the water cistern padlock rattling on its hook.

The two small girls pushed the playpen through the uncut grass of the yard, finally reaching their destination, a young ash tree whose branches provided a slender fan of shade. Ruby began unfolding the playpen the way she'd seen others do it, struggling to hold one side upright while she reached to lift another, to fit a notched latch onto a bolt. She pounded at the latch with her fist, but the pain was too much to endure and so she gave up. She stood for a moment, panting with exertion and listening. Patsy Anne was no longer beating the spoon against the tray.

She sent Sharon to fetch a rock from the back of the yard, while she returned to the house to investigate the lack of noise. But when she entered the kitchen, she paused on the doormat and wondered, why had she come? A hand seemed to press against the bump at the side of her head, a steady warm pressure that felt like a caress. Then, as quickly as it had descended, the hand lifted and the release of pressure made Ruby feel weightless. She felt that if she jumped, she'd float to the ceiling. The cherries on the wallpaper jiggled and steadied. The fruit plaques marched across the wall with their usual vigour.

The kitchen brightened with the fullness of Patsy Anne's grin. Bee Bee, she called, and Ruby remembered why she'd come. Patsy swivelled her hands in anticipation of being freed from the belt securing her to the highchair, just as all the Vandals squirmed and strained to be free of what held them down. Wanting to run before they could crawl, and winding up with bruises and chipped teeth and nightmares of wolves and bears.

Just as Emilie had squirmed against the stricture of a tie binding her to a chair in the cellar. Bound and left in the dark so that she might contemplate, without being distracted, the reason for the energy that propelled her through the rooms of the house, leaping from one piece of furniture to another for an entire day, or why she had cut apart a pair of curtains to make a costume, or had been sent to the store to purchase puffed wheat cereal and had returned with a bag of marshmallow Easter eggs, or had filched slices of cold cuts from a parcel of meat so that, at mealtime, there wasn't enough to go around. Emilie had learned how to breathe in abject darkness, to enjoy the sweetish musty odour of last year's potatoes going to mush in the vegetable bin.

Bee Bee, Patsy Anne called once again. Her face had been wiped clean of oatmeal smears, hair dampened and teased with a soft brush into a wave cresting the length of her head. Ruby pronounced her own name, loudly, so that Patsy Anne would realize she was trying to teach her something. Not Bee Bee. Say, Roobee. Patsy tried, the word coming out as Booby, and Ruby laughed. Then she assured the baby, Yah, yah, Ruby's going to take you outside to play now.

Ruby didn't recognize that when she said, Yah, yah, she was mimicking her aunt Katy. Because Katy's voice was soft, Ruby believed that her *ja, ja* expressed a desire to comfort. She was too young to interpret the nuances in her aunt's voice. *Ja, ja* could be a chastisement, expressing a sadness that had the power to make a grown listener cringe with guilt. *Ja, ja* could be spoken with an undertow of anger. Uttered as a threat.

Alvina had cleared away the breakfast dishes and put them into the sink before rushing off to her typing test. The countertop was free of toast crumbs and butter smears. But she hadn't turned off the radio. Ruby silenced it, then listened for a creak in the ceiling that would mean that Sara was up and moving about. But there was no sound. Either she was sleeping or she had died, as people were sometimes known to do.

The kitchen darkened suddenly, the water truck having arrived and going past the window, backing slowly along the driveway. Then the room lightened, the sun illuminating the plaster plaques, the lime-green tiles again reflecting the legs of chairs set around the table.

When Ruby stepped outside with Patsy Anne, the truck was already backed up to the cistern. She went round it and saw the water man folded into the grass beside Sharon, fastening the last of the playpen's sides into place. He got up slowly and stood looking down at Ruby, his length and angularity reminding her of a grasshopper. Or a woodcutter come to rescue a gobbled-up grandmother. The creases and folds on either side of his face were like ropes of pull-taffy. He took off his cap and scratched at several strands of hair on his otherwise bald head.

I'm Ruby, which was what Ruby usually told the water man, when he asked. And that one? He'd point and she'd say, Well, that one is Sharon. Same as the last time.

Patsy Anne is the baby, she'd tell him, but without hope that he'd remember. She would recite, Alvina, Norbert (Sonny Boy), George (The Other One), Ida, Emilie, Simon, Manny, Ruby, Sharon, and the baby of the show—Patsy Anne! *Diddle-diddle dumpling, my son John, went to school with his pants undone.*

But today the water man didn't ask Ruby who she was. Today, just when she knew the total of their years, he didn't ask. The total of the Vandal kids' years amounted to ninety-seven. She'd figured it out before hoisting Patsy Anne out of the highchair. Then, when she looked at the clock, the clock said to her, Ruby, it's 9:39. And she said, What? And looked about the room, because the voice was old, like her uncle Ulysse's, and she expected he might have come into the house without her hearing. But of course he hadn't. Then the clock said, It's 9:40. Ulysse wasn't in the living room or dining room, or in the pantry closet, where Sara kept the flour barrel, the floor polisher and a dough-kneading pan. When Ruby returned to the kitchen the clock didn't speak, but just the same she knew that it was saying that the time was 9:42.

Where's your mother? Stevenson asked.

Ruby shrugged. I don't know, she said, because she knew there was no money in the sugar bowl.

Here girl, he said, and reached for Patsy Anne, who whimpered with objection when he peeled her out of Ruby's arms and put her into the playpen.

Okay now, you kids stay clear, he said. He had to connect the hose and then put it down the hatch.

The key's where it usually is, Ruby told him.

How come you know that, and you don't know where your mother is? he asked, a soft smile playing at his mouth.

He didn't want an answer, she knew, as he went over to the cistern and began clearing away the clutter of roller skates.

Ruby gave Patsy Anne a basket of clothes pegs, a bracelet of rubber sealer rings to play with, and led Sharon over to the sandbox adjacent to the house.

Then she returned to the kitchen, the clock saying that it was now 9:55. She intended to fetch a book and a chair, which she would set beside the playpen. She intended to look at pictures and at the same time watch over Patsy Anne, see to it that she didn't ingest a bug, or the ribbons on her sun bonnet, while Sharon played in the sandbox and sang a made-up tune. She sat down at the play table, her thick braids shifting across the smocking of her yellow dress. She felt the vibration of the refrigerator as it hummed, saw the hands move across the face of the clock, while outside in the yard the slender shade of the elm tree shortened, and the entire yard filled up with sun.

EIGHT

Alvina's examinations

THE TEACHER'S FOOTSTEPS receded as she went down the stairs, taking with her Alvina's speed test, the addressed envelopes and correspondence she'd been required to type. *Dear Sir, The price of steel has increased so much during the last six months, that we believe we ourselves shall soon be forced to increase the price of almost all of our products. Gentlemen, I am the owner of the house at 211 Ottawa Street, which is covered by fire insurance that you wrote last year.*

She had managed to stop quavering like a stray dog and had gathered speed as she went along, shutting out the distraction of an entire class in the room below chanting, *Tiger! tiger! burning bright in the forests of the night, . . . What the hammer? what the chain? In what furnace was thy brain?* Their droning pace was about thirty words per minute, which made Alvina want to scream and get it over with, as Sonny Boy had earlier suggested. She had barely begun to type, it seemed, when the bell dinged and Miss White called, Time.

Now the room felt chilly and about as welcoming as an impending ice storm. The blackboards were worn to a sheen that reflected the cold light shining in the windows; above the boards, depressing and ghostly shapes paraded across the wall where pictures, graphs and maps had once been. So, what's up with your sister Emilie this morning? Has she been kept home today? Miss White had hesitated before speaking, as though having second thoughts about inquiring.

Search me, Alvina said, and shrugged, affecting a nonchalance that her pleated skirt and cardigan sweater denied. She preferred that people didn't assume she was her sisters' and brothers' keeper. But of course they did, and of course she was. The teacher's query was about to bring on stomach cramps.

That Emilie! Alvina scrolled a sheet of paper into the Underwood and typed her sister's name, prefixing it, as usual, with the word *that.* And then she notice a misspelled word, *juztaposition,* imprinted on the ribbon. She resisted the urge to scroll out a carbon loop of sentences and look for other errors. The Underwood had been threaded with a new typewriter ribbon and she didn't wish to chance carbon smears on her fingers. A virgin ribbon for a virgin who, barring a kibosh, was about to embark on her virgin voyage as junior secretary for Monarch Industries, the General Hospital or one of several law firms currently advertising in the *Winnipeg Tribune.* Alvina didn't know that, despite the distractions, *juztaposition* was the only error she'd made, and she'd just earned her one-hundred-words-per-minute speed pin.

That Emilie, she thought. The words embodying all that Emilie was—a cause for both vexation and envy. During the war, Emilie had thrown Sara's entire ration of clothes pegs down a hole in the privy, and she'd required special dispensation in order to purchase more. On a dare Emilie had come to school barefoot in minus-twenty-degree weather. Had wandered off at a Sunday school picnic at the Winnipeg Zoo and had been found half a day later at the bear pit, unaware that she was lost. But she hadn't been absent from school before, without Alvina knowing why.

Fart. Something, someone, would put the kibosh on her future. There was news of polio on the radio this morning. Stay out of the sun, away from public swimming pools. Hah. As if she'd ever get near a swimming pool. But still, think of her friend Edward, his leg withered to a stick by polio last summer, and he hadn't been to a public pool. Holy. Think of one of the kids becoming feverish, a headache, stiff muscles. Poliomyelitis, infantile paralysis. How would she get her siblings to agree to play only in the shade this summer? She'd have to come up with something to keep them quietly occupied, so they wouldn't get overheated and susceptible, and wind up with iron lungs.

At recess Miss White would return and dictate the shorthand exam. Why not read while you wait? she'd suggested, and with a snort of laughter had indicated the magazines Alvina had wedged under the desk to give her a level surface. Miss White wasn't much older than Alvina, her study of science at the University of Manitoba interrupted by a need to earn money. Like most teachers who passed through Alvina's dreary life, she was on her way to something larger than teaching. The chemise dress she wore, and the flamingo-pink nail polish, made Alvina feel as fashionable as a chopping block.

The Underwood belonged to the teacher, as did the magazine shims Alvina had borrowed from a stack of various periodicals on a shelf beneath a window, which Miss White had brought to school to be sorted and placed in classrooms to make up for the lack of a library. The young woman had also arranged for a classroom to be made available to Alvina three mornings a week, so that she might have relative peace and quiet to study English composition, literature and commercial by correspondence.

Alvina's too sensitive, her nerves are bad. No one's going to hire her, Alvina had heard Sara say to Florence Dressler. Alvina had recognized the truth. If she wasn't running for a bathroom, she was coming out of one. When her stomach wasn't babbling, her head was. Babbling throughout the long and dark forests of the night: make the shitty beds, fold the shitty laundry, be sure they wash behind their shitty ears. Scrape the diapers. Don't chew your nails. Please, please, don't overflow your cornflakes.

Now she breathed, Please don't let Emilie be throwing herself down the tubes. Emilie was a bee buzzing at a window to get inside a house and then frantically buzzing to get back outside. Alvina got up and went over to the window, thinking that perhaps Emilie had followed the creek to the monastery and was now returning, on the run, her socks harbouring a field day of wood ticks. She prayed to see that girl, her feet skimming across the ground as she came flying through Zinn's field. Please God, just once, please, Alvina would like to feel her feet leave the ground in the way Emilie's seemed to do.

The stretch of land near the horizon was yellow with sunlight, and interrupted by bold strokes of trees concealing the presence of the monastery and its collection of buff stone buildings. From a distance the monastery brought to mind a holy city, but up close the air stank of pigs and cattle like any farm; blowflies buzzed over manure piles, the geese came hissing and running at her if they got a chance. Below the window, the west-facing schoolyard looked rainy-day dismal in the shadow of the building.

The new grass in Zinn's field, beyond the baseball diamond, was as yet unbent by a wind or flattened to a path where someone had come tramping through it. The grass sometimes grew thigh-tall, could conceal a person fallen to the ground. Tipped into a gopher hole, suffering from a burst vermiform appendix or an exploded bladder. Alvina knew from Oliver about a woman who'd been a fool to hold back her water out of embarrassment. She didn't want to interrupt the square dance, to tell her partner, and so she died on the dance floor when her bladder couldn't take the load. Never hold back, Oliver had instructed. This is something you shouldn't fool around with. You got to pee, you go pee.

A thin falsetto, *boo hoo,* rose up from a classroom below, someone crying, the sound winding up to a full-blown wail. Boy or girl? Alvina couldn't tell, as they sometimes sounded the same. Judging from the direction, it was one of the younger students. And there was nothing put on about the crying; this was not a seeking for attention, but a mixture of hurt and anger.

The wailing intensified the dismal appearance of the schoolyard, which looked abandoned, as it would be within months, the rock-hard path between the bases on the diamond overgrown with pigweed and thistles. The eleven years Alvina had toiled in the sinking edifice would vanish when the wreckers came and smashed it down and carted off the rubble for salvage. Alvina would be recalled by former teachers as having been a brick, a co-operative and diligent student. A chubby-cheeked and wistful-looking child who, in the first grade, had unfortunate accidents that required mopping up. Alvina "Saggy Pants" Vandal. The source of her nickname being a nervous bladder and the navy fleece bloomers an aunt had provided by the dozen. While the bloomers did sop up a considerable amount of wetness, they grew heavy and drooped beneath the hemline of Alvina's skirts.

The teachers couldn't know that the brick, Alvina, was an ancient grandmother awakened in the night by spirits running from room to room, knocking on doors and bumping into walls. She woke to any tension building in the house, and heard Sara's groans, snorts, her sighs, coming from the bedroom. A twisting and turning in bed that meant she'd been awake for hours, waiting for Oliver to come home, and that sometimes ended with her feet meeting the floor in a thud. Alvina recognized the sound of Sara dressing hurriedly, felt her presence in the doorway of the girls' bedroom, her shadow falling away. Alvina held her breath in order to hear when, downstairs, the key unlocked the door.

She had learned not to turn on a light, as the darkness enabled her to better see beyond the yard and into the tunnel of the street, where the branches of crooked and stunted trees hoarded the night. The trees attended the street and the yards of several houses, the vacant lots in between them. Within moments the hiders appeared, slinking from tree to tree, their long black coats grasped tightly around their narrow bodies. Alvina counted to a hundred to ensure that her sisters and brothers would not awake. Two hundred, at most three, brought Sara the seeker back, a small figure hurrying towards the house, while behind her the hiders emerged, darting from trunk to trunk.

Alvina had learned to count in order to make the time pass, to protect Sara, to keep from crying. The sting of Sara's crabbiness when she found her daughter up and waiting was diffused by her light touch, her fingers cool against Alvina's face. Can't you sleep? she would ask, her voice going lullaby-soft, as it was when she sang to a baby while towelling it dry after a bath. German songs. Naughty songs about pooping and farting. As naughty as the way she paper-trained the babies, grasped them beneath the knees, their bums suspended over a piece of newspaper, while she commanded that they go *uh, uh.* Go *uh, uh,* she urged, the sound like a grunt that the baby might imitate, while the rest of the children crouched round the paper adding their grunts. They crooked their heads to better see the baby's pink flower-bud anus unfolding, and reported the progress of an emerging turd, cheering when it dropped to the paper. Sara nuzzled the baby's neck, fondled the creases of its legs. Oiling, powdering, smooching the babies until they began to walk and talk, and then she turned them over to Alvina. If you can't sleep, Alvina, just say your prayers, Sara would say when she returned and found Alvina up and counting. That's what I do.

Alvina searched through the drawstring bag at her waist, her fingers shaking as she pushed aside a folded sanitary napkin to get to the bottom of the bag. Finding and discarding a bundle of bobby pins, a Chap Stick and several coins. Downstairs, the crying went on and on and on. As it did sometimes at home, Sara shutting out the sound with pillows while Alvina lay in bed seething, expecting to be called.

Alvinnaaa? Waiting for the summons became in itself unbearable, so she would swing down from the bunk and go to the crier before she was told to go. She soothed away nightmares, rubbed stomachs, whispered *Tooralooraloora, tooralooralee,* spoke the words to the Irish lullaby until the child fell asleep—spoke and not sang, as she believed she couldn't hold a tune.

She found what she was looking for, a small tin that held tiny pink pills that rattled as she drew it from the bag. The nerve pills were a gift from Florence Dressler, to smooth out the bumpy spots in Alvina's life until she could make her getaway. One a day kept the shakes away.

Don't think I don't know what goes on over there, Florence had said as she stepped down from a kitchen chair, bringing a sugar bowl whose lid she removed, and took out the tin of pills. The pills had carried Florence through some tough spots, and although they were old she believed they'd still work their magic.

I've been thinking about you, Florence said. Instead of going to the refrigerator for the butter Alvina had been sent to borrow, she invited her to sit down. This was new since last winter, the first of what would be many short chats between them. A conspiracy that sent Alvina scurrying home through the highbush cranberry, carrying a cinder block of guilt for having listened to Florence say, Lots of women have large families. My own mother had thirteen. But she managed quite well, without there needing to be so much hollering and screaming. Without keeping certain girls home from school to help out. You have to think about your future. Start planning, Florence said. On the day she offered Alvina the pills she asked, What do you want for yourself? The question was not dissimilar to the familiar What do you want to be when you grow up?

Alvina wanted to remain what she was. A virgin. That was as far as she'd got in determining her future. In goes the prick, out comes the shitty little papoose. That was a law. When she didn't answer, Florence sat down at the table across from her. She resembled Tugboat Annie, broad-faced and plain-looking. Plain-speaking, too. Florence said, I've got something to steady your nerves. But you've got to promise not to take more than one a day. I think you can be trusted.

Alvina licked a finger now and pressed a pill up from the tin. She pooled spit on her tongue, set the pill into it and swallowed. One a day kept the shakes away, but this extra one was for the sake of the shorthand test yet to come. To iron smooth the wrinkles of the crying downstairs. To take the edge off her worry for Emilie. Then she left the room and went along a dark hall towards a rectangle of light shining in the window of the fire-escape door. The crying grew louder, and then ceased for a moment and continued anew, louder, as though the child had needed to stop to take in air.

The closed classroom doors vibrated with the absence of the voices of her classmates. A class of six students hadn't warranted hiring another teacher, after the previous high school teacher resigned in order to enter dentistry college. As she passed by an empty room, she imagined Edward's deep baritone; his broad shoulders stooped over his desk, his smiling face turning towards her, slick with oil, and a rash of pimples blooming on his generous forehead. He limped now, a steel brace fixed to his withered leg. The other silenced voices were those of her friends Ruth and Shirley, who, like Sonny Boy and George, were driven each day to the high school at Alexander Morris.

Alvina intended to go out onto the fire escape and look towards town on the possibility she might see Emilie. She worried about the kibosh, about the shorthand test yet to come, about diphones. *Two vowel sounds, one coming immediately after the other, are expressed by the sign*  *or* .  *is used where the first of the two vowels is a dot vowel.* She reviewed in her mind, words such as along, alone—*where the outline begins with a vowel and L is followed by a simple horizontal stroke, L is written downwards.*

Absolutely, of course Alvina should complete high school, Oliver had said, agreeing one hundred percent with Miss White when she came round to the hotel, wanting to talk. I'm all for it, he assured the young teacher. Surprising himself with his gusto, and being pleasantly surprised when, several days later, Katy sided with him.

Sara had been anticipating Katy's arrival, was anxious to voice her indignation that the young teacher had gone behind her back to sweet-talk Oliver. On the occasion of an infrequent mid-week visit by her sisters, Sara had instructed Emilie to freshen the threshold with a coat of white paint. Alvina washed the door frames, light switches; she upended chairs and scraped pads of dust from their feet, while Sara poured lemon into pie shells and beat egg white into a stiff glossiness, glancing out the window, fearing that her sisters would arrive sooner than expected, as they sometimes did. Hoping to find her and the house in disarray, no doubt. To catch sight of beer bottles lined up on the porch windowsill.

The sisters were late that day, let off in front of the house by a neighbouring farmer who had business in Union Plains. They brought a pint of heavy cream and speckled eggs, a bundle of leaf lettuce they'd picked that morning. Sara received their gifts and regrets at not having arrived on time with an uncertain smile, while motioning to Emilie that she should go and fetch Oliver. Acts of kindness, the bestowing of gifts, made Sara awkward, left her flailing for a fitting way to respond. She had changed into a dress of cotton sateen that was patterned with flowers, the colours matching the bouquets of flowers on the table.

The aunts' faces were softened by their inherent kindness, Annie quietly jubilant for some reason, and flustered as she kissed Alvina. Katy drank in Alvina's features, took her hands in her own and squeezed. So, Alvina, what does it? Katy asked, meaning, how are you doing?

Shitty, Alvina thought, but smiled and ducked her head. How did she know that her life was excrement? By the world around her, naturally. Ruth and Shirley. Cool bedrooms, cool mothers. Hollywood-style, diamond-tufted pink vinyl headboards, satin quilted spreads. A wall of shelves in Shirley's bedroom holding a collection of seventeen dolls, one for each birthday. Untouched, unspoiled by grubby hands. Their mothers—one a former teacher who spoke evenly and in full sentences, the other a chubby bubbling presence, her sentences laced with terms of endearment. There were families out there comprising as few as three children. Alvina, Sonny Boy and George. That would have been perfect.

She's such a fine girl, Katy said to Sara, and failed to notice Sara's drawing inward, a flicker of irritation in her grey eyes.

When the greetings petered out, Sara led her sisters into the dining room, while Alvina remained in the kitchen. When it became necessary, she was expected to replenish the china pot with coffee from the battered aluminum percolator on the Rangette. She was to bring the china pot into the kitchen and fill it there. She was required to head off a child screaming into the house with a bloodied nose, a skinned knee, a whining complaint of unfairness, all of which would usurp the aunts' attention and turn Sara tight-jawed and critical.

Oliver entered the kitchen, sweating, short of breath and bringing the odour of the hotel, a mustiness that made Alvina want to sneeze. He turned to the mirror above the washstand and drew his fingers through his hair; then, seeing Alvina's reflection, he grinned. So, the sourpuss, she's here, eh? God bless her. He winked and slapped his pockets and said, Now, where did I put my sardine-and-onion sandwich? Oliver loved to tease Annie, but he seemed to almost fear Katy. Okay, let's get this show on the road, he said. When he entered the dining room, the aunts' voices rose in genuine pleasure to greet him.

Sara had mentioned the teacher's proposition as soon as they were seated, and once Oliver joined them, Katy said grace and waded in, not taking the time to admire the table. The wedges of lemon pie set on plates, their meringue perky and evenly browned and beaded with droplets of sugar. An arrangement of pickles, salty buns and cheddar on a star-shaped plate. The white and mauve lilacs and sprigs of Boston fern, set at each end of the dining table in identical etched-glass vases. Ida had polished the silverware, and the dessert forks gleamed against starched linen napkins, their satin-stitch corners embroidered with the initials S & O, the handwork of Alvina. Morningstar knives, teaspoons, a butter knife, arranged in the way Penny, the downstairs maid, had set afternoon tea at the home of Emily Ashburn.

There's no future in keeping house, Katy said. Alvina is much too smart a girl to wind up housekeeping.

There was a moment of charged silence, Sara's eyes brightening, her chest rising, while Oliver sat at the head of the table craving a smoke, sensing that his wife and Katy were about to have a set-to. Annie sensed it too, and quickly rummaged through a knitted satchel as though working on a piece of smocking would stave it off.

Of course there's no future in keeping house. Tell me something I don't already know, Sara replied. I was too smart a girl for housekeeping too. She drew herself up and squared her shoulders. At least Alvina doesn't have to go down the road and stook hay for Low German peasants, she said. I had to work for people who couldn't speak English any better than I did, even though they were born here. Don't I ever know what it's like to be taken out of school too soon, yes? I went from the second grade to the sixth in two years. Two years. That's how fast I learned. But was I allowed to continue? No, I was not. Your Kornelius could afford to buy more land, cars and whatnot, but still, he sent me to work for peasants. The word *peasant* was spat out in a puff of sound.

Then I was made to empty piss-pots for the rich, while you stayed home and kept house for your dear Kornelius.

Washing his back. You think I didn't know what was going on behind that curtain in the middle of the day? I was wearing my fingers to the bone in your kitchen, while you were laughing. Both of you, all the time, laughing. I could barely stand to be there. And I'll have you know, I was the smallest person working in that field. Hardly taller than this table, and it was a job to lift a stook, not to mention throwing it up onto the hay wagon. And where were you? Washing his back.

Sara, what has this to do with Alvina? Katy interrupted in astonishment.

From outside came a loud rattling. The wagon one of the boys pulled through the yard was filled with stones, and Katy seemed relieved at the diversion.

But when the noise passed, Sara continued. Instead of going to school, I was sent to do a man's work, and for the kind of people we wouldn't have stood for at home. Papa never would have approved of that. He wouldn't have approved of my not continuing school, either. Unlike her sister Annie, who had completed high school, she didn't say. The fact that her young sister now worked in a bank in the large town of Steinbach was a stone in Sara's shoe.

Listen here, who emptied piss-pots for the rich? Oliver interjected.

Katy became larger with indignation, interrupting Oliver when it appeared he wanted to say more. *Ja, ja,* there's lots of things Papa wouldn't have approved of, she said, while Annie's eyes filled.

I beg your pardon, Sara said. Don't say that. Don't you dare blame me for that.

Who, then? Katy said.

It was you who made me come home. You decided that I shouldn't work for the Ashburns any longer. She liked me. She said that if I ever wanted to return, I should come and see her. That's likely the real reason you wanted me to come home. You thought, there must be something wrong with that woman, if she appreciates Sara so much.

Sara got up from her chair, as though she wanted to run away but couldn't decide in which direction.

Alvina listened to the ensuing silence, electricity humming in the wall clock, Annie's sniffling. Oliver repeating, Who emptied piss-pots for the rich?

There's some truth in what Sara says. Annie spoke quietly, the words interrupted as she began to hiccup. I, for one, didn't think that such a fuss should have been made over Sara wearing earrings. Even the pastor's daughters wear cosmetics now and then. Her voice grew in conviction as her hiccups subsided. There was no reason to send Sara to work in Winnipeg in the first place. Kornelius could afford to pay our passage fees.

Sara interjected, But think of it. If I had stayed in Winnipeg, I likely wouldn't be here now, would I? But no, you couldn't do without my help. So what gives you the right to say that I should do without Alvina's help?

Katy got up and went over to Sara, reached for her as though to embrace her, but Sara jerked away. *Ja, ja,* Katy said. She sighed and returned to her chair, unfolded the napkin and spread it across her lap. She said softly, to no one, I didn't need your help. I was better off without it, but I thought you needed mine.

Wait a minute, Oliver said. He chose to ignore the implications of what Sara had said. The fact that, if she hadn't been made to return to the farm, they would not have met again, they would not have married. Instead he went on to say, I understood that you were a store clerk.

Sara turned her back to them, and Katy's sorrow became palpable.

Sara, Sara. What next? What else? You're like a windmill in a storm. We have so much to be thankful for. If it wasn't for this country—

We'd all be living in a hole in the ground, in Siberia, Annie finished, in a wry tone that Katy missed.

Yes, a hole in the ground. Look at what you have here. Katy indicated the room, the house around them. You've been blessed with wonderful children. She hesitated, and then she said, And you've been blessed with a good man. Papa would have approved. Our future was decided by others, but at least our children have a chance. We should give them that, *yes?*

What Alvina wants to do is a good thing, Alvina heard Katy say.

Hold on a darn minute. You told me that you worked in Ladies' Wear at the Bay store, Oliver persisted.

Sara continued to ignore him.

Impulsively, he picked up a plate of lemon meringue pie and set it on his head. I used to be in the circus, he told Annie with a wink, as she looked on in astonishment. He crossed his arms against his chest and began to wiggle his scalp. The sisters gasped as the plate wobbled.

Sara cried out, *Eeeeeeee,* then leapt and caught the plate in mid-air. For a moment it appeared she might throw the pie at him. Oliver, for Pete's sake, she said. If you ask me, I'm the circus performer around here.

That's my girl, Oliver said with a grin, as Sara set the plate down in front of him. Now how's about we get this show going, I've got customers waiting.

There was a moment of silence, interrupted by Katy's chiding, There are people in the world who are starving, and you make fun with food.

The crying in the classroom downstairs grew louder as Alvina neared the fire escape, and she realized it was coming from the second-grade room. Miss White came hurrying up the stairs. I think you'd better come down and see what you can do with Simon, she called.

Alvina found him lying beside his teacher's desk; when she saw the scatter of foolscap papers around him, the crashing of her heart diminished. Her little brother was red-faced with anger as he knocked his heels against the floor.

How many? Alvina asked the teacher, who stood with her back pressed against the blackboard, her young face betraying frustration. Several students were gawking, but most were going about their business. He got two mistakes, one of the boys volunteered, and was shushed by the teacher, who crouched and began picking up the papers.

Alvina knelt beside her brother, loosened his collar and began rubbing his breastbone. Moments later he reached for her, his hands hot against the back of her neck. She scooped him into her lap, amazed as she always was by the amount of heat from such a small body. She believed she felt the blood flowing in his limbs, the electricity firing his muscles, cells multiplying and radiating energy. He was a complication of tissue, sinew, skin and bones, and at his centre was a pulsating, transcendent amoeba, his spirit, Simon.

She knew not to try to persuade him that two errors on any test were not a cause for rage. Instead she set him onto his feet, snared his bow tie from beneath the teacher's desk, tucked in his shirt and poked the bow tie into a trouser pocket. She sent him back to his desk with the promise to help him correct the errors during lunch.

Then Alvina was back upstairs, where she stood at the window and leafed through a magazine. Feeling as though her scalp had been peeled back like a lid on a can, her brains a pile of worms writhing in the exposed air, as she took in the images of a photograph. She turned the page and saw another image, and another.

At first she thought she was looking at an explosion, a heap of debris, a pile of boards in striped pajamas, scattered about like pick-up sticks. Then, in the foreground, she noticed a hand. Its fingers curled, a wrist, a forearm, that led to the face of a child and its blackened mouth opened to the sky. The pile of exploded debris was human. Hundreds of cadavers strewn about in a black pit.

Holy, holy, holy.

The page closed, and the magazine was gently taken from Alvina's hands. I'm sorry, but you weren't meant to see that one, Miss White said. I should have gone through the magazines before I brought them to school. That happened during the world war. They were Jews, she said, in answer to Alvina's unspoken question.

NINE

Female matters

OLIVER EMERGED from the river path into a clearing by the light-spangled water and saw the ferry nudged into the ramp on the opposite shore. Thoughts of his quarrel with Sara, the call he'd heard while going along the path, vanished. He went down to the landing, the clay shore crazed and crunching underfoot, wafers sliding away and revealing the sweating ground underneath. He picked up a tire iron leaning against a post and banged on a guide wire, making it hum.

Moments later Ulysse ducked out from the far motor shed, his red shirt a splotch of welcome. I seen you coming, he'd likely say, although it wasn't possible. He waved and returned to the shed. The engine coughed and sputtered to silence. A sound of metal striking against metal rose up, and Oliver dropped to his haunches, prepared to wait.

Throughout all of Oliver's young life, Ulysse had been either coming towards him or going away, as he did on the ferry. Coming more often and staying longer after Oliver's father had died. During those times, Ulysse had brought with him a whiff of the places he'd been, the smoky grass odour of the North Saskatchewan, of spruce forests and mushrooms, a green smell of the Waterhen marshes. He brought the voice of Oliver's father, and a way of being near to Oliver without seeming to take notice of him.

There were times when he would enter the kitchen in the early morning, expecting to find Ulysse asleep on the floor beside the stove, and be left as hollow as a reed to discover that the pad of blankets his mother had stitched together for Ulysse's infrequent sojourns had been rolled up and fastened with cord.

Yes, you can be sure he's left. It's beyond me why you should be surprised, his mother said. She sipped hard on the remains of a cigarette, took a lid off the cookstove and dropped the butt into the embers. A fire Ulysse had likely built before departing. She poked at the embers with an iron, as though she was angry. Her dark hair was gathered in a large smooth bun at the back of her head, shining as always, but the crescent-shaped impressions beneath her eyes betrayed the sickness faintly present under her skin.

She unrolled the pad and went out into the yard to pound it against the side of the house, and then hung it on a line to expose it to the elements. When next the bedroll was needed, Ulysse would sleep more soundly with the scent of the outdoors, she said, explaining the care she took for his uncle's comfort. She understood the need for the familiar to help a person fall asleep, as she was a woman who'd been left too young without a man.

Ulysse has always been a strange one, him, she said. The strangeness had been wished upon him by an Indian woman. A Sioux had lost her child when a stray bullet passed through her tent during the troubles at Batoche. She took Ulysse to replace her loss. She grabbed him from his mother's arms and made off. Weeks later she returned him, tucked down into a backboard and left in a meadow to be discovered by children out picking berries. From then on, Ulysse was known to be strange, she said. His first walking steps took him through the flap of the tent and across the hunting camp to the edge of it. Before he'd reached his tenth birthday he went for a walk that lasted a year, which became his pattern. It wasn't until Oliver's mother died that Oliver discovered the true story of Ulysse among his grandmother's remembrances, stored in a tobacco can.

My home was at St. Norbert, and I was at the Garry fort when a message came that soldiers had reached Selkirk. They were coming to take the country. I started for home across the Assiniboine River, and when I got to the bridge I noticed that it had been punctured so the water was coming across. This had been done by enemies. This was about three o'clock in the morning. I remember I was so frightened.

After the trouble at Red River was over, Joe and I married and later, we settled near to Aubigny on land given to us. Then my husband took sick, and we moved to Fish Creek as I had a sister there. Now the trouble started again at Batoche. It seemed that trouble was following me through my life.

The leaders of the rebellion ordered all families into Batoche for safety. For ourselves, my husband didn't take part in the rebellion, as he was against that. But we were at Batoche with the others, because he was so sick. The battle was on for three days, starting at 7 A.M., and leaving off at 6 P.M. The soldiers got orders to fight and take Batoche as the rebels were getting out of ammunition. When the soldiers entered, we all hid alongside the river bank. All the families and children were camped there. We could hear the leaders commanding the soldiers, and the bullets were going over our heads into the river, just like hail. Some of the tents were shot through. Once I went for water for the children and I saw something strange. So my sister and I pulled it out. Afterwards, we found out it was a cannonball.

But my real worst experience, to me at least, was when I nearly lost my Ulysse. There was an Indian family that I used to feed before the rebellion. I was really frightened of them. When we were getting away from the fighting with our children, I had Ulysse in my arms, and Narcisse by the hand, Isidore and Marie-Ange being big enough to follow me. This same Indian woman happened to pass me, and she saw that I was in difficulties handling the children. So she grabbed Ulysse and made signs she was going to help me. Putting the child on her back, she started off. I hadn't looked, and when I did, she was almost a quarter of a mile ahead of me. When I got to her I grabbed my boy. I told her she was running away with him. The squaw said yes, and took out some bannock and gave a piece to him. I never saw this woman again.

Ulysse sometimes spoke the Red River tongue Oliver had heard while growing up. Its sound was a balm that became more profound when, one by one, his friends, his brother, left him for wives and children. Oliver's aimlessness hadn't been expunged by his own marriage, but rather accentuated by Sara's purposeful nest-feathering, his children always wanting to claim him.

There was nothing on the other side of the river for him any more, except for Alice Bouchard and the memories he had of the many Sunday afternoons whiled away round a piano at the Bouchard home. Alice practising the prerequisite hour of scales and exercises, until Madame Bouchard bustled into the room in mock irritation and stilled the metronome, demanding that her daughter slide over on the bench.

She would immediately begin playing a waltz, a polka, stopping moments later to insist that Oliver take her place, as she had done ever since coming upon him in the parlour waiting for Alice, picking out the melody of a song Alice had played earlier. He was unable to listen to music without some part of his body moving in time to it. On those Sunday afternoons Madame Bouchard sang in a wobbling vibrato to Oliver's accompaniment, If You Knew Susie, Ain't She Sweet, I'm Confessing That I Love You, as Alice's sisters drifted into the room to join in. He recalled leaving those musical Sunday afternoons feeling satiated, as though he'd had more than his fill of a good hot meal.

Oliver sometimes went wandering through Aubigny thinking he'd missed a detail of that old place—a spectre from the past might present itself, and his self, the boy he'd been for such a brief moment, would be restored. When he wound up at Alice's house after the meeting at the school he realized that he'd sought her out. She was younger than he was, but from the beginning of his awareness of her she had seemed older. In a room filled with people, at a dance, a mass, he had only needed to be at her side to feel himself settle into his skin.

From the time they were children they had sometimes spoken one another's thoughts. Oliver, staring at her looped braids as she sat at the front of the classroom with the younger students, would will her to turn and acknowledge his presence. Stop daydreaming and get on with your lesson, her look told him, as though he owed her because they could read one another's minds. Oliver would think of her suddenly and fling down the axe halfway through a chore. Leaving the yard, he'd see her hurrying along the street in search of him.

He was fifteen when his mother died, and Alice came to him at the graveside, took his hand, and his tilted world grew steady. My mother's prepared a meal, she said.

Afterwards, Oliver and Romeo sat on the veranda steps at the Bouchards', smoking, listening to the give-and-take of conversation going on in the house between the three sisters and their mother as they cleared away the remains of the meal in the dining room. Oliver's ear was tuned only to Alice's voice, as he still felt the pressure of her mouth against his, her breasts, small and hard, against his chest. My poor dear Oliver, she'd said, coming up behind him in the hall as he was about to join Romeo outside. He turned to receive her embrace. Dear Oliver, she said again, the words a tickle of warmth against his neck. She kissed him, her mouth a brief pressure against his, and then once again, more softly, as though she'd been dissatisfied with the first attempt.

He hadn't anticipated the kisses, and a shiver played his body as he sat with Romeo on the veranda steps. Oliver and Alice had been startled by footsteps entering the hall, Alice's mother coming upon them in their embrace. She was a quick-witted and humorous woman, but in this instance she was at a loss for words, unsettled by what she'd just witnessed. Then she took a deep breath and said, I want you to know that you and Romeo will always be welcome in this house. Don't be shy.

Oliver felt Romeo's dark brooding, at the same time as he was imbued with the promise of Alice's kiss, Madame Bouchard's invitation. His eyes followed Romeo's gaze, a team of chestnut horses and a wagon waiting in the street in front of their house while their sister and brother-in-law packed up those of their mother's belongings they might have use for in their own house.

Scavengers, Romeo said. He couldn't stomach thinking about the brother-in-law arriving at the funeral in a wagon, intent on carting away the pickings afterwards. When Oliver suggested they go and oversee the packing up, Romeo snorted. What's the point? he said, defeated before he'd set out, as always. Oliver would be grateful to find that they'd left him his bed, a table and two chairs, dishes in the cupboard, and on the top shelf a rust-bitten tobacco tin holding the scrip documents, and the newspaper clippings of his grandmother's remembrances as told to a reporter of the *Winnipeg Tribune*. They'd also left the collection of animal traps, hanging in the woodshed.

Father Carrière, who'd said the mass for their mother, came along the sidewalk towards them, and Romeo swore under his breath. He flicked a half-smoked cigarette into the grass and got up, and Oliver followed. The priest raised his hand as though to call them over. Then he seemed to change his mind, and sprinted up the steps of the church, his black cassock caught by the wind and billowing around his legs.

Oliver hurried to keep up with Romeo, who went down Main Street and struck out along the ferry road. The sky became suddenly alive and loud with geese and Romeo stopped to watch the flock pass over, the sound striking a too plaintive chord in Oliver's chest as he came up beside his brother. They mounted the crest of the road and saw the ferry at the landing, the operator hailing them with his half-empty sleeve. As they came near the landing, Romeo veered off from the road to walk along the riverbank and collect small stones that he sent skipping across the still water.

You and me, we sure as hell weren't dealt a good hand, Romeo said. Oliver was disquieted by his brother's comment. He recalled Alice's endearment—my dear Oliver—her mother's promise that the Vandal boys would always be welcome. On the contrary, he thought, he'd been dealt a strong hand.

There was a jalopy on the other side waiting to cross the river, and a hay wagon and a team of horses, but the operator didn't seem to be in a hurry to get underway. The car doors opened and the passengers got out all at once, women, children, several men. A child scooted off down to the river's edge, and an adult shouted for her to return. There was something similar about the look of the people, the way they moved, hesitant, as though thinking they might need permission.

The brothers went over to the ferry; the operator was a distant cousin on their father's side who, since returning from the war with his amputated limb, uttered no more than a few words at a time. And so Oliver was surprised when the bandy-legged and tough-looking man spoke to him. He'd heard a rumour that a butcher at Alexander Morris was looking for someone to train. You could do well there, he said.

Yes, but my English isn't strong, Oliver was going to say, but only nodded. Alexander Morris was farther south than he cared to be away from home. The thought of home made his stomach lurch, as though he were about to step from a bridge into the air. Before he could reply, the jalopy's horn squawked, *hooga, hooga,* a sound that made Oliver smile.

Oliver and Romeo rode across the river, and when it came time, Romeo took it upon himself to guide the car onto the ferry. On the first attempt the driver stalled the engine, and then revved it too much, and the car lurched erratically towards Romeo. Oliver feared the car wouldn't brake in time, and held his breath as it pitched to an abrupt stop within a foot of his brother, who didn't flinch but stood stiffly, a palm extended, his long dark hair streaming across his face in the wind.

The men on shore laughed and shook their heads as the driver, a stocky blond man, emerged from the car with a grin and shouted something to them in German. As the engine started up, the blond man went over to the motor shed to investigate. The children were herded all at once onto the ferry by a woman. A young girl among them would not be tugged into place, choosing instead to stand a distance from the others. She wore a hat that was too large, and hid her face. Now she took it off and gazed at the sky, her brow furrowed as though she was about to cry. She looked the way Oliver felt. Stricken. Off balance, but determined not to show it.

Mennonites, the ferry operator muttered under his breath, having pushed aside the man peering into the motor shed, in order to exit. He pronounced the word *minnanites*, as most people did, his tone derisive as he gestured towards them with his half-arm, his shirt sleeve folded and fastened with pins.

The Deetch, other people had named them. And seed-eaters, after the sacks of sunflower seeds they invariably carted around with them, shells flying from their mouths as they talked, littering the ground about their feet like sawdust.

Several men in the parish of Ste. Agathe had given their lives, while others had lost their minds and limbs, fighting Germany in the Great War. Just as the ferry operator had. The fact that many Mennonites claimed the right not to go to war was a topic that raised disgust.

And now, in the early 1920s, the government had welcomed even more of them, thousands of Deetch-speaking minnows fleeing Russia after the revolution. The people on the ferry that day were among those refugees, had joined their ilk already living on vast tracts of land the government had designated for their use. The East and West Reserves, those areas were named, situated on either side of the Red River. Rich black soil, breadbasket earth, designated for people who preferred to keep to themselves, to conduct business with their own. Among them the cowards who'd refused to take up arms in the Great War.

Romeo and Oliver crossed the river on the ferry, Romeo standing with his legs apart and arms akimbo, staring down the broad channel. He was almost twenty years old, a slight and bony young man wearing a rumpled and mismatched suit, the wind making his eyes tear. He was seemingly oblivious to the children, to the women, who'd formed a circle and were quietly talking among themselves. He was oblivious to the anxious glances cast in his direction by one of the women, a tall person in a long navy coat. She went over to the girl who was standing apart and tugged at her arm, her motion conveying, Come away, you're too near to the edge.

The car disembarked and soon it was gone from view in a billow of dust, and Oliver and Romeo struck out across open country, walking without speaking. No doubt they were thinking of the fresh mound of earth in the cemetery in Aubigny, thinking that their time as a family had been too short a season. After a while, Romeo stopped and took off his jacket and spread it across the ground, Oliver following suit, the two of them disappearing into the tall grass, feeling the warmth of the earth against their bodies.

You can't come with me, Romeo said. Even if Oliver lied about his age, he wasn't sure he could get him on at the meat plant in St. Boniface, where he'd worked for a year now on the killing-room floor.

Oliver felt a pressure in his ribs. I don't want to, he replied. Henri Villebrun had offered him work at the hotel, in exchange for a small weekly income and room and board.

I've got a girl, Romeo said.

So do I, Oliver thought.

The sun pressed down on them and they drifted into sleep.

They awakened as the day began to end, the wind quiet now, a breeze that held the scent of a field of freshly mowed hay, the sky turned royal blue. Oliver thought they would return the way they'd come, and was surprised when Romeo headed away across the land. He followed without speaking. Soon they began to hear cows calling, the echo hailing them from the opposite direction. And then another sound rose beneath it, thin and wavering.

When a grove of saskatoon bushes grew large on the horizon, Oliver realized that Romeo's intention was to visit their grandparents' old farm site. A kind of farewell, likely, before he set off to live his life in St. Boniface. The log house began to take shape beyond the bushes, the place that had been their father's boyhood home and now was home to pigs rooting about. The first time Romeo had taken Oliver here, he'd boosted him up to a window to have a look, but there was nothing more than a room lit by the daylight passing through the chinks, and a floor covered in soiled straw.

Today they carried on towards the two-storey wood house built by the Mennonite settlers, and came upon the jalopy they'd seen on the ferry, nudged into a row of hollyhocks growing alongside a plank walk leading to the house. The sound they'd heard proved to be singing that would suddenly fall silent and then rise again. They followed the sound, skirted several small outbuildings, made their way towards a barnyard, which cows were crossing single file. Romeo feared a dog. Once when he'd come here, he'd been chased by a collie and forced to climb onto a shed roof until the animal lost interest. The blades of a windmill above the barn clattered and seemed to throw off sparks.

The people they'd seen on the ferry had been joined by others, a crowd sitting on benches and chairs arranged in a semicircle. A table set before them was covered with a white cloth, and on it the remnants of a meal. Their joyless song began again, and continued for a few moments before breaking off. A man standing in front of the singers began speaking quietly. When he'd finished talking the people took up the song, and Oliver realized that he'd given them the next words to sing.

Banshees, Romeo said darkly. That was what the stop-and-go singers brought to his mind: crows, or a large grey owl, keeping watch in a tree just beyond the house all of one night, soothsaying the death of Romeo and Oliver's family. They went round the barn and emerged onto a field where children played at making a human tower. Several of the older boys had become the base of the tower, and were hauling the younger ones up onto their shoulders. A sudden teetering brought about screams of laughter.

Romeo stopped to watch, a wistful smile pulling at a corner of his mouth. Sunlight glanced off a dugout pond, and there was a tree beside it where another group of younger children played; the girl Oliver had noticed on the ferry was climbing high up into its branches. A seed broadcast by the wind years ago had grown to this mature elm, whose wide crown had likely provided shade for their father. Perhaps he too had climbed it. Oliver was impressed by the young girl's agility and courage.

His thoughts were interrupted by the barking of a dog. Romeo swore as they turned to see a black-and-white animal bounding through the grass towards them. They broke into a run at the same time, Oliver slower, anticipating the nip of teeth at his calf. Someone whistled, calling the dog away.

Holy mother of Christ, chased off of our own bloody land, Romeo said, when they'd stopped to catch their breath. By these Germans, and another of their kind before them. By the Bouchard family, whose dealing in real estate had caused their grandparents and others to lose their land. It hadn't been automobiles that had made the Bouchards rich. Their money had been made in dirty land dealing, Romeo said, in what had been denied their father, and now them. In the coming years Romeo would fan the embers of his anger over the injustice meted out to his grandparents, so as not to dwell on the injustice that had been done to him by a priest.

Their father had always said that their grandmother was unable to manage the farm without a man, and so she'd let it go. When Oliver came into possession of the tobacco can and her remembrances, he discovered that Romeo was the one who possessed the truth.

After the battle at Batoche was over, we had very little to eat and our clothes were badly torn. No blankets or bedclothes. While we were there beside the creek, Louis Riel came to us. All his moccasins were torn and my sister gave him a pair. He wrote out his surrenderance papers and then the three went to meet the soldiers and give themselves up. Riel said that he took these two with him to witness that he was surrendering, and so that no one could claim the reward for his capture. He said he had left Montreal in 1870 at the age of twenty-three years to defend his country and religion and in 1885, he said, he was obliged to close his eyes for the North West Territory.

The next day the captain arrived with two soldiers and an express wagon and took us to Clark Crossing, where all the army camps were. I became their cook. They then gave me supplies and clothing for a year and we went back home to Manitoba. With my five children, my sick husband and myself, I started out in my express, driving the team. I camped by the side of the road, and while my husband and children went to bed I tied my ponies and kept watch all night as there was lots of horse thieves at that time.

I travelled for seven days, not seeing nobody and no houses. The eighth day I arrived at Qu'Appelle valley. We met two friends of my husband. They reported to the Catholic mission that a family from Batoche had arrived. Curiosity brought them all to see who it was. They thought my husband was wounded in the rebellion. A man bought my ponies and rig for sixty dollars so I could take my sick husband on the train to St. Boniface. Then I went back to the farm with my children to take up the work. The first thing I seen was a house that hadn't been there when I left, and someone's wash hanging on a line.

I went to see the Father at St. Norbert, and he told me that we had been away too long a time. There was nothing to be done.

Oliver sat on his haunches beside the river, waiting for Ulysse to bring the ferry across, thinking that he'd first met Sara on the ferry with her people, and not in Winnipeg, as she believed. He had never mentioned that meeting because the day itself was too painful a memory. He wouldn't say that the scrip documents he kept in the pocket of his army jacket proved that the land Kornelius and Katy farmed rightfully belonged to his grandparents. Their farm had been stolen out from under them when they'd gone up to the North Saskatchewan.

The ferry engine roared to life, and moments later Ulysse emerged from the motor house through a billow of blue exhaust, a gnarled-oak man, sinewy and impervious to the elements as he had been when, years earlier, he appeared at the hotel to voice his opinion about Sara. Sent, no doubt by Romeo, Oliver had since concluded. Coming upon Oliver lost in the familiar rhythm of mopping up the previous night's stickiness from the parlour floor, and not hearing the opening and closing of the back door.

Oliver knew that the ordinances governing drinking establishments made it against the law for anyone going past the parlour to be able to look inside. Nevertheless he'd knotted the curtains and let in the pale winter light that illuminated the wet trail of the floor mop, the tabletops shining with ring marks, and deeply scarred, as you'd expect them to be after so many years of service. He sensed a presence, glanced up and was surprised to be confronted by Ulysse. His hands and face were windburned, a plum blush underlying a complexion turned smoky-looking from campfires, from road dust.

You leave them people alone, Ulysse said. He'd carried the words on such a long journey, and wanted immediately to set them down. His mukluks looked the worse for wear, wrapped in strips of a wool blanket and bound with *babiche.*

I always told your brother, don't bother going over there. The past is gone. Now he tells me that you're tangled up with one of those, there. You're running around loose with a Deetch woman, Ulysse said.

Beyond the window, Oliver saw Sara coming yet again, plunging knee-deep through snowdrifts in the vacant lot, her coat unbuttoned and flapping, a plaid headscarf framing the pinch of worry in her features. Surely she hadn't come on foot, not in this cold. He stepped sideways, as though to remove himself from an invisible circle on the floor. He wished that he hadn't knotted the curtains.

She's not Canadian, she's not even Catholic, Ulysse said. Their society isn't acquainted. They've got their ways, that don't mix. His voice trailed off as he sensed Oliver's distraction.

Oliver spotted Kornelius's car parked one street over, in front of the creamery, its exhaust white and roiling. Her brother-in-law was behind the wheel, waiting, as Sara hurried towards the hotel, hugging herself against the wind. She cupped her eyes and pressed her forehead into the window, straining to see into the dimness at the back of the parlour, where he stood; then crooked her head, craning to catch a glimpse of the poolroom.

Oliver willed Ulysse to remain silent as Sara's silhouette dropped away from the window. Moments later, there was a noise as she tugged at the latch of the lobby door. He breathed a silent plea that she would not go round to the back.

She's in the family way, he heard himself say. He was relieved when he saw Sara go back across the street, kicking through the snow in the vacant lot.

I'll take care of things in my own time, Oliver thought, as he'd been telling himself for weeks, the promise not holding any more weight now than before.

Her? Ulysse said. They watched as Sara got into the car and was driven away.

A *bibi?* Ulysse asked. Oliver nodded, and Ulysse turned away in disgust. By golly, I thought you were the one with brains. Don't you know that when a man puts more than his hands under a woman's skirt, that's usually what comes out? His voice went thin and crafty as he asked, What kind of woman is she, anyway? You sure it's your family?

It's mine. Oliver spoke emphatically, the words slamming into his own chest.

Holy mother. She's not even English. Me, I'd sooner bunk down with a squaw. She knows how to take care of herself. And if she doesn't, she isn't likely to come tracking you down.

Soon after, Ulysse left. Talking had worn him through, he said. And he did look suddenly fatigued and deflated, gaunt in the face. He wanted to go sit beside a fire and be quiet. For some time now, he'd been seeing a white bird near a thicket at

Cranberry Portage. Wasn't like any bird he'd ever seen, the way it acted—strange, circling low over the treetops; its wingspan was as large as that of a hawk. The bird always appeared near sunset, he said, and he believed it might be Martel, a man who'd disappeared while hunting during winter in that same area, near to ten years ago.

In the early hours of the following morning, Oliver dressed and left the hotel, going down to the riverbank, where he strapped his skate blades onto his boots. Ice crystals streamed from his nostrils and mouth and the light of a headlamp illuminated his hands and the snow. While there were government ordinances that dictated how he conducted hotel business, laws could be made to take the shape of necessity. When it came to female matters, there was no bending.

Oliver was obliged to do what a man of conscience should do. For him not to be able to look at his reflection without shame was worse than seeing his shame in another person's eyes. As he buckled the straps he recalled the strength of his father's fingers tightening the leather, and it finally became real to him that he was about to become a father.

He followed footprints leading down to the middle of the river, where the impressions in the crusted snow held blue shadows. The ice cracked, the sound travelling away from him, but he knew he was safe. Safer than he'd been as a boy when he had gone tramping cross-country over snow ridges that could suddenly give way. He might have crashed through to his shoulders, with no chance to throw himself onto his back and swim out of it. As a boy he had feared a white smothering, and from time to time had dreamt about it. Dreamt that he was sinking and being held by the weight of the snow, unable to move as it closed in over his face.

Tonight he skated towards the lights of Aubigny with his hands clasped at the small of his back, leaning into the long push and glide of his strokes. His trouser legs began flapping as he gained speed. The light of the headlamp swayed across his path, and it seemed that the winter world glided by while he remained fixed, even though his thigh and calf muscles were cramping with the effort and the cold. Across the highway stood the hotel, its windows darkened and all the houses of Union Plains laid out beyond it, also in darkness.

He was coming near to the backside of Main Street, the houses strung out along the shoreline, woodsmoke streaming from the chimneys along with a yellowish smear of coal smoke, the odours both pleasant and harsh. Moments later the headlamp illuminated a red danger sign, and Oliver knew that a ramp where ice blocks were loaded onto wagons or truck beds loomed in the distance. Open water lay beyond that ramp.

When the ice harvesters had finished cutting for the day, he and Romeo used to join other boys in a game of daring, venturing out amid the litter of ice spears crunching underfoot like glass. They dared one another to take a running slide, arms extended for balance, knife in hand, to see who could come nearest to the edge of open water. The others carried their knives for show; Romeo was the only one ever to use his. He sometimes purposefully misjudged the slipperiness of the ice, his momentum, and at the last moment twisted his body and fell onto his stomach, digging the knife into the ice to stop his backwards slide. Once he had slipped over the edge, waist-deep in the black icy water, the knife blade holding him in place until he could scramble back out, while Oliver looked on in admiration and fear.

Oliver thought of the open water beyond the ramp, his legs scissoring round a gentle curve and the skate blades biting into the surface as he picked up speed, the wind a sheet of cold pressed against his face and body. He expected a shock of wet cold, so sudden and profound it would, in a moment, knock him unconscious. That is not the way, an inner voice told him. He let himself fall to the ice in a slide, rolling onto his back, his knees drawn to his chest. He felt the ripple of an ice fissure through his jacket, saw the lamp's weak shaft of light dissolve into the dark and brilliant starred sky.

He flailed his arms to slow himself down, then clutched at the ice in a futile attempt to stop, his fingertips raw and pulsing. In desperation he lifted his legs and slammed his skates onto the surface, their tips gouging a gutter of white; then rolled onto his stomach so that he might raise his head towards the downwards plunge in the water. Then a skate blade caught on the edge of a crack. In a sudden jerk he was swung sideways, sent spinning off the clear ice and rolling across the packed snow.

He lay for a moment, panting with relief, realizing that he was feet away, not inches, not anywhere near to the brink. Unlike his brother, he lacked the courage to truly court danger.

He took off the blades and left them on the ice, his legs trembling now as he plunged through snowdrifts wind-banked and hard along the river's edge; half-running, stumbling, the air burning like fire in his chest. He struggled up an incline at the back of the Bouchard house, clutching at tufts of weeds to pull himself along; pushed through a cross-hatching of bushes that bit at his hands and face. The kitchen window was lit and illuminated a path of trodden snow between a garden shed and the clothesline stoop. The remainder of the windows along the back of the broad house were in darkness.

The winter world pressed through his panic, the rasp and thud of his breath and heart. Snow squeaked loudly underfoot as he went up the stairs to the back door. Three light raps were always enough to bring her.

A dog barked across town, likely announcing the presence of its own shadow, but just the same raising the hair on the nape of his neck. A reaction gained as a child from the tales he'd been told about dogs knowing when a soul was about to depart a body. Superstitions that had nothing to do with who he was now. He believed that neither animal nor so-called holy man could call down the unseen world, but nevertheless here he was, reacting like a child to the hubbub of a lonely dog—a grown man who was often tongue-tied in the presence of a priest.

He breathed into his cupped hands, holding the white fog and heat against his face. Moonlight glistened in a cape of snow thrown over the roof of the garden shed, and in hoarfrost coating the clotheslines strung from the stoop. Footsteps approached behind the closed door, and Oliver's uneasiness at the sound of the dog's barking was replaced by an uneasiness over what he'd come to say.

He sat across from Alice at the kitchen table, a dim light shining in the hall illuminating a staircase, its balusters casting a ladder of shadows on the wall. She was a silhouette, her pretty features unreadable in the darkness, while Oliver felt exposed. He resisted an urge to yawn and ease the tension in his jaw.

He'd only been there for a moment when a familiar sound came from the lit hall, its ceiling creaking beneath someone's step. One of her sisters, her mother, perhaps, had come to stand at the top of the stairs. To cough, to clear her throat and let him know she was aware of his presence; there was a scuffle of slippers against wood as the person retreated. Some things remained the same. As promised, he'd always been welcome in this house—and always welcome to leave.

Alice encircled a cup of tea with her hands as though to warm them, the presence of the cup causing Oliver to wonder if she had been waiting. Throughout their long courtship the three light raps would always bring her, but he hadn't been altogether certain whether tonight would be the same.

I wasn't cut out for city life, Oliver said to her.

You didn't come here just to go through all that again, Alice said, her voice low and impatient.

True.

From an adjacent room came the sharp ticking of a clock.

I'm sorry. That's what he'd intended to say. He cooled his burning fingertips against his forehead.

She exhaled loudly and then breathed in deeply, as though she was starved for air. What are you sorry for? she asked, and he was startled to realize that he'd spoken.

The basket of eggs. He remembered Sara's basket of brown eggs resting on the floor inside the door. Remembered

Sara perched uneasily on the edge of his cot, hair undone and brushing her white shoulders. The fullness of her breasts, pale nipples gone flat and as large as silver dollars. She got up from the bed, the curve of her spine giving way to plump buttocks.

She looked up at the sloped ceiling as the piano music began, hearing Alice counting out the beat of the song. Oh, her, Sara said, knowing that Alice had rented the Villebruns' former suite of rooms. The two women had come upon each other once, as Sara was leaving his room and Alice was descending the stairs, both of them equally surprised. Alice took in Sara's attempt to smooth her dishevelled hair; the egg basket in her hand. So it's Sara, the egg girl, she said, with a tight smile, connecting the egg girl with the Sara she'd met for the first time at Romeo's party in the city.

Oliver wondered if Sara suspected that Alice's presence in the suite upstairs was why he'd coaxed her into his room, petted and kissed away her protests until she agreed to a hurried bit of love, while her sister Katy went about town delivering pints of cream. He wanted Alice to be playing the piano, Moonlight Sonata, Drink to Me Only, or a student of piano to be plinking up and down the scales, which would mean that Alice was present on the bench, her pencil poised above the keys, ears turned to the sound of their shenanigans. Put that in your pipe and smoke it, Oliver thought. He was giving Alice something to chew on.

The buffalo robe where Sara had sat, and the insides of her legs, were streaked with semen as she shivered into her clothes, mouth soft from their hard kisses while her eyes remained a blur of anguish, worry, fear.

He was sorry for that.

And he was sorry for Sara's longing, such an intense smouldering that he feared it might suck the air from him. A longing he felt even when she wasn't present. Do you love me? Her question seemed to mean so much more than that.

And he was sorry for a particular afternoon when a timid and halting rendition of a well-known song in Villebrun's suite had suddenly turned him angry. He swore, heaved himself over Sara and up from the bed. He pulled on his trousers, ignoring her whispers, her alarm that he intended to leave the room shirtless and in bare feet. He'd gone thumping up the scale of the stairs, astonishing Alice when he burst into the parlour. She stepped away from the piano, a rash of blood rising in her neck as he nudged the inept piano player aside on the bench.

He demonstrated as he played by ear, and with a flourish that was entirely his own, how the piece was meant to be rendered, as the student shrugged into her cloak and rushed from the room, armed with a new tale of Union Plains' most-talked-about bachelor.

Goodnight, Irene, Für Elise, Claire De Lune. Oliver played on, his fingers knowing which notes to reach for, the sharps and flats, the ascending and descending harmonies. He possessed strong and nimble fingers, a muscular yet slender body suitable for the back of a pony, or to pull oars for two smokes of the pipe without tiring.

Oliver's people had once been known as the true people of the west, admired and respected, but with the arrival of the Orangemen they were cheated, humiliated, murdered and chased off the land. Ignorant men from Ontario pressed their inferior stamp on everything and everyone, proud to be strutting around in the dung of their vulgarity. Some of his people had gone to the rodeo circuit in America as ropers, trick riders, sharpshooters. Those who were whiter of skin and clever enough melded into the streets of St. Boniface among the self-important French, who, should they catch a whiff of smoked meat among them, would turn up their aristocratic noses. Most of the Metis disappeared into cities and northern towns, into bushland, or parked their tents along road allowances and dug in for a life of poverty.

Alice stood at the window while Oliver played, her face working as she watched the student hurry across the street to a waiting car. Yes, you have talent to burn, Alice said to the window. Whatever you put your hand to seems to come easy. But you're all show.

She turned to him, her features swimming with emotion as she gathered music books from a side table and held them against herself as though for protection. Oliver began playing a nickelodeon song with a plinking lightness he didn't feel. It was true, he was jack of all trades and master of none.

As easy as breathing, he told her when he'd finished. A person doesn't need to go to an academy to learn music. He'd spoken in English, because she had come over to the English side of the river to teach piano to English-speaking kids. When in Rome.

This he had learned while working for a short time as a barber in Winnipeg, with people who said *bison* when they meant to say *basin*. Say, Oliver, old chap, why don't you bring me a bison of hot water so I can shave this man? He'd learned to speak like them, and while doing it almost ruined his hands, swollen twice the size by the end of the day. He'd been so naive to think that the barbering trade would make him a suitable candidate for Alice's husband. He found himself working in a tiny room with four chairs, the space between them hardly large enough for a man to pass through. He'd paid an arm and a leg for his tools, for the laundering of barbering clothes and towels. He came home at the end of the day with the stink of other people's hair on his body, an odour that made dogs growl and bare their fangs when he passed. And so he'd put his hand to driving taxi, where a man could be his own boss.

I don't need to do this, Alice said now, as she reached the door. The nuns send me as many students as I have the time for. I don't need to come here for the pleasure of teaching the tone-deaf. Her throat clicked as she swallowed.

He heard Alice open the door, he would soon hear it close. And so why did you? he asked.

There was a pause. Through the tightness in her throat, she said, I thought it might be a way for my father to get used to the idea of my being over here. The door closed behind her.

Oliver suddenly thought of Sara in his room under the stairs, waiting for him to whisk her out the back door, listening to their talk. He thrummed the piano keys—a sound of impending danger, a train rushing towards a woman bound to railway tracks, a car speeding through a busy street about to crash into an unsuspecting woman. Oh bugger, oh for the love of the Good Maker, all he'd wanted was a little piece of life.

—

You stink, Alice said to him now.

For a moment he thought she was teasing him in the old way, when she had made a show of waving him off when he went to embrace her, clearing the air of the fumes he'd brought with him, the dankness of the hotel, the odours of malt and cigar. Then he realized she was angry.

Again footsteps crossed the upstairs floor, and Oliver was surprised to find anger rising in him too. He wanted to pace, to raise his voice, let those upstairs hear, he didn't care. He was a man of twenty-five years, what did she expect, keeping herself away from him? Demanding that he measure up to some mark her father had put on a wall. What in hell was a man of substance? If not a barber, or a driver of a taxi, then surely it was a man who'd been given the opportunity to run a hotel.

I'm not meant for the city, he'd told her as they walked among a grove of trees beside the academy in Winnipeg where she studied. The sanded path was strewn with leaves; a crisp sound underfoot heightened his awareness of her cool hand inside his, the way her shoulders were squared—against him? Against her need for him? He didn't know. He'd been struck silent by the henna in her hair when he'd come upon her in a practice room. He didn't care for the colour. It made her look handsome, almost mannish, and too pale. The green cape she'd taken from a coat tree in the front hall and flung around her shoulders concealed the shape of her body, as much as did a nun's habit.

He didn't tell Alice that he feared that, if he remained in the city, he would become a drinking man. What began as a get-together after work to let off steam degenerated quickly into a determination to get soused. After several drinks Romeo's lopsided grin gave way to surliness, his pupils dilated and became tunnels of black. Meanwhile, several drinks imbued Oliver with a love for the entire world. He left Romeo to simmer and went visiting among the tables, encouraged by the laughter his joshing roused, his generosity stretching beyond a sensible limit if he should happen to notice a man who had drunk down to the last bit of change on the table and still nursed a deep thirst. He seldom turned aside a challenge at billiards, and although he usually went away with empty pockets, he refused to be bothered by it. It's just money, is all. There's nothing a person can do with money, except spend it.

On too many occasions, he'd awakened to find himself on a sofa in a house he didn't recognize. A half-dressed child staring him in the face, its inner arms crusted with eczema; a baby going about unattended in a sopping diaper, whimpering to be fed. He'd awakened to the sight of a woman's breasts spilling across the sheet beside him, and not known who she was. He worried, the days following, lest there be signs of the clap.

When Alice had gone to study music for a year at the academy, Oliver had followed her, hoping that the distance between Winnipeg and Aubigny might weaken her father's influence. Although he'd found many opportunities to go past the academy while driving taxi, he'd never turned into its long driveway, or climbed the stairs to the second floor, until now. He followed a mishmash of music erupting from the practice rooms. A soprano voice sighed up and down a scale, while several pianos competed to be heard. He followed the music, an odour of incense, its scent hinting at the secret lives of the nuns lived out above the classrooms, as mysterious as the dimly lit corridors branching off from the practice rooms.

He wanted to pull Alice into himself while he told her about Villebrun's offer to let him manage the hotel so he and Madame could retire to Florida. But he found himself stirring through the leaves with his foot as he blurted the news outright, instead of doing as he'd intended, asking Alice to come to Union Plains as his wife.

But Oliver, you'd still be nothing more than a joe-boy to that man, she said.

Hours later, Oliver sat in the darkness of a movie theatre, tears streaming down his cheeks as he watched Charlie Chaplin eating a piece of watermelon. His muscles ached from laughing as the clown dug watermelon from his ears, speared a turkey off a banquet table with his walking stick. When he danced with Miss Moneybags, his legs flew out from under him, or else he kicked himself in the arse. Oliver began to anticipate the laughter of the audience, felt the joy that lingered after the moment when it erupted, a lightness in the air. There was something good to be said about a person who could do what Charlie Chaplin did.

He emerged into the glare of the day feeling hollow, but the ache put there by Alice was gone. He went to the taxi garage, washed and polished the car and gave notice that he was leaving. Then he donned his uniform in a curtained cubicle, for a last time, and set off for the remainder of the day and evening. He thought he would stop in at the barbershop on Main Street and put another dollar down on what he still owed there. There was no reason for him not to see Sara bounding into the street in front of his car, except that one moment she wasn't there, and the next she was. The little DP girl he'd seen on the ferry had become a woman seemingly throwing herself in his path.

The heat in the kitchen made his eyes grow heavy, and he noticed that light was beginning to dawn in the window. Some kid, or the ice cutter, would soon venture out onto the river and come upon his skate blades stuck on end in the snow and wonder why they'd been left. He couldn't afford to come too near the edge again. Drinking or otherwise. He breathed in deeply to gain the courage to say why he'd come.

You stink, Alice had said, the words riddled with hostility. Now she said, with a flatness, The woman is pregnant, isn't she. It was not a question.

Yes. That she is. She's in the family way, Oliver answered. And he was the family-maker. Whatever had kept him tethered to Alice throughout the years snapped. He hadn't anticipated this flooding of relief, a sudden light rising as it now rose in the window. Daylight.

Her hands flew up to her face, she bent over the table, and he realized that she was weeping.

Don't, he said. But he felt none of the attending rush of anxiety, the need to squat beside her while she cried; to pick bits of gravel from a scraped knee and sponge it with warm water.

I'm going to die here, she said, the words amplified and distorted by her cupped hands. They want to keep me here for the sake of their old age. I'll go crazy.

Do something, she had pleaded on a winter day long ago, when a dog had got into a rabbit hutch. But he couldn't undo the ripped-apart bodies, the bits of fur and spatters of blood on the snow. And so, in anger, he'd chased down the dog and shot it. Well, there was no way he was about to do the same to himself.

The chair scraped against the floor as he got up to leave.

I've always loved you, she told him when he'd reached the door. I'll never stop loving you.

Yes, but unlike Sara, she had never loved him enough in the here and now. Unlike Sara, she'd not been willing to go against her family's wishes in order to take a flyer on the likes of him.

He returned from Alice shortly after sunrise, his body aching for sleep. He planned to rest, to eat, and then he would strap on his snowshoes and travel along the river to the farm and put an end to the shame of having evaded Sara all these weeks. The snow on his trousers had melted in Alice's kitchen and froze on the walk home; the trousers became stiff and beaded with ice. His fingertips still stung like fire. He didn't recognize the horse and wagon parked across the street from the hotel, but he could guess who they belonged to.

Where I come from, we have ways to deal with matters such as what you've done to Sara, Kornelius said. Those being his first words when Oliver stepped into the hotel foyer. There was a horsewhip lying on the floor between his feet.

Rusty sardine-can lids, a straight razor—Oliver was familiar with the means and ways by which a man could be persuaded to take up his responsibility; in his case it was an unnecessary persuasion. He knew it wouldn't matter what he said. Forever after, Kornelius would believe that his visit had been the deciding factor. Oliver told him, Sir, there's no need to get your shirt in a knot. I intend to do the right thing.

TEN

Two weddings

A HOUSE ISN'T A HOUSE without a piano, Oliver decided, recalling the many Sunday afternoons spent at the keyboard in the Bouchard living room. And so it should not have been surprising that the second purchase he made for the house was a piano, the first being a wood-burning stove. He continued to live at the hotel during the week leading up to the first of his two weddings to Sara, and made daily trips to the small house to stoke the fire, and went again during the night, to ensure that its walls warmed sufficiently by the time the instrument arrived at the train station.

Oliver had chanced upon the piano in a second-hand store in Winnipeg, a bell tinkling above the door as he and Romeo stepped inside to a confusing display of household paraphernalia. Romeo had met Oliver at the train station, anticipating that they would play billiards and then he'd treat his young brother to a meal at a snazzy restaurant, and they'd join up with the meat-packing crowd at the Belgium Club. Treat Oliver to what was to be his last roaring time as a bachelor.

On Romeo's advice, Oliver sought out the second-hand store in the hope of finding a wedding present, as he'd already spent a considerable amount at a tailor shop for a suit, shirt and tie, and put out good money for his first pair of proper shoes, black oxfords that seemed flimsy and treacherously light on his feet. After walking the distance of an aisle and back, he declared that they were just what the doctor had ordered. I'll take them, Good Sir, he said, his tone matching the proprietor's enthusiasm, while Romeo looked on in amusement.

The upright Heintzman sat against a wall, surrounded by paintings and photographs. Landscapes of misty, meandering streams, flower-dotted meadows, old-world scenes whose subdued colours seemed too soft to be actual depictions. Portentous-looking people glared out at the clutter of housewares and furniture, their photographs put on show for the value of the picture frames.

The piano was covered in dust and the top of it was being used as a display shelf for various items. The instrument had seen better days, its keyboard spent. Consequently its touch was too light and its tone jangled, a sound suited for honky-tonk, the proprietor said. Oliver played several chords and allowed that it was blown out, but imagined himself playing waltzes, teaching Sara to play a duet. Romeo looked dubious, questioning his brother's wisdom in considering a used-up piano as a wedding gift. He thought Oliver should be perusing jewellery, in particular a bracelet of cut glass that sparked different colours when Romeo turned it to the light in the window.

But that was Romeo, a jackdaw, inclined to be seduced by a bit of shine. Oliver was Oliver. Romeo's house would never know a bookshelf holding volumes of *The New World Encyclopedia, Fairy Tales of the World, The Books of Knowledge, Uncle Arthur's Bedtime Stories, A Child's Illustrated Stories of the Holy Bible.* A refinement that the infrequent visitors to the Vandal house attributed to Sara. But Sara's eye was for decoration, for arranging furniture and painting the walls a different colour every five years or so, whether they needed it or not. Oliver was a soft touch for any salesmen who landed on the doorstep wanting to sell conveniences for the lady of the house, or an enhanced future for his children.

It was Oliver who purchased the latest in kitchenware and appliances: the brightly coloured melamine dishes, which proved to be truly unbreakable when hurled as a discus against the side of the house. The gigantic Servelle refrigerator, with its faulty door handle. The real McCoy, the Rangette, which according to the salesman required less juice to heat than the new electric ranges. Its oven proved to be uneven; anything put into it came out either undercooked or burned to a crisp. It was Oliver, too, who purchased a perpetual-motion drinking bird and set it on the windowsill above the younger children's table, so they'd be entertained while they took their meals. For a time, a young red fox rescued during spring high-water streaked through the house, darting out from behind the furniture to nip at the children's socks—again, Oliver's doing.

The Heintzman in the second-hand store would cost most of the money Oliver had in his pocket, with enough remaining for him to claim the wedding suit, which was being altered. Enough to have the piano shipped to Union Plains. He made the arrangements and left the store, while Romeo dallied over the bracelet he'd admired and was finding difficult to resist.

Oliver rocked on his heels, contemplating a playbill posted outside the entrance of the second-hand shop while waiting for his brother. The picture on the playbill, of a man seated at a grand piano, had captured his attention. A family of musicians, The Musical Eckhardts, were performing at the Pantages Theatre. He recognized a familiar longing, but a stupid unreasonable timidity told him that such events were meant for others and not for him.

Romeo joined him, flushed with pleasure over having bought the bracelet for Claudette, an early Christmas present. Abruptly, Oliver pointed to the playbill and said, Whatever's my pleasure, right? Your treat? He made his brother's promise sound like a dare. This was how he wished to spend his last night out on the town as a free man, by going to see The Musical Eckhardts, he said. But he'd no sooner spoken than he was beset by doubts.

Romeo surprised Oliver by not arguing against it, hiding his reluctance with an exaggerated shrug, indicating that while he didn't understand the odd request, he'd indulge his kid brother. He would meet up with Oliver at the theatre, he said, leaving him on his own to wander about the snowy streets looking in windows, to eat a meal in a greasy spoon, not the snazzy meal Romeo had promised. Romeo was getting back at him for not going along with his plans, Oliver thought, regretting having changed them. One more little toot on the town wouldn't have hurt, Sara being safely tucked away on the farm with her sister and not any the wiser.

Oliver was surprised when Romeo hurried towards him outside the theatre, on time and freshly shaven, dapper-looking in a slouch chapeau Oliver hadn't seen him wear before. The hat, along with a paisley scarf knotted at his neck, gave him a debonair appearance, and as Romeo purchased their tickets Oliver realized that his brother was handsome in an offhand way. Then Oliver smelled liquor on

Romeo's breath, and understood that he'd needed to fortify himself. His brother lit a cigarette and Oliver noted a tremor in his hands, a wariness as he surveyed the milling crowd in the foyer, as though he expected someone would come over and request that they leave.

Attending picture shows hadn't prepared Oliver for the rows and rows of red plush seats, the chandeliers shedding light on the people sitting in gilded recessed arches. At the picture show an audience became noisier and fidgety when curtain time drew near, while the atmosphere in the theatre felt charged with a quiet and expectant waiting, the shuffling sound of paper as people read through their programs. Geez, it's like a church, Romeo muttered. He glanced up at a balcony directly above them. Anyone spit on me, I'll be up there before they can say jackrabbit. He laughed nervously. When Oliver didn't reply he slouched into the seat, his chin propped in a hand as he stared straight ahead. As he would for the entire concert.

The theatre darkened and the stillness was instant. The curtain rose, and the audience around the brothers vanished. A young man walked into a spotlight and stood for a moment looking out, then cradled a violin under his chin, raised his bow, and began to play. As he listened Oliver remembered the blinding dazzle of sun on snow, trudging knee-deep through it, his feet plunging down into the footholes where Romeo had broken trail among the red osiers. Wanting nothing more than to be outdoors after a two-day storm, to feel the clear sky moving away from him. Hear a school bell ringing in the distance, the church bell calling. His throat tightened with an almost overwhelming desire to weep.

When the applause ended, another young Eckhardt came on stage to join the first one in a violin duet. As would happen for the remainder of the concert, one after another family member appeared to play various brass, wind and stringed instruments. Midway through the concert a young blonde woman seemingly floated onto the stage in a pale green gown. She sang an aria, her voice an incredibly high warble; when the applause faded she was followed by a banjo-picking black-faced brother performing a vaudeville routine. The audience murmured and shifted in their seats, the young man's Al Jolson act causing excitement.

Near the end of the concert the Eckhardt father appeared, a tall poker-stiff man, his tuxedo shirt a glowing white breastplate leading him across the stage. He sat down before a grand piano, and after a pause to adjust the stool and another pause to set his hands above the keys there was a great crashing and swelling of music. The piano concerto unfolded with a magnificence a man would be a fool not to recognize. Oliver's hands grew clammy and he began shaking as the music washed over him in waves. He was carried away by its force, by its over-large, if not overblown, European beauty. The last note faded and the audience leapt to their feet in applause. Oliver rose hesitantly, followed by Romeo, rumpled and grey in the face, caught half-asleep, startled by the sudden commotion.

The brothers moved with the flow of people towards the exit and stepped outside, threaded their way amid an ebullience of chatter, clouds of exhaust billowing from automobiles idling at the curb. Oliver's face burned, his head rang as though he'd been on a long train journey. They went along

Main Street towards the city of St. Boniface, where Oliver would stay the night at Romeo's, two loose-jointed slim figures disappearing into the darkness between the lamp standards and reappearing in a circle of warm light moments later. Oliver elastic in step, filled with energy. Finally he couldn't resist: What did you think of the concert?

So that's how the other side lives. The mucky-mucks, Romeo said, the effects of the liquor worn thin. He loosened the scarf at his neck and almost angrily took it off, stuffing it into a coat pocket.

Oliver stifled his reaction—pity mixed with disappointment—making allowances for Romeo's moodiness, as he had done as a child. Romeo kicking Oliver away in anger when he tried to curl against him in bed for warmth; the nightmares that had Romeo thrashing and calling out, and left him dark and silent the following day.

They crossed the bridge over the river into St. Boniface, a scattering of lights from houses shining among the wintering trees beyond, made soft by a mist that overnight would paint the city white. Oliver sensed now that by insisting on going to the concert he'd caused a distance to come between them. Romeo's children spoke French while Oliver's would speak English. I guarantee you that, Oliver had said. Spelling it out clearly for Sara. Speaking French would not get them far in Union Plains and speaking German wouldn't even get them to the starting gate. Sara had agreed.

But there would be no guns, she said. No liquor, no dancing, no worshipping of idols. Crucifixes, she clarified, when he wondered. Within a week they would be married by a priest, as Romeo had insisted, fearing for the souls of Oliver's children. The following week they were to be married by a minister of Sara's religion, as her sister had requested. Oliver was agreeable, wanting to clear all the hurdles in their path. When it came to religion, as long as the kids were baptized, Sara could raise them up on her side, it was no skin off his nose. He knew, however, that even though Sara had agreed to the Roman Catholic wedding, the distance between him and Romeo was bound to grow wider.

There's a photograph wedged between the pages of a German hymnal that Sara keeps on a shelf on her side of the closet, a photograph that Alvina sometimes takes out and ponders. Oliver is seated on a piano bench, his hair thick and ropy and flipped up at the ends like tiny wings. He leans forward on the bench to nuzzle Sara's neck, his eyes half-closed. It appears he intends to sniff a corsage pinned near to her shoulder.

He's inhaling this moment, inhaling Sara, who perches on his lap, her dress hiked to display a strong-looking calf. The leg of a milkwoman of Flanders, which is where Sara's ancestors originated. They were Anabaptist martyrs who fled from the Roman Catholic church, going north to the Baltic, where they worked under the protection of a nobleman in fields overshadowed by an imposing red castle. So, perhaps Sara is part Teutonic, especially her work-woman legs. Or her legs may originate from a later migration of the Mennonites into what was south Russia—perhaps she's descended from a Cossack. But that is highly improbable. Sara's people, unlike Sara, were slow to mix their blood with others. Whatever the case may be, Alvina is relieved that she didn't inherit Sara's plodding, tree-trunk legs.

Where was the picture taken? Alvina wonders, as Sara unexpectedly and soundlessly enters the bedroom. This particular photograph—the way Sara's head is turned, exposing the length of her neck, her features obviously embellished by cosmetics, a tendril of hair falling in a C shape on her forehead—causes Alvina to realize that once upon a time her mother was a woman, and not a mother whose rolled-up Wallis Simpson hair is at odds with the pink shirtwaist dress she wears, spotted with large white polka dots, an Eaton's basement special. Her breasts are flat, two drooping pears, Alvina knows, from once having come upon Sara stepping out of the bath.

Where were you and Dad when this picture was taken? Alvina asks.

Oh, it's just a picture, Sara says, with a dismissive air. Now put it back. And how many times do I have to tell you to stay out of my closet?

Where was I? Alvina burns to ask. I can count, you know. I was a six-month baby. She suspects her mother is ashamed of this fact.

Or perhaps Sara cherishes the moment of the photograph, and is reluctant to give Alvina even a small part of it. This all too brief moment when she had Oliver to herself.

In one such brief moment, Sara and Oliver set off on a brisk winter day to the cathedral near Romeo's house, to be married. Sara tucked her arm firmly beneath Oliver's as they followed Romeo and Claudette along the icy walk. The cathedral's twin spires were their magnetic north on the compass, guiding them towards holy matrimony. As they came near the church Sara had to crane her neck to take them in, to see the birds circling and coming to roost at the base of a spire and then flying away. She thought, *spire*. The word was now as familiar as the word *sky*, its winter face above her distant and wan. She could also say the correct word for the white column pouring from a chimney stack across the river in Winnipeg: *steam*. A tram bell echoed across the frozen river; there were bird tracks dotting the dirty snow around a tree. Sparrows.

They entered the churchyard and were headed towards the entrance of the St. Boniface Cathedral when Romeo veered from the path. He wound his way among gravestones and moments later called out, Here it is. He squatted and cleared snow from a foot marker. Come and see where Louis Riel is buried.

Sara refused to go, not wanting to look at graves on the day of her wedding. Her mouth quivered with cold, with nervousness, as Oliver and Claudette obliged Romeo. The twin spires seemed to pierce the winter sky, and her eyes teared from the cold. Months would pass and she wouldn't think of her family. Now she imagined that her parents rose up from among the gravestones and stood before her. Her father doffed his cap, his weathered features softening with a smile; the fringes of a shawl around her mother's shoulders fluttered in the wind.

I'm here, Sara told them. As though they'd been looking for her. As though it were she who had gone away and not they. She said to herself, Papa, give me your blessing. The baby moved, a gentle shifting to one side, and she put her hand against it. If falling to the ground, pounding her fists against the earth, if screaming, if weeping would bring them back, then she would do it. She held her breath and waited for the others to return. By withholding her tears she kept her parents somewhat present, even as they faded into the snowy yard.

Our grandmother knew him, Romeo said to Oliver, meaning Louis Riel.

But their father had cautioned them not to mention Riel's name, as—like many Metis—he was fearful that people would think his family had had anything to do with the man, that their family might be branded traitors to the crown of Britain.

The brothers and Claudette rejoined Sara and they continued on towards the church, Romeo picking up on what he'd been saying to Oliver. The Orangemen had been hell-bent that Riel be executed. When Oliver sent him a warning look, Romeo said that it was important that Sara know about Louis Riel. Despite her growing nervousness at having to stand before the priest, Sara wondered but did not ask, who are the Orangemen? She imagined the name had something to do with the colour of their skin.

Oliver steered Sara away from the front entrance and along a narrow path cleared in the snow leading to the rear of the church. Twice before they'd gone to the small varnished room, once to request that the priest marry them and then to receive his answer. Sara refused to call the man *Father*. The ceremony proved to be swift, and throughout it, Sara, accustomed now to Oliver's almost shy demeanour in the priest's presence, was subdued too, her voice monosyllabic and barely audible.

They left the churchyard as husband and wife, Sara animated, while Romeo and Claudette were like children set free from school, giddy and relieved to be away from the saturnine man of the cloth, who had smelled faintly of mothballs. They scooped up snow and threw it at the bride and groom, laughing raucously.

The priest doesn't like me, Sara said, and then astonished Oliver by saying that in her opinion the marriage had been held at the rear of the church because the priest feared the sanctuary would be soiled by her Protestant presence. I could feel he didn't like me, she said, wanting Oliver to dispute it. When he didn't reply she asked indignantly, How can that man call himself a Christian?

Oliver wondered what the connection between the two might be. There were people you liked and others you didn't. He wasn't accustomed to speaking his thoughts when it came to matters of religion. The man's a priest, of course he's Christian. He certainly isn't Mohammedan or Jewish or heathen, he said.

Not everyone who calls himself Christian is a Christian, she replied, with an authority Oliver hadn't heard from her before. He couldn't recall ever having used the word *Christian* in a conversation.

They went away from the great stone cathedral, along a snowy walk, and then Romeo sprinted towards a busy intersection where the traffic was constant, bound for a taxi stand on the corner. Claudette set down a bulging cloth bag while she waited for Sara and Oliver to catch up. Refreshments, she'd explained somewhat mysteriously when she and Romeo had met them at the train station.

Hey, you two, she said now, meaning that she was happy for them. Her scarlet Cupid's bow bled into the chapped skin beneath her nose. Once you got around the strange appearance of her pinched-looking nose and accustomed to the nasal sound of her voice, you could see that she was really quite nice-looking. She waited on Romeo hand and foot. She walked with tiny and cautious steps, her fur-topped boots shuffling cautiously, while Romeo careered mindlessly across the polished snow to the taxi stand, slipping and sliding, whooping as he nearly fell. Moments later a taxi entered the street and Romeo called out to them from the back seat.

They quickly left the city behind, motoring east along the river on the narrow and wind-drifted road that Kornelius had taken when he'd driven Sara in and out of the city. There was nothing to be seen for miles around except the road reaching on into a white blaze of light, the grooves worn into its surface by sleigh runners, the snow glazed and yellowish like a callus. The whiteness of winter in the countryside was relieved now and again by copses of shrunken-looking oaks, bunches of beige eyebrow grass and wild oats poking through snow banked along the fence lines.

On one side of the road the land was farmed in narrow strips, affording those early farmers all they required of water, wood and hay land. Land that Kornelius had recently acquired. On the other side of the road the land was divided into squares, each a quarter of a section intersected by a grid of dirt lanes. Where Oliver's grandfather had built a Red River log cabin, post-on-sill construction, a design brought to the prairie from Quebec.

Oliver and Sara were bundled in the back seat of the taxi under a blanket, while Romeo sat between the driver and Claudette in the front, nipping at a flask he'd taken from Claudette's bag even before they'd got out of the city. The windshield began frosting over and Romeo was kept busy for a time, scraping it clear on the driver's side. But as his features grew blotchy and his speech careless, he switched places with Claudette, who took over the task while Romeo slouched in the window seat and drank in earnest.

Oliver grew silent, turning his face to the frosted window as though it were possible to see the landscape beyond, the muscles in his jaw working when Romeo offered the driver a drink. The cabbie was a red-haired Scotsman whose accent was so thick they could barely understand him. You people back there stop breathing, Romeo said with mock severity. Meaning that Oliver and Sara were the cause for the windows frosting up. He turned to offer Oliver the flask, and Oliver took it and put it into his coat pocket. Romeo was about to protest, but Claudette nudged him and he remained silent.

They arrived at Union Plains at noon, sunlight touching all the rooftops of the houses lined up along the few short streets, the red brick school standoffish and solitary-looking on the edge of town. The hotel had been shut down for the day, one of only a few times in its history, a sign in a window announcing that Oliver had gone fishing.

They came to a stop in front of the Vandal house. A freshly shovelled path led to the front door. Smoke poured from a stovepipe at the side of the house, evidence that the fire had been recently fed. Beside the door lay a pile of chopped wood.

You can expect that from the people around here, Oliver told Sara as they approached the house, although the gesture had taken him by surprise. He wanted to believe that the good deed was recognition of his new status—a family man.

The walls of the main room streamed with rivulets of condensation that ran through the red stick figures, and Romeo's pointed silence gave way at the sight of them. Holy cow, he said, being near to sober now.

Sara gasped, her eyes growing wide when she saw the Heintzman parked in the centre of the room.

It's just a small thing, there's more where that came from, Oliver was about to say, when he saw the other furniture. A new bedstead and a bureau, set against a wall.

Katy, Sara said, as though she couldn't believe it. The bed had been made up with plump pillows, and the feather quilt she recognized from her grandmother's bed. Katy and Kornelius had obviously brought the furniture, had chopped wood, fed the fire. A braided oval mat lay on the floor beside the bed, Annie's handwork.

Oliver fell silent as he took in the room, a crocheted runner placed on top of the piano, a framed sampler hanging above the bed embroidered in German. *Thy word is a lamp unto my feet.* Sara read the sampler first in German and then in English. Little Annie, Katy, she said, her voice filling and almost spilling over.

Years later, Oliver would joke that, like insurance, their second wedding was a necessary evil in the event the first marriage fell apart. The second wedding was held a week after the Roman Catholic affair, and not in the Mennonite church, a square sturdy building built on a farmer's field miles from nowhere, but in Katy and Kornelius's parlour.

Sara was impatient for the weddings to be over, impatient to begin arranging the two-room house, just as she was for Annie to be finished with measuring the adjustments to be made to her dress, its hem requiring letting down in the front and easing out at the sides to accommodate the swell of her stomach. The second wedding was necessary; Katy insisted they must be joined together in front of believers, their pledge confirmed publicly and before God.

No guests, Sara said, and was surprised when Annie blushed and said, Some.

A few, Katy admitted. She'd invited several people they knew from the old country. It's what Papa would have wanted, she said, as a means of stopping discussion.

Katy had been surprised and moved when, weeks earlier, Oliver had come calling to ask for Sara's hand. Asking Katy and not Kornelius, his manner courtly and shy, his soft dark eyes steady on her face when he said, If Sara will have me, I'd be honoured. By the time he'd reached the end of the lane, she'd resolved to try to do all she could to make him feel welcome in the family.

Look at me, I'm showing, Sara protested. You think I want people staring at me?

That's nothing to be ashamed of. You listen to me, Sara Vogt, Katy said quietly. In the old country there were girls younger than you. They were taken against their will, and so very brutally. Even so, some of them wouldn't agree to their babies being cut out from them. A baby is not something to be ashamed of. A baby is a blessing.

Sara couldn't argue about the baby being a blessing, and so she dropped her objections to the guests. She couldn't argue against being blessed, although this wasn't the kind of blessing she desired. This blessing was about to clamp onto her life for good. She was expected to feed it, to teach it how to be a person, to love it more than herself.

On the day of the second wedding, Kornelius arrived to fetch them earlier than expected and caught Oliver in his undershirt. Although his beard was such that he could go two days without shaving, he was less presentable than he'd hoped to be. Sara had melted snow on the stove and sponged his trousers, which were still damp when he put them on, and soon wrinkled. Throughout the journey to the farm Oliver felt a coolness in Kornelius, an unwillingness to meet his eye.

Sara was silent, the motion of the car sending her into Oliver's side, grateful for his heat and solidity as she recalled the light of another November morning years ago, when she'd gone with her family across the compound of the estate—the last time she would ever be with them—feathers falling from the sky all around, like snow. Her ribs began to ache, and a band of muscles in her abdomen tightened as though to hold the baby more securely against the rocking motion of the car.

She wasn't expecting to enjoy the second wedding any more than she had the first; neither did she imagine that it would turn out to be a celebration. She entered Katy's house and was greeted by the sight of spruce garlands looped about parlour windows and the door. There were pans of fruitcakes cooling in the kitchen, bowls piled with sweet buns, platters of meat and cheese spread out on the table in preparation for a wedding meal. Her lips quivered as she took it in, becoming self-conscious as her sisters anxiously looked on.

We've invited only a few people, Katy assured Oliver, who, with an unease that was palpable, took in the chairs lined about the parlour walls, cups and saucers on a dining-room sideboard.

To his chagrin, as the guests arrived he noted that he was one of only a few to be wearing a suit and tie. He was introduced to men dressed in everyday kinds of clothing, plaid flannel shirts and twill trousers, the exception being several city dwellers, a man who later told him in broken English that he'd once been a photographer and now was a sheet-metal worker, another man was a grocer, the last, a teacher whose eyes passed across Oliver's face too quickly to take him in when Sara introduced them. Peter Goosen, a friend from Winnipeg, she said, but the man had already turned to the room and begun to hold forth in German, as he did most of that afternoon, falling silent only when the minister spoke.

Oliver was equally surprised to find that the man of God was clothed the same as the others. He was a farmer turned preacher on Sundays, who'd agreed to marry them providing Oliver would allow Sara and their children to attend his Mennonite church. Oliver readily assented. The priest had elicited a similar promise from Sara.

Midway through the afternoon, Sara and Katy plopped their feet into the first boots they came upon at the back door and left the wedding guests to go to the barn. They half-ran across the barnyard, made awkward by the large footwear. They squatted in the warm and moist air over a gutter full of manure and straw between the horse stalls, their skirts hiked up and buttocks exposed.

Katy had left the barn door partly open for light. A mist of warm air escaped into the outdoors, and through it Sara saw Oliver come out of the house and cross the farmyard. He stopped to look in the direction of the lane leading from the farm to the road.

So, Oliver bought you a piano, Katy said.

Yes, Sara said. I'm not musical, she had protested, when Oliver had forced her to sit beside him on the bench while he attempted to show her the simple fingering of a melody called Chopsticks. They posed for Claudette as she took their picture, and then they went off to the hotel to consume the meal Claudette had taken care to bring in the cloth bag.

Ja, ja, for sure, it's nice to have a piano, Katy allowed, although she did not possess one. But usually we wait for such, yes?

Usually we do, Sara agreed. But she and Oliver were not Katy and Kornelius. Oliver was a far more generous man. She inhaled the steam rising from the hot puddle foaming between her feet, noticing again that since she had become pregnant, its odour had changed.

Oliver turned towards the barn, and although Sara knew he couldn't possibly see her, something passed between them. Just as something had moved between them almost all of that long afternoon. When she went past the doorway of the room where the men visited, she felt his eyes rising, felt his question—what was expected of him? Later, he came to the doorway of the dining room where she sat with the women, transmitting his desire to leave. His presence was like a tap shutting off the flow of conversation. The women's eyes moved between Oliver and Sara. What did he want and how would he phrase it? How would she respond? All of it would indicate whether or not Oliver was a hard man. Who would wind up wearing the pants in their household? Rumours abounded that Sara Vogt had fallen for someone wild and unpredictable. A handsome man who resembled a Turk. He had got into her blood, a man who was part Indian. When Oliver left the doorway without speaking, Sara knew that the women had decided he was soft, and that some envied her, while others did not.

Oliver had spotted the half-open barn door and looked as though he was going to come investigate. Sara was about to call to him when Kornelius appeared. He quickly bridged the distance between himself and Oliver. The two men spoke briefly and disappeared from view.

Katy crooked her head and peered at Sara in the sepia light of the barn, a shy smile pulling at her mouth. What did she want? What? While the barn was warmer than the privy, its odours held no attraction, nor did the thumping and snorting presence of the large draft animals.

So, little sister, tell me. What do you think about all the fuss that's made over relations between a man and a woman, eh? Katy spoke in a conspiratorial whisper, as though they were still in the room filled with women, and not shaking their haunches over a gutter to free the last droplets of urine before hitching up their undergarments.

Katy didn't wait for Sara to reply. In her opinion, she said, intimate relations between a husband and wife weren't what she had thought they would be. They're not all that much, she admitted, with a wry bit of laughter.

Sara was startled to silence, recalling the noises behind the curtain of Katy and Kornelius's room. The gasping and calling out that had left her wondering if sex was painful, only to discover that not having sex was painful. She had a gnawing hunger to be filled with Oliver. To feel him moving inside her, his swelling, just before it was finished. To be lost for moments and then return, thinking that she'd been on a long journey inside of herself. Now that she was expecting, Oliver tried to remember himself. He'd be gentle, until she pulled him into her hard, her heels jammed against his buttocks.

Did Katy really want Sara's opinion, or did she want Sara to agree and in this way perpetuate the notion of a woman's tepid desire for sex? In the same way Katy had presided over her children's growing up, she had presided over Sara's and Annie's childhood. She had smelled their breath for signs of illness, watched for evidence of unseemly character traits such as a quick temper, pigheadedness, a need to stretch a story into something larger than it was. Sara had awakened to the presence of Katy hovering over the bed, listening to her breathe. It was an almost impossible feat, a triumph, when Sara managed to conceal the onset of menstruation for close to a year, to become a woman without her sister knowing exactly when.

She decided that Katy hoped for a revelation. For something she might hold up to her own experience.

Oliver's member is so very large, she said.

Katy's eyes widened and grew uneasy with a question.

In comparison to Kornelius, Sara said. She realized immediately that Katy wondered how she would know there might be different sizes. Once she'd seen Kornelius after a swim in the dugout pond, she quickly explained. His cut-off trousers had not concealed a thing. He might as well have been naked.

He was likely cold from the water, *ja?* Katy asked. When Sara appeared not to understand what she meant, Katy burst into laughter. As she rose from her squat, her white thighs gleamed. Even if that's so, it seems to do the same work, *ja?*

Oliver followed Kornelius across the farmyard, noticing once again that his legs were short for his body and his gait bow-legged, though he seemed tall and his shoulders and back were muscular. They went towards a small building on a path beaten into the snow. It turned out to be a woodworking shop, tools hanging along one wall, blond curls of wood scattered across a work table that held a plank that appeared to be freshly planed.

Oliver was surprised when Kornelius reached into the rafters and took down a bottle.

Plum brandy, he said, and offered it to Oliver.

Suit yourself, but I don't take a drink in the afternoon, Oliver replied, believing this was a test to measure his thirst for liquor.

I do, Kornelius said abruptly. He drank, wiped his mouth and put the bottle back. Then he went over to the work table and ran a hand across the smooth plank.

Oliver noted that several fingernails on Kornelius's hands were blackened with pooling blood, and that reddish blond hair, like fur, covered his knuckles. There weren't many people Oliver didn't take to, but this man might be one. He thought of Romeo and his refusal to attend the second wedding. Have you any idea whose land this shed is sitting on? Oliver was about to say, when Kornelius interrupted his thoughts.

You likely don't know that Sara's parents were murdered, do you?

When Oliver, stunned, failed to reply, Kornelius continued. Well, you should know, he said bluntly. Sara's parents, four brothers and a sister. In the aftermath of the tsar's abdication, near to three thousand Mennonite colonists lost their lives to violence, typhus and illness caused by malnutrition.

The Whites, the Reds, the Greens, Kornelius said, the front sometimes passed through our colonies twice a day, and there was nothing we could do to stop them from pillaging, from going off with our livestock and our young men. The muscles in his neck were taut, and his pulse jumped against his skin. Oliver turned away from the sight, the man's anger making his own heartbeat rise. He'd heard of the Russian Revolution, the killing of the tsar and his family, but he knew little else.

The worst were the so-called Anarchists, Kornelius said, his voice brittle. That's what they called themselves. But they were no more than roving bands of criminals, followers of a man called Nestor Makhno. Sometimes they took over our towns and stayed until there was nothing more to ruin or steal. But it was the wealthy Mennonites who were in for it, first. The estate owners, like the man Sara's father worked for, they were the first to feel the brunt of the peasants' vengeance.

Oliver's scalp prickled with dread, and although he wanted to flee, the flat drone of Kornelius's voice kept him rooted, his eyes going from tool to tool hanging on the wall.

I went to the Sudermann estate to sell the man some horses. I found their bodies strewn about on the ground beside the house, among feathers, Kornelius said.

The quilts, mattresses and pillows had been cut open and emptied from the second-storey windows of the Big House. The Mennonites' feather bedding was a symbol of all they were perceived to be—privileged interlopers who bought up large tracts of land from Russian noblemen. That the land greened and prospered was another source of envy. Whether or not the Mennonites who employed the peasant people had treated them fairly and with kindness, as Sara's father had done, or harshly, it didn't matter. They all received the same treatment.

Kornelius paced about the small shed as he spoke, the story made more powerful by his dispassionate telling of it. Oliver couldn't know that Kornelius had never told anyone the entire story until now.

Eleven people in all, Kornelius said, his voice wrenched with pain. Seven from Sara's family. They were axed down, beaten to death or shot when they tried to run away. The estate owner's head was severed. And the girl, Margareta, Sara's sister, she was brutally raped, this was very clear.

Oliver turned and saw Kornelius's screwed-up features, his knuckles gouging at his eyes. My God, Kornelius said, and his chest heaved. Their eyes met, his quickly swerving away. I've butchered plenty of animals in my time, but I wasn't prepared, he said.

Sara's father wasn't yet gone. He told me to look in the greenhouse. That was where Kornelius had found Katy and Sara, hiding in a hole their father had dug months earlier, when the lawlessness began. The baby, Annie, was crawling about the floor inside the house amid a rubble of broken glass, her knees and hands cut and bleeding.

Quiet filled the workshop, then a hurl of wind sent snow against the side of the building, the small window—a grainy, threatening sound that quickly receded. Weather drawing attention to itself for a moment.

They should not have been there, Kornelius said, with renewed bitterness. They would have been safer with their grandparents in town. But their father was too good-hearted. He had let himself be persuaded by the estate owner to return to work despite the troubles, in exchange for a small piece of land that he might eventually call his own.

Oliver floundered for appropriate-sounding words. What Kornelius said had happened in another world. Sara had once said that several of her family members had died during the revolution in Russia, but he hadn't pressed her to say more. His parents were gone, and so were hers. They were both orphans, and that was that. He'd attributed Sara's unpredictable flare-ups, her need for him, her constant question—Do you love me?—to the difficult business of learning new ways. Not to this.

Once again Kornelius reached for the bottle of brandy, and this time Oliver didn't refuse. Beyond the window he saw Katy and Sara emerge from the barn, Katy suddenly twirling and swinging her arms in what looked to be a girlish dance. Kornelius came up behind him at the window, both of them watching as a boot went flying off Katy's foot. She hopped like an awkward child through the snow to retrieve it, while Sara stood looking on, as though impatient with Katy to get over her silliness.

Well, just when you think you know who they are, Kornelius said, wryly.

Sara watched as Katy pushed out her chest dramatically, lifted her chin and swaggered in an exaggerated long gait. I'm Peter Goosen, she shouted. Then she stretched her neck, put a hand to her forehead and swivelled her head this way and that, as though she were spying on someone. I'm Franz Pauls, she shouted to Sara in a self-important voice. She snapped imaginary suspenders and then caught herself.

I shouldn't have done that. Her features grew strained, aging her instantly. He was so young to be a teacher. He was my first and my last teacher. But you wouldn't remember him.

Of course I remember him. I remember that you didn't like him, Sara retorted, still smarting from Katy's laughter in the barn.

Yes, and I'm sorry for that, Katy said, her shoulders drooping.

The wedding guests streamed from the house now, led by Annie, carrying a camera. The sisters went to meet them.

Picture-taking, Kornelius said, with resignation. Man, oh man. They can't get enough of it. Welcome to the family.

Oliver flinched as Kornelius clapped him on a shoulder. He wished the man had kept silent. If Sara had wanted him to know, she would have told him, he thought. Forgetting that when they were together they were usually horizontal and in a hurry. In the heat of the moment or rising from it. Until now, Sara had begun and ended there. Welcome to the family. He hadn't the faintest notion of the extent and complications of such a family.

He followed Kornelius across the yard, dragging his feet. I've made a mistake—the realization was a stone dropping to the pit of his stomach, making him want to back away, even as he went forward to join the wedding party for the picture-taking. He took each step with the increasing and sickening certainty that he'd made a terrible mistake.

The wedding guests pressed in around him, some calling out comments in broken English and the others laughing, their odd sense of humour passing Oliver by. He was pulled and jostled to the middle of the group, Sara taking him by the arm. He was joined in marriage to a stranger, was the father of her child, and he'd never felt more alone.

The camera's shutter opened and closed with a tinny decisive click, while Oliver thought, it's too late. He was impatient when Annie held up a hand to keep the wedding party in place. He knew he had Annie to thank for the decorated parlour, for having rehearsed Katy's children to sing a greeting before the minister took charge. But throughout the long winter afternoon he'd grown uncomfortable at how diligently Sara's people worked to be accepting of him, as though he were a piece of real estate to be tilled and seeded and brought to harvest.

And now this. This, this. This information Kornelius had passed into his hands, which left him grappling for something in the depths of his experience that would clue him in on how to deal with it. Once again the camera's shutter opened and closed, while Oliver thought, I've made a mistake.

Just one more, Annie called.

Lay off, Annie, Kornelius said. Enough already. He broke ranks, stepped out of line, and the others followed.

I only wanted a last picture, Annie said, tears welling and then spurting from her eyes like watermelon seeds. One more, that's all, she cried, her voice rising towards hysteria. It's Sara's wedding and Mama and Papa should be here. They should all be here.

Katy hurried over to her, slipped an arm about her waist, while Sara escaped to the house, her pulse pounding in her ears as she heard Katy say, They're here. They can see.

In the wedding group snapshot these ordinary-looking people stand in three rows in a snowy farmyard. Sara and Oliver are in the centre of the first row, both unsmiling. Alvina is taken by how Sara clutches Oliver's arm in a fiercely proprietary manner. She tilts her head towards his shoulder as though to dispel any doubts about them being man and wife.

When was this taken? Alvina has asked Sara on more than one occasion. Soon after we were married. At a family gathering, Sara says, wiping flour from her hands before taking the snapshot and studying it carefully as though searching her mind. I thought I was so grown-up, she once said, as though laughing at herself. He looks like a gypsy. And Alvina thinks, it's true, he does. Oliver gazes off to one side of the camera, his dark hair curling overtop his collar, high cheekbones reflecting light, trousers wide and bagging at the knee. While all around him the others stare directly at the camera. They're fair-skinned, round-faced and solemn people, and pose as though they're aware that at some point, in their lives or in the hereafter, they could be called upon to give an account of this day.

Within hours of the picture-taking Kornelius brought them home, the winter darkness having quickly descended. Here and there, lights twinkled in the windows of the houses in Union Plains, while in the Vandal house a lantern wavered in the draft of the open door as Oliver gathered up an armload of firewood. After the baby came along the house would need to be electrified, hooked up to a source of water and a septic field. Sara was right, he thought, the windows were crooked and drafty, and when the heat from the stove got up, the earth beneath the floor gave off the odour of mice, like the smell that hung about the corners and closets of the hotel, and in the vacant guest rooms.

There's something wrong. What is it? What's wrong? Sara had wanted to know as soon as they stepped inside the house, following him about the rooms. She came to the doorway now, watched him stack the wood against his body, a coat slung over her nightgown, bare feet, toes curling on the sill against the cold. She stepped inside as he came in and set the wood down beside the stove. We need a woodbox, she said, unhappy with the bits of bark and chips littering the floor.

I'll build you one, Oliver said. I'll build you a dandy woodbox. Then he turned away from her and said, Go to bed. I won't be long. I'm going to see a man about a dog. To stretch my legs, is all.

To take the air, to feel the wind. To gather my thoughts. To keep from smashing his fist into a wall, as he would a hammer one day in the future, while hanging a shelf. Pound and pound through Sara's shouting at him to stop, until he'd put the hammer clean through the shiplap.

He told her he was going to the hotel to relieve Cecil. The old gent's gout had flared up, and it wasn't kind to keep him on his feet. After he shut down the parlour, likely he would go for a walk to feel the air. Go to bed, he told her again.

You can't leave me, she said. Her dismay at his departure was replaced by fear. She'd never once slept in a house alone, and wouldn't be able to sleep, not until he returned. She had heard things going on in the house during the night, thumping, an animal's breathing beneath the floor.

Listen here, woman, I can't afford to take any more time off. You know very well what I do. I'm going to work, he told her. You danged well better get used to it.

Three raps at the door brought Alice. They sat in the dark and sipped tea, then a finger of whisky. Inhaled its amber fumes and talked about this and about that. Chewed the fat.

Oliver described to Alice the people he'd met that day, without once saying the word *wedding*. He told her about their strangeness and lack of lustre, not telling her that, before he and Kornelius had joined the others for picture-taking, Kornelius had opened his shirt and bared his back to display a map of scars, several of them pebbled and ridged with proud flesh. Sara's got them too, only they don't show, he'd said.

Those people will laugh over nothing, Oliver said. Alice laughed and said, Like that? They fell silent. The house creaked as the temperature outside fell. Oliver listened for the inevitable footsteps in the upstairs hall, which never came.

Alice's hand rested on the table near his hand, its palm turned up, as though she expected something would drop into it. She flinched when he placed his hand round hers and gave it what was meant to be a reassuring squeeze, while hoping for the same. She drew away from him, got up and switched on a light, took down a deck of playing cards from a cupboard and returned to the table.

Your pleasure, mademoiselle, Oliver said.

Hearts, she replied.

He waited as she shuffled the cards, her small cone-shaped breasts shifting beneath her sweater as she began dealing them out.

ELEVEN

Housekeeping

FOR A TIME a piano man makes calls to the Vandal house to tune the Heintzman, until he pronounces the instrument no longer worth the effort. And so the piano is relegated to the back porch, where its joints loosen, the felts on the hammers harden, its veneer cracks. Most of its ivories are chipped or missing entirely, having been pried loose by restless fingers. Oliver cannot pass by the instrument without feeling wounded, without thinking, what a crying shame.

The letters of the piano keys are labelled in crayon, the work of Ruby, who thinks she doesn't have the ear. Nevertheless, at five years old she's determined to teach herself to play. Thanks to a *Learn to Play Music* book of simple tunes provided by Florence Dressler, who also obligingly wrote the letters beneath the notes of the songs, Ruby toils on. Her pointed tongue flicks across her lips as she searches for a corresponding letter on the keys to the letter beneath a note on the staff. Sometimes she plays the piece of music an octave higher or lower than she means to, until Alvina goes out into the porch and positions Ruby's body on the middle of the bench and moves her hands to the appropriate octave.

Oliver bought the piano reasoning that it would be years before his future children would need to reach beyond the midsection of its keyboard. He didn't take into account music such as boogie-woogie and rock and roll; Emilie plays mostly at the top and bottom of the keyboard, and sometimes with her feet and elbows. The distorted pounding suits her musical taste. Ida prefers to play hymns, improvising as she goes along, embellishing the melody with clever trills up and down the keyboard, but when, invariably, the sounds of the high and low registers fall apart, she becomes cross and says, Shoot! Instead of Shit!, as she would like to but doesn't, because she's playing hymns. The piano keys are mushy beneath Oliver's touch, the tone wavering and offensive to his ears, and he gives up trying to coax a tune out of the instrument. His sons remain indifferent to piano playing, preferring a trumpet or saxophone, if only they had one.

Oliver believed that by the time any of his future children was an accomplished pianist, he'd be flush and able to purchase an upright grand, whose sound was better suited for the classical style. Which, despite his objections to Alice going away to the academy to study, was what he imagined his children would play. He also concluded that classical music could only be truly appreciated, and played with the necessary ferocious power, by a man.

During the almost twenty years that follow their second wedding night, Sara and Oliver find themselves in one another's company for only brief moments at a time. A moment when the bed springs dip beneath his weight and Sara's inner chatter flattens to a straight line. He sheds his clothing in the dark, and sometimes sparks fly off his body with a snap, sheets of static electricity flash with the downward movement of his trousers, across his chest, illuminating him in a sharp blue moment of light. He slides in beside her with a learned stealth so as not to disturb the current baby asleep in its crib, and they have this moment when they lie side by side, not yet touching.

So how was work? Sara asks. By *work* she means how much money was in the till at the end of the night, an indication of the amount she can expect to be in his leather envelope the next time she goes shopping. She's unaware that, as the years pass, more money comes through the hotel's back door than from the ancient cash register, a marble and brass edifice as large as a pulpit. She's never heard the term *bootlegger.*

It was a quiet night, he may say. A Saturday night hockey game in Alexander Morris, a talent contest in another town or a dance in Ste. Agathe means that the parlour is empty most of the evening, except for the old-timers nursing a tumbler of beer for hours, until he takes pity and draws a round on the house. Easy come, easy go, he tells them with an ever-increasing uneasiness.

It was a fair night, a good night, he may say. And come to believe his own optimism, entertain thoughts of dropping in at the car dealership in Alexander and arranging for a loan to purchase an old Chevrolet that has been sitting on the lot for half a year. He'll leave Cecil in charge of the parlour more often, go places. Maybe drive to Emerson and check out the car bingo that is attracting players for miles around, including Indians from the Roseau River Reserve. The jackpots are sometimes near to three hundred smackers.

He'll take the kids to play bingo. For sure. Why not? It would widen their horizon. Drive around the border town for a bit, maybe drop in on cousin Danny and his family.

Danny surprised him by showing up at the hotel one night. The man's a customs officer, he told Sara. He's a high school graduate. The young cousin came through the dimness of the parlour towards him, a clean-looking and neatly dressed man whose soft smile reminded Oliver of his mother. He was surprised when Danny ignored his extended hand and hauled him into a bear hug. Come and see us, bring the family, don't be a stranger, he said when he left. Maybe Oliver will do just that. If he won a bingo jackpot, they could go on a real trip.

Yes. Take Sara and the kids to see Ontario. The forests he saw from the train when he was returning from leave. He made that trip twice on mercy, when Sara gave birth. At the end of two years he returned home for good. An honourable discharge for the old fella, whose burgeoning family needed him more than the war effort did. The train wound through slabs of rock and black forests that gave way suddenly as it left shield country. The prairie lands seemed to descend from the sky, the land and water touched by light and releasing a tension in his body. It was as though he'd been holding his breath for the entire passage through the rock and woods. He'll take his kids to see that black forest and make them appreciate what they have. You betcha.

I'd like to buy me a car, Oliver muses aloud, during one of his optimistic meanderings.

We could go to Edmonton, Sara says, her mind leaping with the possibility. She would like to visit the distant cousin on her mother's side. During the ocean crossing the woman noticed Sara's plight of the too-large stockings, and exchanged them for a pair that fit. A small gesture, but one that Sara has never forgotten. If they had a car, she and

Oliver could go for a spin to neighbouring towns on Sunday afternoons. They'd be able to park in the driveway and have conversations without all the big ears listening in.

Niagara Falls, Oliver says, his imagination up and running. Just you and me. We'd stay in a motel, feed the radio quarters and not get out of bed all day.

In the silence that follows, the clock on the bureau seems to tick louder. A stack of freshly ironed laundry on the easy chair beside the window glows in the light of the moon. A child calls out abruptly in sleep. Sara holds her breath as she listens. Their children cry out to be rescued from ravenous wolves and raging fires. They dream of falling and of flying, of being able to breathe underwater. Who would look after them? she wonders. She can justify needing help to care for them when she's ill, or lying in with a baby. But how could she for a vacation?

They have moments together when they seed the garden; in later years, without the presence of a blanket of children set down in a patch of shade. Alvina tends to the children and the house. They work well together when they plant, there's no need to speak as Oliver hoes a shallow trough while Sara comes behind him, trailing seeds and covering them. Hours later they stop to drink water from a jar and gaze at the sky, Oliver reaching for Sara to massage a crimped neck muscle. She leans into his kneading, wondering at the strength of his fingers, grateful for their heat. When a woman passes by in the street, Oliver calls a greeting, while Sara returns to the task at hand.

It doesn't hurt to be friendly, Oliver says. Smile, Sara, your face won't crack.

I've tried that. They only want to make fun of me, Sara says. The English hid their unfriendliness behind crooked little fingers as they sipped weak tea and nibbled on stale biscuits she wouldn't be caught feeding to a stray dog.

Throughout the nearly twenty years of their marriage, Sara attends weddings and funerals alone because Oliver cannot shut down the hotel, and church, as Sundays are his only day of rest. On parents' day she visits her children's classrooms with the smaller ones in tow, sits with the other parents on chairs placed across the back of the room while the teacher conducts a lesson. She's taken by the busyness of the classroom, the colourful artwork, the earnest look of exercises pinned to the walls, the maps, the scribblers lying open on a display table, which she dutifully inspects along with the other parents. But unlike them, she doesn't understand what she inspects. She doesn't know long division or multiplication, fractions, the simple algebra and geometry exercises, the names for the parts of a flower or the body of a bee. Why must they learn health, she wonders, and about the ancient Greeks—of what use will that information be to them in the future? She bristles when a teacher puts her hands on Sonny Boy's shoulders and steers him over to the blackboard to work on an equation.

She's quietly amazed that her children can recite and point out all the states in the United States, the provinces in Canada and their capital cities, while she strains to find Russia on the map of the world, and fails. She's nonplussed by their politeness and deference to the teacher, their confidence. She knows she should be proud that they're among the achievers, and not envious.

You should be there, she tells Oliver. School visits make her feel inadequate, and she overdresses for them, she knows from the sideways glances of the other women, which makes her chin rise and her smile feel forced, while at the same time she fights against a shyness that wants to pull her chin down, turn her controlled smile into an obsequious one. If she spoke, she would flounder for words that, at home, come so fluently. Oliver only needs to enter a room, and everyone turns towards him as though expecting to be entertained or encouraged, expecting that he knows that someone in their family is ill or has passed away, or has a new baby. Expecting to feel better for having talked to him.

Your Oliver is a real character, Florence told Sara during one of their first visits, as though it was important that she know this. According to Florence, during Oliver's bachelor days he was sharp at billiards. For a time he played a circuit and travelled about the countryside toting a cue in a case engraved with his name. Word of Oliver's prowess reached Minnesota Fats and, unexpectedly, the man came up on a train from Minneapolis to engage Oliver in a game of billiards, and lost. Florence's husband was one of the few men to witness that midnight game, the defeated Minnesota Fats grinding out a cigar on the table and retiring to his room without uttering a peep. Oliver denied the rumour when Sara repeated it, but in a way that hinted that it pleased him.

But there it was, the pool hustler's name appearing on the billboard he erected to attract travellers going by on Stage Coach Road. *Why pay city rates? $6.00 per night! Pool Room and Billiards. Frequented by Minnesota Fats!* What the sign didn't say was that a guest couldn't expect more than a cup of coffee.

Since the health inspector had closed down Florence Dressler's nip-and-chip stand, the nearest place to purchase something to eat was a café in Alexander Morris.

It was also known, Florence said, that Oliver used to float downriver on his back while reading the newspaper. This in face of the fact that he got rid of his rowboat when a fortune teller at the Alexander fair predicted that he would die by drowning.

Sometimes Sara and Oliver go for a walk, the children gathering in the yard to see them off, unsettled at the sight of their parents going away from them, as though Sara and Oliver were embarking on a voyage to a foreign country.

Their shoulders almost touch, they're that close when they walk. Close enough for conversation. However, Sara isn't interested in what Oliver wants to point out during their infrequent rambles onto the land. The things he learned from his father and Ulysse. Moss grows on the north side of a tree, the saucers of mustard-coloured fungus stacked up the side of a trunk are edible. Oliver names the grasses, the trees. There are owls burrowed in the ground five to ten feet down. The nocturnal birds shelter in the holes of other animals, a fact that brings Sara to a halt, her shoulders bunching in fear of an unexpected flapping of wings about her head.

He tells her that before his uncle Ulysse was a ferry man, he'd been a walker, until his legs gave out.

When word reached him at the Roseau Reserve that the municipality was looking to replace the aged one-armed ferry operator, he claimed to be a distant relative with a right to the job, and walked back into Oliver's life one winter morning, stepping into the kitchen suddenly and soundlessly, an apparition wearing layers of what looked like sackcloth. Icicles and snot matted his grey moustache and beard, which moved when he spoke what sounded like French—his mouth being rigid with cold caused the words to come out square. The English phrase *by golly* jumped out of a series of clanking sentences as he held up a string of fish. When he shook it, the fish clattered like wooden chimes.

By golly, nephew, long time no see, Ulysse greeted Oliver when he came downstairs to investigate the commotion. The heat of the kitchen turned Ulysse's cheeks the colour of wine and began penetrating the layers of his clothing. As the various shirts warmed, odours were released—fish, woodsmoke, his unwashed body, his advanced age.

He'd brought the string of fish for Oliver's woman to cook for supper. In the meantime, he'd welcome a hot breakfast. Eggs and bannock. Did Sara have flour in the house?

He stayed for the remainder of the morning, on a chair beside the kitchen cupboards, drinking tea and consuming the bannock he'd made, having taken over from Sara when she appeared not to understand his instruction. As the morning progressed, Ulysse began to draw off layer after layer of clothing, the first being a duffel jacket bound at the waist with a soiled and worn sash, and a pair of leather leggings. Then he removed a flannel shirt whose buttons were missing, the shirt fastened with stovepipe wire. When he peeled down to one shirt, Sara realized that the man was nothing more than skin and bones.

Throughout the morning Ulysse's attention had been taken by the children. Ruby crawling about in a playpen set up in the centre of the room. Simon and Manny amusing themselves at the play table. Ulysse would laugh, for no reason Sara could discern. He seemed pleasant enough, and showed an interest in the fruit plaques on the kitchen wall, and took it upon himself to rearrange them, while Sara was out of the room.

By the time Oliver and the children collected around the two tables for supper, Sara was terse and fierce in the eye. He wears four shirts, she said. Each one of them equally dirty. Their meal of fish was consumed without Ulysse, who had excused himself to go out back to use the privy. When he failed to return, Oliver followed his footprints in the snow past the privy and through Florence Dressler's yard, and onto the prairie. Good riddance, Sara said. She had seen the likes of Ulysse before, in Russia—long-haired and dirty peasants, their fingers stained with nicotine, men who erupted suddenly and made demands, made a shambles of whatever house they entered. Thieves who came snooping and returned later with others, with horses and wagons to carry off what they claimed rightfully belonged to them. Her grandparents' bed had been loaded onto one of those wagons and hauled off down the street.

That has nothing to do with this, Oliver interrupted, speaking quietly, as though he expected Ulysse would materialize through the wall. Oliver wanted to put a damper on what he feared she might go on to say. Sara was a cat dragging a dead mouse to a meal table. Don't bring the old country into this, he warned.

She might have told Oliver that, during the revolution, people her family had known for years had changed. Ordinary men turned into animals, their features swollen with lasciviousness, sharp with cunning or blunted by rage. They'd become evil. She thought of this when Ulysse's features turned hawklike and his eyes ferocious with concentration.

Ulysse had tapped his teacup with a spoon to gain Sara's attention, and pointed at the clock. The hour hand inched across its face, passed through all the numbers, and then it stopped. You see what a person can do if they have a mind, Ulysse said, his English halting as he struggled for the necessary words. As Sara recounted this to Oliver, her eyes grew wide. He made the plaques move in the same way, she said, in a whisper.

What Sara wants during her and Oliver's infrequent walks into the country is to try to understand their children, who seem to resist all her efforts to raise them in a fitting way, in the way her sister raised her children as obedient, mild-tempered and respectful of their elders.

Ours are good kids. They've got strong spirits. There's nothing wrong with that, Oliver says.

Sara has come upon a pack of cigarettes in Emilie's drawer. Where did she get it? No amount of questioning or swatting or pinching will make her say. Sara worries that Emilie hangs around with boys more than girls. She hears herself saying things to Emilie she sometimes wishes she could take back. *You're going to wind up pregnant. You're going to throw your life away. Slut.* She's puzzled and shamed by her cruelty, but it seems that once she gets started, she just can't stop. Not even at the look of bewilderment, Emilie's hands covering her ears.

They all go through that, Oliver claims.

Stealing? Well, I certainly never did. Did you?

Not everyone's the same, Oliver concedes.

Ida got her period, Sara announces.

You don't say. Oliver thinks Ida will make a dandy wife. She reminds him of his sister, anxious for a head start and out the door and married at the age of fifteen.

Don't you think it's time to start a hopeless chest for the girls? he asks. Six girls—ye gads and little fishes! He's never put a thought to the fact that he'll be responsible for six weddings.

Hopeless is right, Sara says, and adds, I never had one.

Twice now, Sonny Boy has come home with what Sara suspects is the odour of beer on his breath.

A little beer never hurts, Oliver says. You let him have one at home now and then, and he won't see the need to go out drinking with the Bogg brothers in the car. It's safer to do it at home than in a car. You're making a mountain out of a molehill.

As usual, he thinks.

TWELVE

Shopping

HOW WAS WORK? Sara asked Oliver, thinking of the trip she would take to Winnipeg tomorrow. The scarf she meant to return to Emily Ashburn lay on the bureau across the room, along with the paper patterns she'd made of the children's feet. She hoped to buy the girls sandals, the boys runners, for the coming summer months. To take the trolley car down Crescent Road and see how the elms had grown. Go as far as the park gates, perhaps, and walk back along the crescent to the Ashburn house. What had changed, if anything? she wondered. She's changed. That's what has changed. She's older, wiser, a woman. A mother of ten children and owner of a house.

Oliver said, *Comme ci, comme ça,* and flicked his hand. While he didn't want her to worry, he didn't want her to entertain thoughts of going on a spending spree, either. I bring the money in the front door and the little woman shovels it out the back, he liked to joke, concealing the worry that sawed away at his ribs. Years had passed since he'd last heard from Henri Villebrun, and then last month he had received a letter, a few lines of greeting and news of Madame Villebrun. News that he feared would bring repercussions tramping down the road.

I heard from Villebrun. The old lady has had a stroke.

She's bedridden, he said, his voice not betraying his feelings, a sense of vindication. He thought, the old sow, she finally got hers. He recoiled from the memory of the woman's powder-caked face leaning too near his own, her lipstick bleeding into the creases of her mouth as she pursed her lips in an invitation for a kiss.

Sara let this reference to a person she'd never met go without a comment. She rose on an elbow to peer at the luminescent hands of the clock on the bureau. It's late, she said. After all these years she was still unable to let this go.

I know. I had me a walk. To the river, to jaw with Ulysse for half an hour or so, he didn't say. Ulysse had heard talk of a bridge being built and the ferry being shut down.

Sara slid a leg against his to draw in its outdoor coolness. He must be fed, she thought. In order to keep him in his usual good mood, she must feed him before she left, and when she returned. While he encouraged her to go shopping in Winnipeg, he was always distant when she came back, as though punishing her for being away. To keep him from wandering, she must see to it that his hunger for sex was appeased. He turned to her, threw his leg over her thigh, and moments later she felt his testicles moving, his member growing thick.

Afterwards he slept immediately, while Sara imagined flowers on the wall, foliage composed of the light and shadows cast by moonlight through lace curtains. She'd memorized the shopping list she had made after supper, and ran through it now. Fishing lures. A brassiere for Ida. She thought of what she would wear tomorrow, something smart and stylish to impress Emily Ashburn.

She thought of Coral, of meeting the woman nearly a year ago at the bus depot when she'd arrived early and, wanting a bite to eat, had gone into the coffee shop. The only information Coral had volunteered about herself, she had offered on that first meeting, when she parked her enormous derrière on the stool beside Sara. She had nodded towards a window and a man coming across the parking lot walking sideways, obviously drunk. Poor soul, she said. I'm from Trinidad. Where're you from? Sara felt her sideways appraisal. From Russia. She was startled to find herself talking to the bus depot's cleaning lady. That makes us both DP—two dumb people, Coral said. Two dirty people, Sara countered, surprising herself. Coral's heavy eyelids closed and she hummed, then stopped, her smile revealing large even teeth. But you know of course, girl, that we're all sheep. And some of us have gone astray, but there's nothing dirty about us when we're walking in the footsteps of the Good Shepherd.

Astray, oh yes, Sara thought. The closer she came to being forty, the stronger was the feeling that somewhere in her life she had taken a wrong turn. If Coral weren't black, she wouldn't have told her stories about her life, in the way rural women were apt to do. It was easy to know who among the shoppers were country women by the way they engaged sales clerks in long tales of their families, their illnesses, the trials and errors of distant relatives. They were oblivious to indifference, the clerk's condescension, which made Sara stare at the back of the talker's head and will her to stop making a fool of herself. But Coral was black, and Sara didn't want to appear reluctant to talk to her.

She recalled telling Coral about Florence Dressler's sister going to the Holy Land, and bringing back the bundle of palm leaves. I want to go there too, she thought, the idea just occurring. She couldn't ever go back to the country of her birth. But there were places she could go in order to find the past. To the manger where Jesus was born, to the hill far away where he was crucified, as described in an Easter hymn. She would visit Bethlehem, Golgotha, and find out if such places actually existed.

How're them kids of yours doing? she imagined Coral asking.

Fine.

How's Emilie?

I love all my children.

That's not what I asked.

Yes, I know. But that was what came to her mind whenever someone asked. I love them all, Sara thought. As though they were eggs in a basket she hovered over in adoration, but thank God—she needed to breathe sometimes—Winnipeg was only miles away, and tomorrow she would board the bus and be there within thirty minutes.

The following morning Oliver walked Sara down the access road to the highway, to wait for the bus. It's going to be a good one, he said, meaning the day. Warm for June. He fished in his back pocket and gave her his leather pouch, and when she put it into her purse, she saw the blue scarf. I might take a later bus home, she told him.

Suit yourself. Don't go spending the money all in one place, he said, which was meant as a joke but this morning didn't sound like one. Both of them turned at the sound of an approaching vehicle.

Stevenson, the water man, cranked down a window of his truck as he came alongside. If they wanted a lift, he was taking a load down to Alexander Morris, he said, all the while knowing that Sara was off to Winnipeg on one of her shopping trips.

He was actually alerting them to the fact that another family had moved out of Union Plains. This here's their stuff, Stevenson said, motioning to the jumble of furniture and boxes secured by a lashing of rope. He told them that the widow Anderson would likely be the next to leave, as her son and his family had driven all the way from Arizona to help the woman pack up.

Sara and Oliver fell silent as the truck entered Stage Coach Road and went south, not wanting to acknowledge that the rumours about Union Plains seemed to be coming true. They waited beside the highway, the air warming quickly as the sun burned mist from the outlying fields.

When the bus came to a stop beside them, Oliver noticed the nuns on board and insisted on escorting Sara to her seat. He stopped in the aisle to greet the two sisters, saying, How do? How do?, old-world courtly and respectful, as though, with this homage, he could stave off whatever uncertainty he might be required to face during the coming months. Sara found her own seat as he lingered to address the nuns in French, his voice softening and lilting with a cadence that, to Sara, sounded put on.

As the bus pulled away she refused to acknowledge his exaggerated salute. He thought that she was stupid, that she couldn't recognize the difference between a joke and mocking. His deferential greeting to the nuns, the snappy salute in her direction, left her fuming.

Hours later she was riding a trolley down Crescent Road, having taken the blue scarf from her purse to fold it and press it between her hands in the hope that its creases would ease. She thought that if Emily Ashburn invited her for tea, she would ask to see the room where she'd stayed. Of course, the messages behind the baseboard would likely be gone, including her own. Sara and Oliver, she'd written, then folded the strip of paper so that their names touched.

But perhaps the bookcase remained in the hall outside the door, along with the pitifully few books she'd managed to finish reading. *Little Women, Lorna Doone, Uncle Tom's Cabin,* novels whose worlds were equally puzzling in their unfamiliarity. She felt a prickle of embarrassment now as she recalled the moment she'd come across a photograph in a book by Sir Walter Scott. A photograph of an enormous oak tree, which had set her heart racing. She had thought she recognized the tree, had taken it to be an old oak growing in her grandparents' town. A tree well known for its age and size, for being a meeting place. Known by most of her kind, who'd dwelled in over three hundred towns and villages spread across southern Russia.

She went hurrying downstairs to show Penny, and found her in the dining room, setting the table for dinner. See, this is what Russia was like. It was very green, I remember, and the trees were huge. She sat down at the table trembling, while Penny read aloud the inscription beneath the photograph, an inscription Sara had failed to notice in her excitement. *The King's Oak, at Woodstock.*

Not many days after, when Sara entered her third-floor room, she saw that a book had been left on her bed. She knew without needing to pick it up that it was a reader. She knew from the two years she'd attended school that it was a second-grade reader. Likely Penny had said something to Emily Ashburn, who had concluded that Sara was unable to read.

There was a tug of movement as the streetcar took off at a stop, empty of passengers now except for an elderly man sitting near the front. She felt the heaviness of her purse resting on her lap, the burden of the bulging shopping bags wedged between her feet.

The trolley car passed by the Ashburn house and Sara noted a flagpole on the front lawn, a Union Jack snapping in the stiff breeze, and couldn't recall it having been there. You dumb bunny, she thought. Fool. How ridiculous to think she would ring the doorbell and be invited in. Likely Emily Ashburn had forgotten she'd ever worked there.

She rode to the end of the line and returned downtown, stepping off where she'd boarded, into the roar and impatience of traffic. The day had warmed considerably, and as she went to the Metropolitan store, where she hoped to purchase running shoes, people were streaming from shops and offices without their winter attire. She entered the flow of pedestrians, her shopping bags setting her apart from the clerks, the stenographers, the business people. Light wavered in puddles beyond the curb, and when a vehicle approached, the people around her swerved to the inside of the sidewalk, called out to the driver and ruefully laughed at nearly being soaked.

Sara felt their exuberance at being freed from the bulkiness of winter, and gave in to it. She unbuttoned her coat and enjoyed the wash of warm air against her throat; the papery crackle of the bags afforded her a sense of accomplishment. She'd already purchased underwear for the girls, tea towels, the prescribed connect-the-dots and colouring books; a corselet, as several stays on the one she wore had worked through the cloth and poked when she moved suddenly; a jackknife for Sonny Boy.

She found herself among several women at an intersection, waiting for the traffic light to change. They were on their coffee break, likely, going to a luncheonette, a diner or perhaps the cafeteria at Eaton's. Young women whose hair was teased into stiff twists and smooth domes, their ears covered with pearly-looking plastic earrings fanning halfway across their cheeks. She'd seen similar earrings in the Met and thought of Alvina. But she couldn't imagine her wearing them. And so she'd purchased an angora collar instead, hoping it would soften her daughter's perpetually sallow complexion. Where, oh where had that come from? Certainly not from her.

She had bought a bottle of Evening in Paris, and a jar of Pond's vanishing cream. Given how quickly the jar emptied, the cream seemingly did vanish. She suspected Emilie applied it to her warts, but of course the girl denied doing so. She bought a flannel shirt for Oliver, whose spring bouts of bronchitis were becoming a worry; and several cards of fishing spoons. Manny and Simon had taken the fishing rods and reels outside to practise casting and had snagged the telephone wires. Oliver had had to cut the line in order to free the rods. If you boys want to go fishing so badly, why didn't you just say so? Oliver had promised he would take them soon. He didn't recognize his sons' antics for what they were, a reminder of the promises he'd made in the heat of generosity, just as the holes in the backyard shed windows were a reminder that he had promised to take them target shooting with their air guns.

Days might pass during which Oliver only vaguely noticed he had children. He was sometimes so far gone into his thoughts that he didn't hear their questions, or their quarrelling for attention. He afforded them vague answers, a shrug, a turning away, and Sara fumed over the luxury a man had to be able to shut things out. And then suddenly he arrived at the meal table one evening fully present and engaged, eager to visit. He blew smoke rings for them to slip their fingers through, was tickled by their antics, hauled them onto his lap to inspect their school notebooks.

The traffic light changed and the women around Sara moved forward, only to come to an abrupt stop in front of a store. Sara caught up to them and saw the display that had captured their rapt attention: three spring brides in a show window. The gowned mannequins were framed by a trellis intertwined with artificial apple blossoms and cotton batting fluffed against the window glass to resemble clouds. The gowns gleamed with a whiteness of organdy, satin and tulle, adorned with lace and beads.

Alvina and Ida pestered her to know what she'd worn on her wedding day. She replied, A green dress. Your aunt made it. It was winter and Annie thought green would be nice. But she knew that they wished for a description of a gown such as the store mannequins were wearing. A fingertip veil held in place by a tiara of mother-of-pearl sequins. The bridal trains were arranged in a half-circle on the floor around their feet, and sprinkled with confetti, champagne glasses tipped onto their sides as though just emptied in a toast.

Oh, my. How nice. How very, very nice, she thought, hearing her own sarcasm through the silent awe of the young women around her. They lingered a moment longer and then broke away all at once from the bridal spectacle, resuming their quest for coffee, she assumed, while she remained, absorbed and shaking. *Here comes the bride, all flushed with pride.* Or embarrassment at being the centre of attention. Yes. Go ahead and enjoy it, missy. Because it's not going to last very long. The extravagant show put on at weddings these days made her furious, because it made her want to weep.

She'd spent the night of her real wedding, her second wedding, waiting for Oliver to return. Hours passed and the supply of wood he'd left for her ran out, the fire dwindled and dampness began to engulf the room. She ventured outside to replenish the wood and stood for a moment hugging herself against the frigid air, searching for the sight of him. Across the street, a blob of darkness hovered above the ditch. She called out, but the shape neither came closer nor retreated.

Throughout the previous months she'd nestled into Oliver's sticky embrace in his room under the stairs, and had come to know their mingling yeasty odour. Tonight she hadn't recognized the arrangement of his features, their severity, when he told her she'd better get used to him being a working man. She was rattled by the sudden retraction of goodwill.

She chewed at the skin of her knuckles, rather than give in to a desire to weep. Water only meant more water. A gushing tap was hard to staunch. She felt Alvina move inside her, a heel sliding down, grazing the wall of her womb. *Peter, Peter, went into the water. When he came out, he let out a poop.* The Low German ditty came to her, the sound of her mother's singing chant, her laughter, as she dipped a baby into its bath. She returned to the house and dressed, pulled on a pair of Oliver's pants over her nightgown.

I'm going to see a man about a dog. The old gentlemen want a game of cards after closing. A late customer held me up. I was jawing, is all, Oliver would say in the coming years. Chewing the fat, listening while a fella took a load off. A man's got to be sociable; especially once Oliver's second source of income, the after-hours and Sunday trade in liquor, became necessary to provide for the growing number of Vandals.

When he didn't return at the expected time she would put on his curling sweater, a tar-stained parka, a rain slicker, and go out into the dark as she had done the first time he'd left her. Later it was jealousy that drove her out in search of him, but that first night it was fear of being alone. The night of her real wedding, fear heated her pulse and drove her into the unknown.

Within a few swift years she was no longer alone, but surrounded by small bodies with beating wild hearts and muscles twitching in sleep, her children continuing in dreams the journeys they had begun the moment they emerged from her body. Straining to be off and away from her, no matter how tightly she swaddled them.

Her belly muscles jiggled after a recent birth of a child as, stomach unbound, she went out into the night in search of Oliver. Vowing that this time she would venture far enough to determine if a window at the hotel blazed with light as the card players went about their game in an upstairs room. Or whether, as she suspected, the hotel was shut down and Oliver had gone walking to see that woman.

When she was lying in after a birth, he deemed it necessary to stay at the hotel to make way for Annie, who came to cook and tend the children, houseclean with a fury and sew new curtains. Annie layered the kitchen floor with coats of paste wax, glossing it to a hard shine that hurt the eyes. At the end of a day, she gathered the children about the dining-room table and taught them a German prayer, a song; required that they read aloud from a German reader she had brought with her. She put the girls to work learning simple daisy-chain stitches of embroidery to render the store-bought tea towels in a kitchen drawer respectable, while Oliver stood in the doorway looking on. Having arrived silently and unnoticed, and leaving the same way. Sara worried that Oliver used these periods of freedom to see Alice whenever he liked.

In the nights Sara had never been able to get as far as the hotel. But if she had, and had then discovered the squat, demoralized building in darkness, she would not have been able to find the narrow trail that went along the highway and down through bush to the ferry. Or crossed the frozen river to determine whether or not Oliver was with the woman. If she had, she might have come upon him as he was returning, bringing with him a shopping bag filled with shoes, which he would claim Alice had sent to the hotel earlier in the day.

The darkened houses, the sound of the wind in the trees, a dog barking, quickly diminished Sara's determination to uncover the truth, and her angry words settled to the bottom of her stomach. Inevitably she returned home to a house of sleeping children, or to discover that a light had been turned on in her absence. Alvina's round face peering out from a window. Alvina, drowned in sleep like all the others before Sara left the house, often awakened as the door closed behind her mother. Knowing, somehow, that Sara was gone.

Sara stared at her reflection in the bridal-store window, a woman approaching forty years, her coat hanging open, her suit creased across the front—a beast of burden laden with shopping bags, and she still had to buy four pairs of running shoes before the late afternoon bus departed for Union Plains. She had given birth to ten children in less than twenty years. But if she fixed her eyes a certain way, she could imagine a beautiful and youthful woman whose features were soft and unbound from the determination to make something of those children. Especially the boys.

She had just rearranged her features when she became aware of a woman in the store hovering behind the display of brides. There was no mistaking the distinct pixie-like features, the small brilliant eyes accentuated by mahogany curls across her forehead and hugging her ears. Sara's scalp tightened. Alice Bouchard. She immediately thought, my feet. She was wearing Alice's shoes. Then she looked down, flooded with relief that she had kept her rain boots on over the shoes. The sidewalks were gritty underfoot, and so she'd decided against stowing the overshoes in a locker.

She felt anger rising, words she'd never used coming

unbidden. You whore. Bitch, thief of my husband's mind. Oliver's bouts of preoccupation were likely brought about by an anticipated visit with this woman. Of course. Why hadn't she realized this before? He went to see Alice to be immersed in the language of their time, their history, the people they had in common. Immersed in each other's bodies, for all she knew. She'd once smelled an odour on Oliver when he'd returned late during the night, a spicy scent that she didn't recognize.

His shaving soap, Old Spice, he said. She'd bought it for him as a Christmas gift from the kids. He'd shaved at the hotel before coming home so he wouldn't need to do it the following day. That way he might get at things around the house sooner. Tar the roof of the back porch. Putty the windows. Sara wanted to send Alvina to his closet under the stairs to scratch the bar of shaving soap, bring its scent home under her fingernails so Sara might know for certain. Yes? No. No, yes. Yes, yes! Oh God, the see-sawing of dread, of peace; of an enfolding tenderness in her gut when she thought, I'm wrong.

Alice turned away from the window. Moments later, the shop door opened and she stepped out into the street carrying several packages. She was not wearing overshoes, but rather red pumps with needle-nosed toes, a beige suit, its Joan Crawford shoulder padding squaring her frame and making her waist look even tinier than it was. Her perfectly drawn features and ivory complexion brought to mind a porcelain doll. She went over to a new two-tone Buick parked beside the curb, and was about to open the trunk when she became aware of Sara and turned, her small brilliant eyes sweeping across Sara's body, a slight mocking smile forming.

Then she put the packages inside, closed the lid and went on down the sidewalk.

Sara was almost certain as she watched that figure mincing off down the street, a shoulder bag bumping against her hip, shorn head held high. The defiant click of her stiletto heels against the sidewalk seemed to tell Sara that Oliver had been there. He'd put his sex into that woman's narrow body and then had come home and done the same to her.

Only she wasn't sure. And if she had been, what could she have done?

I wanted to hit her, Sara told Coral at the bus depot later. Smack that look right off her face, she said, without confessing what she *had* done. She raised her voice in order to be heard above the sound of water running in one of the cubicles, a toilet tank leaking and constantly refilling. A moment passed.

That's reasonable, honey. The Almighty, he sure do understand anger.

Oliver says they're friends from way back. Maybe they are just friends, Sara said, with more hope than conviction. Do you love me? she asked him, and always he said, I married you, didn't I? Would I still be here if I didn't? He refused to say the word.

Honey, where's your brains? Men and women can't be just friends, Coral said. It's a law of nature.

Yes, Sara thought with a sinking feeling, that sounds like the truth.

The washroom held an antiseptic odour from a recent mopping of the floor, and its hexagonal tiles were still wet and shining. The shopping bags took up the entire area of Sara's cubicle; a third bag had been added, bulky with the running shoes she'd come across in a bin at the mail-order as she went up and down the aisles, her heart burning, trying not to imagine Oliver and Alice joined together. Thinking, the whore got what she deserves.

But it's wrong, she said now, her voice too loud and echoing. He's married, he's a family man. Disloyal, dishonest, dissolute, lying son of a bitch.

Yah, Coral agreed. That's men. They can't help themselves. A stiff prick's got no conscience. The Almighty understands your anger, wanting to hit that woman. But that doesn't make it right.

I beg your pardon? Sara asked. She undid the clasp of a rainboot and kicked it off. Then stuck her foot under the cubicle into the next one. Do you see these shoes? She gives them to me as a way to keep her hooks into Oliver.

If you think that, then why do you wear them? Coral asked.

Because, she said. Because I like the way my feet look, she thought. Her feet had stopped growing too soon in life, and she had been forced to wear children's shoes throughout her adult years, until Oliver brought home the first bag of Alice's footwear. She felt finished then, her tiny foot admired and complemented rather than being a peculiarity; which was what she had been, a peculiarity, until she'd left the old country. A person who'd been spared death, while her family had not. Was it wrong to want to look like everyone else?

She was angry again. Angry that Coral would dismiss her with a platitude—God sure does understand, but that doesn't make it right. Huh! I have every right.

The graffiti she had come to expect on the walls of the cubicle, the crude but direct expression of desires, the declarations and curses, had been recently painted over. But there were two new angry-looking slashes in the fresh paint. Sara understood the intensity of an emotion that would press that hard with a sharp object.

With her shopping bags set about her feet on the street, to obscure her activity from passersby, she had tried to puncture a tire on Alice's car; but the jackknife she'd bought for Sonny was too blunt for her anger, or else she lacked the strength as she jabbed and twisted at rubber that proved to be impenetrable. She became aware that she was being watched, glanced over her shoulder and saw a teenaged boy leaning against a light standard, looking on with bemused interest.

You need help? he asked. And when she didn't answer, he came over and dropped to his haunches beside her. He was about the age of Sonny Boy, she guessed, his face freckled, with short brushlike eyelashes that flickered when he saw the jackknife in her hand. You need more than a peashooter, he said. He brought his hand forward and a blade flashed from his fist. His arm jerked and there was a sound of spurting air that quickly became a quiet, steady hiss. He went round the car to the street side and she heard a similar sound. His face appeared above the car, a nonchalant query accompanied by a smile. Do you want me to finish the job? he asked.

No, that's enough, she said. She fumbled with her purse, thinking she would give him a dollar, but he was gone, drifting off down a narrow alley between the shop and another store. The first tire had gone flat and the car sagged to one side. A bus approached in the street, sending a wash of water over the sidewalk and the side of Alice's car as it passed by. Its brakes sang as it glided to a stop beyond the intersection, and several people waiting for it surged forward while others disembarked.

Quickly she gathered up her bags and walked away, resisted the urge to go faster than necessary. Good, good, good. I've done it, she thought, and felt a momentary jab of triumph. Done what? What had she done? she wondered. The heels of her plastic overshoes felt spongy against the sidewalk, and gave her a buoyancy that she did not feel.

THIRTEEN

Alvina contemplating

ALVINA CAME OUT onto the fire escape at school, chilled and gulping for air, hugging herself against a shiver she'd gained from the closed-down classroom. The images in the magazine of the human pick-up sticks, the corpses in their striped pajamas, followed her outside. *A thing of beauty is a joy forever: Its loveliness increases; it will never pass into nothingness.* She recalled the poem and instructed herself to appreciate the weather, the sun like a warm hand against her brow. Rah, rah, rah. At this very moment its rays were manufacturing vitamins on her skin and preventing pimples vulgarious. A meadowlark piped from a fence post in Zinn's field, a bouncy flute song that failed to raise her spirits. She heard a question in the bird's trill, Where the hell are you?

Contemplate the beauty around you, the poem suggested, and not your feet, a monk had once told Alvina. Unless, of course, you find your feet to be particularly inspiring. She'd approached the monastery from the creek side, and through a windbreak of saplings she had seen him tending bees on the far edge of a large garden. The next moment, his long shadow had moved towards her across an apron of mowed grass.

The monk had come to inquire about her reason for being there. She saw his looming shadow and looked up into what she thought might be the face of an angelic being, made indistinct by the veil of a beekeeper's hat. A face darkened by the sun, she realized as he lifted it. His brows were white baby-bottle brushes that almost concealed his eyes. Have you lost something? he asked. The way Alvina kept her nose to the ground when she walked, he thought she must be looking for money. Lift your head, look around you, he said, and then recited the poem. Contemplate a thing of beauty. A joy forever. A quiet bower of sheep and daffodils. He had returned to the hives, leaving her to contemplate the rash of mosquito eggs clustered on the syrupy-looking creek, the dwarfed trees providing a hollow for a plaster figure of Christ. She had considered the silence gathering under the willows bending near the water.

The meadowlark was a blurred spot perched on the wire fence separating the outfield of the school baseball diamond from Zinn's field. Earlier, she'd hoped to see Emilie coming on the run through that field, late as she sometimes was but at least present and accounted for. Emilie's unexplained absence, Simon's temper tantrum over two mistakes on an arithmetic test, Sara coming down with what was likely another shitty baby, no longer seemed relevant. The bodies in the pit were like sticks because they'd been starved. Shot by firing squads. Gassed.

She looked towards the highway, a buff ribbon of concrete that at the height of summer would shimmer in the heat. Sometimes she peered into the shimmer and saw people walking down the centre of it, watery ghosts colliding into one another, melding, coming apart and being made whole again. A mirage, Oliver had said. He'd once seen a herd of glass buffalo crossing the highway—he'd been able to see right through them. Alvina became aware now of the cars sporadically passing by. From the distance they appeared to be toy cars, determinedly going south to the U.S. border and north to Winnipeg. They didn't even slow down when passing the access road to Union Plains.

Where the hell are you? the meadowlark gurgled, heralding the onset of summer's heat. Superimposed on this day, on the birdsong, was a black-and-white image. A negative image of human beings heaped in a mass grave. The meadowlark's question was pertinent. She'd been awakened this morning from a deep sleep. Left shuddering and chilled and wondering, what was the point? What was the point of the shorthand and typing exams? She only wanted to pass commercial in order to escape the putty knife. To gain her own space. A space about the size of a desk, its drawers repositories for the minutiae of her shitty life. A life that so far amounted to a denim drawstring bag bulging with metal hair rollers, a Chap Stick, a sanitary napkin, a Vicks medicated inhaler, a bottle of pearl-white nail polish and the little tin of get-happy pills.

Throughout the years—while Sara called out during the night, Alvinnnaa?, and Alvina trundled downstairs to make certain the locked door was really locked, while she made up the beds and scoured the scale from the piss-pot with a lava stone, buffed Bon Ami from windowpanes—she imagines that millions of people were being gassed, shot and starved to death. Men, women and children thrown into a pit, peering down and up through the strata of other deaths, staring with blackened eye sockets at the sky. Why were they so thin, like sticks? she asked, as the teacher took the magazine from her. Miss White folded the periodical with more energy than necessary and jammed it firmly under her arm, as though to prevent the images from sliding out onto the floor. They were starved. Hitler didn't see any point in feeding people he planned to wipe from the face of the earth, she said.

There hadn't been any pictures of starving people among the photographs in Katy's trunk one summer long ago, when she had taken Alvina upstairs to see them. There were no fat people in those days of hunger, believe you me, Katy had said. We stopped taking pictures then because we didn't like how we looked.

Alvina and Katy had been alone in the kitchen, elbow-deep in a tub of dishwater. Beyond the window, people sat out in the yard on chairs and benches, consuming a noon meal. Among them were Sara and Oliver, and a distant cousin who had motored from California in a large truck whose box was fitted with a canvas roof. The truck was used for hauling fruit and had been lent to the cousin by the owner of an orange grove. The cousin and his family had camped along the highway during their trip, like a pack of roaming gypsies, the man kept saying, until his listeners ceased to laugh. His presence had precipitated an unusual number of people attending the summer gathering, and so there was a need to eat in shifts.

Before the meal began, children were called to recite and sing for the visitors in German, which had Sara craning her neck in search of her own. The land sizzled with sound, clouds of grasshoppers rising to go on to another field and strip it clean. Oliver frowned and said, For God's sake, Sara. Let the kids play. Alvina had stepped out of Sara's line of vision. It appeared her brothers and sisters had done the same. And so she was just as surprised as her mother when, moments later, Annie came from the house trailing a quartet of Vandals. On cue, Simon, Manny, Emilie and Ida lined up and began singing.

Immediately the land grew quiet, and a crow calling from the elm beyond the dugout pond lifted up and flew away. The Vandals were singing in French, a round song that asked, *Are you sleeping, brother John? Morning bells are ringing.* Annie hadn't said they would sing in French. During the performance Oliver's face grew swarthy with emotion as he stared at his hands, his brown fingers laced together over his paunch. The song ended in a soft echo of bells, *ding, dong, ding.* There was applause, the people around Oliver smiling and nodding, signalling their approval and pleasure. Oliver swiped at a wetness on his face and went over to a woodpile across the yard to have a smoke.

As he got up, the stricken Annie raised her hands. I thought he would like it, she said.

Well ding, dang, dong, you're wrong, Emilie replied.

Sara rose from her chair, colour radiating in her cheeks. Shame on you, she called after Emilie, who had quickly run away. Emilie went across the farmyard and climbed up onto a threshing machine, where she could keep her eye on Oliver until he returned.

Alvina scrubbed dishes in the kitchen while Katy rinsed and dried, hurrying to prepare for the second shift of diners. Only then would the children be allowed to approach a table overburdened with roasted chickens, a shank of ham, a boiler swimming with chunks of farmer's sausage. Alvina had helped carry the food, the pots of perogies awash in white gravy, platters of cheese and watermelon, a crock of plum soup. Still to come were trays of cream puffs, fruit pies and dessert squares.

I'm starving, Alvina had moaned as she washed dishes, and had quickly found herself being whisked upstairs to Katy's bedroom, her aunt taking a key from a drawer and unlocking a huge trunk on the floor under a window. Her keepsake trunk, Alvina realized, which had come from the old country.

Moments later the lid rested on its hinges, and scattered in the lid were photographs Katy had taken from a wooden box inside the trunk. A box that had once belonged to her grandfather. Alvina's great-grandfather, she explained, in a voice that had become less efficient in tone.

These are my parents, your grandparents. This picture was taken on their wedding day, Katy said. A woman stood beside a man sitting on a chair, her hand at rest on his shoulder. Her expression was one Alvina sometimes saw in Sara. A proud look, a lifted chin, and eyes saying that she wasn't interested in what was going on around her. The man leaned forward, his large hands splayed across his knees. His expression was soft and almost sad.

This is your aunt Margareta. Greta, we called her. Katy pointed out a young woman among several others. The face leapt forward. It was a face Alvina might have recognized, if not for the fact that she'd been told she resembled her father. And that's your aunt Annie, see? Annie was a baby in a flowing white dress, held in her father's arms, the only recognizable features being the pale blue eyes and frizzy cloud of blonde curls. Alvina's eyes were drawn to a small girl standing beside Annie's father, her chin tucked into her chest. She has Emilie's smile, Alvina thought, self-conscious, shy. Could this be Sara?

And those are my brothers, Katy said, before Alvina could ask. Her aunt's voice broke, and her finger trembled as she pointed out four blond boys of various heights. Two stood at their father's knees while another two stood behind him. Alvina barely had a moment to take them in before Katy put the photo away. She gathered up the remaining photographs in the trunk lid and stacked them in a pile.

Who were the others? Alvina had caught glimpses of groups of people, couples, people lined up in front of houses. There was a picture of people lying in what looked to be narrow coffins, their hands folded across their chests.

What happened to your brothers? Alvina wanted to know.

They're gone. There was a war and bad times. What's important to remember is that they're with God, Katy replied. She knew exactly what had happened. But she believed there was nothing to be gained by dwelling on the past.

I was a little girl when they died, and I hardly remember them, Sara would tell Alvina when she asked. They were all taken on the same day. By bad men. Killed. Don't ask me how or why, because I don't know. They're safe in the arms of Jesus, Sara said, and Alvina recognized the words of a hymn.

Katy put the wooden box of photographs back into the trunk and locked it. She slipped the key into an apron pocket. She went over to a window and looked down at the people gathered in a circle, eating what she and the other women had prepared. There came a time when everyone was hungry. At least those little boys were spared that, she said to Alvina. We stopped taking pictures because we didn't like how we looked, she continued, after pausing to dab at her eyes with a corner of her apron. There weren't any chemicals to develop them, anyway. They were used up in the war.

She beckoned to Alvina to join her at the window. She pointed to the cousin who'd driven from California, a stub of a man whose face shone with perspiration. He had buried twin boys just before he left Russia. The babies had died of malnutrition. That woman over there? Katy indicated a nervous-looking woman who might have been Sara's age, except that her hair was stark white. Katy said, She was your age when she saw her father being killed. Then her entire family died of typhus. The people in the yard eating so much food with apparent relish knew first-hand the meaning of the word *starving*. The words *hate, murder, maim*. I never want to hear you say starving, because you don't know what it means, Katy said.

Well excuse me, what are you, a cop? Alvina thought, being only fourteen years old, and immune to the implications of her aunt's stories.

According to Miss White, the deaths of the people in the open grave had been planned. Someone had penned or typed the dictate that they should die. Alvina imagined the word *extinguish* imprinted on a typewriter ribbon. She'd thought of that word because of the sudden depth of darkness in a room when a candle's flame was quenched. What happened when people died? What happened to their memories, all the thoughts they'd ever had? She couldn't fathom all that being frozen inside their stopped brains, the thundering, calcifying silence of everything they had felt, dreamt and hoped for.

Then she thought about Sara's parents, a sister and four brothers, all killed. She didn't take into account that they had died in a different time, in a different kind of war from the one she had happened upon in the magazine. She only thought that they'd been killed during the violence of a war, and her mind logically placed them in the pit among the corpses. Holy. Now she understood. She would not be able to say *kill, murder, maim,* without thinking about them.

Dust rose along the access road, the water truck churning it up as it went towards the municipal compound. Stevenson was likely returning from filling the cistern, she thought. When she got home she needed to take the key from the hook and put it back on a top cupboard shelf, where the little kids couldn't reach it, on the chance that one of them might figure out how to undo the padlock, unthread the chain from the cistern lid handle and lift aside the iron cover. She must remember to sprinkle and roll up the clothes that needed ironing and put them in the refrigerator. Her thoughts slid to one side of her head and then to the other. She grabbed on to the railing to keep from keeling over. Nausea whelmed up from her stomach and, with it, a gush of salty-tasting water that filled her mouth. Her ears began to ring and her face ran with perspiration. She should not have taken the second pill. One a day, Florence had cautioned. Never take more than one.

Where the hell are you? the meadowlark piped again. As far back as Alvina could remember, she'd always been surrounded by voices. A house filled with voices, as when, before supper, she would sneak away for a nap. She would creep upstairs hoping Sara wouldn't miss her, up to her bunk bed, and immediately pass out to the sound of muffled voices downstairs. A cotton comforter of sounds that would still be there when she was roused by someone sent to fetch her. Voices were a buffer against oblivion, against the silence embraced by the willows bending near the creek. Now the silence she sometimes craved was a wall of darkness rushing towards her. Was this what it was like to die? A wooziness, a retraction of reality, the world as though viewed through wavy lead-coloured glass? Was this the Lord taking away?

Her legs trembled with weakness and she was unable to will them to carry her downstairs to a classroom, where she would be safe among the children. She wanted to go home, to enter the house to the sound of her sisters' shitty little voices. Alvina! If this is going to be your last thought, it should not contain the word *shitty*. From now on, let shit be shit, and not an adjective or a verb smelling up the air and your mind. She vowed never to use the word that way again. Just please, please, please. Save me. She was thinking that she would slide backwards into the darkness, when someone called her name.

The world swivelled back into focus as she saw Emilie coming through Zinn's field, arms flailing in a butterfly stroke, her hair streaming out behind her. Then Alvina saw Manny on his knees at the fence, crouching over a pile of dry leaves heaped against it. He leapt up, then stood staring, entranced by the yellow lick of flame consuming the edges of several leaves, a tendril of smoke.

Manny! Jesus Bloody Murphy! Alvina yelled, and he turned, spotted her on the fire escape and stomped out the beginnings of his bonfire, while stuffing Oliver's loupe into his pocket.

You're going to get your ass tanned, Alvina shouted—an empty threat, she knew. A fire lit against the backyard shed, in the garbage barrel, hadn't resulted in a tanning. While Sara believed in spanking, she didn't think it was right for her to spank the boys, and left that to Oliver, who objected to having to carry through on her threats. What kind of a homecoming is that? he asked. The kids scared out of their wits for me to step in the door? Do your own dirty work.

You get back inside before someone catches you, Alvina called, and Manny took off at a run. Just then Emilie vaulted the wire fence, and there was an attending flash of yellow as the meadowlark lifted from the fence post and flew away. Emilie sprinted across the baseball diamond, and Alvina became aware of the cool metal of the fire escape against her hands and stomach. Sonny Boy, George, Ida, Emilie, Manny, Simon, Ruby, Sharon, Patsy Anne. *Ten little, nine little, eight little Indians, seven little, six little, five little Indians.* She couldn't sing, and so she chanted the counting verse to her sisters and brothers while she put them to bed, making them hold up the appropriate number of fingers. She required them to say their prayers—*Now I lay me down to sleep. Our Father who art in heaven. Forgive us our debits.* She remembered the polio warning on the radio this morning—*Do not get overheated, do not perspire.*

Stop running! Stop! You're supposed to walk, only, Alvina called to Emilie. But would Emilie listen? Of course not. Thank God the nausea had passed, Emilie had returned, the world remained the same.

At last Emilie had reached the fire escape and stood on the bottom step looking up at Alvina, her ribs heaving, the fringe of white bangs pasted against her forehead. For all the rush, she seemed at a loss for words. Why had she bothered to show up when the day was nearly half over? She's so fragile, Alvina thought. Pale skin stretched over tiny sharp bones, and a smile that was too wide for her narrow face, and never reached her eyes. Emilie looked hungry. Alvina wanted to gather her in an embrace, but she knew Emilie would only strain against it, as she had never been one to cuddle.

We're going home, she said, her footsteps rattling the fire escape as she quickly descended. Relief made her light-footed. One a day, she vowed silently. She paused on the bottom step and looked down at Emilie, who seemed confused. Her nervous smile had faded, and her brow had wrinkled with puzzlement. Her thin arms came up to hug her body, and to conceal a smudge of dirt on her shirt.

I'll do her hair, Alvina thought. I'll wind it up in rollers and see if I can coax it into a pageboy.

It's not time to go home, Emilie said.

It doesn't matter, Alvina replied, propelled by the urgent need to get there.

FOURTEEN

Seeing about a dog

OLIVER WAITED as the ferry unravelled the water between him and Ulysse, thinking that he would ride until as late as noon, when his uncle, unmindful of vehicles waiting to cross, would open a can of creamed corn or herring, maybe both, although that would mean he'd need to go into town earlier to replenish his larder. They would eat in silence, their communion punctuated by an otter sliding down the bank and splashing into the water, a fish tail smacking the surface of their thoughts.

A distant humming of a vehicle approaching on Stage Coach Road sounded like a finger being drawn along the rim of a bowl, the green bowl of vegetation he found himself in, the river unwinding along its bottom. The hum became a ringing as the vehicle passed by and then the sound faded. The steady *putt-putt* of the ferry's engine pecked away at the silence. He planned to board and cross over and back, to do so for as many times as was necessary for the wind in his ribs to subside.

The Red River and not Alice Bouchard was actually ABC the Goldfish. ABC the Goldfish being *Abe, see the gold fish*. The saying had originated with the old gents, and referred to a travelling salesman, Abe Solomon, who had once sold needles and thread in the towns along Stage Coach Road. He claimed to have seen a school of gold-coloured fish the size of bread-and-butter plates, hundreds, churning upstream as though disturbed by an eggbeater. Although Oliver often went walking in the night, he dropped by Alice Bouchard's house no more than twice or three times in a year.

Ulysse was the man Oliver went to see about a dog, whenever the glass eyes of the worn-out buffalo head on the parlour wall seemed to follow him about the room as he cleared away the tumblers, emptied ashtrays, washed and wiped, as though the animal were impatient for him to be finished and get started on his real life. Chief Fine Day oversaw the abandoned parlour with a proprietary air that sometimes became mocking. At such times Oliver stopped what he was doing, looked about the battered establishment and realized that this was his real life, his future. He was living it.

He also went to the river to escape, on the days when he was fortunate enough to spot Emilie hurrying along the street, riding the ferry for as long as it took her to give up on her search for him and return home. Or wherever it was his kids went during the day in order to stay clear of Sara. In winter he kept his snowshoes ready at the back door. When he reached the river he strapped them on and went for a tramp along the wind-blasted channel, his lungs on fire with the cold, his body elastic with a youthful vigour, his corpuscles plumped with oxygen.

He had heard from Sara the Biblical story of there once being a race of giants on earth, the offspring of angels who'd cohabited with the daughters of men. He hadn't said that he'd heard a similar story, that the first of his kind, the true Canadians, were seven and eight feet tall. They were burly, broad-shouldered and barrel-shaped men who hunted a breed of giant buffalo, of which the bones of several had been unearthed within miles of Union Plains. The first of his kind had been giants, while the women had also been known for their size, petite and dainty as meadow buttercups, such as Oliver's mother had been—comely and dark-complexioned, with dimpled cheeks and strong white teeth.

The ferry nudged into the landing and a wave washed over the toes of Oliver's boots and retreated. I seen you coming, Ulysse called, as he ducked out of the engine shack. He stretched tension from his body, rose on his toes and lifted an arm, his palm turned upward as though he were a pillar holding up the sky.

How come you didn't see me coming last night? Oliver teased, referring to his uncle's sixth sense. He'd been startled to find Oliver and the two girls waiting on the shore.

It was dark, Ulysse said, as though Oliver should know this, leaving Oliver chagrined and at the same time puzzled.

The ferry shuddered as they drew away from the landing, churning up the yellow clay bottom that muddied the water in the way thunderclouds murk a horizon before a storm. And then they were into the deep, where the algae particles dazzled like sequins on a figure skater's twirling skirt.

Oliver took down an apple box from the roof of a motor shack and upended it, his usual seat, but his uncle didn't claim his chair. He seemed lost in himself as he scanned the approaching shoreline, his walnut features crinkling in a squint against the sun. There she be, he said, and moments later a car appeared on the crest of the ferry road. The old maroon Chrysler swayed and squeaked as it descended towards the river.

Old man Villebrun, Ulysse said. He plucked his pipe from his shirt pocket and jammed it between his teeth as though to prevent himself from saying more.

Look who you see when you don't have a gun, Oliver said to cover his turmoil. The car appeared to be driven by a child. Villebrun's hands grasped the steering wheel at the level of his ears, so that only the brim of his hat was visible above the rim. The car horn blared, a hand waved and Oliver felt the man's penetrating gaze. He was on his own, so Madame Villebrun was likely still bedridden, or perhaps she had passed on.

Oliver got up from the box, as though wanting to flee, but there was nowhere to go except to meet him head-on. He imagined himself saying, Business has been slow. An explanation for not having written or even sent a postcard throughout the past five, six years. Maybe more, he allowed, as, moments later, Villebrun's car brought its roar onto the ferry.

You've got to understand, Oliver thought, feeling the heat of the car as it idled for a moment; its engine gave a final kick as Villebrun shut it down. The door opened with a wrenching creak of metal, a white golf shoe appeared, a brown trouser leg and then the whole man.

Merde, a cadaver, Oliver thought, as Villebrun's pale face turned towards his own, his features indistinct, as though dusted with a powder that absorbed the light of the sun.

Oliver, my good man, I was on my way to the hotel to see you, Villebrun said, and extended a trembling, liver-spotted hand. Its clamminess and the tissue-paper thinness of its skin turned Oliver queasy.

I was on my way to the hotel to see you, Villebrun said again. His voice was toneless, rusty-sounding and cracked.

He'd left his hat in the car and Oliver noticed that his silver hair was long, slick with pomade and tucked behind his ears.

Oliver had to lean towards him in order to hear. You saved me a trip, Villebrun said. His brown-suited body exuded an odour of decay, like the mould-encrusted vegetation lying in pockets in the underbrush where the land never had a chance to dry out.

The ferry started up and Villebrun teetered with the sudden but gentle motion; he grabbed for the car and leaned into its fender. He had never been tall, but the years had shrunk him to less than five feet.

How are things in Florida? Oliver asked. He knew Villebrun lived in a trailer park outside Palm Beach and near a golf course, and that was all he knew. The correspondence that had passed between them throughout the years had amounted to several lines on a postcard, and the brief notes Oliver sent with an even briefer accounting of the business midway and at the end of each year. An accounting of the intake and output, the resulting profit and what he had managed to deposit at the caisse populaire. Brief letters explaining why he hadn't sent an accounting, why there wasn't any profit, the dwindling receipts, and then he didn't think there was any point in writing.

Alligator, Villebrun said, and with some difficulty he opened his jacket to reveal a shiny leather belt. Got one in the car for you, he said. His obvious pleasure at the happenstance of coming across Oliver on the ferry subsided. We have to talk, Oliver, he said. We have to talk about the business.

You betcha. For sure, we'll have a talk, Oliver said. By and by they'd have a meeting. But first he'd have to get the books in shape. He'd ask Alvina to sit down one night and sort through the hat boxes of receipts. Enter them into the accounting book and add up the columns. She had a good head, a flair for numbers. Emilie had a flair for words and for causing trouble. She had written stories for him, verses, which he sometimes read. War stories, verses about the war, about battlegrounds she had imagined coming to life in the flash and boom of a howitzer.

What do you want to go and write about that for? he'd asked. What he knew about the battlegrounds of the last war would fit into a thimble. Emilie knew even less. You don't know anything about that, Oliver told her. But I can imagine, she said. No you can't, he said. No one can imagine what it's like to be in a war. When you make things up, you're telling lies.

He had Sara's fruitfulness to thank for his own lack of experience of the real war, his honourable discharge coming just as his regiment was being shipped to Hong Kong, creating a worm of bitterness that he nursed during the long train trip home. A thick and flesh-coloured worm the size of a finger, curled at the bottom of a glass of clear water—the thought of his comrades, the older chaps he'd come to appreciate, going off where he couldn't go. He still nursed a bitterness, tinged now with a begrudging gratitude, knowing that he likely would not have got through the internment that only a few had survived.

Oliver's thoughts went this way and that to avoid beginning conversation with Villebrun, who'd gone over to Ulysse to exchange a word. Now Villebrun had returned. I've just come from the caisse populaire, he said. I closed the account. You should know this, Oliver. You should know that as of today, I have shut down the hotel. She's closed. I'm going to arrange for a transfer company to come and empty her out. I shut her down, Oliver. I shut her down for good, he said again, and nodded. Oliver, my good man, I'm here to tell you that.

Look here, I've got three lodgers, three old gentlemen. Where're they going to go? I've got me ten kids, Oliver said, hearing his English come apart in the presence of this man as though he were twelve years old, stumbling for words because it was this man's money he carried home in his pocket.

In the silence that followed, Villebrun didn't seem to know what to do with his hands. He put them in and took them out of his pockets, flicked at imaginary lint on his jacket, scratched at the silver stubble on his chin. Then he said, Holy Mother of Jesus, by now some of them must be old enough to go out to work, eh? Couldn't you put them to work for you?

Sonny Boy and George were years older than what Oliver had been on the day he had left the schoolhouse for the last time. His kids wanted to know how far he'd gone, what grade had he achieved? He suspected they would deduce from that what was expected of them. He told them, I went to school three days and both days the teacher wasn't there. They never seemed to catch the joke; he surmised from their bewilderment that they took what he'd said as fact. He'd attended school four years, and then, like most boys of the day, he had been out becoming a child of experience. He had nothing whatsoever against that, except that he wasn't fussy on his sons gaining the type of experience he'd gained while indentured as a joe-boy to Madame Villebrun.

She's bad, Oliver. She costs me a mint for Madame Villebrun's care. I'd just as soon strangle the old bitch and get her over it. But as you know, there's a law going against that. Villebrun's lips parted in a smile, colourless and glazed-looking. He laughed, his thin shoulders jerking inside his too-large suit jacket.

He wiped his eyes with a crumpled handkerchief, stuffed it back into a breast pocket and continued, The old lady can't so much as go to the bathroom on her own any more, but wouldn't you know it, she still has all her marbles. She still runs the show, Oliver, like always. She says to tell you, don't take this serious. She says to tell you that she will always think of you as being a son.

A declaration that had come before, too soon after his mother's burial and Romeo's departure to St. Boniface, while Oliver lived alone in the almost empty house, the days interminably long and silent. Oliver had awakened thinking he heard his mother's footsteps, the chattering of a lid on a cookpot. His breast had been swollen with such a hard ache that he could barely swallow as he ate the food he sometimes thought to prepare.

Oliver had noticed a dusting of snow on his mother's grave one morning, a forecasting of the pending winter. He hadn't thought of the season changing, until then. There was movement around him in the earth and the wind, changes that had gone unnoticed, which would bring about a closing in and closing down, the earth frozen solid, the snow banking up the sides of the tiny house while he hunkered under the buffalo robe, thinking he heard his mother's footsteps. While he waited for the Bouchard family to return from their winter spent in Boca Raton.

He had been grateful when Henri Villebrun had come

with a horse and sleigh to help him transport his few belongings across the river. A gratefulness that had given way to trepidation as he felt Madame Villebrun's finger in his back, directing him across the room, as he was urged towards a table and the chairs set around it. I want you to think of this as being your home, she told him. The budgie bird screeched and rocked on its perch inside a cage hanging before the window. Marcel, hey, sweetie, you remember Oliver, yes? Marcel likes you, she proclaimed, when the bird came over to the door of the cage and began nipping at its bars.

The ferry nudged into the landing, and Villebrun pushed himself away from the car and went over to its door, signalling that their business meeting had ended. Near to thirty years of Oliver's life was finished, a marriage of sorts was over, leaving him nothing and nowhere to go. The ferry strained against the guide wires, tugged sideways by the current near the shore, and Oliver thought, cut her loose. Let the whole shebang drift downstream. He felt like an abandoned child, except that his body was not that of a child. It had lost its resilience, its ability to fly down a snowy hill on a piece of cardboard without him feeling every bump in his spine. The years had aged him faster than what was necessary to remind a person that the Good Maker had promised human beings a lifespan of three score and ten.

Villebrun was about to climb back into his car, hesitated and then returned. He reached inside a jacket pocket and brought out a wallet, a wad of money unfolding like an accordion as he thumbed through it.

The way she stands, Oliver, it's clear that you owe me. But there's no point in trying to get blood from a stone. I'm not one for that. Ten kids, my God—I guess once you learned how, you couldn't get enough of it. He leered, his lips stretching tautly across his large yellow teeth. Madame told me that I'm to give each of your kids ten dollars, he said. You can bet your britches she didn't know what she was getting into when she said that. A hundred smackers, he added, with a wry chuckle. Tell you what. You shut her down for me. I've sold the furnishings to a junk dealer I met in Florida, a fella from Winnipeg.

I know, Oliver said. I've met him. He came round yesterday. The man in the cream-coloured suit and his moll, he thought.

I was going to write and tell you, Villebrun said, looking away. Then I thought I should come and see the old girl before she's closed. Listen, the man wrote a cheque on the spot, a thousand bucks sight unseen, I couldn't refuse. You make sure everything goes smoothly, eh? Especially that the men at the transfer company take special care with those mirrors. You see to that, Oliver, my good man, and I'll consider us square.

The ferry drifted to a stop. It bumped into the platform, the swell of water rising and falling under Oliver's feet. He was surprised to discover that the bills were warm from the man's body, surprised when once again, just as Villebrun was about to get into the car, he hesitated, then returned to Oliver with the alligator belt. A little remembrance, he said abruptly, shoving the belt into Oliver's hands before turning away, as though not wanting to risk a display of emotions.

Oliver should have stayed in Winnipeg; like Romeo, he might have found a steady woman who understood his ways.

They might have frequented the horse races, a bingo hall, taken in the picture shows and an occasional celebration of the Eucharist. If Romeo could turn a blind eye to the hypocrisy of a sinning priest for the sake of his soul and those of his children, then surely Oliver might have too. Stay away from that one, Romeo had warned Oliver of Father Carrière, he's a bugger, that one.

He chose to think this and to forget about his brother's deep pain, his need to numb it with alcohol; his own despair when, after a night of partying, he was given a bum's rush out into the street, the words *drunken half-breed* tossed out after him.

He imagined now, with mounting acrimony, that his life might have unrolled into an ordinary carpet of events if it hadn't been for Alice's father. Human nature caused a person to strain against a dictate such as the one given by her father, that Oliver must prove himself, prove he was good enough, become a man of substance in order to win Alice's hand. His life would have evolved differently if his own father had been present to tell him that just being who he was was already good enough. His and Alice's future had been determined by a man who was now unable to control his own bladder.

Villebrun's car sprang to life, followed by the engine of a truck parked beyond the landing, waiting to embark.

Oliver watched as Villebrun drove away and the truck lumbered onto the ferry. He decided that he would travel across with it, as he needed time to collect his thoughts before returning to Union Plains. Sara was in bed, flat on her back with what was likely morning sickness, and a sickness of his own gripped his body. He sometimes joked that he was aiming for twelve children because he'd heard that they were cheaper by the dozen, but he hadn't aimed for anything. The Vandals had just happened; they had happened to him while he was out seeing a man about a dog.

Oliver wound the belt Villebrun had given him around his hand and felt the bite of its stiff leather. His eye was drawn to a radiation of ripples where a fish had surfaced. He thought about being near to the age of forty-five and having nothing to show but an expanding waistline and regret. He unwound the belt, swung it about his head and let it fly. It came down near the rippling circle and he watched it sink, imagining the fish swerving, darting down into the hidden world.

The ferry landed and as the truck drove off, Oliver followed it. Without thinking, he took the usual route to the Bouchard house, a path running parallel to the river and Main Street, which branched off at the various houses along the way to go up an incline and through a growth of chokecherry, coming to an end at the edge of yards. When he travelled this path during the night, he was guided by the lit windows, moonlight shining on a roof beyond the trees. Today, through the trees, he was afforded a glimpse of the backyard sheds and privies, what remained of his childhood.

The river gave off a slippery odour of the bullheads he had once caught just to feel their slimy tough skin before throwing them back. Then a faint whiff of effluence reached him, and grew stronger with each step. He could see a patch of colour moving in the Bouchard yard, and as he went up the incline through the bushes, he realized that Alice was on her knees in the garden. He was surprised by that, as he'd never thought she was one to put her hand to growing things.

He hesitated before opening the gate. He'd come without a piece of news to entertain her. He wasn't about to tell her about the hotel closing, either. He always imagined that she was hungry for news, that since her aging parents had stopped travelling to escape the winters, she'd become the Rapunzel of a child's fairy tale.

He might tell her, A man took his own life. He went into the barn after supper one night and hanged himself. What was strange about it was that his wife didn't notice him gone until morning. Oliver didn't know if he envied or pitied a man whose wife didn't miss him for an entire night. One Saturday evening, a car had gone off the end of the ferry into ten feet of water. Luckily none of the passengers, all of them kids, had suffered anything more than a scare. But the accident had fired up talks about there being a need for a bridge, and of shutting down the ferry.

He might say to Alice, there was this kid whose father died, and his mother soon after. A skinny and scared orphan kid. He woke up and found himself on a couch in Madame Villebrun's parlour, and in the woman's drunken embrace. His head rocked and his mouth was thick near to choking with the sweetish taste of sherry. He found himself pinned by her arm slung over his waist, his nose buried into her bosoms, which was why he'd come to. His brain was starved for air.

What Madame Villebrun thought would make him chirpy was to sip at a finger of sherry. She knew from rumours that the mothers of his kind calmed a baby's colic with a twist of cloth filled with sugar and dipped in brandy. They filled their babies' milk bottles with beer so they would sleep more soundly in the barn, bundled into a bed of straw, or in a sling cradle hung from the rafters, while their parents wore their shoes out dancing.

On Sundays after his mother died, Oliver had been invited to share the Villebruns' meal of a boiled chicken, an anemic-looking bird splayed across a platter, arranged with potatoes or turnips, or carrots Oliver pulled from the hotel garden. A garden he'd set to growing behind the livery; he'd learned from Johnny, a young Hutterite, to store the root vegetables in bins of sand in the cellar. Weekly, Johnny delivered a live hen in a gunny sack, which Oliver butchered, drew and plucked. When he'd finished scrubbing a week's filth from the parlour floor, he bathed in the kitchen sink, washed the bird in the same sink and cooked Sunday dinner. He took it upstairs to the Villebruns, to be consumed with a bottle of sweet vermouth.

Every Sunday he'd cooked and dined on boiled chicken, and afterwards, while Villebrun slept off the meal and the vermouth in the bedroom, Madame Villebrun had tried to seduce him. The patting, the light touches that were meant to seem motherly, fed her own need for affection. A need that brought her to his room to sit beside him and stroke his forehead, his shoulders, his stomach.

Until he'd got wise and thought to empty his glass into hers, and put a hook on the door of his room. That stopped her flat. But he'd never been freed of thinking about those encounters.

To this day Oliver can't stomach the smell of boiled chicken, a pot rimmed and swimming with grease. It speaks to him of dirt left in corners, mildewed closets, a woman whose body is in need of a good wash, covering her scent with too much cologne.

It took all of his weight to push open the gate, whose hinges were rusty. At the squeal of metal, Alice exclaimed and got to her feet. She was wearing the burnt-orange dress she had worn last night, the front of it and her hands streaked with soil. For some reason, Oliver found this appealing. She hurried to meet him, glancing back at the house several times, and at him, her eyes holding a familiar pleading.

A plea that he stitch together the mangled bodies of her rabbits when a dog had got into the hutch, that he somehow breathe life back into them. That he rescue a kite caught in the high branches of a tree; that he remain loyal and at the same time stay on the periphery of her life, sustained by a treacle of words—*My dear Oliver*—and a girlish, tentative kiss on the day of his mother's funeral, which she'd renewed from time to time with occasional pecks at his mouth and cheeks. Her kiss last night, however, had been hard and urgent, a woman's kiss.

He had come unprepared, without news to ease them into one another's presence while he watched for signs that would tell him she had changed, had taken a beau, perhaps. Her travels had put more than miles between them. Recently he had found that the everyday wear of the years was polishing her heart to a hard smoothness. And so he was taken by this old softness in her, this pleading in her eyes, a shakiness of uncertainty over someone having vandalized her car.

Why my car? Alice asked him, and Oliver thought, as usual, we can read each other's minds.

There were other cars parked where I was parked. And they weren't touched. Why mine? she asked, and gave him her hand.

FIFTEEN

Fending for themselves

SARA HAD HEARD OLIVER and the children leave the house when they went off to school, and she'd wanted to leap up and rap hard on the window, but it was as though a hand pushed her backwards onto the bed. Yes, go ahead, she said, make a show of being a father. She sliced the air, imagining that she was splitting herself and Oliver apart as though this were possible. As though during their first night of lovemaking they hadn't left something of themselves behind in a newly formed creature, Sara and Oliver. It had come into being during the mingling of their breaths, heartbeats and thoughts, and in their absence it cried out to them like an abandoned child needing its parents in order to be complete.

Her stomach had lurched when she'd said the word *father*. Papa, father. She was near to being forty years old and her throat clogged with a longing to be taken onto her father's knee. She'd heard the radio in the kitchen going silent, Patsy Anne banging for attention, the arrival and departure of Stevenson, the water man. For near to an hour now the house had been quiet, and the clock's ticking on the bureau seemed louder as its hands moved closer to noon.

The sun rose up the sharp slope of the roof and turned the whites hanging from Florence Dressler's clothesline even whiter. Florence squinted against the brightness as once again she came from the house and walked the length of the line of laundry, touching the clothes although she knew they had dried. She used the laundry as an excuse to peer through the spaces between the cranberry hedge and into the Vandals' yard.

She gnawed her lip at the sight of the baby still asleep in the playpen, and the sun growing hotter. Stevenson had alerted her to the situation before he'd left, and she had taken the liberty of covering the playpen with a sheet from the line to provide shade, all the while watching the kitchen window for signs of Sara, apprehensive that she might take the gesture as a slur. Sunburn is sunburn, Florence reasoned, and for the sake of Patsy Anne she was willing to take the risk.

She was puzzled that Sara's clotheslines weren't hung with the wash, that she didn't hear the slosh and chug of the machine in the back porch. Even more puzzling had been Sharon, the three-year-old, digging in the garden wearing nothing more than a pair of underpants, her pink dress in a heap in the sandbox, where she'd taken it off. Sharon, having learned how buttons and fasteners worked, was of the age to disrobe for the pleasure of having the option. For the pleasure of causing the kids to go screaming into the house to tell Sara that she had done so, and of having Sara come running out in a fluster of embarrassment. The swat on Sharon's backside being worth the effort of undressing because of the excitement she had sparked.

But Sharon was no longer in the garden, Florence noted, and the pink dress no longer in the sandbox. She reasoned that Ruby must have taken her into the house.

—

Sara lay on the bed thinking that the quiet in the house meant Alvina had hauled the stroller out of the backyard shed and gone walking with the girls. The quiet seemed to be a person, a stranger moving through the downstairs rooms and into the front hall, ascending the stairs. A sudden quiet often preceded a crack of thunder, the screams of one of the kids being injured. Silence usually meant that Manny was up to something and the rest of the kids were in collusion, or Alvina was at the mirror in the girls' room, dabbing lipstick on her mouth, shoving out her chest, practising looking like a hussy.

Silence meant that The Other One was at the table in the dining room, perspiring and chewing his fingernails ragged as he studied for a test. Sonny Boy was about to take a chance for the sake of it, as he had done ever since being able to walk. Climbing onto the roof, riding his bicycle with his hands in his trouser pockets, stealing vegetables from the widow Anderson's garden.

Last Halloween Sonny and the Bogg brothers had attracted the attention of Constable Krooke when they hoisted a teacher's car onto the roof of the creamery. Sonny Boy liked showing off to girls, Alvina had reported. She'd heard that he and the Bogg brothers were picking French girls up in Aubigny and the boys of that town had challenged them to a game of chicken on Stage Coach Road. The details of the car-racing game had passed Sara by, as she'd become rooted on the word *girls*. Sonny Boy and girls. At sixteen? She began noticing his irritation when she came near him, that he shrugged her hand from his shoulder.

Sara could not have imagined that at this very moment Sonny Boy was teetering along the hand railing of the Morris Alexander bridge, a two-storey-high structure spanning the Red River near the town. The current was swift and the channel still swollen from spring high-water, and sometimes animals venturing into the shallows to drink were swept away and drowned. The Bogg brothers were among several other high school boys who paused to watch as one of those hapless creatures, a cow, came floating towards them, rolling onto its bloated side as it emerged from under the bridge and cast them a look with its opaque and sightless eye, giving them the shudders.

Their mouths hung open when Sonny Boy reached a crossbeam and hiked up onto it, his hands gripping its sides as he half walked and half crawled up its slope to a girder. Then he stepped onto the girder and inched across it to another crossbeam, and pulled himself up to the second of several level girders, where most of the boys who were watching had already, at one time or another, etched their initials in its silver paint. B.B. T.B., Sonny read the Bogg brothers' initials aloud. K.M. sucks cocks, he read, which brought a round of laughter.

They expected he would take his knife from its sheath and scratch his initials into the paint, and were as surprised as Sonny was when he grabbed hold of a cable and swung himself up onto another crossbeam. He straddled it and humped up its cold length, noticing that the higher he went, the narrower the river seemed to be, a yellow sluggish snake of water. The cow's carcass looked like a rusted barrel as it rounded a curve and floated out of sight.

The top beam of the bridge vibrated with the river's flow, and Sonny Boy felt it behind his knees as he sat, his legs dangling, not daring to look down at the treetops or the sprawling town beyond, or at the composite high school downstream and near the river, a new two-storey stucco building on a rise of land. The wind had grown stronger the higher he climbed, and he could hear the girders and cables humming. Nausea clutched at his stomach, and his hands were cold and clammy as he fumbled for his belt and the knife, at the same time fearing that the pressure needed to scar the paint would put him off balance.

Sara's fussing at Sonny Boy when she straightened his collar, her anxious eyes watching as he consumed the food she'd prepared, her eyes following him throughout the house had sent him racing across the fields towards the horizon, sent him shimmying up the bridge to the top span, where no one else had gone. His knuckles whitened and his hand shook as he scratched the letters N.V.; then he raised his arm in triumph. The boys cheered, stuck their fingers between their teeth and whistled, the shrill sound resounding in the steel around Sonny, echoing from the school grounds of Alexander Morris Composite and a moment later being answered by the harsh buzzer signalling students that it was time to change classrooms, time to return.

The boys watched Sonny's slow descent; Sonny watched himself descend, the careful and exact placement of his hands and feet belying the nature that had been attached to him—devil-may-care, dauntless. If anyone tried to get Sonny with a bowling ball, he, Norbert Vandal, and not the Bogg brothers, would see to it that they paid. Norbert, not Sonny

Boy. The nickname was becoming a relic, like the buffalo on the wall in the beer parlour, which had been patted and fondled and admired near to wearing out.

Sara did not for a moment think that the silence creeping through the rooms of the house was Ruby, going about on tiptoe lest she awaken Sara. She'd crept up the stairs and down the hall, and peered into the room and saw her mother, the bedsheet tucked around her body, eyes closed and hands folded on her bosom.

Mom.

Mom.

The ladybugs had come back, they were coming through the wooden splinters of what had been the kitchen doorsill, under the doormat and across the floor, and disappearing under the refrigerator.

Mom.

When last Ruby had looked at the clock, it had said the time was 11:20, which she knew was near to twelve. *Hickory dickory dock, the mouse ran up the clock, the clock struck one.* I'm leaving, the water man had called into the back porch. Anybody home? he had asked, startling Ruby into realizing that she was sitting at the play table on the chair she had intended to carry outside and set beside the playpen, turning the pages of the storybook she'd planned on looking at while watching Patsy Anne.

The water man's truck rumbled away down the road, and the kitchen grew silent except for the steady *plop, plop* sound of the perpetual drinking bird dipping its long beak into the glass of water. Ruby noticed the ladybugs, like spatters of paint moving against the white splintered wood and across the lime-green floor.

Mom, she whispered, and when Sara moaned she tiptoed back down the hall.

Good morning to you, we're all in our places with bright smiling faces, Ruby thought, as she wrenched the vise grips on the refrigerator door and felt the clasp give way. *Oh, this is the way to start a new day.* As she would sing when she started school. Sit up straight, make a church steeple of your hands and put them on the desk in front of you. Good morning, boys and girls. Good morning, teacher. *She'll be riding six white horses, when she comes, woah, back!* No, no, Ruby. That's a grade three song. You'll sing that in grade three.

If Ruby needed to go pee she would raise her hand. If she needed a drink of water, she'd do the same. The water cooler was in the cloakroom, a big upside-down bottle with cone-shaped paper containers. You pull one of those paper cups out of the holder, you turn the little tap on the water cooler and you'll get water. If you spill some, you're in trouble.

The heavy refrigerator door swung open on its hinges and crashed into the wall. She took out a plate stacked with leftover flapjacks and set them on the table, then a half-filled bottle of milk. Going between the refrigerator and table carrying a jar of pickles, rhubarb jam, struggling with a two-quart jar of butter soup that Sara had intended for their supper meal, the leftover bowls of porridge that Alvina, in her rush to be away, hadn't put into a container. Ruby took out the blue bottle of milk of magnesium, which Oliver sometimes gulped down without bothering with a spoon; a piece of stinky feet cheese wrapped in wax paper, which no one but he would eat.

She pulled a chair over to the cupboard and climbed up onto it, opening the cupboard doors and taking down the melamine plates, mustard-colour for the boys, maroon for the girls, her eyes travelling up to the second shelf and the third, where, she knew, was the statue Aunt Annie had given to her mother following a trip to New York.

The Umpire Skate Building, Ruby thought as she took it down, not anticipating its heaviness, and it slipped from her hands and tumbled to the floor.

Oh, no, oh no, oh no. Sharon played with it, Ruby thought, as she bustled down from the countertop, onto the chair and then to the floor, thinking, I didn't do it, Sharon played with it, and then she thought, Sharon?

The porch door swung shut behind Ruby as she stepped outside and saw that someone had made a tent out of the playpen, and the stillness inside it told her that Patsy Anne was asleep. The tires of the water truck had flattened the quack grass and weeds from the front of the house to the back and the water cistern. Whose lid was pushed aside, the chain curled beside it and the key still in its padlock. You kids stay away, that's not something you want to fool with. There's five feet of water in there, which was higher than Ruby or Sharon, or Manny or Simon. It was up to Emilie's eyes, they had calculated, and if ever Emilie fell into the cistern, she would need to bob up and down on her toes in order to breathe, until someone rescued her.

Ruby knelt on the cement and stretched out on her stomach, the cement cool now that the cistern was full. She pulled herself along on her elbows, inching near to the blackness of the water, the light shining on its surface making it look even blacker. She saw her head, she saw what looked like a cloud of pink hollyhocks floating just beneath the surface of the water, which she knew was Sharon's dress. And then suddenly Ruby was yanked upright by the arm, and looking into Alvina's terrified face.

Go and get Dad, Alvina shouted to Emilie, who took off running. Then Alvina crouched over the cistern hole and yelled, Sharon! As though she expected the three-year-old would swim to the surface and hold up a hand. And not come stumbling out of the backyard shed, as Sharon did now—half-naked, her cheeks spots of colour as she rubbed sleep from her eyes.

SIXTEEN

Unfinished business

OLIVER HAD LEFT THE HOUSE that morning intending to outdistance his shadow, and wound up entering a backyard garden shed with Alice Bouchard. The shed door closed behind them. A hook clinked into an eye as she locked it, and Oliver became acutely aware that they were alone. They were enclosed in a sepia-coloured light, a confinement of the sun's heat, the air full-blown with the odour of the earthen floor. An atmosphere that was similar to being in a tent, a containment, an aura of secrecy that was an aphrodisiac overcoming whatever doubts Oliver might have had about the wisdom of being there.

He reached for her and she skittered out of his hands, her laughter girlish as she turned away from him to swiftly undress. Her clothes lay in a scented pool at her feet—a flower, he thought vaguely, roses—as she faced him naked in her narrow body. Her skin was prickled with gooseflesh and the colour of worn porcelain, breasts like small firm pears, and she wore them high. Wait, wait, she said, as Oliver went to caress her.

Her flanks flashed white in the half-light when she reached under an overturned wheelbarrow and brought out a Hudson Bay blanket encased in plastic. She unwrapped it quickly and spread it across the floor in a way that suggested she'd thought about doing so. She had prepared for this moment by clearing space in the centre of the floor, had stacked plant pots and wooden seeding flats around the perimeter of the walls.

Of course, Oliver had thought about this happening. It had always been there between them when they sat in the kitchen and in the dining room, with only the dim hall lamp shedding its tepid light, the glow of a fish tank illuminating that withheld desire. Oliver might have hinted that they do more than talk, than play cards, if he'd thought there was the slightest chance she could be persuaded. And yet he felt a sudden shyness as he knelt beside her on the blanket. He shed his trousers and boxers in one swift movement. As though, if he didn't, he might not shed them. As though he was determined to defeat whatever doubts he might have. He peeled off his shirt without unbuttoning it. She opened her arms to receive him in an embrace, her smile self-conscious, hesitant. Yes, she said quietly, and then a resounding Yes!, her face leavened with desire. He climbed onto her at once because he was mindful of his paunch. She pressed her mouth against his shoulder and moaned, her body grew taut and quivered against his.

And then it was done, and Oliver lay beside her, his heartbeat growing quiet. From the river came a harsh cry that sounded like a heron, but he hadn't seen herons in years. A person had to go farther north, near the delta, up where the river emptied into the lake, in order to see herons and cranes. He'd gone with Romeo to his summer camp once and seen those birds among the reeds. His brother had cupped his hands and made the sound of the birds and they had raised their heads. But not here. Not now.

A desire for sleep was a woollen hood that kept wanting to slide down over his brain. He'd once seen a whooping crane in a store window, inside a glass case. Those birds were gone, the passenger pigeons too, the buffalo. Conjured away by the priests, according to his grandmother's remembrances. He recalled Romeo's hand sweeping across the land. Geez, must have been something to see, eh? Sometimes, at the plant, they call me Old Buffalo, Romeo said. Why not stay for a day or two? Wouldn't kill you. Oliver turned away from the urgency in his brother's voice. Romeo wanted the two of them to camp, but the tug of responsibilities was too strong for Oliver to deny. This is as close as I come to being Old Buffalo, Romeo said, smiling to hide his disappointment. Perhaps Romeo had wanted to talk about the priest, Oliver thought now. His brother had wanted to tell him what he already knew from rumours, and from what other boys had said. Unlike Romeo, they'd been able to jeer and draw pitiful caricatures of the man of the cloth.

What is it? Alice asked, as Oliver sighed deeply. He remained silent.

She lay beside him, her head cradled in the crook of his arm, the scent of her hair making him want to sneeze. Minute by minute he was fading, sinking into a sadness, and his throat tightened. He might have admitted to Alice now that he'd been jealous of her music training. Or he might have said, You were right. I was nothing more than a joe-boy to Henri Villebrun. Which was exactly what he would have been to her father, too. He remembered entering her father's garage with his cap in hand. Hearing the man say, And what would you, a person without training do, sir? Not mechanics, that's for certain. And I can sweep my own floors. When a person is about to dish out big money for a car, it's a man's reputation that sells it to them. What the man stands for in the community. The weight of his word with the manager at the caisse populaire, the Bank of Montreal. Go and prove yourself elsewhere and on your own time, her father had said. A man's reputation, apparently, was determined by money, and the influence he wielded because he had money.

And not by wisdom, fair play and generosity. The success of any man's livelihood used to depend on such traits: honesty, courage, loyalty, fidelity. Traits that made for a successful buffalo hunt. Oliver yearned to have been alive during those times, when good traits were a necessary part of everyday life. He sometimes longed to have been part of a hunt, to have experienced the time his grandmother had described in her talk with the *Winnipeg Tribune* reporter.

It's strange, Alice said. It doesn't seem to matter how much time goes by, I still feel the same about you. I've been missing you more and more, not less.

You don't say, Oliver replied, her words causing discomfort. He purposefully did not imagine what she might be doing or thinking as she went about her life across the river. Her name, uttered by someone in passing, was a stone that made him stumble momentarily, and then he got on with what he was doing. Sunlight passed through cracks in the garden shed, illuminating a slash of skin on her ribs and a sprinkling of tiny red moles. He'd known her all his life. And yet, while he had adored her, he hadn't really known her. Her leg, crooked over his hip, grew heavy. An ache rose in his back, an uncomfortable dampness gradually seeped through the blanket. He might have fallen asleep for a moment, as it seemed that the angle of light coming through the cracks had changed imperceptibly, enough that he felt the shed had become larger.

From across the yard came a sound of a door opening and closing. Oliver turned his head towards it to listen, and saw that there was something moving near the base of a plant pot. What looked to be a patch of dark colour became a swarm of insects. A writhing and churning bed of ladybugs crawling overtop and under one another and up the sides of the pot. Hundreds of ladybugs of various sizes and shades of red, their glossy bodies looking as though they'd been painted in nail varnish. The insects had been brought to life by the uncommon heat of this June day, and meant to spread out, to mate and establish themselves in the world of the shed. As Sara feared they would do in the kitchen.

The kids. Sara. Word would reach them about the hotel, if it hadn't already.

Alice? Madame Bouchard called from the back step, her voice a pigeon's coo. Alice?

Alice rose up on an elbow, her fingers against Oliver's lips. She gestured to the door, its hook being fastened.

Hoo, hoo, Alice? Madame Bouchard called.

The clot of ladybugs had come apart, and strings of bugs were crawling off in all directions across the earthen floor and up the sides of other pots. Several were within inches of the blanket. The buggers could bite. Just before they clicked their hard shells and took off with their orange fingernail-clipping wings, they would take a chunk out of you. Oliver swore and pushed away from Alice, not caring if her mother heard.

Mama! For the love of Christ, go away, Alice called out in anger. Spoons of wetness shone beneath her eyes, smudged with mascara. She looked older than what she was, and tired.

That's no way to talk, Madame Bouchard said reprovingly. Who's that with you? Alice? she asked, when Alice didn't reply.

Oliver was gripped by panic as he tucked his shirt in and fastened his belt, recovered his boots from the edge of the blanket and stuffed his socks into a trouser pocket. He had to get home before the news broke. He fumbled with the bootlaces, his fingers gone stiff.

When will I see you again? Alice asked.

I can't say, he said. Don't wait, he thought to say, because he didn't know what, if anything, was certain any longer. He reached the door and undid its hook. It occurred to him that he'd put a similar hook on the door of his room under the stairs, in order to keep someone out. He was certain this hook was there to prevent them from being happened upon. He recalled Alice's kiss last night, her tears. A hooligan had vandalized the tires on her car and she was feeling small. Feeling the waning of her beauty, perhaps. As in the past, she had counted on him to rescue her. To rescue her from the boredom of caring for old people.

He burst through the shed door with an urgency to return home, without acknowledging the presence of Alice's startled mother. He didn't stop to close the gate, and went careering down the embankment towards the path, grabbing on to branches to keep himself from stumbling on the knots of tree roots. He hurried along, pursued by a dread that soon caught up with him and rode on his shoulders. He was remembering the call he'd heard earlier. The piercing sound of it.

He was remembering long ago, a sparrow landing on a snowy windowsill to announce that his father's spirit was departing. Oliver entered the radiating cold of an ice house and, through the fog of his own breath, saw his father laid out on blocks of ice. Then he went off to school, hoping that he'd find himself there, but the boy he'd been the previous day had vanished. The birdlike call he had heard while heading towards the ferry earlier had been like that. It had been an announcement that something irredeemable was about to be lost.

The ferry was midway across the river and moving towards him as Oliver came down the slope of the road. Ulysse, seeing him, seemed to grow taller. He put his hands to his hips as though asking, what has kept you? He was coming without ferrying a vehicle.

They didn't speak until they were well underway, Ulysse folded into his chair and sucking on an unlit pipe. His tan-coloured clothing, rumpled and blotchy with new and old oil stains, brought to mind a cocoon that had just been vacated. Ulysse broke the silence by saying, What in hell are you doing taking up with that rice-powdered woman? It wasn't a question but a gruff chiding. That's no way to do it. There's no answers to be found at the bottom of a bottle. Or at the bottom of a woman, either.

Despite his anxiety, Oliver grinned. You're a joker, he said. He realized that he hadn't put on his tie, that it lolled from a shirt pocket like a maroon tongue. He swiped at his mouth with the back of a hand; he could smell lipstick and so, likely, he was wearing it. Once again he thought of the hook on the garden door, and wondered now whether it was new, or had it been there for years and used for the same reason it had been used today? To keep Alice from being interrupted while she entertained? He chuckled inwardly at the thought. That steamy old girl. She'd found a way to skin the cat, and right under her parents' noses. God bless her.

Listen here, Ulysse said. I just seen Roger Delorme. He says to tell you there's a chair waiting for you in Alexander, if you want it. He's getting too old. Gonna quit. He says he'll train you to get your licence. He's a master at barbering. You could take over from him, Ulysse said.

Anger raised the hair at the nape of Oliver's neck. God damned hell to Christ and Mary. If the barber in Alexander Morris had heard he'd be out of a job, likely everyone in the entire Red River valley knew it too. Everyone had known before him that the hotel was going to be shut down. It's like I'm a kid to be talked about. Discussed. Someone to be pitied, or humoured, or allowances made for what he might lack. The people around him had the luxury to choose their own way, while his course had been set by circumstances and chance.

He struck out along the highway, going south, energized with the determination to keep walking until his legs failed him—all night, the next day, if possible. He'd shelter in a farmer's shed, or a stack of crumbling straw bales, hunger making him stronger, not weak. His body nourishing itself—he'd heard of some prisoners of war gaining weight just thinking of food—but he'd need to find potable water. His hair would clean itself, his unwashed body would become acidic with a natural poison that thwarted germs.

A vehicle approached from behind and he turned to face it. Why not? he thought, and stuck out his thumb. The young man was taking a load of gravel to Alexander Morris. That's as far as I'm going, he shouted over the noise of the engine as they took off. I know you, don't I? he asked, a young man about the age of Sonny Boy, a decent hard-working fella, son of a farmer. I know your dad, Oliver said, despite his vow not to become engaged—a foolhardy vow, he realized, given that he was known up and down the valley. We're going to Texas next harvest, the young man said. Me and my dad, and my brothers. We're going to combine and make some good hard cash.

The youngster drove with his arms hugging the wheel, peering into his destiny, bright-eyed and bushy-tailed. Texas, as far as that, Oliver thought. He'd spent his young life traversing the goddamned river. They rode the remainder of the way to Alexander Morris in silence, Oliver mulling over the young man's words. Yes, why not go as far south as Texas?

When they entered the town, Oliver got out on Main Street, a broad paved street that was shiny with store picture windows, red and blue plastic flags fluttering on the car dealer's lot. Main Street was lined with garages, cafés, banks, the red-brick post office and elementary school. Kids such as Sonny Boy were attracted to its bowling alley and movie theatre. The dairy owner had bought a machine from Switzerland that dispensed soft swirls of ice cream that were then dipped in chocolate. Two traffic lights had been installed on Main Street when the high school went composite. Kids such as his own, who were driven and bused into town, strolled downtown at lunchtime, frequented the drugstore, the poolroom, the several cafés, and caused a traffic jam.

Oliver came near the hotel, a three-storey building that had recently been painted, and a neon sign hung over the entrance. *Eat Here, Get Gas,* the sign invited, which always made him chuckle, but today he thought, the hotel's got no business dealing in gasoline. The proprietor had his fingers in too many pies, including the barber-shop space he rented to Roger Delorme. Oliver crossed the street, rather than go past the large window and be seen.

He might have dropped in on Delorme, as he did once a month to have his ears lowered. He might have jawed with the man to see what would transpire. But he recalled too vividly his short and unprofitable stint as a barber's apprentice in the city. As soon as he'd revealed his barbering experience to the army, they had slapped him into another shop, and he had given up hoping he'd receive some training—mechanics, perhaps medical, something he could put his hand to if he decided not to return to the hotel. He recalled the festering splinters of hair embedded in his shoulders and chest. The need to groom his body with tweezers, his stomach going queasy over the thought of other people's hair sprouting from his pores.

Minutes later he had reached the cemetery and the town's southerly limit, his resolve to keep walking gaining strength. South, and not east, where he might find work on the lakers, as he'd heard of others doing. South to St. Paul, where Metis traders had once taken their hides and furs. Once again, as a vehicle approached, he stuck out his thumb. This time, the driver was going as far as St. Jean.

Minutes later they arrived at the small community and, on a whim, Oliver went roaming through the several short streets. He soon found what he was looking for. He knew his grandmother's house was now occupied by a bachelor, a man named Sabourin. He was in his eighties, but it was rumoured he still went trapping. Years ago he'd come to see Oliver at the hotel, to express an interest in acquiring the traps. Oliver had declined, without thinking. He planned on using them, he said. Now he wondered, why hadn't he let them go? The traps had become badly rusted, the chains almost eaten through in spots. He suspected they were no longer of any use to anyone.

He went past the house, noting that its yard was overgrown with bushes. In his mind he saw his grandmother seated on her bed, and spread about her on a patchwork quilt were pieces of fur and leather. Her stomach rested on her knees, her thick lips shone with saliva as she called to him to come and sit beside her. Her voice was broad and soft, its nap always brushed high with good nature. Her words rang in his ears.

I was blessed to grow up during the golden years, when there were still many animals and the Indians were pacified. Sometimes you couldn't see the land for the amount of buffalo. The passenger pigeons were as plentiful as the mosquito, then. We caught hundreds of those birds with nets.

In the golden days there was always enough meat in a pot, elk, rabbit, partridge and deer, too. There was visiting around a fire in the evening, the men talking their stories. Making their plans for the following day. And there was always time for music-making. When the sun went down, the missionary, he came through the camp. He rang his bell to call us to his tent for prayers. I remember this being the sweetest time of all, as we kids came running, going through the dark to pray in the priest's tent, just as the dew was gathering in the grass.

The whooping cranes are gone now. Some say that the Fathers conjured the animals and birds away. They prayed away the pigeons because of their all-the-time calling that some people found to be a bother. And the cranes, because they could be a nuisance. Many children were attacked when they got too close to a crane's nest. The bird could run fast and would peck out your eyes if it was mad enough. Our Fathers prayed away the buffalo, so that the hunters would stay home and become farmers. But I believe that the golden days came to an end because the animals didn't care to return.

At that time there were men going around. It was their job to see who had come of age and were old enough to sell their scrip. These agents were given a list by their employers of the names of those who held scrip that hadn't been taken up yet. They went looking to buy it from young men who thought a few dollars was good pay for a piece of paper. When their pockets were empty, some of them became scouts. Others were hired to ride the country doing to others what had just been done to them. Those boys that went to Montana looking for work soon forgot their prayers. They came back hard or beaten and spoiled by women.

My man passed away and I had no land to farm with my children. Early in my life I had noticed that when you lose something, other things can be found. I found that I could work with furs and so I put my hand to that. At first I trapped small animals, until frost got three of my toes. Then I sewed furs. I sewed muffs and hats and later I fashioned pretty jackets for the English women. I made moccasins and gauntlets and tobacco bags.

I am now seventy-seven years old, and I live in St. Jean. I have had a very good life.

Her words were a hollow whistle of wind passing over the top of Oliver's life. *I had noticed that when you lose something, other things can be found.* Oliver looked out across the vast fields, his knees trembling. He felt numbed, as though what he'd come through today had happened to someone else.

He walked for several hours, the miles between him and Union Plains opened up as the dwindling sunlight touched the land. The air smelled like ice, clean, scented with the new growth on fields that were about to burst and greet the summer in full swing. A meadowlark perched on a fence post, its yellow breast a flash of colour as he passed by. Man alive. It was as though he was seeing the breadth of spring for the first time, and realizing what he'd been missing. He knew that families were sitting down to the evening meal, and he thought of his own kids, the little ones seated at the play table beside the refrigerator. He was heading down the highway, going even farther south and away from them.

SEVENTEEN

—

A family gathering

THAT EVENING an odour of woodsmoke brought Florence Dressler to her back door, and to the sight of Kornelius's car parked alongside the Vandal house, the place lit up like a ship at sea. There was a bonfire going in the Vandals' firepit, Emilie hovering over it, poking at the flames with a stick. Sparks flew up, sailed over the cranberry hedge and drifted towards the line of laundry Florence had hung out in the morning.

The laundry would smell of smoke, but she lacked the will to reel it in. This lethargy, a feeling that she was wading through molasses, had slowed her down earlier in the day and she'd realized: of course. On this day eighteen years ago, a section man had failed to close a switch to a side track, and at ten o'clock in the morning a Great Northern train had come roaring through the station and into a grain car shunted onto a siding. Two men had perished, one of them being her husband.

The Vandal house, with its tacked-on back porch, resembled a boot more than a ship at sea. How did Florence cope with being neighbour to that wild bunch? several women of the Women's Workers Club had asked in various ways throughout the years. Monkeys swinging from clotheslines and bringing them down. Contortionists, acrobats; they chanced broken limbs while walking across a rope they'd strung between trees. They were artists painting the unripe pumpkins in the garden a glossy orange enamel. When the girls inherited their brothers' hockey skates they painted them white.

The Vandals went fishing and caught themselves. Fishhooks in a calf, a finger, a cheek. They swam in water-filled ditches and came home with whooping cough, pleurisy; leapt from the shed roof into snowbanks, Ida snagging her lip on one of the half-dozen clotheslines. Sara had said to Florence, Ida's being a cry baby over needing a few little stitches. Sara, pretending to be as tough as nails, when she hadn't got over her unreasonable fear of washing her hair without an adult being in the room. They can cry all they want, Florence thought. Give me just one of those monkeys.

Emilie sat on a log at the edge of the garden, beside the bonfire, whipping the air with the stick. In no time, Florence would put meat on her bones. Sonny Boy and George emerged from the house and ambled off into the darkness. The interior light of Kornelius's car came on, its dim halo illuminating the heads and shoulders of Simon and Manny. Any of the four boys would do.

Whatever was going on over there was none of Florence's business, but she hadn't seen Sara all day. The playpen was still out in the yard; thank the Lord, Alvina had had the sense to bring the baby in out of the sun. The playpen pad would absorb the night dew and become a breeding ground for bacteria, for bugs to set up shop. Bugs had set up shop in the mattress of the carriage Sara had bought second-hand when Sharon was a baby, and Sara had not been able to understand why Sharon had resisted being put to bed in it. Why she awoke so often during the night crying. On Florence's advice,

Oliver had shone a flashlight into the carriage and what Florence suspected had proved to be true. Bedbugs.

There wasn't much to be seen through those windows to spark the curiosity of anyone going past the Vandal house. Two living-room windows through which a person might see the pictures of flying geese in salmon-coloured frames hanging above the sofa. Where Kornelius usually parked himself and read newspapers while waiting for Katy. He was too cheap to purchase his own, Sara said, and so he asked her to save them for when he picked her and the children up for church. Dived into the newspapers first thing, whenever they came to visit.

Sara had appropriated the colour of the flying-geese picture frames for the living-room and dining-room walls, and during the evenings, in the light of the floor lamp, they glowed like twilight and were cozy, but throughout the day the colour was muddy and draining.

The hotel's going to be shut down, Alvina had said to Florence earlier in the day. She'd come over to the hedge with Patsy Anne on her hip, her large flat eyes fearful and hurt-looking as she glanced up at the bedroom window above the back porch. Her eyes asking, now what are we supposed to do?

I know, Florence said. She had heard earlier, when she'd gone to the store for her mail. Everyone in town knew about the man who'd come to take inventory of the hotel, telling Cecil that he now owned the contents. He'd gone through the place with a clipboard that very morning, counting, sticking pieces of paper onto items.

How's your dad taking it? Florence asked, and noted the evasive look in Alvina's eyes.

Who knows? she said with a shrug. Then she said, Anyway, I called my dad's brother and my aunt Katy. Florence knew that Alvina wasn't telling her everything.

Because they had visitors, the Vandals had eaten supper in the dining room. There was a sunset going on when they sat down, and lambent light swam across the salmon-coloured walls, mirroring the children's quivering determination not to notice that their parents' chairs were vacant.

Throughout the meal they felt the prod of silence, Romeo's exacting politeness in the presence of Katy and Kornelius. Yes sir, no madame, he said, refusing to pick up any thread of conversation either of them offered. Refusing to eat anything other than the food Claudette had brought with them on the train. There was an embarrassing moment when Katy and Kornelius bowed their heads and prayed before eating. Praise the Lord and pass the ammunition, Oliver might have said, if he'd been present. Sonny Boy commented *sotto voce* to George that Romeo looked as though he was passing hot coals.

What's that, eh? Romeo asked, his cheeks becoming the colour of cranberries. By cracky, don't you be a wise guy, he added, unusually surly. He shook his fork at Sonny but really he wanted to speak his mind to Kornelius. He'd promised Claudette to remain silent, so instead he said to Sonny, If you're so smart, why don't you bring back your daddy's livelihood, eh?

I can tell time, Ruby said later, following Claudette around the kitchen with adoring eyes as she and Alvina cleared up after the evening meal, which had been held late in hope that Oliver would arrive home. It's 7:22, Ruby announced. Oliver should have eaten supper by now and returned to work. The atmosphere in the house was like a mousetrap set to go off.

Ruby was being a pain, Alvina thought. She'd been unwilling or unable to explain how Sharon's dress had wound up in the cistern, and Alvina had let it go because she didn't want to think of either of the girls being so close to danger as to throw the dress down the hatch. The water man forgot to close the lid, Ruby said accusingly. A mistake he'd made in his worry over the little ones being left to fend for themselves. Alvina shuddered as she thought of the terrifying seconds just before Sharon had come stumbling out through the door of the backyard shed.

Huum, Claudette replied absent-mindedly, and patted Ruby on the head. Claudette's hair was a cloud of auburn, her cheeks highly rouged, the skin of her eyebrows shiny from being shaved, the brows painted on in black. The sleeveless dress she wore was patterned with crimson flowers, her ears glittering with rhinestone earrings. In contrast to Alvina's grey cardigan sweater and pleated skirt, Claudette was a lit-up Christmas tree, a fact Sara had sometimes pointed out.

Claudette and Romeo had surprised them, Simon and Manny the first to spot them coming down the street from the train station, Romeo having left the packing house early in order to catch the four o'clock. Did you check the basement to see if his gun's there? he blurted upon entering the house, and then, seeing the fear in Alvina's eyes, was sorry for having asked. He affected a nonchalance as he went down the stairs into the basement. When he returned moments later, he said, I thought maybe your dad went squirrel-shooting. Give your uncle a kiss. His eyes watered and he smelled of hops and his cheek was feverish when Ruby kissed it. Mad money, he said to Alvina, and gave her a dollar. Just don't go getting mad at me.

The unexpected arrival of Romeo and Claudette failed to draw Sara downstairs. When Katy and Kornelius got there she had dressed and wound up her hair, but had remained in her room. Katy cooked some rice soup and took it up to her. She had brought a canned chicken, a jar of potato salad and buns. At the sight of the food, Claudette grew flustered. You and me were thinking along the same lines, she said with a bashful smile, and produced a package of coconut-coated marshmallows from a shopping bag, and several pounds of bacon, which she went on to fry to a crisp, along with two dozen eggs she scrambled in the grease.

Everything will turn out all right, wait and see, Claudette reassured Alvina once again as they washed and dried the supper dishes. Ruby sat on a chair beside the radio, thinking, *She'll be coming round the mountain when she comes, when she comes. And we'll all go out to greet her when she comes.* There were footsteps in the room above, Aunt Katy walking to and fro saying, *Ja, ja.*

Alvina was unaccustomed to such blatant optimism and she thought Claudette was charming but naive. As much as she doubted that everything would turn out all right, she was grateful to her aunt for making the effort. Ida hung around in the doorway, looking for a chance to horn in on the adult talk, and Alvina shooed her off to the dining-room table to do her homework, and Ruby outside to play with Manny and Simon.

Claudette poured two mugs of coffee and took a flask from her handbag. She carefully measured a scant cap of rum into each of the mugs and then indicated that Alvina should join her at the table. What's sauce for the gander is sauce for the goose, she said, and winked. As soon as the meal was finished, Romeo had rushed from the house to go to the hotel. He'd said he wanted to see for himself that an inventory had been done. And to be there on the chance Oliver showed up. To get sauced, Claudette said. She sat down at the table and leaned back into her chair. The chalkiness of her deodorized armpits glowed white as she ran her fingers through her tousled curls. Then she lit a cigarette and set it into a saucer. That's it, the kitchen's closed, she announced.

Which meant that she was prepared to spend the next several hours visiting, while all hell broke loose around her, and she expected Alvina would do the same. Alvina had already put Patsy Anne and Sharon to bed on the floor in the girls' room, Patsy having graduated from her crib in Sara's room because Katy and Sara needed to talk. She still had to tuck the others in, read to them, listen to their prayers, set out their clothing for the next day of school. Simon required tutoring in arithmetic to recuperate from his test, Manny needed a good talking to about the dangers of playing with matches, although she had not found any matches on him. Claudette pushed the mug of spiked coffee towards her, her eyebrows arching towards the ceiling as the murmuring of Katy's and Sara's voices rose.

That morning Oliver had gone for a stroll and failed to come back. Oh my Lord, Sara had exclaimed, when Emilie returned from the hotel with the news. The girl didn't say that she'd been there once before, or that she'd seen him going along the path to the river that morning. The decrepits swore on their hearts that he hadn't been there. A city slicker driving a flashy Caddie had come in looking for Oliver and had then gone through the hotel as though he owned it, making notes on paper. I do own it, he'd said to Cecil. Everything inside it, that is. Including the chairs you old geezers are sitting on.

Sara had grown strangely serene. Like an exhausted boxer, relieved when a referee steps into the ring and halts the match. The bedroom closet doors were open and their shelves in disarray. Scattered around her on the bed were the letters she and Oliver had exchanged during their almost two years of separation.

In the silence of the day she had gone in search of nuances, a tone, something she might have missed years ago when her understanding of English was lacking. She looked for evidence that Oliver had been unfaithful, and found none. She looked for signs that he took her for a ninny, or that she had read more romance into the lines than he'd intended, and found herself lost in his lilting voice and beautiful script; its flourishes and curlicues were the movement of his body across the page as he composed who he was at that particular moment. She was entranced by his account of the people he'd come to know, could picture them and hear their voices; his descriptions of the destruction that still existed twenty-five years after the explosion at the Halifax harbour were captivating and vivid. His writing mirrored the way he stood with his hand at his waist, its palm turned up, as though he were on stage, about to give a performance.

In comparison, her own handwriting was unimaginative, uncertain and spidery. It was influenced by the German Gothic script she'd been taught in a village classroom in Russia, the letters clumsy-looking as she pushed through to achieve a goal. *The boys will need a wagon to deliver the papers. A cabinet maker came to measure for kitchen cupboards. Today I put up two dozen jars of pickles. Annie is a big help.* Her letters were filled with accounts of the progress of home improvements; she wanted him to be part of it although he was so far away. *I think I may be that way, again,* she'd written, meaning that she was likely pregnant with Emilie following his most recent leave. She had not written that the bed seemed too large, that even amid the constant chatter and duties of the day her heart sometimes lurched with longing for the sound of his footstep.

I was just a child, Sara thought. I was going around in a fury of activity from morning to night in order to keep loneliness at bay. Dog-tired but awake and staring into the darkness of the room, thinking she heard voices, feeling that the room was cavernous, its walls porous and riddled like a dried-out bone. She was a child wanting to hitch a ride out of the constant throb in her chest; out of an ochre-coloured cave on an Easter day, the sun shining on the river below while the people around her hid their faces in their hands and wept. Away from all of that, and into the polished sky beyond the cave, the get-up-and-go of a country called Canada.

This was as far as Oliver had been able to take her. Union Plains, Manitoba. Ten children, and near to twenty years of being irritated and preoccupied by the constant buzz of jealousy. And over what? From the back Oliver still looked good, his shoulders square, his hair thick and not a single grey among the black. But when he stood sideways, that was another thing. His girth gave her a secret glee that she fed him well; he was taking on weight and less and less would she need to worry that someone might steal him away, that he might leave this little German immigrant girl who still couldn't say the word *very* without it sounding like *wery*.

She'd come to realize that his knowledge of the world was suspect, his wisdom a cloak he put on and took off at will. He wasn't who she had thought he would turn out to be once she became better acquainted with the ways of the land. Like her, Oliver was a displaced person. He was out of place and out of time, as much as were the Indians she had seen haunting the periphery of Kornelius's farm.

I wanted to hit that woman, Sara said to Katy, without admitting that she had tried to vandalize Alice's car. Below, in the kitchen, Claudette and Alvina visited, while Sonny Boy and George sat out on the front steps, not speaking, waiting for the Bogg brothers to arrive and take them to Alexander Morris and a movie.

Once Sara began to talk about Alice Bouchard she was unable to stop speaking her fears, suspicions and imaginations, unmindful all the while of the look of distaste growing in Katy's face, as though Sara, in the telling of Oliver's supposed indiscretion, was besmirching herself. She told Katy about the spicy odour Oliver had once brought home on his skin. She told her that she had been sorting the laundry one day and had come upon a pair of his undershorts clotted with semen, a pinch of hair stuck to it. I don't think it was his hair, she said. It seemed finer.

We don't hit people, Katy interjected, warily.

We? Sara said. You hit your children.

I spank them, I correct them. That's different, Katy said. I mean our enemies. We Mennonites, Christians, we're to turn the other cheek.

Oh yes, and where did that get us? Sara asked, meaning the Mennonites in the old country who had refused to protect themselves, and had consequently lost their lives as swiftly as those who had taken up arms in self-defence.

From the front of the house came the sound of an approaching vehicle, then voices, as Sonny Boy and George went to meet the Bogg boys. Katy, relieved at the diversion, got up and went into the girls' room at the front of the house to investigate. She felt short of breath in the face of Sara's intensity, the embarrassing accusations she levelled against Oliver. She reached the window in time to see Sonny Boy and George get into the car. She watched as it went off down the road and turned at the corner. Sonny Boy didn't attend church any more, and Sara hadn't put her foot down, while Oliver refused to be involved. *Ja, ja,* Katy said, with a sigh. And so it goes.

Ja, ja, a small voice chimed out of the darkness, startling Katy. She realized that she had barely missed stepping on Patsy Anne and the little rose, Sharon. The girls stared at her from their made-up bed on the floor, their eyes following her now as she went across the room. Their tuners were set to the tension of the house, which kept them awake yet afraid to venture beyond the perimeter of their mattress. Children gave off what they took in. At the end of the day, when her own children had been particularly cranky, Katy examined her behaviour to find the reason for it. *Schlaft, Kinder, schlaft,* she whispered.

When Alvina had telephoned, Katy had set out for

Union Plains thinking she was coming to tend to an illness, to comfort and reassure Sara that the hotel's closing might prove to be a blessing. Not to witness the end of a marriage. Kornelius's plan to build a new house was timely, and until it was finished the farmhouse would suffice to hold them all.

She returned to Sara and the maroon easy chair on one side of the window, unsettled again by the clutter of her sister's room. She'd needed to clear the chair of clothing before she was able to sit, to step over the pile of shoes at the end of the bed. No matter how clean and ordered the rest of the house, this dishevelled room revealed something about Sara that was a cause of unease. You've spoiled her, Kornelius once said, and perhaps there was some truth to it. But how could she not? Beyond the window she saw Emilie arranging wood on the bonfire. The girl's expression was always shifting, sharp with impatience or dreamy or troubled. But so far she'd not seen in any of the children the kind of anger she sometimes saw in Sara.

Following supper Romeo had left the house quickly, wanting to be away from Kornelius, and his own desire to bring out the land documents and lay them down in front of the man. Give it to him in black and white. He waved to Emilie, who for some reason had been exempted from cleaning-up chores to go outside and build the fire. She sat beside it, hugging herself.

Hey, you there. We had a good time at camp, eh? You want to come with us again this year? Romeo called.

Maybe, she said.

He ambled over to Kornelius's car and watched for a moment as Simon and Manny played games of tic-tac-toe in the dust on its doors. You boys sure are making a mess, he told them, in a way that suggested it was an achievement. Before leaving the yard he called again to Emilie, If you need someone to twist your arm, just say so. You're always welcome to come with us. But you have to let me know in good time so I can pack extra beer.

Despite what she was feeling, Emilie grinned. Okay, she said.

Romeo went off down the road, whistling to cover his anxiety over his brother.

Emilie watched him go, thinking that playing in the shells of rusted-out cars and in the sand dunes might not be as much fun the second time round. Or berry-picking, either. Remembering how the sand held the sun's heat when she'd buried herself in it as protection against the evening mosquitoes, how darkness over the lake became complete. A fire crackled near the tent and the shadows of her older twin cousins playing cards inside it loomed against the white canvas. Beyond the beach, the high voices of her three younger cousins echoed among the trees as they went with Romeo to shine a flashlight on an owl. Claudette dipped fillets in flour at a picnic table, the fish Emilie and her cousins had caught in the early evening while casting from a dock. The fish could not wait, it had to be eaten immediately or why bother fishing? Romeo said. A week-long vacation at this camp on Lake Manitoba slowed Romeo down. It steadied his hands and cleared his eyes. Left him on an even keel to tackle going back to the killing floor.

Emilie fell asleep buried in the sand that night to the sound of waves foaming up the beach, and awoke to the sound of wind buffing the sides of the tent. The fire had been extinguished; Claudette hadn't awakened her to eat the midnight meal of fish but had let her sleep, covering her head with a towel to protect her from the no-see-ums. Emilie felt betrayed, as children sometimes do when they awaken and find themselves in an unexpected place. She felt a momentary flash of anxiety in the sudden awareness that she was alone in the dark. And then she grew calm in the velour darkness of the night. The covering of stars became brighter the more she looked at the sky. She was pleased to know that she wasn't afraid. She freed herself from the blanket of sand and crawled inside the tent, feeling her way among the warm shapes of her sleeping cousins, whose bodies shifted beneath a quilt to make room for her.

In the morning she happened upon several Metis girls berry-picking in a thicket of saskatoon bushes, their mouths smeared with red juice, their voices like twittering birds that broke off instantly when one of them noticed her coming along the sandy road. Seeing the Vandal cousins behind her, they burst out of the bush like a flock of chickadees to greet them. Immediately Emilie found herself surrounded and petted, their fingers like suede as they plucked at her white hair and clothing.

The children belonged to several families who lived in tarpaper shacks, Romeo explained. There was a name for them, Road Allowance People, half-breed squatters who camped along strips of land designated to become roads. It's a hard life, he said. Emilie recalled the girls' dusty hands patting her arms, their heartfelt confession that they loved her and wanted to be her friend. Oh Emilie, Emilie, I love you so much. Emilie, you're so pretty.

But they wouldn't want to be friends with a slut. A slattern, the dictionary defined the word. A slovenly woman, a prostitute. Corrupted. These were new words to be added to the list of reasons why people didn't appreciate Emilie Vandal. Everyone knows what goes on at your house, Charlie's brother, Ross, had said. Everyone knows. You guys sleep all together like sardines in a can.

Charlie's brother wanted to go sightseeing in Winnipeg. Yeah, sure. What Ross really wanted was to sightsee her.

The realization was a rude bolt of lightning parting the air and revealing a world carrying on behind the one Emilie had taken to be real. She was as astonished as she was chagrined to have been so clueless. But since then, she'd hauled out the dictionary. Chagrin and astonishment had made way for disquiet. Slut, slattern, prostitute?

I just can't take it, the sickening thought that Ross had intended to stick his thing into her. And now this, Oliver not coming home for supper. Who do you want to speak to? Madame Bouchard had asked, when Emilie called from the hotel. I am looking for my father. Is he there? Who? Who? she asked, sounding like an owl. Oliver Vandal. You know. We were there last night. I'm sorry, but you 'ave the wrong number, the woman replied, and hung up. Liar, Emilie thought.

Oliver had never failed to show up for supper, or to put Cecil in charge if he wasn't going to be around to open up the parlour. A snow of paper squares had jumped out at Emilie from the dusky light of the beer parlour. From the wall sconces, the walnut panels, the trays of tumblers stacked on shelves behind the bar, the bar itself. The cash register. The door of the broom-closet office was ajar and Emilie noted that the linens on the shelves had been disturbed and also ticketed. So had a box of toilet soap, Oliver's commode and shaving mug. The buffalo robe that should have been hanging from hooks inside the door was gone.

The pieces of paper had shouted at her, The End. The end of Oliver as she knew him. Today a door had opened a crack, and Emilie was now wiser about what might be going on across the river. She would leave. Run away, rather than live in the house without Oliver. She didn't need to know he was home to feel his presence. There was a lightness, the walls expanded with his goodwill. She stabbed at a burning log with a stick and sparks flew up around her shoulders and went skittering across the yard in a confusion of air currents. The log fell apart, its embers exposed and roiling with an intense heat that she felt in her face and arms, and in the warts clustered beneath the Band-Aids on her hand.

She knew that when Ross had come up alongside her in the car, she should not have got in. But she'd sent Charlie away, school had already begun, and she had thought, well, I know how to find Portage Avenue. She could show him that. And the zoo. But they hadn't been on the highway longer than minutes when he turned off it and onto a country road. His sly smile, the word *cutie,* gave way to his real creepy self as he grabbed at the front of her shirt and wrenched at the buttons, his hands hurting the swell of flesh that was becoming her breasts. Tits, he called them. Show me your tits. Come on, cutie. You've done it before. If you can give it to little Charlie, then you can give it me. No, no and no, she said. He wouldn't stop until she bit him. Slut, he shouted.

But he didn't follow when she took off running from the car, thinking, there's that word.

A scuffle of voices rose up from across the yard now, and the interior light of Kornelius's car came on and went off, illuminating for a brief moment the light and dark heads of Simon and Manny. They'd opened the car trunk and Ruby, like an inquisitive cat, had climbed inside it. She sat cross-legged, an impertinent silhouette whose thick braids seemed to be slats of wood bracing her head. Ruby believed that the opened trunk lid protected her from Alvina, the Grim Reaper, who would eventually come to hook them out of the corners of the yard and put an end to their day. She didn't know that Alvina was sipping a rum-laced coffee and feeling that her arms had grown longer. Today Ruby had learned how the seconds ticked off the minutes, the minutes the hour, the hours a day. Alvina was learning how time could stand still.

There was this little boy? Claudette said to Alvina. He lived two houses down from us? He was ice fishing, and his dad had no sooner turned his back when he fell into the hole. By the time they got him out, he was frozen stiff as a board and his heart had stopped beating. While others were planning his funeral, a nurse at the hospital where they took him thought to try and thaw the boy out with hot water bottles and enemas. It worked. His heart started beating. You never saw anything worse, but it turned out fine. He's the same as he was before the accident. That's the way things can sometimes go. Things can look terrible, but turn out fine. She reached across the table and squeezed Alvina's hand. I've known your dad longer than you have. He'll be okay.

Yes, but will I be okay? Alvina wondered. And why was it that the frozen little boy hadn't died, while others had? Sara's four brothers, that child lying in the pit strewn with bodies. She had begun the day worrying that someone or something would put the kibosh on her dream of becoming a Girl Friday, not dreaming that it would turn out to be the hotel being closed. And now she was ending the day wondering why some people were chosen to be saved from harm, while others were not.

Light from the kitchen window illuminated the car's interior, where Manny and Simon investigated its workings. This here's the brake pedal, Manny demonstrated to Simon. During their trips to and from church, Manny sometimes sat between Katy and Kornelius. He'd studied his uncle's movements, his foot coming down on the clutch pedal, his hand shifting the gear on the wheel. Down, up, down, towards you and down. He knew that his uncle kept the key in the glovebox, and how necessary the key was to start the engine.

This is the gas pedal, the shift stick. That there is the glove compartment he said, and inside it, not gloves but a bag of peppermints and the ring of keys. They helped themselves to the candy, crunched them quickly, one after another, until a sugary saliva dripped down their chins and their jaws ached.

What're you eating? Ruby called from the trunk, where she sat on a bag of seed near the spare tire, tools, a gasoline can.

Nothing, Manny said.

I can smell something.

Shut up, you want Alvina to come?

Dipstick, Simon added.

Ruby remained silent. They were eating something that smelled like Chiclets. Just before she'd left the house, the kitchen clock had said 8:45. It was almost an hour past their bedtime.

See this? This thing is for lighting cigarettes. Watch this, Manny said. Kornelius never used the cigarette lighter, or allowed anyone to smoke in his car. Using it drained the battery, he'd explained to Manny when he'd once caught him trying to light a twist of grass. Manny pressed the glowing coils to the dashboard, and the curl of smoke gave off the odour of a cow barn.

The ceiling light in Sara's bedroom obliterated the image of the windmill in the picture hanging beside the door. Sara had purchased the sombre and unattractive print because it reminded her of a windmill she'd seen on a hill overlooking the town of Rosenthal, where her grandparents had lived. Katy relished pointing out to Sara that the windmill in the print stood near to a lashing sea, and not on a green hill overlooking a valley of roses.

No, we don't hit people, Sara said, picking up where they'd left off when Katy had left the room. What we do is run away. You and I.

The words hung between them for a moment, and then, with a bat of her hand, Katy said Phfft! Why bring that up? It's over, finished. She wished now that she had thought to bring some mending.

But not forgotten, Sara said softly. We ran to the greenhouse, and there was screaming. It seemed to go on forever, she thought, even after Katy had pulled the lid over the opening of the hole, and they'd held on to one another in the darkness. She must have fallen asleep, because when Kornelius came to free them, the greenhouse was filled with sunlight, the yard of the Big House beyond was quiet, shapes strewn about on the ground, not moving. A bird came flying across the glass roof. Sometimes when she would work compost into the garden, the odour of humous would start her heart racing, and she suspected that had been the odour of the hole where she and Katy had hidden.

You didn't hear any such thing, Katy said. She leaned across the chair arm to look out the window, vaguely realizing that her hands had grown cold.

Oh, yes I did, Sara said. I heard people screaming, as clear as if it were going on inside the greenhouse and not across the yard where her parents, her sister and four brothers had met their end. I heard men, shouting.

Katy saw Florence Dressler out on her back step, illuminated by a light above the doorway. Coming through her yard was that filthy ill-kept man who ran the ferry, Oliver's uncle.

You were Ruby's age, she told Sara. You're imagining things.

Papa told us, if there was ever any trouble we were supposed to run and hide in the hole in the greenhouse floor, Sara said. But you wouldn't run, Katy. I had to make you go. Isn't that so?

Throughout the years Sara had been careful about what she wanted to remember. She remembered the Taras Bulba cave, the windmill. A dressing table and a clock striking the hour. Now she remembered pulling at Katy's hand, her father screaming at them to run.

Yes, that's so, Katy replied softly. I was too frightened to move. But you weren't, because you didn't know what was really happening. You were just doing what Father told us to do.

I beg your pardon, Sara said. Don't you go and say that my experience wasn't as real as yours because I was the age of Ruby. Don't you tell me anything. I was there.

All right then, Katy said quietly. Why don't you say what you think you remember?

A saxophone began playing and Florence realized the music came from the Vandals' kitchen. Someone had left the window open and tuned the radio to jazz. She saw Sara's sister at the bedroom window above the porch, and then she went away. Now Sara went past the window and returned, again and again, pacing.

There was no pretense that might account for Florence dropping in at the house without her needing to explain why she was still up and roaming about in the dark. There were no blooming flowers that required her compliments, reciprocated with an invitation for coffee, as it sometimes happened, and she would go inside the house and admire the children who came like cats from all corners, hanging over the back of her chair, crouched beneath the table, furtive smiles tugging at their mouths as they eavesdropped on what passed for conversation between her and Sara.

Just then Emilie emerged from the house, carrying a pail. Of water, Florence guessed. The girl planned on dousing the flames. But the pail contained potatoes, not water, and Emilie began dropping the tubers into the hot coals of the fire. She went to the wood stack, returning with an armload of wood, and arranged several pieces teepee-fashion over the embers. Within moments the flames were licking skywards. The car's headlights came on and went off, lighting for an instant the new crown of growth on the highbush cranberry, and Ulysse sitting on a kitchen chair near the fire, smoking his pipe.

The bowl burned through the darkness as he inhaled and sucked back saliva. He had appeared before Emilie through a haze of smoke, his eyes slits in his raisin face as he took in the house and Kornelius's car parked beside it. By golly, he muttered, and fell silent, staring into the embers flaring in a circle of stones.

How're people getting across the river? she asked.

They don't always need to get where they're going, Ulysse replied. He studied her for a moment and said, What're you keeping there under those bandages?

Emilie resisted the impulse to cover her hand, tuck it in her armpit, sit on it. There were eight meaty-looking warts under the adhesive strips. The mother wart was surrounded by a colony of lesser warts of various sizes and colours. Some were pale white, while others were white with a yellowish tinge. The new ones were flesh-coloured. Several of the larger warts looked to be made up of segments that moved when she nudged them, revealing what appeared to be black threads at their cores. In the past she had painted them with nail polish, thinking to starve them of air. She'd soaked them in hot water and tried to pick them loose. Painted them with wart remover, which had burned off the tops, but they always grew back and spread.

Warts, she told Ulysse.

What're you doing with those things? he asked.

Living, she answered. Having a party.

Ulysse sent her to the house to fetch a potato and she assumed that he intended to roast one and so she brought a pailful. If Sonny Boy and George ever returned, or Romeo and Oliver, they might appreciate something more than bread and jam before going to bed.

You bring me one of those *patates,* Ulysse called, when she finished stoking the fire.

He smelled like the mouldering potato bin himself, the sprouts fingering the air for light. He cut the potato in half with a penknife and Emilie thought he meant to eat it. She was surprised when he set the pieces on the ground.

Give us your hand, he said.

She extended it and flinched as Ulysse stripped off the Band-Aids. She felt naked, and shivered the way she did when she got out of a washtub set down in a circle of towel-draped chairs. Like the warts, the parts of her body normally kept covered were more sensitive to the air, which seemed to underline Sara's admonition that her daughters must keep their seats and chests covered at all times. Seats, chests, she said, as though those body parts were pieces of furniture. She required that they wear underpants beneath their pajamas and that the underwear itself never be seen. Except when hung out on a line, and then only on the middle lines, so the apparel was concealed from the yard and street, and whisked into the house the moment it dried.

The sensation of air passing over the warts made Emilie think of insects, their feelers waving to read the direction home.

You want to keep those things? Ulysse asked. His eyes swam with cloudiness. Cataracts, Oliver had said.

Another stupid question. When she didn't answer he rubbed the cut potato on the warts, the starchy wetness making her skin contract. Then he gave the half-potato to her and told her to bury it in the garden.

She dug a hole with her heel, dumped it in and covered it with earth. When she returned Ulysse had finished eating the other half. He wiped his mouth on his sleeve and then opened his hand to reveal a pool of coins. He stirred through it and gave her several. The warts now belonged to him, he told her. He'd just bought them, and within a short time they'd take up house in the potato she'd buried.

Her knuckles tingled as she stirred the embers with a stick to cover the roasting potatoes more deeply. She thought, the ugly duckling is about to turn into a swan. She was too old to believe in fairy tales, but she felt awake all of a sudden, as though Oliver was nearby. She imagined him coming along the highway in the darkness, whistling.

Emilie would not have believed that at that moment Oliver was going farther away from them, the lit-up town of Emerson beckoning. There was a small hotel there, he knew, and a café where he would get something to eat. Then he thought perhaps he would bypass the town and cross the border, go to Pembina, where he'd heard there was a tavern. Leastways, there had been years ago, and a woman named Ma Shorts who ran it. She had a room at the back, and for a price she would let people sleep off a drunk or have a quick romp, whether or not the couple was married. The night air had chilled him through, and he was no longer inclined to sleep under the stars.

Headlights swung onto the highway and bore down on him, the vehicle approaching swiftly. He felt caught in the sweep of light as the car passed. Going no place in a hurry, he thought. The squeal of brakes made him turn. The car had stopped and was coming back towards him. The ditch was broad and shallow, and the grass not grown tall enough to conceal him. People spoke about the danger of picking up hitchhikers, but he felt exposed and vulnerable.

The car came to an abrupt stop beside him, its door opened and the interior light came on to reveal his cousin Danny.

I thought I was seeing things. What in God's name are you doing way out here? Danny called.

I had me a walk, Oliver said, feeling foolish, as well as relieved.

Some walk, Danny replied, as Oliver came over to the window. You could get hit. It happens. Get in, you're so darn close it would be a shame if you didn't pay us a visit.

Country and western music twanged from the car radio as Danny and Oliver headed towards Emerson. Twilight, a pink band of silt, had settled on the horizon, and Oliver gazed at it, only half listening as Danny elaborated on the car bingo taking place at a curling rink in town. As many as two and three hundred people attended some nights. The loudspeaker broadcast the bingo numbers to the cars parked in a field around the curling rink. You win, you honk the horn, Danny explained. So far, he'd won an ironing board and a kitchen clock. Cashwise, fifty bucks on a four-corner game. If you want to go, just let me know. I'll drive up and get you. Next one's on Thursday.

Soon Oliver was seated on a couch among warm and accepting bodies in Danny's darkened living room, at ease on a sofa, surrounded by Danny and his wife and their four children. Light flickered in their faces as they watched television, the program being *I Love Lucy*. The intensity of their attention was contagious and few words had passed between them since the comedy had begun. A toddler cradled in Danny's arms was mesmerized, her eyes swivelling towards the screen while she nursed on a bottle of milk.

The signal came from North Dakota, Danny had said. The border town of Emerson, where he lived and worked as a customs officer, was too far south to bring in Winnipeg. He explained how he'd aimed the antenna on the roof so that its arms scooped the images from the air and gave them *I Love Lucy* and Milton Berle, whose show, *The Texaco Star Theatre*, was his favourite program. The wife preferred *Toast of the Town*. Of course, Oliver had seen television before. There were TV sets in appliance stores in Winnipeg, and a garage in Alexander Morris had one going in its show window. But he'd never sat down in a living room to watch a program, much less while eating a meal. He couldn't remember the last time he'd been to a picture show, had enjoyed the zany antics of Charlie Chaplain, laughed until he could have died. His sides ached from laughing now. The humour of Lucille Ball tickled his funny bone, and the cramped living room, Union Plains, the hotel, the man in the white Cadillac, Sara, his children, all had disappeared.

His stomach was satisfyingly full of roast pork, mashed potatoes and apple pie, and the several beers Danny had pressed on him. Snack tables were pushed to one side of the chairs and the couch, dishes left unattended until the program was over. No need for hurry, to jump up and pull the plates out from under a person the moment they'd swallowed the last morsel.

Laughter broke out around him, prolonged and agreeable. Oliver realized that, except for Christmas morning, he hadn't ever sat down with all his kids in the living room for the purpose of entertainment. Its clutter of doilies, the polished varnished surfaces discouraged relaxation, unless a person was desperate. Sometimes he played Chinese checkers at the kitchen table, the kids arguing among themselves over whose turn it was to play with him. His girls pulled long faces on the occasions he took the boys fishing. They went across the river in pairs on summer vacations to Katy's farm. Or to St. Boniface.

Unlike Romeo, he hadn't been able to take them all on a vacation, much less sit down in the evening as these people were doing. All these years he'd been hitched to a dowdy, toothless old woman—married to the hotel, as Sara had once put it—while his kids were growing away from him. Sara had recently heard about a church summer camp and had wanted to send at least three of the kids, get them out of her hair for a short time, if the money could be found. They were all going off somewhere on their own. They would soon all be gone. Once again the room filled with laughter as Lucille Ball struggled to free her foot stuck in a bucket.

The headlights of Kornelius's car came on, and this time they remained on. The lights beamed through the hedge, casting a mosaic of shadows across Florence Dressler's lawn. Perhaps

Sara's sister and brother-in-law were leaving, she thought, although she hadn't seen either of them come out of the house. The car's engine started and revved, long and high. The sound brought Emilie to her feet and Katy over to the bedroom window. The car lurched forward and then suddenly stopped. The trunk lid slammed shut, awaking Ruby, who had curled up inside and fallen asleep. Kornelius woke with a start on the couch in the living room, and batted away the newspaper collapsed about his head.

The engine roared and his car shot backwards, streaked off from the house and out of the yard, narrowly missing Romeo returning from the hotel. Romeo, paralyzed with astonishment, watched the seemingly driverless car snake backwards into the ditch then up onto the street, across and down into the opposite ditch. A breathless moment later, there was a solid *thud!,* the sound of glass breaking as its taillights shattered. The headlights beamed across the face of the Vandals' house, bathing the girls' room in light. The engine stalled and Ruby began to scream.

Honk the horn! Simon yelled. He reached across the stunned Manny and punched the horn to bring someone quickly. He'd banged his head on the dash and feared he might bleed to death. Ruby might suffocate and it would be their fault. At any moment the car would burst into flames. Through his terror, he saw Romeo's face at the car window. And then Kornelius, as he pushed Romeo aside and opened the door.

What the devil's going on here? Kornelius shouted in German. I have told you boys a hundred times to stay out of my car. He grabbed Simon by the arm and dragged him outside, lifting the petrified boy off his feet as he took a swing at his backside. Don't hit me! Don't hit me! Simon screeched as he twirled about his uncle's legs, drowning out Ruby's muffled screams. The harder Kornelius swung, the more Simon turned and the less effective was the wallop.

Hold on, mister, Romeo shouted, his features dark with anger. He yanked at Kornelius's arm and was shrugged off.

You little devils. It's time someone taught you a lesson, Kornelius said in English, the harshness of the words measured out between swats as Simon thrashed and his uncle struggled to remain upright in the slippery muck.

Claudette and Alvina came running from the back of the house, Alvina in the lead. She stopped dead at the sight of the car tilted into the ditch and clapped her hands over her mouth. Her eyes were large with fear as Claudette joined her.

By Jesus Christ! Romeo shouted at Alvina. Go to the basement and get the goddamned gun! Go on, go and get it!

And then what? Claudette muttered. She tugged at Alvina's skirt. Don't you go. He doesn't mean it. He's just making a show.

As Simon's howls grew louder, Romeo ripped off his jacket and threw it to the ground, raised his fists and jabbed the air, startling Kornelius. Simon broke loose and fell to the ground between the two men, his face streaked with tears.

Romeo! Don't be a fool, Claudette called out. He's going to get creamed, she said to Alvina, when he failed to answer.

Ruby's screams got louder and Alvina took off for the car at a run, her feet shooting out from under her as she went down the slope of the ditch. She slid the rest of the way on her behind, soaking her skirt and smearing her legs with mud. Cold water oozed into her loafers as she rescued Manny from the car, took the keys from the ignition, and freed Ruby from the trunk. She gathered her sister and brothers around her, pulled their shivering bodies into her own. It's okay, don't be scared, she comforted Simon, who'd scrambled out from between the men to run round the car to the safety of his oldest sister. Don't be scared, she'd said, for her own benefit, as she took in Romeo, whom she had known as soft-spoken and good-natured. He'd become a crouching menacing stranger, a dog baring fangs.

You've got more to answer for than you know, mister, Romeo snarled, as Kornelius turned away from him, went over to the car and shut its door.

Or maybe you do know, eh? Maybe you don't give a good God damn about the people who were here long before you came. You took what belongs to someone else. Land that rightly belongs to Oliver and me, eh? Our family farmed that land for years. You gave our house to pigs!

Kornelius was stopped by Romeo's words. I don't know what you're talking about. Put away your fists and I'll listen, he said.

Cowards, Romeo spat. The whole damned bunch of you, you Deetch, getting fat on other peoples' land. Some of our people gave up their lives for this country while you got rich. But what do you care, eh? All you people care about is yourselves and your big fat purses. You're nothing but skin flints and cowards.

Say what you want, Kornelius said wearily. His shoulders sagged as he stepped away from Romeo's jabbing fists.

Romeo lunged and swung and Kornelius's head snapped

back with the impact and the squishy sound of his nose being broken.

They were both stunned for a moment. Romeo rubbed his knuckles while blood gushed over Kornelius's mouth. Kornelius swiped at his face, his hand coming away smeared red, his shirt spattered.

His face buzzed as he dug in a trouser pocket and brought out a crumpled hanky, which he pressed against his nose. Go ahead, have your say and be done with it, Kornelius said. You won't get a fight from me.

No, you'd rather have a go at a kid, eh? Someone who can't fight back. Romeo lunged again, this time punching Kornelius in the stomach. Kornelius doubled over and clutched himself.

Stop it! Alvina cried, and Ruby began sobbing anew, while Manny and Simon turned their faces into Alvina's stomach and clung to her skirt.

Kornelius came up for air, pain swelling in his cheekbones. His way to the house was blocked by this bobbing scrawny bantam rooster. What possessed the man, why was he so angry? Let me be, Kornelius said.

Let's see you do more than talk, Romeo taunted, as Claudette came ploughing through the mud towards him. She flung herself at him, wrapped her arms about his ribs and hung on. Instinctively Romeo jerked loose and sent her flying. She fell backwards, crying out, water splashing as she landed flat on her back, her dress flipping up about her hips, revealing her white rayon mound.

Romeo shook his hair from his eyes and swiped at snot running from his nose. You prefer to hit little kids, he said, not realizing that Kornelius's stolid demeanour had given way to disgust.

Go and take care of your woman, Kornelius said sharply.

Romeo followed his gaze and saw Claudette floundering in the mud, and found himself locked in a bear hug. Then Kornelius's knee jabbed at the back of his, and he fell onto the ground.

Claudette struggled to her feet and implored them to stop. For God sake, look at what you're doing, she said, pointing at the road where Emilie and Ida stood watching, their arms wrapped around each other. The car headlights bored through the darkness illuminating Sharon's small white face framed by the window in the girls' bedroom, peering down at them.

And then Sara came bursting out the front door, crying, Oh God, Oh God, as she sprinted across the yard and down into the gully of the ditch and up onto the road. She was bathed in the glare of the headlights, her hair undone and sticking out around her head as though she had pulled it loose. She saw Alvina, Ruby, the two boys clinging to Alvina's skirt, their faces pressed into her stomach. Sara remembered: an axe swinging, blood the colour of molasses splashing to the ground. The horror in Margareta's face as she backed away from the sight of a man being butchered, the small brothers hanging on to her nightdress. Sara remembered the animal sounds of violence, the cries of the women and children, her father's contorted features as he screamed at her to run away.

Papa!

Sara's wrenching cry froze them. They watched as the long darkness of the road took Sara away, away from Katy up in the bedroom covering her face with her hands, Katy thinking, it isn't possible for her to remember. She was only five years old.

Sara ran headlong into the darkness, the calves of her legs flashing white like the heaving underbelly of a fish caught and dragged onto land.

Oliver left the access road where Danny had dropped him off and entered town, carrying an apple pie wrapped in newspaper. As he grew nearer, he noted that his house was one of the few with its lights still beaming. Maybe he'd be lucky enough to find ice cream in the freezer compartment. He'd get the kids out of bed. Wake up the whole famdamily and treat them to a piece of pie and ice cream. My cousin's wife made it. You'd be pleased to meet her, she's quite a jolly person.

Probably they'd heard about the hotel and were waiting up for him. He'd tell them first thing that his next big purchase would be a television set. Any fool could see that there were good things to be gained from watching it, a belly laugh, for one. And television could prove to be educational, to be sure. A TV could take you places you hadn't been. Then he thought, holy, something's coming. He could hear a sound, a humming.

The humming became a high, singing wail. A banshee. He stood still, the hair on his arms prickling, heart going to beat the band. A cloud passed from the face of the moon and he saw Sara running towards him.

They had a moment before the sun rose beyond the curtains, a moment to lie in each other's arms, their bellies spilling together. My little pig, Oliver murmured into Sara's hair, fighting against sleep, which wanted to at last claim him. She shuddered and turned her face into the pillow, which was damp with her tears. Her ribs ached from crying.

Sara had liked to say, to the point of crowing, that she never cried. It might have been better if she hadn't started, as her crying was hard to listen to. Its sound was as rough as the splintered doorsill, bitter as the taste of earwax, but nevertheless it evoked sympathy. A tightness gripped Oliver's throat as he thought of his own loss; a child's marvelling at the world he found himself in; his own small wavering voice saying, Oh God, oh God, while the stars wheeled across the heavens.

Whose house is this? Sara had wanted to know right off the bat.

It's ours, Oliver thought. She's ours.

EIGHTEEN

—

Moving day

STAGE COACH ROAD follows the course of the Red River, a yellowish clay-heavy channel that curves inland near Aubigny and glimmers through the trees. A municipal truck leads the convoy of vehicles inching along the highway, its lights on and flashing. WIDE LOAD, a sign on a second truck proclaims, front and back. Alvina supposes that a house is a wide load. The Vandal house has been pried from its footings and perches precariously on a flatbed, hanging over its sides. It's being dragged down Stage Coach Road and into the twentieth century.

Waiting for the house in Alexander Morris is a vacant lot beside the United Church of Canada, and a basement already poured and ripened. A recreation room will be built down there and furnished so that the Vandals will have a place to entertain themselves on rainy days and during hard winters. The Wrecked Room, Oliver has already named it. That's where the television set will go, and perhaps a ping-pong table. Anything to keep Sonny Boy home. Kornelius chose that particular lot because of its proximity to the Alexander Morris Composite High School. He purchased the land for the Vandals because he understands from his old-country experience what it means to have land pulled out from under your feet and claimed by others.

A third truck in the convoy carries their possessions, the roller skates flung into a crate, the piano swaying, the washing machine jammed against it in an attempt to keep it steady. Chairs and tables, bunk beds, mattresses; melamine dishes clatter like bones in a box. Sara's china dishes and Morningstar silverware are rolled into bed linens and crammed into the Servelle refrigerator, which is bound shut with skipping ropes.

A fourth and last truck is the water man's one-ton vehicle, its tailpipe spurting blue smoke. Some of the Vandals ride in the back, while Sara and Oliver and the two youngest girls ride in the cab. Sonny Boy and George walk behind the truck on the lookout for traffic approaching from the rear, their job being to direct it to go round them. Manny and Simon, like Alvina, watch Union Plains recede, while Ida's and Emilie's faces shine with anticipation of the town of Alexander Morris rising from the earth.

Emilie thinks that, should people in their new town make a list of her characteristics, well, at some point in her future she may need a dose of smarten-up pills. That's what Oliver called the rabbit droppings clustered around the hotel's foundation. You see those? You take one of those, and you'll get smart.

Dad, how can a rabbit turd do that, eh?

Well, you take one and likely you won't take another, right?

Why not?

Sheesh. Presumably you'd be smarter, that's why.

Of course. Of course! Emilie laughs now at her own density, finally getting the joke. Because of the taste, that's why she wouldn't want a second one. And presumably she is smarter now, and will not get into a car without knowing where she's really going. Slowly, inch by inch, the Alexander Morris grain elevator rises on the horizon, and she imagines going to a café after school with friends, sipping an Orange Crush float and eating chips with gravy.

Alvina watches Union Plains growing smaller, Ruby wedged between her knees, and she tries not to pay attention to Sara snuggled against Oliver in the cab of the truck. She's crying, Alvina knows. Crying even when she smiles. Your mother's been cranked up to cry for years, Oliver has explained. Just let her go and eventually she'll run out of gas.

Alvina tucks Ruby's braids into her T-shirt to prevent them from gathering dust, while Simon and Manny sit on sacks of potatoes, their hands and arms smeared with dirt. Simon wanted to bring his school desk, and Manny a young rabbit he'd spotted coming out of a burrow beside the hotel, and Sara allowed them that. A rabbit each, which the decrepits, before leaving to live in a veterans' home in Winnipeg, had helped them snare. They made crates for the rabbits, which the two boys now hold firmly between their feet.

Alvina knows that for a time she will have to settle for singular, disconnected beads of silence. Moments snatched here and there. Moments when everyone is asleep and she can study in peace with The Other One at the dining-room table. In September she'll begin matriculation at the high school, a year behind, but nevertheless, she thinks. Nevertheless.

For moments she's been seeing a thin trail of grey smoke climbing across the sky above Union Plains. Now suddenly the smoke balloons into a tarry-looking roiling cloud, and she sees orange flames.

She leans over Ruby to rap at the back window of the truck and calls, Dad! A fire! Look.

Oliver turns, glances at the sky, which rapidly turns black. He shouts, I can't stop. Not without chancing a rear-end collision with some maniac driver in a hurry, his kids going shooting out the back of the truck like bowling pins.

Everyone but him look towards Union Plains now, Sonny Boy and George walking backwards, while Manny thinks, I didn't do it. It wasn't me. His hand wraps around Oliver's loupe in his pocket, and he brings it out, concealed in his small fist. He pokes a hole in the half-rotten gunny sack of potatoes, and pushes the eyepiece in amid the mush of last year's spuds.

Is all, Oliver thinks, as he turns his attention back to the highway and the vehicle in front of him. The whole shebang. The past is past. He'll hang out his shingle with Delorme after training in Winnipeg at the Marvel School of Beauty. Oliver Vandal, Master Barber. It will be his first diploma and likely his last, but better late than never.

Flames shoot out the hotel windows, lick up its velour curtains, consume the buffalo head on the parlour wall. The image of Chief Fine Day turns brown, and as the glass melts the photograph curls and becomes ash. Oliver's broom-closet office is the first to be obliterated, the stairwell above it collapsing as everything inside it burns or melts.

I didn't do it, Manny says, this time aloud. In the distance the sound of a siren rises and grows louder. Of course you didn't, Emilie says, without knowing what he's referring to.

She pats Manny on the shoulder and feels his relief. He turns and flashes her a grin. Constable Krooke's cruiser screams up from the south on Stage Coach Road, coming to investigate the fire. Someone has called. The volunteer brigade from Alexander Morris will soon follow in their red truck.

Good riddance to bad rubbish, Oliver thinks as the cruiser approaches, its lights flashing.

Sit down, you'll get us all in trouble, Alvina yells to Manny. She fears that the constable means to pull them over. The absolutely, positively shitty man is going to give Oliver shit again. But the cruiser speeds by and goes on and on. When it turns onto the access road at Union Plains, it disappears.

ACKNOWLEDGEMENTS

I am indebted to the authors whose books I have turned to during the writing of this novel, among them: *The Métis: Canada's Forgotten People,* by D. Bruce Sealey and Antoine S. Lussier; *Vanishing Spaces: Memoirs of Louis Goulet,* by Guillaume Charette, translated by Ray Ellenwood; and *Buffalo Days and Nights,* by Peter Erasmus.

I am grateful for the remembrances of my great-grandmother, Mrs. Estienne Desmarais. Several paragraphs in Chapter Six, "By chance," appeared in a short story, "A Necessary Treason," published in the collection of short stories *The Two-Headed Calf.*

I would also like to acknowledge the assistance of The Canada Council and The Saskatchewan Arts Board.

And a special thanks to Anne Collins, for her insight and gracious patience, and to Denise Bukowski, whose enthusiasm and wit came at the right moment. And thank you, Jan Nowina Zarzycki, my partner and friend, whose passion for story is as fierce as ever.